Kiwayu
Faza
Kizingitini
Siyu
Ras
Mtangawanda
Pate
Shanga
Pate
Swahili Seas

ALSO BY YVONNE ADHIAMBO OWUOR

Dust

The Dragonfly Sea

The Dragonfly Sea

A NOVEL

Yvonne Adhiambo Owuor

Alfred A. Knopf
NEW YORK
2019

THIS IS A BORZOI BOOK
PUBLISHED BY ALFRED A. KNOPF

Published in the United States by Alfred A. Knopf,
a division of Penguin Random House LLC, New York,
and distributed in Canada by Random House of Canada,
a division of Penguin Random House Canada Limited, Toronto.

www.aaknopf.com

Knopf, Borzoi Books, and the colophon are registered
trademarks of Penguin Random House LLC.

Grateful acknowledgment is made to the following for permission
to reprint previously published material:
Daniel Ladinsky: Excerpt from *The Subject Tonight Is Love: 60 Wild and Sweet Poems of Hafiz* by Daniel Ladinsky, copyright © 1996 by Daniel Ladinsky.
Reprinted by permission of Daniel Ladinsky.
The Permissions Company, Inc., on behalf of Shambhala Publications Inc.:
Excerpt of "Like the Morning Breeze" from *Drunk on the Wine of the Beloved: 100 Poems of Hafiz* by Hafiz, translation by Thomas Rain Crowe. Translation copyright © 2001 by Thomas Rain Crowe. Reprinted by permission of The Permissions Company, Inc., on behalf of Shambhala Publications Inc., Boulder, Colorado (www.shambhala.com).
Shahriar Shahriari: Excerpt from "Ghazal 374" by Hafiz, translated by Shahriar Shahriari. Reprinted by permission of Shahriar Shahriari (hafizonlove.com).

Library of Congress Cataloging-in-Publication Data
Names: Owuor, Yvonne Adhiambo, author.
Title: The dragonfly sea : a novel / by Yvonne Adhiambo Owuor.
Description: First edition. | New York : Alfred A. Knopf, 2019.
Identifiers: LCCN 2018020711 (print) | LCCN 2018023670 (ebook) | ISBN 9780451494054 (ebook) | ISBN 9780451494047 (hardcover)
Classification: LCC PR9381.9098 (ebook) | LCC PR9381.9.098 D73 2019 (print) | DDC 823/.92—dc23
LC record available at https://lccn.loc.gov/2018020711

Jacket image: *Seaside* (detail) by Ben Bonart.
Private Collection/Bridgeman Images
Jacket design by Linda Huang
Map by Christopher Ganda

Manufactured in the United States of America
First Edition

For you, La Soledad.
&
As always,
The Family
Matriarch, Mary Sero Owuor
&
The father we dearly miss.
&
My siblings,
&
the most iridescent of lights:
Hera, Hawi, Gweth, Sungu, Diju, Detta, and Sero.

Author's Note

In 2005, also the six hundredth anniversary of the Ming dynasty's great Admiral (Haji Mahmud Shamsuddin) Zheng He's (1371–1435) first voyage around the Western (Indian) Ocean, a young woman from Pate Island, Kenya, obtained a scholarship to study in China. The award was given based on family claims and DNA tests that suggested that she was indeed a descendant of a Ming-dynasty sailor who had survived a storm-wrought shipwreck, who, with others, had found refuge and a sense of belonging on Pate Island. *The Dragonfly Sea* is inspired by this historical incident, but it is necessary to emphasize that it is *not* this young woman's story, lest the character plot points be ascribed to her. Though the story incorporates current news and historical events, this is a work of fiction, and the chronology of several events has been altered. Names, characters, places, and incidents either are products of the author's imagination or are used fictitiously. Any resemblance to actual events, or persons living or dead, is entirely coincidental.

Take this amulet, child, and secure it with cord and honor.
I will make you a chain of radiant pearl and coral.
I will give you a clasp, fine without flaw, to wear on your neck . . .
Wash and perfume yourself and braid your hair;
string jasmine and lay it on the counterpane.
Adorn yourself in clothes like a bride, and wear anklets and
bracelets . . .
Sprinkle rosewater on yourself. Have rings on your fingers and,
always, henna on the palms of your hands . . .

—Mwana Kupona binti Msham,
translated by J. W. Allen and adapted by Yvonne Adhiambo Owuor

Roho ni mgeni.

The soul is a visitor (stranger).

[1]

To cross the vast ocean to their south, water-chasing dragonflies with forebears in Northern India had hitched a ride on a sedate "in-between seasons" morning wind, one of the monsoon's introits, the *matlai*. One day in 1992, four generations later, under dark-purplish-blue clouds, these fleeting beings settled on the mangrove-fringed southwest coast of a little girl's island. The *matlai* conspired with a shimmering full moon to charge the island, its fishermen, prophets, traders, seamen, seawomen, healers, shipbuilders, dreamers, tailors, madmen, teachers, mothers, and fathers with a fretfulness that mirrored the slow-churning turquoise sea.

Dusk stalked the Lamu Archipelago's largest and sullenest island, trudging from Siyu on the north coast, upending Kizingitini's fishing fleets before swooping southwest to brood over a Pate Town that was already moldering in the malaise of unrequited yearnings. Bruised by endless deeds of guile, siege, war, and seduction, like the island that contained it, Pate Town marked melancholic time. A leaden sky poured dull-red light over a crowd of petulant ghosts, dormant feuds, forfeited glories, invisible roads, and congealing millennia-old conspiracies. Weaker light leached into ancient crevices, tombs, and ruins, and signaled to a people who were willing to cohabit with tragedy, trusting that time transformed even cataclysms into echoes.

Deep inside Pate, a cock crowed, and from the depths of space a summons, the Adhan, crescendoed. Sea winds tugged at a little girl's lemon-green headscarf, revealing dense, black curly hair that blew into her eyes. From within her mangrove hideout, the scrawny seven-year-old, wearing an oversized floral dress that she was supposed to grow into, watched dense storm clouds hobble inland. She decided that these were a monster's footsteps, a monster whose strides left streaks of pink light on the sky. Seawater lapped at her knees, and her bare feet sank into the black sand as she clutched another scrawny being, a purring dirty-white kitten. She was betting that the storm—her monster—would reach land before a passenger-laden *dau* now muddling its way toward the cracked wharf to the right of her. She held her breath. "Home-comers," she called all passengers. *Wajio.* The child could rely on such home-comers to be jolted like marionettes whenever there was a hint of rain. She giggled in anticipation as the midsized *dau*, with *Bi Kidude* painted in flaking yellow, eased into the creek.

Scattered, soft raindrops.

The thunder's spirited rumbling caused every home-comer to raise his or her eyes skyward and squawk like a hornbill. The watching girl sniggered as she stroked her kitten, pinching its fur in her thrill. It mewled. "Shhh," she whispered back as she peered through mangrove leaves, the better to study the passengers' drizzle-blurred faces—a child looking for and gathering words, images, sounds, moods, colors, conversations, and shapes, which she could store in one of the shelves of her soul, to retrieve later and reflect upon.

Every day, in secret, she went to and stood by the portals of this sea, her sea. She was waiting for Someone.

The girl now moved the kitten from her right to her left shoulder. Its extra-large blue eyes followed the dance of eight golden dragonflies hovering close by. Thunder. The *dau* drew parallel to the girl, and she fixated on a man in a cream-colored suit who was slumped over the vessel's edge. She was about to cackle at his discomfort when a high and harried voice intruded:

"Ay*aaaa*na!"

Her surveillance of the man was interrupted as lightning split the sky.

"Ay*aaaa*na!"

It was her mother.

"Ay*aaaa*na!"

At first, the little girl froze. Then she crouched low, almost kneeling in the water, and stroked her kitten. She whispered to it, "*Haidhuru*"—Don't mind. "She can't see us."

Ayaana was supposed to be recovering from a morning asthma attack. Bi Munira, her mother, had rubbed clove oil over her tightened chest and stuffed the all-ailment-treating black kalonji seeds into her mouth. They had sat together, naked under a blanket, while a pot of steaming herbs, which included eucalyptus and mint, decongested their lungs. Ayaana had gulped down air and blocked her breath to swallow six full tablespoons of cod-liver oil. She had gurgled a bitter concoction and been lulled to sleep by her mother's dulcet "*do-do-do.*" She had woken up to the sounds of her mother at work: the tinkle of glass, brass, and ceramic; the aroma of rose, clove, *langilangi*, and moonflower; and the lilts of women's voices inside her mother's rudimentary home-based beauty salon.

Ayaana had tried. She had half napped until a high-pitched sea wind pierced and scattered her reverie. She had heard far-off thunder, but she had pinned herself to the bed until the persistent beckoning of the storm proved irresistible. Then she rolled out of bed, arranged extra pillows to simulate a body, and covered these with sheets. She squeezed out of a high window and shimmied down drainpipes clamped to the crumbling coral wall. On the ground, she found the kitten she had rescued from a muddy drain several days ago, stretched out on their doorstep. She picked it up and planted it on her right shoulder, dashed off to the seafront, and finally swung north to the mangrove section of the creek, from where she could spy on the world unseen.

"Ay*aaaa*na!"

The wind cooled her face. The kitten purred. Ayaana watched the *dau*. The cream-suited elderly stranger lifted his head. Their eyes connected. Ayaana ducked, pressing into the mangrove shadows, her heart racing. How had that happened?

"Ay*aaaa*na!" Her mother's voice was closer. "Where's that child? Ay*aaa*na? Must I talk to God?"

Ayaana looked toward the boat and again at the blackening skies. She would never know what landed first, the boat or the storm. She remembered the eyes that had struck hers. Would their owner tell on her? She scanned the passageway, looking for those eyes again. The kitten on her shoulder pressed its face into her neck.

"Ay*aaaa*na! *Haki ya Mungu . . . aieee!*" The threat-drenched contralto came from the bushes to the left of the mangroves. "*Aii, mwanangu, mbona wanitesa?*" Too close. The girl abandoned her cover, splashed through the low tide to reach open sands. Ayaana scrambled from stone to stone, with the kitten clinging to her neck. She dropped out of sight.

The stranger, a man from Nanjing, saw a small creature soar against the backdrop of a black sky, hover, and then fall like a broken-off bough; as she did so, a long chortle erupted out of him. His fellow travelers, already sympathetic about his chronic seasickness, glanced at him with unease. It was not uncommon for seasickness to turn previously sane persons into lunatics. The man focused on the land, eyes active in his placid face. A cataract in his right eye gave it a luminosity in his balding head on his tendon-lined neck. He turned at the sound of a woman's voice calling, "Ay*aaaana*!" Stomach roil. Craving the sense of land, he tried to measure the distance between the boat and the jetty, hoping that they would dock soon.

Fifteen minutes later, ill-fitting suit aflutter, the visitor stepped off the boat. He had to wade through shallow water to reach the black sand shore. Even though anonymous hands helped him forward, he stumbled. His hands touched the soil. He swallowed air. Here were the rustlings of ghosts. Here was the lonely humming of those who had died far from home and had for too long been neither sought nor remembered. A brown hand dangled in front of his face. He took it. One of the sailors helped him up before handing over his single gray bag. The man intoned, "*Itifaki imezingatiwa*," and then chortled at a secret joke.

The traveler blinked, uneasy and engulfed by redolent evening scents; *oudhi* spattered enchantment. His breath discerned bitter orange, sweet balsam, and the sweat of the sea blended in a dense air that also heated his bones. Succumbing, inhaling. He then tilted his head toward the hubbub of human arrivals. He heard the music of a rolling tide. He glimpsed an almost storm hovering on the horizon. *What was this place?* He ambled forward, heels rotating as if his toes had roving eyes. Pale light shone on a pink petal falling from a solitary and slender wild-rose bush. The man faltered. He waited for the petal to settle on the ground before reaching for it. Only then did he lift it to his lips, enclosing it in one hand while the other adjusted the condensed contents of a life that fit into the canvas bag hanging from his shoulder.

Mwenda Pate harudi,
Kijacho ni kilio.

One who goes to Pate does not return;
only a wail resounds.

[2]

The morning when the man from China entered Kenya—inside a spacious lime-washed bedroom within a wood-and-coral two-story house located in a twelve-house maze in Pate Town still chiseled by trade winds named *kusi*, *matlai*, *malelezi*, and *kaskazi*—an aging seaman, Muhidin Baadawi Mlingoti, dreamed, again, that he was circumnavigating a gigantic sapphire mountain at the bottom of the sea. He carried a map in the dream. It was inside a dark brown book, and contained arcane words that lit up as if inflamed. The real version of his dream map was under his bed, inside an ornate mahogany Lamu chest, bundled up in a dark green cloth.

Five years back, Muhidin, the sun-blackened, salt-water-seared, bug-eyed, and brawny descendant of Pate Island fishermen and boatbuilders, had swiped this book from one of thousands in the private library of a Dubai-based war and sea bounty collector to whom Muhidin would sometimes sell contraband artifacts. Inside the book's pages he had found a beguiling yellow-brown parchment with maplike markings in a cryptic language that featured the emblem of an archaic compass that indicated the east as the starting point for movement. When Muhidin first examined the parchment, he had imagined it was written out in musical notation. Later, he saw that, when exposed to dusk's light, the parchment emitted an intimate attar that evoked sandalwood. What was it? A memory map's paean to trade winds, ports, and travelers? What if the fragment was a flavored piece from a foolish tale, one of those interminable *Alfa Lela Ulela—Thousand and One Nights*—gossip sheets? *It is nothing*, Muhidin told himself to assuage his lust to know. *It is nothing*. Still, whenever Muhidin fell foul of the haunted realms of his heart, he would automatically reach under the bed to retrieve the book and touch the parchment for reassurance.

Long, long ago, when Muhidin was no more than a boy, a fierce song had burned into his being. It had clung to him like an earth-stranded ghost. It would later re-emerge as dreams that woke him up with a craving for unnamable things. The song would turn an illiterate island boy into a seeker, traveler, reader, and sleuth—a hungry truth-hunter. Muhidin Khamis Mlingoti wa Baadawi had been orphaned when a Likoni South Coast ferry sank with his parents and five siblings. Through this tragedy, his childless relatives—Uncle Hamid, a *zumari* player and master boatman, and his wife, Zainab—acquired a punching bag and an indentured servant. However, during a four-day fishing trip with his uncle, in the middle of a thrashing, rolling, wrestling match with an enraged giant black marlin, goaded by his uncle's baleful threats—"Dare you lose my fish, dare you"—the terror-stricken fourteen-year-old had slipped into a state of high concentration, inside of which whisperings, as if from the Source of Life, bubbled forth. In these he heard a palpable sea-song, which sucked him into the soul of a single wet note made out of the contents of time. The song penetrated his young heart, which proceeded to shatter and scatter as portions of infinite sun across chilled worlds. From that moment, Muhidin would be struck with perpetual homesickness for an unknown place.

Suddenly docile, the fish had yielded its life.

Afterward, a desultory silence. Then Muhidin had tumbled about the boat, keening, the bitter sound drenching his wrinkled uncle Hamid, who contemplated Muhidin with very old, very dark, very cheerless eyes. "It's nothing," the uncle grunted five nights later. "The disarray of wind." But the uncle and his wife never touched Muhidin again.

The emotion of the event had later pressed Muhidin into the sea's service, where he would work nonstop, an enchanted captive. Whenever he reached land, he darted after illusions as if they were fireflies. He dredged dark nooks in port cities, buying, bartering, stealing, and scrounging for maps and riddles. He scoured arcane notations, hoping to signpost existence. Destination: certainty. In this quest, Muhidin rubbed skin with both man and matter, and, finally, they, not the sea, would rip the fabric of his being.

So many sea years later, a world-bruised Muhidin, buffeted by endless solitude, would again encounter reverberations from that odd day. He was aboard his merchant vessel on a frigid, vile-tempered, night-blackened Atlantic. He had, as usual, assumed duty on the ship's storm watch when, from within seething seas, he glimpsed blue spherical lights gamboling on water. He had blinked as they disintegrated into fractions of the ghost song he had once heard. He had leaned over the railings, baying, "Who are you?" A two-story wave had swamped the ship's deck and drenched him before retreating. Muhidin was at once overcome by a yearning for the island home he had abandoned. Everything he had found so far only hinted at what the ocean's formless song was not. He had no high faith to find shelter in either. This he had earlier offloaded in an Alexandrian souk where an alabaster-skinned vendor of everything, with a sepulchral hawknose, had delicately avoided contact with Muhidin's skin.

The souk.

A call to prayer had resounded. The warm-voiced invitation to souls to gather clashed with the chaos of small, bad human habits. Like the word that the trader whose goods Muhidin had spurned had then let slip: Abd. Slave. And inside Muhidin, something had detonated. He had ground his teeth. "Bloodthirsty djinn! Executioner! Gobbler of souls."

The trader's glassy-eyed smile. His stuttered, "Abd . . . my friend . . . You know . . . my friend, brother, it means . . . means . . . submission to the will . . ."

Muhidin had roared: "Stop, thief! Atone! Stink of putrefaction beneath white robes, walking cemetery. *Mtu mwovu*. Imbiber of human blood . . . Atone! Parasite! So you won't touch my hand? Its blackness condemns you? Atone! Thief of land and soul! Atone!"

Fear had distorted the trader's face. Licking his lips, he had whispered to Muhidin, "Look! Look!" He zigzagged backward. He did not close his stall. His arms pointed in all directions. But the others in the market pretended neither to see nor to hear, their faces lowered to avoid Muhidin's incandescent gaze. Muhidin had stomped away, clutching his *halua*. His body's trembling had dislodged the vestiges of faith to which he had clung.

II

Abd.

Muhidin's uncle had called him Abd for most of his life, until the day of the fishing trip. It was the name he knew from growing up on an island where spoken words could become a covenant and a bond. "*Kuffar,*" his uncle had added—"heathen." Using such soft tones while he thrashed Muhidin, and Aunt Zainab just looked at the bleeding boy as she slurped down heavily sugared ginger coffee. This was the face of loneliness, then, the substance of his present disquiet. Images: Uncle Hamid, musical fisherman crouching in white-robed prayer, a *zabiba* on his forehead, hiding the truth of a bloodthirsty will.

Abd.

Muhidin had stridden through that souk, the *halua* perfuming him with sweetness, and a vow on his tongue: *Between religion and my black skin there shall be a sky's distance until the day I hear the Call to Atonement.* Inner weightlessness had followed his vow. Restlessness. He began to pace like the caged black leopard he had seen in a Qatari oilman's vanity zoo, neither happy nor sad. While he was hauling goods or raising chains, he observed himself, as if detached, and wondered why he did what he did. Loading, securing, stowing, unloading, Muhidin clamped down on his thoughts and refused to consider meaning. Unfettered, he soaked his senses in unlimited indulgences: wine, women, words, drugs of assorted flavors, and ceaseless political discourse. He developed an opinion about everything. In this way, Muhidin massaged his unease until the day when, after twenty-eight years, three months, eight days, and seven hours of fealty to the sea, on a simple humid June morning in 1992, his Panama-registered ship reached Zanzibar Harbor.

The morning sun on Unguja Island had been golden and fierce, and its piercing had caused Muhidin to cover his eyes. When he could look, he gaped at Zanzibar Island as if seeing it anew. On the docks below, at least twenty-six emaciated, runny-nosed harbor cats purr-meowed while the flimsy veils between worlds made time brittle. Colonizing crows, wind, warmth, and voices. Muhidin glimpsed a forgotten self amid all the others he had accumulated: fisherman, stevedore, able-bodied seaman, junior engineer, utility man, lover, temporary husband, man with nothing to graft himself on to, salt on his face as the

East African air entered him. Two translucent insects chased light in front of him, and a nameless merchant, into whose body numerous worlds had embedded their stories as deep wrinkles, pointed at him and waved. Tears had dribbled down Muhidin's bearded jowls and fallen into the oil-stained water of the Zanzibar port. Muhidin clutched the guardrails, and a preternatural desolation gnawed him. A second later, a large piece of machinery clanged. His shipmates' voices called him, wrapping his name in fond abuse. The chief officer yelled at him from a height. He turned to grab the nearest out-of-place object, a half-empty water tank, to heft up, carry away, and use to hide his face.

Yet, later, under obsidian darkness, Muhidin slunk away from his life at sea. Muhidin bribed two harbor "rats"—boys of unknown age, who scrounged for anything, and who circled the harbor like djinns bound to one place—to help him haul down five gunnysacks laden with the repositories of his sea exile: books, maps, bottled attars, calligraphy ink and brushes, incense, dried perfumed blood, dried herbs, tree resin including frankincense, two shirts, shorts, a hat, and a large coat. He carried his money in a thick leather pouch strapped to his body. Muhidin and the "rats" had skulked along the shadows and depressions of the new harbor to cross into Stone Town through a hole in the fence. They huddled along coral walls, and re-entered the labyrinths of in-between worldliness to the sound of Algerian *raï*. He remembered the perfumed, wide-eyed women wearing black *buibui*s. Now they glided past him with the single fluttering gaze and bracelet-tinkling seduction perfected here. Food smells. Muhidin inhaled biryani, pilau, coconut-flavored aromas; chutney, pickles, yogurts, peppers, *mbaazi*, and *mahamri;* custard apple and avocado juice offered by a baby-faced vendor. "*Shikamoo*," a pigtailed girl said in greeting as she curtsied before an older rotund man dressed in a gleaming white *kanzu;* he heard Kiswahili cadences and ubiquitous whispers, reggae by Bob Marley and Peter Tosh; he saw dim doorways that veered off the maze. Muhidin's sudden laugh had been a basset hound's bark. They hurried toward Old Dhow Harbor, and stopped along an ancient stone ledge that skirted the sea unevenly.

Muhidin saw a lantern-lit midsized vessel floating a short distance from the docks—a dismal behemoth bulging out in unusual places. It looked as if it should have been burned as an act of mercy at least a century ago. It had been hopefully named *Umm Kulthum.* Its *nahodha*—or captain—stood in silhouette as if welded to his vessel. *"Masalkheri"*—Good evening—Muhidin called, his voice a grit-speckled gravel of underuse.

The *nahodha,* a colossus, detached himself from his boat, slipped into water that came up to the top of his thighs; as he waded toward Muhidin, he asked, in singsong mellifluence, *"Nani mwenzangu?"*—Who is my companion?

"Muhidin Khamis Mlingoti wa Baadawi."

"*Du!* Such a name! What do you want?"

"To spout poetry to the stars with you. What do you think, man? To go."

"What's your problem? Where?"

Pate. A phantom-calling invocation. Memories crawled over Muhidin like arachnids sneaking out of forgotten crypts. "Pate." Muhidin shuddered. Surf breaking, speckled light-in-darkness sea spray filled holes of decrepit silences.

The captain had grumbled, "Only fools and criminals cross the sea in this season."

"Then I'm a fool," Muhidin had growled.

The boatman grunted. "True. What'll you pay?"

"Anything."

"Passport?"

"You need one?" Muhidin countered.

"No."

"Neither do I."

"What're you carrying?"

"Simple things."

"Don't want trouble."

"None from me."

"We leave at dawn." The boatman had turned toward the bobbing *Umm Kulthum.*

Muhidin had called, "Wait for me. I'll be in the boat."

"You're mad, man."

"Maybe."

Muhidin and the urchins had hauled his goods into the *dau.* Before dawn, six other travelers and three deckhands had joined them on board. They set off with the morning's high tide.

. . .

Some of the passengers had disembarked at some of the small half-living ports along the way—Tumbatu, Pemba, Kilifi, and Shimoni—but when together, the men shared the crew's tasks of balancing or patching up the vessel, and bailing out water over the six days and nights required to navigate changing currents and tides, trusting in the goodwill of winds and reaching Northern Kenya waters. At around 2:00 p.m. of the sixth day, the *nahodha* turned the *Umm Kulthum* toward an old sign on a protruding rock that indicated the way to Pate Island. This also marked the waterway that elephants once used to island-hop at low tide. They had turned into the Mkanda Channel, avoiding the riskier deep-sea passage. When they passed the mighty mangrove thicket, Muhidin's heart started to ache. The white tips of sandbars. Faza, reshaped by a fire, Ndau Island, and, before long, the black sand shore of Ras Mtangawanda. Soon Muhidin became one of few arrivals stepping onto Pate Island. *Returning to what?* His knees had weakened as he crisscrossed invisible boundaries that outlined the past, his and the island's. Then easy laughter, the relativity of time. He walked and stared at the frontiers that marked crumbling graves, shrines to scholarship, vestiges of shipbuilding yards, tombs of saints, the syncretic signs of previously confident gods; a sturdy mosque that shared its space with all other worship. The people, his people. An old face crossed his path, and it was familiar. Seconds later, Muhidin's heart had burst; it let out a howl. Children playing close by stopped their game. Three brave boys ran over to see what had caused the sound and discovered a supplicating man on his knees, a man who had just learned that a long, twisted road through vast realms had arched right back home.

That was then.

As for the yellow-brown parchment Muhidin breathed on, today he was certain of only two things: all it offered was that he had it, and, like everything else he touched, it was crumbling before he could decipher it.

15

. . .

"Allahu Akbar . . ."

Another day, night, day. Herald of promise, easing an ancient brooding island into wakefulness.

"Allahu Akbar . . ."

The song ripened.

"Al-salaatu khayrun min al-nawm . . ."

And a high-pitched wind from the sea whipped up sand particles. It sprinkled these on the things of life. Crowing cockerels. The tunes of morning jammed Muhidin's recurrent dream-reel of returning to Pate, which ended with a question he needed to ask but could never articulate. Even though Muhidin had given up God, he attended to these summons to life with the pleasure of an aesthete.

"Allahu Akbar . . ."

From the balcony of a top-floor gallery in his coral house, Muhidin watched a *ngarawa* flotilla. Early-morning fishermen crouched and rose, crouched and rose, digging long mangrove-wood oars into the ocean to the pulse of the dawn's light, which spilled like molten silver over the water. He adjusted his embroidered *barghashia* and casually wondered if he should open up the downstairs window into his shop, Vitabu na Kadhalika—Books and Other Things. The morning sun was an intimate touch on hands that gripped the balcony's worn rails. He listened to the quavering bass echoes from the muezzin's dawn hymn. The salt aroma from the ocean was sprinkled with a blend of spices, seaweed, and unknown ocean herbs.

Allahu Akbar . . .

The Adhan here was still borne in the voice of a man, two men—Omar Abdulrauf and Abasi Rashid—to be precise. Rivals, each bore a rock-hard conviction of his particular vocal giftedness while offering faint praise for the other's efforts. The island still resisted the taped, exact, and washed-out coats of sound offerings made in dour Saudi Arabia that elsewhere had replaced that timbre of truth that a living voice offered.

"Ash-hadu an-la ilaha illa llah . . ."

Muhidin climbed down broad steps, ears buzzing from Omar Abdulrauf's bayed summons: *"As-salatu Khayrun Minan-nawm . . ."*

Muhidin wondered about offering a honey-clove-ginger gel to

the crier, whose baleful countertenor suggested the mating of whales. Muhidin hastened across the inner courtyard and shaded his eyes from the light pouring in.

He waited.

Three minutes.

There it was.

Patter of footsteps behind the north-facing house. After a few minutes, a child's voice chanted: "*Kereng'ende . . . mavuvu na kereng'ende . . .*"

Kereng'ende? Muhidin scratched his beard. Dragonfly season. He glanced skyward. The short rains were coming. The air was thick with humidity, the clouds sat high in the sky, and large shoals of fish were showing up from spawning grounds. There were new currents and undercurrents. Muhidin turned to the sea.

Splash!

A child gurgled, piling on laughter. Muhidin listened for a while before rubbing his whiskers as he wandered into his lower-floor kitchen, and switched on the kettle. He laid out a chunk of honey *halua* and *mahamri ya mbaazi* on a rusting round tray that had once featured pictures of kittens. He poured hot milk into a large mug, added a spoonful of masala, and imagined that the evening dhow from Lamu would come bearing some *mkate wa mofa*, which he needed to get. Somewhere in the water, the child laughed again. Her glee crinkled Muhidin's eyes. Secret laughter for Muhidin meant that a secret could be transferred with a glance across a gallery's turquoise balcony. A secret could be born when a man witnessed a dance that the rest of the world would never see. A secret could be felt or held in a minuscule smile that was no more than a tic on an aging man's upper lip, or a glimmer of starlight in a bastard child's eyes. Before the child had seen him, she used to twirl in the ocean's shallows and sing a loud song of children at ease:

> "*Ukuti, Ukuti*
> *Wa mnazi, wa mnazi*
> *Ukipata Upepo*
> *Watete . . . watete . . . watetemeka . . .*"

Unseen, he would listen. Other times, he saw her just combing the beach. She hauled in driftwood, dead eels, dead birds, dead starfish, a sealed bag of pasta, a hockey stick, a baby doll's head, and a blue plastic turtle. Then she had discovered he was at the balcony at dawn. So she sang in softer tones, but the morning breeze still brought her tune to him.

"Sisimizi mwaenda wapi?
Twaenda msibani
Aliyekufa ni nani? . . ."

He had seen her long before her dawn adventures entered his life. It was over an oil-exuding, large, lobed, scaly fat creature, the size of a short man, with four leglike lower fins that one Yusuf Juma, fisherman, had hauled in and dumped on the jetty. People had gathered to stare, and some fishermen remembered that a similar beast had been found before. The little girl had appeared. She had crawled under the assembled adults' arms, and was kneeling close to the thing, arms looped across her knees, when Muhidin, who was on his evening walk, the tap-tap of brogues with steel heel and toe caps announcing his approach, had pronounced, *"Ni kisukuku. Alieishi tangu enzi za dinasaria."* He repeated a message from a poster he had seen about the coelacanth. He added, "Netted one once when I was at sea. Can't eat it. Return it to the water. The sharks will rejoice." As he glanced over, he briefly noted the intense wide-eyed, openmouthed gawking of the girl in oversized rags. His eyes had glazed over, preoccupied as he was with completing his evening stroll.

As the kettle now hissed and spat water at Muhidin, he heard her voice:

"Sisimizi mwaenda wapi?
Twaenda msibani . . ."

He knocked the kettle's head as if it were a disobedient pet, and poured the dark, bitter coffee into the mug. Chewing on coffee grounds mixed with cardamom, cloves, and cinnamon, he carried his tray upstairs to his room. He looked over the balcony to scan the sea, scrutinizing the red-edged clouds and uneven blue waters. *Storm tonight over water*, he predicted. The girl was playing in white-froth waters. She dived under the surface. *The current*, he worried. Muhidin counted the beats of his heart, looking for telltale dark, rippled signals of an undertow. Then the child popped up. She had surpassed her previous two-minute underwater feat by seventeen seconds. Muhidin wiped his nose on his sleeve. Wasn't as if it should matter to him. Not his business. Mouth twitch. Two minutes seventeen seconds!

An early-morning creaking and shuffling had disturbed Muhidin's sleep one night more than a year ago. It had been dark when he reached for a watch he had put together from the remains of past watches. It chirped, cricketlike, and pinged once every three hours. Restless for the usual unremembered reasons, he had retired to his balcony to wait for the sunrise. He had noticed the glimmer of light in the magenta slashing across the sky. In that luster, he had glimpsed a being leaping in the ocean, cavorting like a baby *pomboo*, a dolphin. It had dived under water and emerged several meters away. It was not that Muhidin *believed* in the existence of djinns, but, as an explanation for the specter in the water at that hour, the shadow of the idea crossed the wall of his mind. He hurried downstairs, crossed an inner courtyard, cut through the reception space he used as his shop and dispensing booth, walked past the foyer and out through the porch. On the street, he trotted down to a corner that would lead to the beach. Then he recognized the waif.

His disappointment had surprised him. *Desperate for ghosts, Muhidin?* he chided himself. *Kweli avumaye baharini papa kumbe wengi wapo*—many kinds of fish in the sea. He had scowled as an inner debate curdled his thoughts. Should he haul the child out? There were unstated rules about who could and could not swim in the sea. A child: not without supervision. A girl: hardly ever. *But.* He also knew how the sea was with certain people, how it needed them, and they it. It was like that for him. But it had been expected of him. His late father, and his father before him, had been sea keepers—they had read the water in all its seasons, and had kept its rites and rituals. Even though they had died before he could learn from them, he had retained an instinct for the calling. In his youth, he had been one of only seven who could dive in the middle of the night to find fish, oysters, and crabs from the deep with only lanterns on boats to light their way. He had been stung by jellyfish and electric eels, and lived. He could name swells, tides, and currents by look or sensation. When a riptide had swept him into deep seas, he had not been afraid, merely curious. Ever since he had returned to Pate, three times he had snapped awake, only to find himself in the water at night, without knowing how he had left his bed and house to reach the tides.

[3]

The dirty-white kitten wrapped itself around the little girl's tiny shoulders as she watched passenger boats dock. She was waiting for her father. She had never seen her father, nor did she know what he looked like. Everything she believed he was had arisen from her imagination, where she had demanded that he reveal himself in a tangible form today.

Just as she had expected that he would yesterday.

And the day before.

Whooshing winds, the murmur of the tide.

Today, her father was not among the disembarking home-comers of the morning, or among those who tumbled out of the evening dhow. He did not disembark from either of the two *matatu*s that traversed Pate Island. Ayaana had waited till she heard the night crickets chirp, until there was sudden stillness, as if the world were waiting for her to speak. She whispered to her kitten that she would give her father only one more chance. Tomorrow was his very last chance to find her. The cat faux-scratched the girl's head and purred.

[4]

Time-dissolving floating. Solitude and wordlessness, and everything traveled toward an unknown beckoning. Even she did. But underwater she did not need to worry about labeling things in order to contain them. Feeling, sensing, experiencing—that was enough for knowledge. The sea had many eyes, and, now hers were another pair. A passing fish stared. A human looked back. She drifted with the currents, with the things of the current. She drifted until it was necessary to surface for air.

Laughter echoed.

Muhidin leaned over the balcony to listen to the child with the sea, the child in the sea. Would she learn that the ocean, like the world, was unpredictable? *But.* Not his business. He had returned to his house that first morning. Still, he looked out for the child every dawn. On some mornings, she did not show. On others, she shimmered into view before cockcrow, tiptoeing into the water, bouncing through the shallows if the sea was in ebb, and jumping into waves when the sea flowed. Months later, as she scurried back to her house, she had tilted her head up at him as if she knew he would be there. He withdrew from the balcony. A month later, she slowed down as she crossed the area below his balcony, walking with her head low. Days later, she stopped and breathed. She caught his look. She then pulled her ears down, crossed her eyes, and stuck out her tongue. And then she was gone, making tiny holes in the sand, as if a duiker were crossing.

When she reappeared the following week, Muhidin returned her salutation in full. As he did, her eyes grew bigger, and then she clutched her stomach and screeched, before covering her mouth. Her mirth made her execute three cartwheels and then collapse on the beach, overwhelmed by the too-much-ness. Her merriment inside dawn's protective shadows had infected Muhidin, who started to guffaw as he clung to his balcony railings. Then she was gone. *Paff!* Tiny steps on dark brown sand.

Ayaana.

The child's name was not common to Pate. Ayaana—"God's gift." Of course, Muhidin knew her story. Everybody did. The child had come to the island one high tide seven years ago. She arrived in the arms of her then skeletal, mostly vanquished, on-the-tail-end-of-a-scandal mother, Munira, daughter of prestige—pale-skinned, narrow-eyed, as slender as a bird's foot, and just as delicate. Her previous haughty, loudmouthed, angular, and feral beauty had been sheared off and dimmed by whatever it was she had tangled with in two and a half years of life away from the island. She had drifted back home, a broken, rusting anchor. *Ayaana* was Munira's only explanation for the raw-skinned thing she carried. It bawled at a wild, fire-streaked dusk as its mother disembarked from the leaky fisherman's *ngarawa* she had chartered from Lamu in exchange for her last two gold bangles. When Munira landed on Pate Island, "Ayaana" was a plea for mercy on her lips. Those who witnessed their arrival, as they would an approaching cortege, did not renounce "God's gift," the babbling evidence of one woman's washed-away dreams.

"Who is the father?"

". . ."

"The father, Munira?"

"The wind," she cried out, harrowed, hollow. "He is a shadow of wind."

And the answer, throbbing with the hint of horror, incited the family to organize schemes that would cause the situation to vanish. They promptly identified a groom for Munira: an austere scholar with a thin beard that touched his concave stomach, whose numerous attempts at serial marriages had failed—each bride fled and was never seen again. His first and only wife had also willed herself into muteness. The man was determined to merge with Munira's patrician family and enter into its ancient, intricate, and extended business tentacles, which touched most port cities of the world. He was already starting the process of changing his name to theirs—a part of the deal.

In response, Munira had rushed to the promontory, clutching Ayaana to her body. She prepared to jump. Her suicide threat compounded the scandal, entrenching the certainty of her incorrigible madness, her cursedness. Many, many years later, in one of their lucent moments, Munira would tell Muhidin the smaller details from that time: how she had handed her heart over to nothing—"I don't believe in man"; how at every moon tide she would vomit out hope; how she rated some days' quality by the quantity of insults received—the fewer the kinder. "But you can't outrun your shadow," she would say to Muhidin. He would reply, "You can ignore it." She would scoff, "Stop it. We *know* the truth. Even as we lie." She would say, "We will speak of death before we dare to speak of our loneliness. *Dua la kuku halimpati mwewe*. But I'm alive. Isn't that good?" She would laugh at herself.

After Munira threatened suicide, her cherished father, to save face, declared her *maharimu*—anathema. He had also preceded her name with the word *mahua*—the deceased—saying, "You, my firstborn, you trampled on my holiest dreams, you, to whom I gave everything. You have squandered your right to our name." His eyes had been red with grief. Munira's father, to the resentful regret of the archipelago—he had been a significant job-creator—had at once moved his harborage business and household five hundred kilometers away, to Zanzibar. Munira's spurned suitor and his family went with them. "Please, die," her stepmother suggested to her on their way out, "but do it after we've gone."

They abandoned Munira in Pate with her child.

Munira mourned them. She would live, but her name became a byword for faults, a caution used to threaten bold or rebellious girls, a reason to remember why there were fewer jobs available on the archipelago. She was *kidonda*—a walking wound.

In spite of his anguish, Munira's father had, supposedly in error, left behind the keys to one of the family's smaller houses. Munira had cautiously moved in and waited to be evicted. That did not happen. She retreated into its shelter with her daughter. She emerged in the early light with the child wrapped on her back and cleaned houses, cooked, washed and braided hair for pitiful shillings, with which she fed herself. She then started a garden of flowers, spices, and herbs, which she tended one plant at a time, burying her hand into the difficult loam and churning it with manure until it became fruitful again. Her beauty-therapeutics work sprang gently from this.

Munira was marooned on her island. But twice a month, and only at night, she wandered over to a cove or sought out one of four large sea-facing rocks from which to look out at dark horizons into which she could implant secret dreams, safe from the jagged, gnashing teeth of an unappeasable world. There, within the shelter of night, Muhidin had thrice glimpsed Munira. Two years into his return to Pate, Muhidin, wandering in the darkness, had sighted a fluid shadow under the silver-light moon. The vision had frosted his soul. Then, to his breath-restoring relief, a human body glided after it, an unveiled moonstone woman. In another month of another year, in an equally dense hour, Muhidin's and Munira's sea-sprayed shadows crisscrossed, merged, and separated again: two isolations tiptoeing on an ocean's boundaries, ears tilted inward, straining toward unknown phantoms and old promises that tempted them into an interiority where they could rest. Muhidin again spotted Munira crouched within an onyx-shaded hollow close to the sea. Not once did either of them acknowledge the presence of the other. At the previous New Year's, while trying to strip himself of the ocean's hold on his soul—he had, again, woken up to find himself in the water—Muhidin had run toward Munira's house for no reason. He had leaned his head against the pillars of her door. Ever since then, he had tried to avoid even the thought of her.

[5]

On some Pate Island nights, conversations among men converged on the island square. In the absence of a reliable television service, these *mabaraza* were Muhidin's news roundups. The men, mostly retired civil servants with rolled-up two-day-old newspapers whose every word they pored over, merchants, nondescript workers and scholars talked. Children played, and women murmured and tittered, and voices gentled by the day's end debated Kenya's contorted politics, its brothel-opened approach to everything, and English Premier League scores. There were three main groups unfairly distributed in support of Arsenal, Manchester United, and Chelsea. A few clung to a much-mocked nostalgia for Liverpool. They spoke often of Kenya as if they mattered to it, as if it had not at once lost its memory of their existence.

Muhidin gobbled sweetmeats with these men, sipped hot, bitter coffee, played dominoes, mocked nearby Lamu Island's self-importance—Pate had once dominated these seas, had been a maritime hub, making and selling warships to the nations of the ocean. The men outdid one another's monster-and-mermaid tales, and dissected visitors, such as the old man from China who had taken over a fishing hut and was planting a vegetable garden. They clucked about scavenging *watu wa bara*, mainlanders, and the native-born *nyang'au* who were Kenyan politicians. They whispered about secret oil and gas and gold finds on the island. They traversed the memories of their broken island; picked up shards of fragmented, shattered, potent yesterdays. They exchanged tales of happenings in ports and sniffed the aromas of white flowers—lady of the night, orange blossom, lilies, jasmine—under the trillion eavesdropping stars. These Pate nights had reduced the volume of the thousand and one moans plaguing Muhidin from hidden places of his soul. The men would often rib Muhidin about his flirtations with heresy and his wild-tempered avoidance of public prayers and sacred events. "The Apostate," they had nicknamed him. Yet Muhidin was also treated with cautionary wonder. Not only was he an augur who soothed secretly proffered fears with mysterious elixirs, but also, with one Pate eye perpetually cast on imagined worlds beyond the sea, the men saw in Muhidin one who had lived their every unmet dream.

In the *mabaraza*, after their evisceration of politicians who, they agreed, went to Nairobi garlanded in dreams and promises and returned to them as shape-shifting djinns—devious, untruthful, and ravenous—the chattering men would often target an island resident to broil, roast, and chew over. To Muhidin's suddenly increasing dismay, he observed how often Munira, the little girl's mother, was fodder. *Kidonda* entwined with major human follies, with a focus on lust, mannerlessness, sloth, and vanity. *Kambare mzuri kwa mwili, ndani machafu.* She had outer beauty but inside dirt, proclaimed a middle-aged merchant with a penchant for watermelons and lewd insights: "Have you seen how that one spins her head?"

"How?" Muhidin barked, irritated by his irritation. *Not my business*, he scolded himself.

The merchant's eyes roamed as he said, "Nose high up. Scandalous daughter of fire, she even speaks with her hands." He lowered his voice. "You've seen the gap between her front teeth? She ensnares men with potions." His head moved in an arc that pointed northward.

Munira had been seen wandering in the direction of the arc, where Fundi Almazi Mehdi lived. He was the almost mute shipbuilder and long-ago wind-whistler—one of the few who could summon sea winds by intent and melody—whose grandfather had moved to Siyu from Kiwayuu. Mehdi repaired broken sea vessels. His wife, sons, and daughters had lives elsewhere, in the Middle East, where Mehdi had also been before returning to Pate alone. He was sometimes heard to whistle to the memory of sea winds. His radio knob was permanently set to the meteorological channel, with which he kept abreast of the state of tides.

"Fundi Mehdi?" Muhidin restrained his amusement.

"God protect us," the merchant sighed.

Muhidin let go a belly chortle. "Dear man, you sound thwarted. Were you hoping to be 'ensnared'?" The others laughed at the man. Muhidin added, "*Du!* Yet that woman's garden is alluring. The soil loves her hand. What flowers! What herbs! What spices!"

The island's mobile-phone services provider protested. "But have you asked yourself what sort of person cultivates plants near a grave, eh? I swear she employs djinns, eh?"

Djinns? Muhidin said, "Decayed flesh is also manure, brother!"

The man sniffed.

A week later, Muhidin felt his body edging away from these night conversations. He had been about to jump into the conclusion of a debate about Arsenal versus Manchester United, in praise of the Chelsea Football Club, when he realized he was on the outside looking in. The same thing happened three nights later. As the island's oldest tailor was boasting and calling his wife "a flower of flowers," Muhidin had stretched his arms. Faking casualness, he pursed his lips to whistle. He wandered off, looking about him as if for a pee bush. But as soon as he was out of sight of his companions, he dashed all the way back to his house.

Muhidin felt his way up the stairs and into his bedroom. There he showered before falling into bed, where an odd electric sensation seized him. *What am I doing?* He tossed about in dampening sheets. "Where is your wife?" those men had once asked him. He had lied. He had looked roguish when he said he had made full use of *misyar*, the traveler's marriage—a legal temporary arrangement between a consenting man and woman. "Countless Nikah mutʿah," he announced. The men gaped at him in wonder. He had compounded the lie to extract sympathy: "The one I most loved . . . she got sick. To spare me grief, she left me"—he dropped his head and choked—"to die."

The men made sympathetic sounds.

One observed, "It is good you are here now; our women are beautiful."

Now, lying in his bed, Muhidin evoked the women who had been actual intimates in his life. After his first wife, he had temporarily married three others—lush beings. He had disappeared on them. One was in Pondicherry, another in Mocha, and another in . . . was it Beira? Far too many gaps, he grunted. He had lost the threads of the lies he told to gain access to soft, scented, sultry bodies, and the lies he wove to extricate himself. With a piercing pang, he wondered about his children—those he knew about, the ones he had abandoned. A shuddering in his heart: condensation of unspoken fears. He murmured into that night: "Am I, then, to die alone?" He had lived hard and unfettered. He had sought this way—preferring it to the possessive disorders of erratic jealousies, overwrought demands that passed for love and its suffering. He had never been able to give himself over to stifling domesticity. He read it as insanity. Fortunately for him, fresh horizons always beckoned. He was a man most himself when roaming the contours of life's riddles. But time had turned on him. Time had handed him over to the shapes of his ghosts. They were of the texture of his unchosen life.

Now—"What am I waiting for?" An opposing proposal—"*Who* am I waiting for?" Muhidin turned over in his bed, leaning away from the encroachment of memory, but not succeeding.

Raziya, his first wife: he had divorced her when he was nineteen and she eighteen. Raziya was a sweet, trusting, overprotected island girl, vulnerable to the potent flattery—*mndani*, and *mpenzi wangu*—that Muhidin ladled. They had eloped and gone to Malindi, then returned to the island married. Seven months later, she gave birth to twin boys, Tawfiq and Ziriyab.

Three days later, Kenya, the restarted country, lowered the Union Jack and raised a red, green, black, and white standard. Raziya's father, Haroun, an erudite man striving for tolerance, who had almost studied at Oxford University, had tried to embrace his rough-hewn fisherman son-in-law. He turned over one of his houses to his daughter, hoping the cultured environment would have both a cleansing and an enlightening effect on the man, to whom he insisted on speaking in English. The house had indoor ablutions. "Dowry," the father-in-law had told Muhidin.

The house's elegant lines and spaces, rows of bookshelves, and old, delicate Chinese plates had scared Muhidin, who stumbled into and broke a two-hundred-year-old Persian vase on his foray across the threshold. He took to spending days and nights at sea to avoid being near the house. He darted hither and thither to avoid the father-in-law, who was always seeking to improve him. "We are now Kenya," Father-in-Law once said of the new flag fluttering on the pole of the repainted administrative shed.

"So?" Muhidin had replied in Kibajuni. "Will it improve the supply of fish?" He was not being rude; he had simply wanted to understand what "Kenya" meant.

Father-in-Law had tried for two more years before giving up and arranging a more suitable affiliation for his daughter, with a widower, a respectable merchant cousin from Yemen. Father-in-Law then contrived a dawn fishing trip with Muhidin. He had camped next to Muhidin's boat from midnight, waiting for him. "Let's go," he told Muhidin. Mid-sea, Haroun had produced an envelope with eight thousand shillings and an introduction to a ship captain in Mombasa. In exchange, he pleaded with Muhidin to divorce his daughter—"Be merciful in God's name; you are surely most unworthy of my child and her children"—and effect a permanent disappearance from the vicinity of the territories of the East African coast forever. Muhidin had sputtered before squelching a plea to Haroun, to explain that he had been poring over a dictionary of English words, that he listened to the BBC on shortwave radio even at sea. Instead, Muhidin had exhaled, deflated. None of his efforts would ever be good enough for them. Muhidin told Haroun that he was bored with the island anyway, that he was tired of everybody's improvement schemes for him. He grabbed the money and left, cursing the island and its people. He told the scrawny boatman with whom he rowed to Lamu that he would become a beached octopus before he returned to Pate.

Yet, years later, Muhidin had drifted back to Pate, and it looked smaller, shabbier, more derelict, isolated, and even more preoccupied with trivialities. The nation of Kenya's half-century of neglect had consumed the soul out of the land, just as ocean-bed trawlers of many nations sucked up migrating yellowfin tuna and marlin unchecked, leaving the fishermen with scraps and the stocks of fish depleted. Most conversations now were about departures—intended, hoped for, planned, or executed. What still thrived were Pate's teeming ghosts, who jockeyed with residents for the right of abode. What still flourished were those in-between-space realms, their history, memory, and stories—it is to these that most who stumbled back to Pate returned.

What lingered was Muhidin's restlessness.

But that night in his bed, inside the gloom of the decayed glory of a coral house he had once shunned, he mulled over an unforeseen reality: in all his fleeing, seeking, tricking, escaping, negotiating, working, whoring, wondering, reading, lying, learning, wrestling, questioning, seeing, tasting, hearing, and journeying, nothing had suggested a vision of "home" or "belonging" until that light-spattered dawn when he glimpsed a little creature dancing with the sparkling Pate sea.

[6]

Weeks later, within those cryptic violet-orange moments before sunrise, Muhidin was startled into wakefulness by a grating voice hurling "*Ayaaana?*" It was Abasi, the other muezzin.

Abasi was a one-man morality police who modeled himself on a Saudi *mutawwa*—policing morals—and might have given himself over to bearded Wahhabism were it not for his heart and gut's helpless devotion to his island's saints. Today, it seemed, Abasi had glimpsed the ocean's dawn companion. Muhidin threw on an old gray *kikoi* and stumbled down uneven stairs as outside, Abasi bayed, "*Eiii! Mtoooto wa nyoka ni . . . ni nyokaaa!*"—The child of a snake is a snake! Words as blows. Muhidin reached for his carved door. Abasi was cawing like a starved raven, "*Nazi mbovu haribu ya nzima, weeee mwanaharamu!*" Hearing light footsteps on the pavement outside, Muhidin flung open his door. There she was. Little, thin, doe-eyed, intense, shivering, dripping water from a tiny pink T-shirt, wearing faded blue leggings. Her damp bangs covered half her face. Upturned nose. Her eyes were red with sea salt, and fear mingled with mischief inside them. The child opened and closed her mouth like a stranded fish.

"*Mwanaharamuuu!*" Approaching footsteps. The child hunched over.

Muhidin beckoned her into the house as he stepped backward. He pointed to a cavernous engraved hardwood cupboard—made in Bombay before Bombay became Mumbai. It had come via Oman. Its main purpose was to aid concealment. There was a deep shelf inside where Muhidin stored his best books, his attar and blossoms; spice-incense experiments lined up several drawers. Four hidden compartments kept his other secrets. Inside, a two-person red velvet bench snapped into place to create a temporary yet comfortable hideaway. Ayaana scrambled and disappeared inside the cupboard. Muhidin closed his door. He stepped into the room to lock the cupboard, pulled out its long key, and lifted his *barghashia* to place the key in the middle of his head. He restored the *barghashia*. Muhidin heard the grumbling outside—"Today I've caught you!"—followed by a shuffle and an impatient knock. Muhidin took his time releasing the latch, ignoring the flutter in the pit of his stomach. There he was: squat, squint-eyed, big-toothed Abasi, chirping, "She was here," as he pecked at the ground with a twisted stick. Leaning over to look, Muhidin saw tiny, fading footsteps in sand and water leading across the porch and into his shop-home.

"Ma'alim Abasi! *Salaam aleikum, mzee!* A day of sunshine! Who was here?" Muhidin asked, but, moving sideways with a surreptitious gesture, he swept a hand over a shelf weighted down with maps, magazines, and books. These fell with a bang to create a small hill that cluttered the entrance. Muhidin huffed, "A thousand possessed books!" He bent to pick up a book, clutching his back with a grimace. "Oh, my back! Good you are here. Please. Help me capture my many, many vagabonds as we talk . . ."

Abasi lifted up clean hands. He also tried to peer over Muhidin's shoulder to scan the room. "I wondered . . . *em* . . . I saw . . . Did you see? Babu, forgive me, I'd like to help you . . . Did you see a *curs-ed* child, this high?" He estimated Ayaana's height with his hand. "What? The books? Understand . . . were it not . . . Yes . . . You know Farouk, the agro-supplies man . . . not good. The tumor has spread to his forehead. Not good . . ." He was on surer ground now. "I must go."

Muhidin blew the dust from the jacket of another book into Abasi's face. His voice wheedled: "Just a little?"

Abasi sneezed, rubbed his eyes, and took four steps back. "Understand . . ." He was very firm. He hurried off, down the coiling street.

The morning returned to its former stillness.

There was the smell of the sea—a whiff of the illuminated things of life. A bird with a low-pitched voice lifted the morning with a punctuation mark—*tong, tong, phee!* Muhidin unlocked the Bombay cupboard's door. "You may emerge, Abeerah," Muhidin said. "A lazy camel has vaporized at the thought of labor."

After four ticking minutes of nothing, a small creature flung the cupboard door aside, leapt out, and ran smack into Muhidin. It knelt and wrapped its arms around his knees. "I am Ayaana," it breathed.

"I know, Abeerah."

Five ticking seconds.

"*Nitakupenda.*"—I *shall* love you—the small being shrieked, before it sailed over mounds of books on its way out, dashing into a narrow alleyway where it merged with lean shadows.

[7]

She stuffed small pink petals into her mouth, chewing damask roses, while her mother, Munira, was distracted by the buzzing of secret thoughts. The girl studied her mother's faraway look as she tasted the rose hip, its thorniness. Sucking rose water from her fingers, treating scent as taste, and remembering how her mother sometimes dropped twelve perfect globules into their tea, their milk, and, always, the *halua* she made. Sliver of a shadow as the girl's thoughts skipped. Many nights, her mother, struggling in a net of fear of unknown things, would call her child over to her bed. There Munira would unseal a tiny long-necked blue metal *mrashi*, stored under her pillow, and sprinkle its rose water over the both of them as a prayer shroud.

Before the girl found a way to this moment of roses, she had been weeping. She had wanted to fix the terribleness of her existence. That day had collapsed over her. In the morning, during the madrassa session, the recitation had all of a sudden pierced her very core. Lost in the feeling, she had been unaware of a gradual silence enfolding the room. She had not seen the usually immobile and monotone Mwalimu Idris stir and then rise like a fire-fed phoenix. Neither had she heard his pained "*Subhan Allah!*"

31

Ayaana had not expected that the tip of her teacher's stick would beat a tattoo on her head to snap her out of her trance.

Mwalimu Idris had then lowered his head, the better to scrutinize her. He adjusted the lenses of round glasses that made his eyes huge and asked Ayaana, "Are you a djinn?"

Ayaana froze, not understanding. The teacher's stick poked her forehead. "Only the unholy dead yowl as you did; only the damned would sully these, the sweetest of words, with such a caterwauling." He had enunciated his judgment: "You will leave my class. You will not return until such time as I decree that I have recovered from this assault."

Ayaana had fled the room amid the titters. She sobbed, then determined that she would not cry.

Big people!

Later that day, she had worked extra hard to do everything she could to be the "same as" the others: striding like Khadija, rolling words in her mouth before spitting them out like Atiya, raising the corner of her upper lip before smiling like Maimouna, and hunting for crabs in the mangroves and then donating the choicest findings to boys like Suleiman. But that afternoon, Atiya's up-country father had returned to the island and found the children playing in the nearby field. While Farah, Mwanajuma, Rehema, and Ruquiya counted seeds, Ayaana skipped rope. The rope belonged to Atiya, who had started to grumble, impatient for her turn. The father had hissed at Ayaana as if she were a stray dog, and yelled, "*Wee! Mwana kidonda!*"—Child of the wound! He had proceeded to break a twig from the nearby shrub with which to threaten her.

At first, Ayaana's playmates had giggled. But when two of the girls burst into tears, unsure of what Bad Thing had happened, Ayaana had run away, tearing down ancient roadways. She had hurled herself through the half-open door of her house, trembling at the unseen horror she carried that offended others, which she could not fix.

In the early evening, Munira, her mother, returned home, carrying two fish, a new set of *leso*s, and an aromatic plant. She crossed the threshold calling, "Ayaana!"

No reply.

Munira clucked. She was crossing the living room to reach her bedroom when she saw the deformed shape of her daughter, huddled on a faded blue chair. Munira dropped her goodies and approached the form. Her daughter's head was pressed against a shabby green-gold photo album; she bit hard on her lips, and from time to time scrubbed the wetness off her face. Munira's gaze focused on the album, remembering, with the usual pang, the people in there, frozen by light, who were absent from their present, and maybe their future. She had not told her daughter who these were. Later, much later, Munira would again conceal the album in a dark, dank corner of her cupboard, still unable to throw it away, still praying that time or termites would dissolve it for her. Now Munira knelt before Ayaana, tugging at the album until it left her daughter's hands. Ayaana lifted her head and sought her mother's gaze. Munira stopped a howl at the sight of her child's hollowed eyes, the profound grief that pinched her face—the miasma of ancestral sorrows, the inheritance of wounds, of absences. She had choked a little, struggling for the right word.

Ayaana's voice had crackled. "*Ma-e*, I, too, I have a father?"

Munira was silent.

Ayaana asked, "*Ma-e, mababu wetu walienda wapi?*"—Where are our people?

Munira tilted her head.

Ayaana whispered, "*Ma-e*, what *is* the name of us . . . our family?"

Munira shut her eyes and heard, again, her own father's heartbroken curse: "You, you have lost the right to our name." She had honored his grief and judgment, had accepted her amputation from a deep and wide genealogy that had for centuries opened for their family access to secret spaces and places of the world. Broken off. Munira and Ayaana had been consigned to nowhere.

Ayaana gestured, pointing through the door, toward the world: "Them . . . they never want me."

"Who?" Munira already knew, but she asked anyway.

"Big peoples."

"How?"

Within the child, a montage of interruptions: Skipping, stop. Tadpole hunting, leave. Marble playing, get out. Shell gathering, go home. Earthworm digging, disappear. Mangrove hide-and-seek . . . Big people had never reached her among her sheltering mangroves. Turning to her mother, Ayaana then dared to ask the thing she most feared. "Is Ayaana bad?" Scrunching her face, refusing to cry. Tears squeezed through anyway. The child continued, as if reciting a crime: "Bi Amina, *Ma-e* . . . Bi Amina . . . She is saying, Ayaana! *Kidonda*, Ayaana! *Kidonda*."

Munira flinched.

Kidonda: wound. That epithet. An idea oft repeated becoming real. Those familiar tentacles had now turned to hunt down her daughter as well. Witnessing the light being squelched from her child's eyes, Munira felt her entrails roiling. In that moment, she would have surrendered her soul to the first gray-feathered djinn who could teach her how to spare her daughter the turmoil of inherited anguish. Munira gulped down her rising rage. Unclenching her fists, she raised her chin. Defiance. She had the power of words: she would call forth another name, an impossible and immense name. Munira's voice was hard. "We have a name." She paused. "The moon"—she hesitated—"gave it to us." Now she whispered. "A sky name. We do not say it out loud, except at night, lest *they*"—she gestured to the outside world with her chin—"seize it from us."

Ayaana's eyes widened, as clarity dawned and refreshed their light. A sparkle. "A sky name?" she whispered. "What it is? What it is?"

Munira struggled with the ball of salt lodged in her throat, a curse she wanted to spit at the world. She spoke the lie into her daughter's eyes. "Wa Jauza." She repeated the phrase, now planting it in Ayaana's soul through her right ear. "Wa Jauza." *Jauza*. Orion. An entire constellation. "That is our name, our secret," Munira murmured.

Ayaana had pressed her palms together, contemplating the grandness of this. The feeling grew and grew, till it heated up her heart and tilted her face upward. She would never stop looking skyward after that evening.

Munira had then gripped Ayaana's right hand, pulling her to her feet, while announcing in a faux-cheery voice, "Come, *lulu*. Let us hunt roses, *lulu*."

Ayaana had exhaled on a shudder.

Seeking roses, borrowing roses, scents that bled tenderness. Munira's heart-gaze sought beauty as a desiccated soul craves water. Yearning for loveliness, she built on color until the greens became the green they were created to be. She trusted scent; it was for her an unfiltered presence, and therefore truth. She tended flowers and herbs, tugging and caressing at excesses until the plants revealed their essential core in perfect aromas that evoked a particular way of seeing. This was also one of Ayaana's many pastimes, which included counting ripples on ponds and the sea, anticipating swells, watching rocks in the sea turn to shadow just before sunset, and befriending pointy-eared island cats with their large prescient eyes. The cats' inclination to disappear with the onset of new-moon tides forced Ayaana into a cycle of affection and heartbreak and affection again.

Munira and Ayaana plucked small petals from the wild-rose bush draped over the ancient tombs. Its flowering was irregular—sometimes light for sweetness, other times dark for atonement. They gathered petals and dreamed of rose water. Rose water purged shame, filled sorrow's crevices, and rinsed out guilt. Rose water tempered fears and longings. Munira and Ayaana hurried back to their cool, coral-stone home with their floral bounty. Munira rinsed a saucepan so she could boil water for half the roses. She glanced three times at Ayaana, her child of abandonment, child of loss, fruit of lying dreams. The water bubbled. Ayaana's eyes rounded. Now that she was lost in creating, delight displaced grief. She lifted her head to catch her mother's eyes. Munira lowered her face, connecting with Ayaana's forehead. They were eye to eye, eyelashes entangling just like their softly-softly touching spirits. The water was cooling. Munira sighed, "*Lulu*, drop half the petals into the bowl. One at a time."

Ayaana did, folding petals in, stirring the water. Seeing that her mother was distracted, her gaze fixed beyond the sea, Ayaana sneaked the largest petal into her mouth, scalding her fingers. She glanced over at her mother, then returned to watch the petals settle in the water and scooped another clutch to eat. In another bowl, the untouched rose petals waited. Later, they would bleed their essence into heated, pure coconut oil, to be distilled into a costly elixir to serve Munira's work, which was to cover women with beauty, even those who called her a fragrant whore.

[8]

On a Sunday afternoon, Muhidin sauntered from the waterfront, whistling and swinging four just-purchased spring-tide fish. He saw Ayaana squatting beneath the old, bent ylang-ylang tree. There was a shallow hole in the dust in front of her. Her fingers were trained on a chipped bluish marble. He smiled, and would have continued if he had not heard her sniffing and comforting herself, "No! Ayaana, no matter, don't cry."

Surrounded by the resonant cheer of the distant playing children, which bounced all over the land, Muhidin carefully laid aside his fish before getting to his knees. Pretending to ignore Ayaana, he looked about, saw an oval black pebble, and dug it out of the earth.

Her gaze.

Lucid. Unblinking.

At last, Ayaana very slowly retrieved a shiny red marble from her pocket and gave it to him. She took the black pebble from his hand and pocketed it. She wiped her face with dusty fingers, staining it with streaks of mud. Muhidin primed his finger, narrowed his eyes, teeth biting his tongue, and let go. The marble missed its target by a meter. Ayaana's smile was slow in coming. Then it emerged. Misery evaporated. They played marbles for over an hour, giggling over everything and nothing. Through oblique questioning, Muhidin would find out that some children had exiled her from their playgroup. Dura had said that there were far too many for the game and someone had to leave. Maimouna had volunteered Ayaana. Fatuma had protested that that was not fair, and they could all take turns waiting out the game. Suleiman had shoved Ayaana to the ground. She fell, her legs in the air. The children had laughed at the sight of her torn underwear. It was the humiliation that hurt her. Ayaana had picked up her three marbles and run away.

A persistent *tong, tong, tong* drilled into Muhidin's past-midnight dreaming. It took him another six minutes to understand that the banging came from a door that was not within his dreams. His eyes snapped open. *Tong, tong, tong. Tong, tong, tong.* Groggy, livid, grumbling, he wrapped a *kikoi* around his waist and proceeded down the stairs, stumbling against the staircase and stubbing his big toe. "*Makende!*" he yelped. By the time he had dragged aside the lock, caught the skin of his thumb in between the clasps, howled again, and wrenched open the door, he was ready to commit murder.

There she was again. A little girl, shifting from left foot to right with bright-eyed urgency, in a still night under a waning gibbous moon. "*Kuja uone*"—Come see. She tugged at his arms, trying to drag him out.

His bewildered "What?" But he followed her.

"Hurry," she demanded.

An emergency? He raced after her. She was steps ahead of him and kept looking back. *Hurry*, her arms beckoned. *Something has happened to her mother*. He wondered if he should have carried bandages.

They arrived at a promontory. Below them, a tide swirled. A cool breeze provided a bass note for soughing night creatures—an invisible reptile interspersed the melodies with a monotone croak. Night jasmine infused the air, and the sky above tossed lights across eternity, splashing white, blue, yellow, and red sparks in the sky, which was reflected in the black mirror of the water. The child tugging at Muhidin's arm attempted a whisper as she pointed skyward at the moon. "Who has break the moon?" Her voice contained a compressed worry. She turned to peer into his face as if he *must* know, as if she suspected *he* could do something about the lunar vandalism. Muhidin had scanned the earth. He saw the night sky as if for the first time. "Who done it?" Ayaana pleaded. She was holding his face as if his was the most important answer in the world.

So Muhidin lied, because he did not want to seem ordinary in light of the hunger to know in her large eyes. He lied because he did not believe. Muhidin said, "The Infinite Poet." "Almighty," he added, as if he and the Moon Breaker were intimates, "who deconstructs in order to renew." He repeated the word "Almighty" to watch the "ooooh"s take over her face. He hoarded her wonder for himself.

They watched the sky, saw stray night clouds, a fraction of the moon, and traveling stars. "Read," she then said, both her hands gesturing skyward. He waited. "Read more," she commanded. But he had forgotten how. Used to wandering down random trails as he was, he had lost his way. So they watched the sky. Ayaana tilted her head back, squeezing her eyes shut, then opening them. She asked, "And the ocean, she is saying what?"

Muhidin listened. "'Who are you?'" he interpreted for her. "'Who are you?'"

"I am Ayaana!" she screamed to the water below, leaning over the edge. "Now you."

"I am Muhidin," he muttered.

She exclaimed, "Loud!"

"I am Muhidin!" he bellowed to the wind and waves.

They giggled. They watched the sky. They heard the sea ask, *Who are you?* And the broken moon watched them. She turned and held his face again, the better to speak. But she forgot what she wanted to say as she studied Muhidin's face. "A small-of-star-insided-your-eyes!" She stretched out a finger and said, "Can-I-touch?" She did not wait for his yes or no. She touched tears, the star fragments she had glimpsed. And they sat on the edge of a promontory, an aging man and a little girl, spying on stars and witnessing the passage of waves. As she pointed, he saw countries between the stars and heard silences between the ebb and flow of the tide. They sat on the edge and listened to the wind, the man and the girl, and the flow of life caused a tree's tiny branch to mark time with an intermittent *tang*. In the ocean's far horizons, a massive ship made its way, a light-spotted giant shadow.

Ayaana whispered, "Where it is going?"

Unconscious that he had done so, Muhidin squeezed her to his side. "Home," he replied.

"Where it is home?" she murmured.

"*Mahali fulani*"—Somewhere—Muhidin answered.

The child drifted to sleep curled up against his body, cupping her own face. He listened to her breathing and watched stars and listened to the ocean, while a bird whistled at him. He listened to the sea for a long time before it dawned on Muhidin that Ayaana ought to be sleeping in her bed. Hesitant, fearful that she and her dreams might crumble in his hands, he stooped extra low to lift her up. He carried her, walking with slow steps. When he reached her front door, he stood and frowned. If he knocked, she would get into trouble. So he whispered, "*Mwanangu*"—my child. Unbidden thought. He blanked it out. "Abeerah," Muhidin called.

She stirred. She yawned and saw him. When she became aware of their surroundings, she said, "You carry Ayaana? You bringed Ayaana?"

"Yes, Abeerah."

She held his face again. "Now I go," she said. "Don't be scared." He lowered her to the ground. "You wait," she commanded, "till I gone inside."

Muhidin watched as she skipped five meters away from the door. Leg up, she stood on one window ledge and lifted her other leg to stretch across what looked like a string-thick ledge onto another window. A midair leap, and she was clinging to a water pipe, on which she shinnied up to a high window. She squeezed through this. Soon a tiny hand appeared to flutter a bye-bye before disappearing. Somewhere in the distance, a cockerel crowed. Apart from Muhidin's soft, stunned breathing and the sound of the ceaseless waves, everything became calm again.

[9]

It was as long as her middle finger, and as thin as her mother's largest sewing needle. There was yellow-gold and red on its head, and red inside its eyes. Its small chest was olive and brown, and she could see the table through fine wings made of pale-orange light. Muhidin told Ayaana to repeat its name, *kereng'ende*, in four other languages: "*Matapiojos. Libélula. Naaldekoker.* Dragonfly."

Ayaana intoned, "*Matapiojos-libélula-naaldekoker*-dragonfly." She clasped her hands, squeezing them. "Why?" she asked.

Muhidin whispered, "To savor its essence. To do that, you must taste at least three languages on your tongue." Muhidin looked stern.

Ayaana's facial expression mirrored his.

. . .

Lying flat on her belly near the mangroves, Ayaana had waited most of the afternoon for the right dragonfly to show up. Today she did not go to the makeshift jetty to watch for home-comers. When the dragonfly landed on a twig, she crawled, stalked, and captured it. It had curled over to bite at her fingers, but she managed to stick it into one of her mother's small covered bowls. Taking slow steps, clutching the bowl, Ayaana brought it to Muhidin. He was reading one of his books when she appeared at his door just an hour before dusk and called, "*Shikamoo*, Babu."

"*Marahaba*," he had replied, his soul uneasy. She was strolling into his life unsought, unwanted, bearing a fragile heart in her big eyes, and offering all this to him unasked for.

"I finded it," she said, "for you." Darts of stifled delight crackled in her eyes.

He laid aside the book. "Oh?" And sighed.

"See?"

With reluctance, Muhidin took the bowl. He opened it and found a comatose dragonfly inside. It was still stunned when he stretched it out on the flat surface of a low table and knelt to look more closely at it. Ayaana, clinging to Muhidin's shoulders, leaned over. Her right foot, in patched red Bata slippers, stood on his left foot. "You like him?" she asked.

"This luminous presence? I do. Thank you."

Ayaana swung to and fro. "Me, I found him, only me alone." They watched the creature. She watched Muhidin. She remembered something else. "Him bited me here." She showed her finger.

Muhidin touched the finger. He pursed his lips. "She was afraid."

"Why?"

"She is so, so small, and Abeerah is so, so big. See?"

Ayaana's eyes watered at once. She whispered, "Only wanted to give you a pretty." Pause. "Ayaana is not bad. Never wanted 'im to be afraid." She shook her head.

A soft, warm spasm spread across Muhidin's chest. *Abeerah*. Unsettled, not knowing what to do. He then told her to repeat its name, *kereng'ende*, in four languages. After she had, Ayaana had another secret to tell Muhidin. She sighed. She bit her mouth. She clutched her stomach. She sighed again. Big people never wanted to hear what she said. They clicked their tongues. They said, *"Debe shinda haliachi kusukasuka"*—A half-empty tin does not stop shaking.

Muhidin watched moods shift on Ayaana's little face, saw her shoulders rise as if she was elated, and then collapse, leaving an unuttered question dangling on her lips. She swallowed it and rested her face on the table, eyes almost level with the slowly stirring dragonfly. She turned large eyes on Muhidin. *Don't speak*, Muhidin suddenly wanted to beg. *Go away.* Yet another inside voice cried, *What, Abeerah?*

Ayaana held out for another fifteen seconds. Then the child got up abruptly, body stiffening with her decision. She looked at Muhidin. Her voice was firm: "You are now my father." Then she exploded into tears, her body shivering from the shock of hearing the words of her longing spoken out loud.

"Oof!" Muhidin huffed as if punched in the stomach. *What words.* He jerked back, then stood motionless. Now his ears were buzzing. Now his thoughts were lurching. He had traveled long and alone, holding on to nothing. He was used to leaving. He had never been claimed before. She was crying, her shoulders heaving. He stooped over to learn the essence of this, of the nature of words that could tear into a grown man's heart. *This.* Child. Her dragonfly. Those words. She sobbed, bereft, as if she had lost everything. So Muhidin reached over to clasp Ayaana's tiny hand as warning bells pinged all over his body. *This child.* Her dragonfly. Entwined hands. His hands were oversized and wizened. Rough, hairy, knotted, and hard-etched with the memory of profane and obscene things they had sought and touched. He dragged them away from her. *This* child. Her tears. His hands touched a crying child's head. *"Haya basi, haya, Abeerah,"* Muhidin muttered.

Ayaana hiccupped her tears to a stop. She gulped down breath. She looked at Muhidin.

He tilted his head.

She threw her whole self onto him, clinging to his neck, her hands to his face.

Within Muhidin, the waiting and wondering.

She was chatting about something, giggling, her breath warm against his neck.

A rush of liquid inside his skull; he was struggling to breathe. She was changing him. He felt himself changing. She said something else.

It must have been a question. It stopped on a high note. Then she was silent.

This child.

In his arms.

Sighing and drifting to sleep.

He sighed, too. He turned his head just in time to see the red-eyed dragonfly shake itself alert, crawl to the end of a small table, spread gossamer wings out, and fly away through an open window. It blended with the evening's touch-of-red light that dappled the room.

He would learn to always stoop to meet her eyes. She expected this: eye-to-eye conversations. She needed to see everything his soul suggested. She kept her vow: she loved him as he was. Ayaana told everyone—except her mother—that Muhidin was now her father.

[10]

The next dawn, wearing her school uniform and carrying a tattered canvas schoolbag, Ayaana showed up at Muhidin's door.

"You teach me school," Ayaana declared.

"Go away," Muhidin said. "Go to school." He closed the door on her.

When he stepped out two hours later, Ayaana was still there.

"What do you want?" growled Muhidin.

"You teach me." Her eyes were clear.

"Go to school."

"No! School is bad."

"I'm going to Lamu."

"I coming with you."

"You are not."

"You teach me."

"No. Look . . . now I'm going to miss my boat." With Ayaana trailing him, he hobbled in the direction of the *matatu* stop, shouting to others to stop the van for him. "*Dereva!* I'm already late."

When Muhidin returned that evening, he found Ayaana's charcoal lines, curves, shapes, and math sums drawn across the steps leading to his door. Muhidin waited for her the next day with a cloth and a bucket of soapy water. She appeared, with a scrawny dirty-white creature purring on her shoulders. She stared up at his thunderous features. Her voice shook. "Ayaana did bad?"

Muhidin's face softened. "No. Just the wrong medium."

She had to put the kitten down. "What is 'medium'?"

"I'll show you when my stones are spotless again."

After she finished wiping the stonework, Muhidin brought down a patched-together calligraphy set. He had once intended to explore the difference between Thuluth and Naskh forms for himself. He gave her the books and several large white sheets of paper. Ayaana clutched these. "Mine?" she exclaimed.

Muhidin scowled. "Now you can indulge the words you love; at least make them beautiful," he said in their island dialect.

"Kujiingiza." *Indulge:* a word to capture.

So, almost by mistake, Muhidin began to tutor Ayaana's gush of hows, whens, and whos. He told her to take her whys to books, retrieving one or another from amid a dark clutter. He read to her from Hafiz.

"What it means?" Ayaana asked. "In three languages?"

He told her to seek answers in her own words, which was better than speaking three languages. Muhidin told her, "Books are emissaries from other worlds."

"Atoka wapi?"

"When you cross this threshold," he said, entering his new role with relish, "English. *'Threshold.'*" Ayaana learned that this meant *kizingiti*. Another word to keep. Ayaana asked, "Why?"

Muhidin sighed, "School rules." Ayaana nodded. Muhidin continued. "In the world, English has the biggest ears."

Ayaana pulled at her ears, testing them for size. Muhidin then told her that the words of the world were collecting in his shop and plotting to form a single perfect expression, which could contain the meaning of life.

Ayaana believed him. "Is it doned? The word? Has it finished?"

" 'Done,' " Muhidin corrected.

"Yes?"

"No," Muhidin said, "say, 'Is it *done*?' "

"Done." She repeated "done" as she tiptoed into the room with books.

Muhidin inclined his head to listen, then shook his head.

"Lini?"—When?—she whispered.

Muhidin told Ayaana to take her whens into silence.

She returned to his house the next day, and the next. In two months, she was rushing to his house at dawn to tell him of characters in the storybooks she consumed, what they did and thought and said as if these were souls about whom a friend might boast.

Ayaana gobbled up everything Muhidin offered.

"Where are you?" he asked her one day, showing her a torn map.

"Don't know."

Here he pointed. She stared at his finger and at the spot it touched.

"Here," she repeated.

"Pate Island: Faza, Pate, Siyu, Kizingitini . . . and Shanga," Muhidin intoned.

Ayaana was transfixed by the spot to which his finger pointed. Her thoughts were in turmoil. There was such mystery in the idea that a whole island and all its people could be reduced to a spot on a page.

Muhidin, spurred on by Ayaana's hunger for knowledge, prepared for their lessons in advance and rediscovered things for himself: basic classical mathematics, geography, history, poetry, astronomy, as mediated in Kiswahili, English, sailor Portuguese, Arabic, old Persian, and some Gujarati. Ayaana always wanted to know about the sea. Every day she asked, "How you read water?" One Friday, she picked up an atlas to, again, find out where she was in the world. On the map she looked at, there was no place marker for Pate Island. No color brown or color green to suggest her own existence within the sea. So she wanted to know about places that could be rendered invisible.

Muhidin told her that the best and biggest mountains of the earth lived under the sea, unseen. Ayaana contemplated this and her eyes grew round with insight. She asked Muhidin: "Where I am before I am borned? Under the sea?"

Muhidin's lips twitched. Though tempted to laugh, he replied, "Somewhere."

"Where 'somewhere'?"

Muhidin put a finger to his lips.

"Silent?" she whispered.

Muhidin suppressed his chuckle.

"Where . . ." She turned to Muhidin.

"Shhhh," he shushed.

She waited. Only afterward did Muhidin explain to her that wheres were tricky things. They wanted to be experienced. They were never, ever to be explained.

Music amplified what they could not find in books. Ecumenical music lessons. Algerian *raï*, Bangla, *kora*, the symphonies of Gholam-Reza Minbashian and Mehdi Hosseini, and every sample of *taarab* they could get their hands on. No contemporary outpourings, which, Muhidin told Ayaana, were the residues of the disordered screechings of Ibilisi. Thus they roamed soundscapes. Hearing a melody, Ayaana often cried out, "What she sing?" or "Read," while pressing clenched fists to her heart, where a stranger's musical yearnings throbbed. Mid-afternoon, one Tuesday, Muhidin reread to her the poetry of Hafiz. First in broken Farsi, followed by his Kiswahili translation: " 'O heart, if only once you experience the light of purity, / Like a laughing candle, you can abandon the life you live in your head . . .' "

"What it is saying?" she asked.

"One day you'll know. Today just listen."

Ayaana spoke to the books she read, some of which lived under her pillow. "You sit here. Hide, she's coming." Most nights, Ayaana read under her sheets with a flashlight long after saying good night to her mother.

. . .

Lurking in Muhidin's home-shop most of the day, Ayaana also saw Muhidin dispense under-the-counter remedies to furtive people who whispered their needs through shuttered windows, pleading for help in love, hope, fecundity, peace, acceptance, mercy, exorcism, wealth, and health.

Ayaana told him, "Teach me."

"No."

"Yes. Yes. Yes."

"Watch me, then," he sighed.

Ayaana watched Muhidin ease out the inner life of seed, fruit, root, bark, berry, crushed leaves, and crushed petals. She saw him blend anise, basil, chamomile; *kisibiti, kalpasi, kurundu; pilipili manga, pilipili hoho; tangawizi, cafarani, nanaa; langilangi, lavani, kiluwa, karafuu.* Later, she told him that her mother worked with flowers and water and oil, and that on their rooftop tiny white night-jasmine petals—collected at night and drowned in distilled water—were giving up their essence under the sun. She asked if he had ever eaten rose petals, and the next day she fed him four. He told her that the rose was a prophetess among flowers, that when flowers were created the rose was sent to seduce humanity's heart for God. Then Muhidin showed Ayaana how to replenish the drooping heart of herbs with a drop of rose oil.

Muhidin had decided to cobble together the trailing parts of his almost-color television set, which was still attached to an ancient VHS, to prepare a lesson for Ayaana. He rummaged through a pyramid of books, layered with enough dust to grow an herb garden, and retrieved his favorite videos. In these new lessons, just as Muhidin had twenty-three years ago, Ayaana discovered Bollywood.

Haathi Mere Saathi.

She watched it once. Twice. Four times. Muhidin rewound the tape. They sang with Kishore Kumar. They caterwauled every day: "*Chal chal chal mere haathi, o mere saathi.*" Muhidin sounded like a bullfrog inside a clogged drainpipe. That did not stop them. They danced. They sang: "*Hai hai oho ho.*"

. . .

Weeks later, having been worn down by her incessant need to know, Muhidin agreed to teach Ayaana something of what he understood about the sea. They left at dawn to experience how, with the other senses as well as touch, she could discover dimensions in liquid, place, space, and timelessness; how to tell the mood of water, and discern some of its intentions; how to intuit with inner eyes. In their aquatic world, in conversations with water, feeling the currents on her skin and tasting its salt on her tongue, she learned one of the ways of tides, sensed hidden routes, and understood that it was possible to imagine a destination by following the flight path of birds. She sensed something of what the winds desired, heard the variety of their refrains, and felt in these something of what Almazi Mehdi had known to whistle to summon them.

"The ocean I am / How can I drown," Muhidin sang to the water one morning.

Ayaana sang with him. The next moonlit evening, Ayaana felt in her skin how she was drawn to the moon. She went to tell Muhidin.

Muhidin sat with her on the steps to his door beneath a starlit sky. "Iron in our blood," he said. "The moon is sometimes a deranged magnet."

Ebbing: disappearing, becoming of the sea. Flowing: returning, rolling on the sands, returned to earth. Ayaana saw that the sky was a mirror for the waters, and that there were places that could be reached by reading the night; that the texture of the day to come was written in stars: *Kilimia kikizama kwa jua huzuka kwa mvua, kikizama kwa mvua huzuka kwa jua. When the Pleiades set in clear sun, they rise in rain; when the Pleiades set in rain, they rise in clear sun.* Watching ships make their ways to various harbors, Muhidin told Ayaana, "A boat is a bridge."

Ayaana considered this for days.

But, though she started to insist, Muhidin would not show her how to hunt deepwater fish with night lanterns.

"If your mother heard . . ."

"She never know."

"Not yet, Abeerah."

She sulked.

He shrugged.

"Fundi Mehdi will show me," she threatened.

"No, he won't," countered Muhidin.

Ayaana knew he was right. "Can you make a boat?"

"No."

"Fundi Mehdi can."

"Go to Fundi Mehdi, then."

"No!" she yelped.

But, later that afternoon, with Ayaana's kitten following them, they wandered over to the part of the island where the vestiges of its shipbuilding memory still lingered. In the decrepitude caused by time and fate lurked Fundi Almazi Mehdi's cove and the wood scent of boats built and boats to be built from templates resting in old memories. Hammer-on-wood echoes bounced in the air. Mangrove poles lay scattered on the ground, scorched in preparation for their destiny. A radio announcer offered the tide reports. Ayaana saw a solitary man. She dashed forward toward Fundi Mehdi as he worked on the hollowed prow of a *mtungwi*, pouring into it coconut oil followed by fire.

Muhidin caught up with her. Before he could greet the craftsman, Ayaana announced, "A boat is a bridge." She watched the flames scorch the prow. "Why fire?" She leaned over.

Mehdi tried to flap her away.

Muhidin lifted Ayaana into the remains of a nearby sand-stranded, barnacled formerly seagoing boat. The kitten jumped into the boat with her. From inside the vessel, Ayaana squawked to Mehdi, "Why oil? Why fire?"

Fundi Mehdi sighed.

"Why oil? Why fire?" Ayaana sang.

Muhidin then told Mehdi, as he settled himself on a stump, "Greetings, brother. Forgive this imposition. I have no problem extending my torment to you. Now she'll hound you. She'll interrogate you. If you have an answer, deliver it to her, lest you babble out deeper secrets in desperate surrender."

Mehdi glowered at Muhidin. Muhidin shrugged. Mehdi turned to look at Ayaana, who was resting on her belly to dangle off the edges of the jettisoned boat. She then lifted up her hands as if she were about to soar and intoned, "Why fire? Why oil?"

He returned to his firework with the smallest of smiles sitting at the edge of his mouth. Almazi Mehdi started. "So listen. When . . . this boat meets fire . . . on water . . . one day . . . 'twill know . . . what to do."

Stillness.

Ayaana's voice, shrill with awe: "I seened you drowned boats. Many, many, many time." She had spied on Mehdi as he seasoned boats by submerging them in the sea, keeping them underwater for weeks. Ayaana continued. "And so . . . and so, when the boats they drown, and afterward when the water comes inside"—she shook her head—"even them now they don't drown, isentitit?"

Mehdi's exasperated breath came through his hairy nostrils. With an audible harrumphing, he turned to Muhidin, eyes frantic. Muhidin turned to face the sea and closed his eyes. He clamped his mouth shut to stop himself from cackling as Ayaana swung her body to and fro on her boat, asking, "You build a *jahazi*?"

"No," Mehdi grunted after a minute.

Cawing crows. Wood-on-oil scent. Wood shavings on sand. Ayaana reached for and seized a twig, with which she poked holes in the sand, interfering with the passage of ants. "You build a *mtungwi*?" she asked.

Mehdi stared at his wizened hands on the vessel he was repairing with fire. He murmured, "This."

Ayaana's kitten jumped onto her head. She tilted herself the right way up and tumbled out of the boat. She stroked the kitten as Muhidin studied the waves. "You build a *mashua*?"

"Mhh," answered Mehdi.

"A *ngarawa* is small to build, yes?"

"Mhh."

"How many *utumbwi*s you have make?"

Mehdi waited thirty seconds.

"Three."

"A *dau*?"

He gnashed his teeth, shifted his body, and grabbed a small brownish-white sail to stitch up. "Many."

"A *mtepe*?"

A pause. A wistfulness crept over Mehdi. The *mtepe* was the emblematic Bajuni vessel; it had made his family's original fortune.

"Kila chombo kwa wimblile"—Every vessel makes its own waves. "This one . . . is our blood." He tapped his head. "Many of them . . ."

"Even my blood?" Ayaana now poked at her skin. She patted her head.

Muhidin intervened: "Abeerah, you are now drowning Fundi Mehdi with words. In order to be born, boats prefer silence. Enough, girl!"

The kitten mewed and purred and, leaving Ayaana, wandered over to Mehdi, twirling its tail around him. Mehdi paused in his work. A finger stroked the small animal's head. "Name?" Mehdi asked, his voice soft.

"Y*aaaa*kuti," whispered Ayaana.

"Good name," he said. Abruptly, "One day I make a *mashua* for you."

Ayaana whirled. "For me?" Her eyes turned into two bright moons. Still attempting to whisper: "Me and you, we make it?"

Mehdi's two brows met. He scratched his jawbone. "Yes."

She patted her chest. "And then we go and go and go, me and you and Babu and Yakuti and . . . and . . . me. I will drive the ship. Babu, you heared Mehdi and me, us will make and drive a boat, and you can go with us, and also . . . and also Yakuti."

Mehdi's mouth twitched.

Minutes before Muhidin and Ayaana left Fundi Mehdi to his solitude, Mehdi had retreated to a work shed, re-emerged with an object, and approached Ayaana with it, mumbling something. Soon she was cupping a compass set in greening brass that had been passed down from ship to ship.

"*Dira!*" she had exclaimed.

"Yes," Mehdi murmured. "Start with 'nowhere.'" He pointed at the compass, and then at their surroundings. "This line—north." He adjusted her hand so the compass was flat in it. "Ask yourself: *Where am I going?* When you know, go."

Ayaana's eyes were glued to the compass. Muhidin chortled at her expression.

. . .

Ayaana zigzagged, trying to maintain her north, using her gift compass. Muhidin stroked the kitten, which was riding on his shoulders. Ayaana asked, "When you are on your boat, did you drown never?"

He huffed, "The boats I worked on did *not* capsize."

"What is 'capsize'?"

"Boats drowning."

"Capsize": a word to collect.

They made their way homeward; the evening was orange, and its light shone on their faces and on the water.

Ayaana said, "Mehdi, he builded your boat?"

"No."

"Someone else, he builded your boat?"

"Yes."

"Even me, I can build a boat?"

"If you want."

Somewhere in the dimming distance, a woman's voice soared over the evening wind and waves. "Ay*aaaaa*na!" Before Muhidin could say anything, Ayaana had taken off like a hunted zebra in the direction of her mother's voice.

A harried mother spoke as rushed footsteps scrambled into the house. "You are late. What a mess. What have you done to your uniform? Who will wash it? Money for soap—does it grow like leaves? Wash up." Munira sighed. "What a day. That woman! Miserable about everything. Can you believe that she wants *singo*, as if she is a perpetual bride, *du*! Ayaana, you hear me? Change your clothes. There's fish on the fire. Mix the henna for me. Less lime this time. How often am I to repeat that to you? The jasmine water is tainted. Brown. That woman! She must have put something into it when I was outside." Munira sighed again. "Quick, *lulu*, dress up; we must collect some *langilangi* before the sun sets. Ayaana, are you hearing me, or am I talking to the walls?"

[11]

Abeerah. An inflow of unexpected light into a carbuncled existence. Without his knowing it, Muhidin's life waited for the moment every morning when a child appeared on his doorstep, sometimes preceded by an almost white kitten that purred nonstop, and that had learned to scratch at his door to be allowed in. One night, Muhidin started to laugh like an old truck starting up. His voice gathered power, influenced by its own sound. He guffawed as he had never done before, head tossed back, clutching his hurting stomach. Something the child had said. He couldn't recall the words, but he remembered the feeling of it. He laughed until his fingers brushed his face and touched tears, which soaked his pillow. It was during that sleepless, joyful night that he realized the extent to which he had underestimated the force of love, its pain and dreadful persistence, and how much like fear it also was.

[12]

Munira, who through the years had refined the art of cushioning herself from innuendos and insults, did not hear the mutterings about Ayaana's relationship with Muhidin until almost three months later. One Friday afternoon, after prayers, distracted by the heat, cursing the morning's two ungrateful customers, who had haggled her into exhaustion, she walked toward the shops. The sight of Ayaana's schoolteacher Mwalimu Juma Hamid lolling about sparked her interest. It was the school's end of term. She hurried toward him to ask about Ayaana's report, which she had not yet seen. As she approached, without turning, Mwalimu Juma asked Hudhaifa the Shirazi, a fabric vendor and avid reader, if he knew to what school of ill-mannered ease Ayaana had been transferred.

Munira halted.

Fear seized her heart.

She looked from one man to the other, listening.

Mwalimu continued: "Alone! Last week, the creature was loitering in the boatyard. Alone, I repeat. Unconscionable, I say. This morning, the girl was crawling on the beach like a *slug*, and Mlingoti the Apostate, half dressed and unshaven—as usual—*looming* over her. Overfamiliar, I say. What habits. Vulgar. That's what I say."

Hudhaifa, with his perfect black skin gleaming smooth and touchable in the sun, gasped loud enough for Munira to hear. Mwalimu Juma, rubbing his graying hair, continued: "Money shops for mischief. Mischief. That's what I say. To be poor is not a sin, I say. But to offer a child to alleviate . . ." He raised his brows and rolled his eyes, performing woefulness.

Hudhaifa loved story lines, whether imagined or not. He lifted a hand to secure Munira's attention. "Is that you, Mama Ayaana? Mwalimu was just wondering why you plucked young Ayaana from her school. Have you . . ." He paused. Munira had evaporated. Hudhaifa glanced at the slightly hennaed nail tips of his fat, beringed fingers, still clutching Mwalimu Julius Nyerere's translation of *The Merchant of Venice*, which he was reading that year. "There'll be trouble." Eyes glowing, his glee met Mwalimu Juma's sneer.

Imagine a firestorm. Imagine that it is a dust devil. Imagine its fierceness as a growl that also contains a sibilant sound. But first—"Ay*aaaaaa*na!" An insane mother's howling.

There was a corresponding stillness inside Muhidin's shop, where Ayaana had been trying to create pear-shaped calligraphy while Muhidin studied a map of ancient seas, still wearing a faded pink piece of cloth around his waist. It was his approximation of Hussein Fahmy in the Egyptian movie *Khalli Balak Min Zouzou*, which he and Ayaana had watched. She had needed a foil for her performance as the belly-dancing Soad Hosny.

From the outside, another yowl: "Ay*aaaa*na!" Ayaana leapt out of her chair, slipped beneath Muhidin's arms, tugged open the door of the Bombay cupboard, and crawled into it. From inside, she prepared Muhidin: "She kicks doors in, so leave yours open." After a slight pause, she added, "She'll lift you up with your ears, but it won't hurt for long. Rub hard. The pain, it goes away."

Muhidin, still tottering from Ayaana's speedy scramble, asked, "Who?"

She said, "*Mamangu*"—my mother. "You, you'll call her 'Bi Munira.' "

Muhidin said, "I will." A brief silence followed; then, "Abeerah?"

"Yes?" she replied from within the cupboard.

"Why'll Bi Munira lift me up with my ears?"

"Mhhh . . . maybe 'cause she doesn't know you're my father. Ahhhmmm . . . maybe 'cause I stopped going to that school—they don't like me, and I don't like them. Maybe 'cause I didn't tell her I live here, but only in the daytime, so it doesn't matter, maybe."

Muhidin nodded. "Anything else, maybe?"

The cupboard door clicked shut.

Muhidin sat down to wait.

Imagine a flash of lightning from cloud to ground.

Munira materialized on Muhidin's porch, crossed into the foyer, and entered the reception area that was also the shop, Vitabu na Kadhalika. She slipped the niqab from her face and glanced around the space, filling it with the wrath of primal forces. Muhidin tried a preemptive strike: "*Hujavuka mto, simtukane mamba?*"—If you cross a river, won't you meet a crocodile?

Munira's anguish turned into distilled hatred. Eyes red, dead calm, she dropped anchor. Her voice spat icicles. "You?" She stepped closer. "A crocodile?"

Outside, the echoes of receding waves. Inside, Muhidin experienced the encyclopedic scope of Munira's knowledge of arcane and contemporary insults. Muhidin kept his head low and imagined himself a rock in the sea. Ten minutes later, the verbal battering ended and Munira growled, "Where's my baby, you piece of filth?"

Point a finger, start a quarrel. Muhidin sighed. He was old. He was tired. He craved peace. He limped to the Bombay cupboard and flung its doors open. "Out," he snarled at Ayaana. Ayaana cowered, covered her face. "Out," Muhidin howled. "Your foulmouthed fiend is here."

Ayaana crept out, shivering. Muhidin had never shouted at her before.

"My baby!" Munira shrieked.

"Noooo!" screamed Ayaana.

"Ayaana!" Munira lowered the pitch of her voice.

Ayaana reached for Muhidin's hand and grabbed it. He shook it and her away. She returned, clung, dangled, rotated on the limb, and shouted at her mother, "He is my father. Mine. My father."

Muhidin extricated himself by peeling each of Ayaana's fingers from his arm. "Go!" he said, lifting her in the direction of the door.

Ayaana froze, staring at him. "Ah! Go!" Muhidin lifted his hand. Munira rushed toward Muhidin. "Don't even . . ." Muhidin turned to Munira, large eyes popping. "Begone, witch," he said. "Both of you. Disappear forever."

Munira grabbed Ayaana and pulled her away. Ayaana was as still and stunned as a small bird in a toothless cat's jaw. But she grabbed the threshold frame, watching Muhidin, her eyes double in size. She hurled at him, "*You* throw me away. *You* . . . you throw me away."

Muhidin heard a child's shrill, post-storm litany. He heard bewilderment in a mother's voice.

Munira: Why?

I. Won't. Go.

Munira: Who?

He *is* my father.

Munira: What?

He's my teacher.

Munira: How?

Him I love.

Munira: Why?

I'll stay with him forever.

Munira: What?

You go away. You are bad. Bad!

Munira: Why?

A child wailed.
Munira: Ayaana! Stop it this second. Stop it!
Noooooo!
A slap echoed.
Muhidin flinched.
Another one.
He flinched.
Another.
Flinch.
Silence.
End of clamor.

His house was too quiet. So Muhidin murmured, "Abeerah." His house was much too still. His heart split when he saw the incomplete shape of a bird on paper and felt the sensation of a cold, hard knife slicing his guts. An unexpected cramp of sorrow forced him to hunch over his heart. So he murmured, "Abeerah."

For three days, it sounded as if some dreadful easterly wind was stabbing the sea, which, with diminishing howls, succumbed to its wounds under Muhidin's unbroken gaze from a tall balcony window.

A resolute and ceaseless pounding shook his door in the thick of night. Muhidin, who had been struggling to sleep, eased himself out of bed, wrapped himself in a pale blue *kikoi*, and descended the stairs. The pounding intensified as he crossed the courtyard into the foyer. He unlatched the door, looked out, then moved it aside.

Munira's body thrummed with fear and fatigue. Ayaana's swollen eyes searched Muhidin's face. Muhidin cringed at the limpid ache there, at the naked soul in her gaze. He translated her imploring look. He knelt down, eyes level with hers. "No," he said. "No, Abeerah." Her mouth trembled as a teardrop reached her chin. She sniffed. He stroked her brow, saying, "A father to throw away his own? No."

The spillover in Ayaana's eyes dried up. She sniffed away whatever lingered and leaned over so that her forehead touched Muhidin's. Unsmiling, she asked, "Never, ever?"

"Never."

"Ever?"

"Ever."

She stood on tiptoe, a long bird half a second before flight: "Promise?"

Muhidin hesitated, and then he nodded.

Ayaana was now chewing on a finger, her eyes on him. "You are mine?"

Muhidin blinked. A lump filled his throat, choked off his air supply, and made him dizzy. He watched her gazing at him. There was the panic, and then a spark of elation from at last knowing what it was to be seen by another, to be truly seen. Seizing the moment, not the future and its consequences, he let go, wordless. He nodded. Ayaana cupped his face, forehead furrowed, eyes to eyes. Her fingers were near his throat, testing the vibration of his words for truth. "Yes." Backed up by another nod.

Copying him, Ayaana also nodded. She slipped under his arms to return to her desk and finish her interrupted calligraphy.

Munira shifted on her feet, not knowing where to begin. Gesturing toward Ayaana, she said, "She hasn't eaten." Muhidin said nothing. "She has mourned you," Munira added, a catch in her throat. She bent her head. Muhidin remained silent. Munira said, "She wouldn't talk to me." Muhidin watched, silent. "Tell me what to do now?" Munira stepped closer to Muhidin.

He heard her, the huskiness in her low voice, its plea. Saw her direct gaze, smelled her perfume. He did not trust her newfound meekness. Muhidin narrowed his eyes.

"Forgive me. I was wrong," Munira said.

He studied her.

Munira then asked, "How did it happen?"

Muhidin's gaze was steady.

She added, "You . . . her?"

He listened.

"Fix it," she begged.

Muhidin laughed.

At himself.

At her.

He laughed until he had to wipe his eyes.

Munira pleaded, "What will she do when you leave her?"

Muhidin grunted.

Munira looked sideways. "May I sit down?" She collapsed into a wooden chair above which books loomed, about to spill over. She stared at his books, drained, a portrait of befuddlement. Muhidin chose to sit across from her in a tilted chair from which yellowed stuffing was popping out. He watched her, the crushed hauteur—traces of her cultivated youth. Its sullied state satisfied the resentful fisherman still within him. Shadows on her angular shape mirrored the loping geography of their island, and her air of displaced, permanent loneliness blended with the perfume of night jasmine outside. She was hugging her body in this room filled with knickknacks from all over the world, piled up like flaked-off memories. Muhidin's eyes, cameralike, sought and captured small Munira-details from different angles. He leaned forward. He was already familiar with her shadow; now he saw the gap between her front teeth. A subsiding sensation all of a sudden dragged at Muhidin, as if the detritus of an unknown life had fallen upon him.

"You choose *us*," Munira said, making certain he heard the "*us*." She continued, "Choose *us* and you lose your good name and standing." Sarcasm underlined the word "standing."

Muhidin's mouth trembled on the edge of laughter.

She asked, "You don't care?"

Muhidin grinned. It had not occurred to him to worry about "standing."

She misread his look. "We amuse you."

Muhidin at last spoke. "Listen, woman, do whatever you want. The girl, well, since we've *chosen* each other"—he studied Munira; her squirm contented him—"since we've chosen each other, and I'm not going away, we'll share her life. You can live with that, as I must."

A sound from Ayaana. They both turned to look. Ayaana was standing on her toes and using her whole body to color in the script that created a bird, using a red felt pen.

Muhidin did not consider then that Munira had neither agreed to nor rejected his offer.

Munira asked, "How did she find you?"

Remembering Ayaana's pre-sunrise excursions, Muhidin half smiled. "We found each other. The sea."

The sea? Munira wondered, looking for the trick, aware of unstated things, and of Ayaana listening behind her. Munira experienced a pinch in the heart at the idea of her daughter's hidden life, a flare of fury that a stranger was privy to sites that should have been accessible to her alone. But she had to be careful. Ayaana had managed to cry for seven hours nonstop. This was not a feat she wanted to experience again. Munira was cool. "She calls you 'father.' In public," Munira said. "Did you know that?"

Ayaana's pen hovered. Muhidin shrugged. "Then I am."

Ayaana hugged herself.

Munira said, "You don't understand."

"Tell me."

"I'm supposed to be a lustful sorceress, old man, trapping even"—Munira hesitated, looking Muhidin up and down, her nose ever so subtly wrinkled—"the likes of you."

Muhidin's body shook with laughter. Ayaana laughed with him, joyful, not knowing that her mother was shrinking and ashamed that the low-class, wrinkled, shaggy beast in front of her imagined she was beneath him. She stretched out her legs and waited for the laughter to subside. Still stinging, she said, "I wouldn't marry you. Not even for her."

Muhidin retorted, "I won't ask."

Munira retaliated, "So, then, what do I call you? Babu? You're old, but are you old enough to be my grandfather?"

"Call me *mpenzi*?" Muhidin offered roguishly. He waggled his brows, hoping she would choke at the outrage of declaring him "beloved."

Munira was tranquil as she suggested, "Why settle for '*mpenzi*' when I can just call you *nyumbu*?"

With his goat beard and uneven broad body, there was indeed something of the wildebeest about Muhidin. Muhidin grimaced. Such a sobriquet would be difficult to outlive. He offered a truce. "Something else?"

"I'll think about it," Munira answered. For the first time since Muhidin had seen her, she smiled. This caused an unexpected shiver within his heart. He turned away at once, to see Ayaana watching him. She offered him a toothless grin. He waggled his ears at her. She giggled. She selected a green crayon to color her bird's wing.

Munira asked, "What do you teach her?"

"Life."

"You took her out of school?"

"She took herself out."

Munira nodded. It was possible. Ayaana's thrill about school and new friendships had given way to her coming back home roughed up, unspeaking, clench-jawed, and wheezing. She would cough ceaselessly, eyes streaming, and her asthma would flare up on such days. Munira had circled the issue, afraid of complaining. She knew things would get worse, and there were no other schools nearby that she could afford to send her daughter to. She glanced at the book-filled room before asking Muhidin, "Do you know much?" Munira chewed on her middle fingernail.

Muhidin shrugged. "Enough."

"Yes?"

"Mhh."

Munira said, "I'll pay, of course."

Muhidin snapped, "Just stop it!"

Munira's hands fluttered. "Please bear with me. I don't know . . . don't know what to do with all this."

"This what?" growled Muhidin.

"You . . . this situation."

Muhidin went silent.

Munira asked, "You pray?"

"No."

"No?"

A shrug. "Maybe an occasional salute to the Creator of Storms."

"God?"

"Who knows?"

"You don't?"

"Do you?"

Munira bent to stare at her hennaed feet. Wistful. "They say you're an apostate."

"They do."

Munira reached over to touch Muhidin's right knee, eyes welling. "*She* believes. I can't give her all I want her to have, but I can offer her the dream of limitless goodness. Do you understand?"

Muhidin bowed his head, the essence of night jasmine hovering between them. He gave a tight nod.

"Thank you." Munira settled back into her seat.

A clock ticked. Ayaana drew. Munira stared at the room, the books. Muhidin watched Munira. She said, "I hear you've traveled the world."

"Most of it."

"When I was a girl, I intended to travel. I wanted to live in every country for a week." Her face was flushed. "How is it?" She leaned forward.

"People are people," Muhidin answered, struck by the strangeness of the night, by the brightness of curiosity in a cursed woman's eyes.

Munira looked away. Her hands adjusted her head covering. "It's late. I'm sorry. But I just couldn't endure another night of her grieving . . ."

Muhidin suppressed a grin. Good.

An uncertain smile softened Munira's features. "Since my one child is possessed by a desire to treat you as the light in a holy man's camel's eye, and you've tied your fate to *ours*"—Munira raised a brow—"shouldn't we clean up this fortress of dust of yours?"

Muhidin looked around him with a fresh sense of possessiveness. It was *his* dust. He focused a cold gaze on Munira. Her zeal subsided at once. There were boundaries. Her daughter's asthma would have to cope. Let *him* deal with that.

[13]

Yet, within twelve days, these boundaries were breached by a gut-wrenching howl at dawn, a wretched being in elemental agony. Island doors were flung open. Footsteps rushed toward the source and faltered. A mother in a flowing cream robe, her hair disheveled, feet bare, flew to the site of the crime and fell over her thin little daughter, who was cradling a ragged corpse with a crushed skull and wet tail—a dirty-white kitten. The girl was baying, her face mucus-streaked, bloody, and muddy. The mother, hand to head, was sobbing. "Why hurt this useless thing? Who did it offend?" And men and women watched, or turned away. Some sniggered. Others, those who knew, or had seen which of their children had been involved, crept away. Though they would pinch those children's ears, nothing else would be done.

Muhidin appeared. He absorbed the scene. He saw a crushing sorrow too old and too adult for a child to bear. So he seized the child, trying to absorb the anguish. He enclosed her and her dead cat in his arms. Both were still, cold, and frozen.

"Why?" whimpered Ayaana. She expected Muhidin to know. "He done nothing bad. So why?"

Muhidin squeezed her. He glanced at Munira's tear-streaked face as Ayaana said, "You fix him." She told Muhidin, "Tell him, 'Move.' " Her eyes were clear in her certainty of his power over life and death.

Muhidin swung his body to face the thinning audience. "Someone saw something." His hands were fists. No one answered. He roared, "Who is responsible for this? Speak!" No one looked at him.

Within a minute, everyone had slithered away and abandoned the trio and their small corpse.

That evening, after Muhidin and Munira had cleaned up the kitten, they wrapped it up with strips of pink silk and inserted it in a large perfume box. They carried this to Munira's gardens, near the tombs. Muhidin dug a hole next to the light-colored roses. Ayaana's eyes were fixed on Muhidin as he then turned the pages of the Hafiz poetry book he had carried, hiding his helplessness behind others' words. "Abeerah," he suggested, stopping on a page, "read this."

Ayaana closed her eyes.

Muhidin said, "Kitten needs to hear your voice as he jumps to the . . . er . . . stars."

"No!" yelled Ayaana.

Muhidin crouched next to her. "Why no?"

She pointed. "Him, he's not moving. See?"

Muhidin glared at the hollow earth. He lied. He said that the kitten was already a wave, a star, and one of the beats of Ayaana's heart, and that to be these things the kitten had put aside his body. He said now the kitten could even grow into a tree. He added that whether the tree would yield one or many more kittens would be up to the tides and winds.

Ayaana whispered into his right ear, "Even me, I can be a tree also?"

Muhidin almost wept. "Not yet, Abeerah." His arms were on her shoulders.

Solemn-eyed, Ayaana stood inside all her unanswerable questions. Muhidin frowned at the tombstones and waited. Finally, Ayaana asked, "Is this 'dead'?"

The strain for the correct answer distorted Muhidin's face. The "yes" was wrenched out of him. That was the closest he came to howling.

Ayaana asked, " 'Dead' is not moving?"

Muhidin cleared his throat. "Yes."

A ghost of worn human sadnesses imbued with newborn dread-loneliness inched into Ayaana and found a space where it could gaze out at the world from within her eyes. The look would never leave her. She lowered her head. They waited.

"You read," Ayaana at last whispered.

So Muhidin read Hafiz over a small hole in the ground, which would later become a mound, and did something he had never imagined he would ever do—he mourned a kitten.

> "*Greet Yourself*
> *In your thousand other forms*
> *As you mount the hidden tide and travel*
> *Back home . . .*"

He could not continue. Little fingers: Ayaana's hand inside his. They stood silently and waited for nothing. Munira, watching from the sidelines, struggled with jumbled sensations: the oddness of experiencing one battle she did not have to carry alone; the sight of her daughter's fears enclosed and offered solace. Munira bowed her head, still expecting an inevitable blow. Preoccupied, the trio missed another watcher, a stranger who often came to the ancient graves in the evenings to sit close to and address their contents. He turned to focus on the child, whose slanted eyes were shaped exactly as his own.

. . .

Muhidin returned in the middle of the night to cover the grave and also plant a pawpaw seedling. Ayaana, up at dawn to visit the grave, was startled to see that her kitten had re-emerged as a small green plant overnight. She hugged the discovery to her heart while, from the inside of her existence, a dreary thing that had overrun her heart the day before eased away.

A rented morning boat. A man, a child. Muhidin had turned to the sea for help. Now, from the water, the island dissolved into forms and shapes Ayaana could rename, and sear into memory: mangrove train, Muhidin's head, the dancing bird, Munira's foot. Ayaana the latest witness to the old habits of water and winds as these approached her island; giddy right-turning leaps, stealth approach, ambush, groaning tumble. Ayaana absorbed everything. She saw how life moved. They returned with the early-evening high tide. Ayaana drowsed as Muhidin rowed, and the tears that had been racking her spirit dried up.

A few weeks later, Muhidin went to Lamu to collect a parcel, leaving Ayaana in his house, and his keys with Munira. He returned a day later, with a carton of fresh supplies and new textbooks, to find that color had invaded his domain: pinks, oranges, purples, reds, yellows, and lemon greens. Fresh-smelling soft things: cotton, silk, satin, lace. Strings of gold and glass beads dangled off doorways, and his chair seats had been cleaned and mended. His clothes were gleaming and smelled of frankincense. Munira had created flatness where, before, things had been puffed.

Muhidin bumped into Munira on her way out of his house. Her gaze averted, she was going to walk past him when his hand stopped her, and wrapped itself around her left arm. "Thank you," he said.

She shook her head at him, tearful. "No. Thank *you.*"

He dropped his hand.

She walked away.

. . .

Under a fresh spirit of order, Muhidin continued the cleaning process. He started alphabetizing his books, as he had always hoped to. Munira returned two days later to help. Muhidin stiffened. She understood why when she swept down a pile of paperbacks from a shelf and found at least thirty empty and not-so-empty translucent dark and light green, colorless, and amber mini- and half-sized bottles of assorted booze stored amid a jumble of papers and maps. She did not ask. Muhidin did not explain.

~

Pate Island, itself a mutable thing, got bored of its rumor mongering—Munira, the whore, was beguiling Muhidin, the apostate—and resigned itself to the arrangement. But, days later, an anonymous message-sender left Munira a purple-on-white *leso*. She found it outside her door on Thursday morning. The design on the cloth, a cashew-nut motif, was precise. The woven-in aphorism, the message to Munira, was mean: *"Huyo kibuzi mwarika mtizame anavyojitingisha"*—There she is, the stupid goat; watch how she sways. Munira carried the cloth to Muhidin. "Still want to be entangled with us?"

Muhidin read it. "If I were a woman"—he exaggerated a swirl of hips—"I would parade my scorching reply."

Munira's already narrow eyes narrowed even more. She raced toward the door and went straight to Hudhaifa the Shirazi. They scanned his shelves for specific *leso*s. When she found them, she bought two sets. An extravagance. Hudhaifa, thrilled that he had inserted himself into a story line, gave Munira a 50 percent discount. He was interested in outcomes.

Munira needed three days to cut and sew. On the fourth day, the island and some of its gossips watched her swing in elegant flow in the direction of Siyu, adorned in vibrant blue and white, which, as her body swayed, revealed its message: *"Fitina yako faida yangu"*—Your ill will; my favor. The following day, she sauntered over to the vegetable stalls in a brown-and-white ensemble. Embedded within its cashew-nut whorl design, an aphorism in white text: *"Mie langu jicho"*—Mind your own business. Her favorite.

65

Muhidin now accessorized his evening walk with a shiny ebony *bakora*, whose handle, when unscrewed, revealed a dagger. He wandered the island waterfront arm in arm with Ayaana. Flaunting her acquired father, Ayaana looked out for old nemeses from school, especially the boys. In her deepest heart, she also searched the land for the absent father, the one who just might appear from nowhere, but whose view she had blocked with Muhidin's formidable presence.

"Ayaana!" She turned. It was Suleiman, bully-in-chief. She ignored him and told Muhidin the sorry history of his moving her end of the school bench just when she was about to sit, so she fell on the floor. Muhidin paused in order to show her what to do next time. He demonstrated a low kick, a follow-up punch to the nose. *Twa! Twa!* Break the bone. He pointed the ebony stick at Suleiman, accompanying the gesture with a glare. Suleiman slunk away.

Resuming their wandering, they reached the smaller jetty to watch the return of the fishing fleet. They listened to the call and response of men contented with the catch of the day. They watched the water together, and Ayaana, watching Muhidin watch the sea, asked, "What is good about water?"

"Storms."

Ayaana hesitated, unsure. "What is bad about water?"

"Storms."

Silence.

They walked on.

Along the way, they ran into the Chinese visitor, who was fiddling with a small net, a thin cigarette in his mouth, his face in profile to them. The sun and humidity had basted him dirt-brown. "Mchina Nihao" was his first nickname in Pate. His smile, when he met anyone, was broad, his gestures fluttery: "*Ni hao*," he did not neglect to say—hello. But when he had taken up jogging in the early mornings, Hudhaifa the vendor started to call him Mzee Kitwana Kipifit. The name stuck; the visitor now answered to it.

Muhidin and Ayaana proceeded onto a twisted road that would lead to the black sand of Mtangawana, from where they would watch the arrival of dhows and other boats. The golden dusk glittered on the water so that it was like orange glass. Engulfed by light, Muhidin turned to contemplate Ayaana. "Belonging" required a map, he thought. Nothing about it could be predicted. He wanted to call her "daughter." But he said, "Abeerah" instead.

"Y-e-s-s-s-s," she sang.

Luxuriating in the salt air, he watched the rise of the red basket-shaped moon and its mirror image on the water.

"What is his name?" Ayaana asked.

"Whose?"

"Moon on water?"

Muhidin racked his brain. Moon on water. Moon on water. He had forgotten the sense of that. "Mahtabi," he proposed. "Perhaps Akmar."

"Mahtabi. Akmar," Ayaana mimicked.

But this was also a portent, this red moon on the water. Unseen by Muhidin, Mzee Kitwana was nearby with his nets. He had wanted to see the moon on the water, but had been distracted by the sight of Ayaana, who was now standing on her tiptoes, demanding that Muhidin command the winds to lift them both up. The child's presence reminded him of a life he would rather forget, and when she turned her head, or gestured, or settled into stillness before the presence of the sea, she evoked for him something of a child of another China.

Penye shwari na pepo upo.

Where there is calm, there is also a storm.

[14]

Harbingers—the birds borne on the *matlai* wind, sun-tinted dragonflies, moon-dancing swordfish, sand-nibbling parrot fish—spoke of the changing seasons of earth, of its dying stars, and of melting time. Sometimes the debris of people, things, destiny, tragedies, and tales collected around a monsoon. Sometimes these seasons showed up with strangers and left them behind on Pate's black sand shores. Harbingers, like the moon-timed festivals Maulidi and Idd-ul-Fitr, brought souls from the fringes of the seas across island thresholds into communion with one another. Invariably, at least three of those who had entered the island's cult of hospitality did not leave. There were those who, unknown even to themselves, belonged to the island and were covenanted to stay. There were those who tried to leave but never could. And there were far more than expected who left, only to show up again years later. Some entered the portals of the land, sometimes naked, sometimes alone, sometimes naked and alone and even dead. The island renamed these. Some tendered false names; Pate did not mind. Names are mere place markers. Their manners alone established their character, and this determined if they should stay or leave. Other persons crossed into Pate to override its timeless codes. These, the would-be reformers, came, saw, scowled, sulked, scolded, and stipulated that the island transform itself for them. Invariably, the right winds swooped in to sweep these away.

And then there were the men—always men—who wore the beleaguered faces of hurriedly abandoned pasts. They entered Pate Island to disappear. The island hospitality apparatus took over; under the shelter of a roof, they would be cajoled into revelations over shared meals. They were observed as they laughed at well-placed jokes; laughter was a test. A disarmed man showed his soul, and the soul, being naked, revealed essence. And essence was truth. Such men might then be taken over by the guiding spiritual undercurrent of the family and the space. Transcendent expectations were synchronized, and the guest would find another ready to guide him into Pate Island's tenets of belonging. At some point in his Pate life, this person, now linked to a family and treated as such, would make a public pronouncement of Shahada: *Ash hadu anlla ilaha ilallah* . . . Afterward, the new islander, giving his life over to the place, would, after taking a purifying bath to shed the skin of the past, adorn himself in a clean white garment and re-emerge, finally, at home. An island bride might be offered to him then. If the betrothal flowered, the visitor would take up a trade to sustain his home, and find himself written into the palimpsest that was Pate.

Toward the end of 1995, a visitor landed—a fastidious, pale, unsmiling man who said he was from the Comoros, although he did not speak like a man from the Comoros. He had sat in the boat praying throughout the journey. His lips had locked into a stern moue from the second he saw red strings dangling off the boat's mast. As his boat companions hurried through their prayers, he clucked, disapproving of such casualness. His voice was polite when, in Arabic, he asked the three women in the boat to cover themselves. They were beautiful, he said, and such beauty was the preserve of God and their husbands.

Three faces turned to him at once. A woman hissed: "*Huendapo waishipo vyura huishi kama vyura waishivyo*"—When you visit frogs, you live as the frogs do. The others tittered.

The men waited for the dour stranger's reaction:

Nothing.

For now.

The women returned to gossiping about some woman who, it seemed, had not only fornicated publicly and given birth to a bastard, but had also then threatened to commit suicide when asked to reorder her life, and persisted in her unchaste lifestyle; to compound everything, she had recently bewitched an apostate and co-opted him in her dilapidation. The eavesdropping man felt his sacrifice deeply: to endure lewd heretics, infidels, and syncretists for the sake of realizing a new order. He glowered when one of the underdressed women cackled an infidel song, flirting with the boat captain. He told himself that if he had not needed to hide he would not even be here.

The fugitive strolled onto Pate Island, a thunderbolt that would strike an old, grand tree down from its roots. He took the island hospitality as his right. But within a year, he saw and fell in love with a Pate girl—shy, docile, alluring, dainty, and enamored of his stern graciousness. They got married. In time, he gathered youthful men around a football team he named Kabul, without telling the islanders that he had lived and fought there. He turned every sports practice into a religion lesson; he called his players *mujahidin*. He anointed the goal posts "paradise." He stopped the game for prayer.

Fazul's honeyed voice was tinged with Egyptian accents, switched "p"s and "b"s, and replaced "th"s with "zh"s. Fazul wa Misri—Fazul the Egyptian—the island called him behind his back. Fazul prayed over everything. His convoluted knowledge of the sacred perplexed even the sheikhs. In conversations, he was always reasonable, even if he chided islanders for their heretic ways. He offered to destroy the tombs of dead saints. Idolatry. Most dismissed Fazul as they did all transitory madmen. Every so often, some ultra-fervent would-be prophet would sail into town to impose nasty gods upon this arcane, wise, and easygoing land. The hospitable land listened with one ear, and waited for Pate time to penetrate the zealot, who either succumbed or left.

Fazul the Egyptian stayed three years. Then, one night, in the middle of the rainy season, he disappeared. But two and a half months later, on August 7, 1998, at 10:35 a.m., in Nairobi and 10:39 a.m. in Dar es Salaam, bombs exploded and incinerated more than two hundred lives. A then obscure extremist asked, "Why complain? It was only kaffirs who were killed."

After Fazul, a plague, an alien army, landed with force on Pate. Two hundred pairs of marching army boots churned the black sand.

Armed strangers came to look for Fazul the Egyptian, who had gone. Even so, they yelped questions: "What do you know, who do you know?" "Where are they?" The howlers hurled themselves upon ancient doors, upending ancient lives, smashing things, smashing the hearts of a people they would never get to know. This was also how Pate discovered that the country that had appended itself to them had given them over to darkness. The fresh invaders accused and judged and roughed up even Almazi Mehdi for not answering their bizarre English questions fast enough. They tore his blue vest. He bled, from his punched-up mouth. Thickset, thin-minded, empty-souled creatures who seized market women's baskets to search for weapons of mass destruction; who shoved fingers down the mouths of gasping fish in hopes of finding secreted codes, and screeched like demented ibis day and night, and cocked guns at unexpected sounds. On an island whose fabric was interwoven with eternity's ghosts, uncanny sounds were legion. The marauders would later seize two consolation prizes: Fazul's wife's brother and her old father, both fishermen, who left in chains. They would be locked up in a distant Mombasa prison cell. A brutal inquisition would follow, for they did not understand what was required of them when they were informed that they were "terrorists." Sentenced to serve two and a half years in prison. For the inquisitors were unable to endure a simple human truth: that Fazul, the man, had fallen in love with a Pate fisherman's sister, a Pate fisherman's daughter. These post-Fazul arrivals were not the first presumptive ghouls that had hoped to contain the island, nor would they be the last to leave, as others had, bereft. *Maji yakija hupwa*—When the tide has risen, it also falls.

Anyway.

To this day, on the island, rumors still circulate to explain abrupt human absences. Here is one: A quick-growing eight-and-three-quarters-year-old girl as thin and long as a praying mantis was hunting for crabs in low-tide shallows. Lost in her searching, she did not see the stern-faced stranger in a white *kanzu* watching her. She turned. Unused to obscure danger, she misread the presence, and assumed the hospitality that was of her bloodline.

She bowed her head. "*Shikamoo.*"

He replied, "*Marahaba.*"

She saw eyes made of magnetic, solid emptiness. She turned back to her crabs, reached for and almost netted a medium-sized orange one that snapped at her with its pincers.

"Crabs?" asked the stranger.

Ayaana whispered, "A big one."

He said, "Sweet illusions." The stranger reached down to shake her hand, which he twisted and turned so she was staring at her palm. His voice was soft, soft. "There she is. God's little martyr," he murmured. "Chosen. So warm, so beautiful. A good, warm, clever girl, dear to God. Little martyr."

Ayaana's chin dropped. Tears filled her eyes; she was sad about unknown things. She could not move. Then a stream of wind scattered cool seawater on her face. She stretched out her arms, suddenly alert. When she looked again, the man had gone.

But from then on, he somehow knew how to find her when she was alone, and he spoke to her with a tender smile. "God's little martyr," he greeted her, "I'm sorry for you."

She asked, "Why?"

"You are a gem in a nest of apostates, adulterers, and infidels." She listened, lethargic, unsure what to do next. "But your life is assured." The hazy questions droned into her night rest, dismantling her sleep. "Chosen child." Words bounced inside her skull like incomplete songs, repeating in a loop; she thought of the heavy-voiced man, his tenderness, and the softness that had not once entered his eyes.

He found her again the next evening. "You know you are going to do right." No answer. "Little martyr, scent of paradise, soldier of eternity." No answer. "You are good, you are right. You are brave." No answer. "You'll purify filth. Your mother, forgiven, freed. How happy she'll be. Free because of her daughter's courage, and the apostate will change his ways, or the way will change him." The shadow of a smile appeared on his face. "You want that, don't you?"

"Yes." Ayaana nodded.

His voice hovered and fell, slithering all over her. She was paralyzed. She could only hear him. He said, "I'll help you."

She stared, eyes on the dark prayer bump on his pale forehead. He said, "You feel alone. I know." Her body shook. "No one looks for you when you hide. Unwanted. Unsought. Poor little one." Large tears reached her mouth. "Poor child."

The tears dropped on Ayaana's dress.

"There, there. You will triumph, little beautiful one. You'll be victorious over those who hate you. You'll be in paradise, a martyr before them. They will honor you. They will praise you."

Ayaana sighed.

The man's eyes glowed. Tears filled his eyes. "Poor, good child." He leaned over to wipe her tears with a white handkerchief, adding, "But you're chosen, warm flower of paradise."

Warmth crawled under Ayaana's skin, and insinuated itself into pauses between her thoughts. Cold words lingered. Words became incantations, leaching out her will, syllable by syllable. Mesmerizing chants, some of which she was soon mouthing back to the low-voiced man, speaking them to him as if she were falling sleep. She would not remember how she returned home, or when. Although she was young, and on her island this was not expected of her, Ayaana soon took one of her mother's *buibui*s to shroud her body. She took to praying most of the day, head pressed into the earth, the rocks, and the floor—starting over if she was afraid she had been facing a degree off east. She dashed away from Muhidin and ceased speaking to her mother, without understanding why, feeling as if her life were flowing out and her heart was always exhausted.

On their next encounter, the man oozed sadness. "The loneliness of the Almighty, the loneliness of the Holy One," he repeated.

Ayaana said, "Muhidin . . . he knows Almighty."

The man fixed his eyes on her and said gently, "*I* am your teacher. You do not speak until I say you can." His smile broadened as he spoke. He sighed. "The Almighty needs a brave soldier to deliver His gift of wrath." A broken guffaw.

"What's 'wrath'?"

He tapped her wrist, seized her upper arm. "The victory." And the stranger laughed. Though his voice was still soft, the sound was the most alien noise Ayaana had ever heard. Drifting, drifting. The man bent his head to whisper again, and his face loomed larger than her vision, and something in his eyes made her think of drowning—until he made a mistake. He said, "You'll renounce the kaffir, the apostate, Muhidin. You are God's slave destined for paradise . . ."

A jolt inside Ayaana's heart electrified her body and forced light into her mind. Something like power flew out of her eyes. Hands pushing outward, she yelled, "No! No!" She took off, feet soaring, reaching for dark safety. "He's my father. No! My father," she repeated. Yet still she heard the whispery laughter, its sibilance, the essence of hissing: "Sacred secret." A susurration that slithered even when, later, exhausted, she slept.

Muhidin had watched Ayaana fade. He had worried over the now nervy, sullen, dull, and monosyllabic child. He noted her dark, baggy-eyed apathy. She had been tumbling into frantic prayer, diligent about the timing, but would emerge with her shoulders stooped, as if she had been scolded. Muhidin had wanted to approach Munira. But three months later, Ayaana had shoved open his door, thrown off her *buibui*, jumped into the Bombay cupboard, and slammed the door shut. After more than forty minutes of stillness, Muhidin peeked in and saw her curled into a tight, sleeping ball. He closed the door, frowning. It was two in the afternoon. At about four-thirty, she opened the cupboard door. In a meek voice she said, "Please, may I have my math homework?"

During the next Adhan, Ayaana stiffened, eyes darting. She blocked her ears. "You must not listen," she informed Muhidin.

Munira came to Muhidin two evenings later. She paced the room, chewing on her fingers. "Something's wrong, old man."

Muhidin flinched. He disliked the phrase "old man." Munira seized his arm. "When she thinks I'm asleep, she's in my bed. She clings tight."

Muhidin grunted.

"Is she talking to you? She's not talking to me. Is she talking to you?"

Muhidin deflated. "No." Munira started to cry. Muhidin thawed. "Ahhhh, I'll find out. Don't cry."

Munira nodded.

Muhidin nodded back.

. . .

The Adhan started the following afternoon—"*Allahu Akbar*"—and Ayaana was already heading for the Bombay cupboard. "Ayaana!" Muhidin howled, with eye-popping anger. "Come here."

She clung to the cupboard door. "No!" It was a savage croak.

Muhidin strode toward her, intending to drag her out.

She lashed out. "You can't t-touch me. I'm d-dirty but ch-chosen, and I'll be p-purged, and so will the adulterer and th-the apostorate. B-but first he must seize me so I can spread his fire." She covered her face. "I-learn-holy-c-c-courage-by-submission-to-the-high-will." Ayaana started to wail. "But I *caaaaan't*. I hided from the man, and if I pray, Almighty can find me, isentitit? So I *caaaan't*."

Muhidin's mouth dropped so low that his jaw creaked.

His first "*What?*" was a squeak. He sucked in air in order to speak. "*What?*" An explosion, followed by an expletive he had not used since his early sea days. "What?" he tried again. "In God's name, what?"

"Almighty," Ayaana said, hiccupping.

"What?"

She whispered, "He's looking for me."

"What?"

She hung her head. Shame was the heat on her face, her sweat, and her stammer. Muhidin placed a rough hand under her chin. He lifted her face. She saw that nothing in his eyes accused her. They never had. She had promised she would split her secrets in half—one set for her, the other for him. Muhidin stroked tears from her face with his fingers. "You're hiding," he concluded, mostly for himself.

She nodded.

"Someone's looking for you?"

She nodded with vigor, then stuck out her lower lip. Quiet.

Muhidin let go her chin and rubbed his hands. "Abeerah?" he said; more tears were sliding down Ayaana's jaw to soak her long orange-flowered dress.

She looked. Hope was the sight of Muhidin puffing up and looking blacker, fiercer, and even more pockmarked. Muhidin's eyes bulged, his arms curved wide, his hands were two clenched fists. She dared. "Almighty won't catch me never."

Muhidin enunciated his words. "We start again, Abeerah. Tell me slow-slow. Why is the Almighty looking for you?"

"*He* told me not to say."

"Who?" Muhidin grunted.

She was unraveling. Her voice haunted, she struggled to say, "Almighty, he sended the man to find me."

"The man," Muhidin echoed, sounding stupid even to himself.

Ayaana inhaled. "The man *saaays* . . ." Then a rush, "Almighty wants *mujahidat*." Ayaana twisted her fingers. "But, me, I was thinking Almighty better tell me Hisself, isentitit?" Fire-eyed, she looked at Muhidin, outrage in her voice. "The man, he said I leave you. So, me, I said, 'No!'" She paused. No reaction from Muhidin. She continued, "Then I runned."

Muhidin's teeth had started chattering. A chill spread throughout his body. He was mute. Ayaana moved closer to him, taking small steps, one foot after the other. When she stopped in front of him, she leaned forward to cup his face: "Tell Almighty killing peoples, it is bad manners."

Muhidin choked out, "I will." Then, in a tender tone, he asked, "The man? Which man, Abeerah?"

"You know." She gestured with her hands. "Fazul wa Misri."

Muhidin leapt up.

"Babu," Ayaana started. She tilted her head, "Almighty is wrath with me, isentitit?"

Muhidin, who had been rummaging among his shelves and cupboards, emerged with a cudgel. "Never you, Abeerah. His wrath is *strictly* reserved for *Fazul*." Muhidin retrieved the *bakora* with its concealed dagger and lined it up next to the cudgel. He muttered, "Degenerates. Are humans now spare parts?" He struck the cudgel with his fist as he spoke. "You stay here. Go to my room. Sleep," he said. "Open the door for me alone. Wait till I return."

She moved toward him and then stopped. She opened her mouth to speak and then closed it.

"What?" asked Muhidin.

Ayaana asked, her voice shaking, "Almighty is your friend?"

"Yes."

"Fazul?"

"No!" he snarled.

Ayaana nodded, then exhaled and, finally, smiled a real smile.

On a late-May night in 1998, one of Pate's tailors, returning home with his Singer sewing machine perched on his shoulder, imagined he glimpsed seven of the island's seamen hurrying in a determined direction in silence. Though this was an odd occurrence, he did not give it another thought. But two mornings later, it was observed that Fazul the Egyptian had disappeared without saying goodbye to anybody—not his cherished wife, not even the football team he had started. Questioned months later, his Pate wife said that he had left to meet someone one evening but had not returned home.

Muhidin was wrestling with doubt. His right knuckle was sore, and there was broken skin on his hand and face. He was grumpy because of a debate with Munira that he had lost before it started that morning. Muhidin grunted intermittently as he paced the room, while Ayaana, wearing a bright red dress, copied out the seven-times table. Muhidin had carried Ayaana back to Munira's house early that morning. After she was settled in her bed, he had returned to the main room and slumped over a table, facing Munira, to explain. "Sorry I missed it. Would have acted faster," he began.

On Munira's carefully neutral face, a mask slipped, so that he glimpsed a feral otherness, a naked, arcane, female force that threatened to roar. The veil returned. Munira heard Muhidin in silence, her head held artificially high. She plucked the end of her kimono-like robe. Her lips moved, the only sign of emotion. But her self-containment disintegrated again. A short guttural sound escaped her as Muhidin repeated to her Ayaana's words. Tension mounted in his shoulders. His throat itched. His voice was miserable.

Gaunt-faced, she had hiccupped, "Has God the Almighty become a butcher to make of the world a slaughterhouse now?" She then clasped both Muhidin's hands with hers, sorrow pooling inside her eyes. Muhidin could not look away. "Thank you. Again," she had coughed. Then she wiped her face with a little square white cloth. Afterward, she took his bruised fist in her one hand while reaching for a jug of rose water with the other. She poured scented water over broken skin, a blend of rose and clove oil, and then spread a black cumin-seed salve. "Your swollen eyes." she said.

"I hurt him first," Muhidin murmured.

As Munira administered the concoction, Ayaana's tiny snores punctuated the tense silence. Soon after, Munira served rosebud tea sprinkled with cinnamon, and small portions of *mbaazi* and *mahamri* coated with coconut. Her *mkate wa mofa* was unlike any other, he noted. Munira asked him, "What do I do now?" In the pale light sprinkling the room, they both stared out at the sea. They savored the snack and avoided answers.

"Is this now the world?" Munira asked Muhidin. Tears shimmered in her eyes.

Silence.

And then Muhidin, gaze distant, spoke to her of things he had once seen. In 1985, two weeks before Ramadan, he explained, he had found himself in Misrata, Libya, on Tripoli Street, he told Munira. He had been making his way back to the emerald seafront of Tawergha, where his ship waited. On one of the side roads, a strangled voice made of disgrace had screamed at him, "Negro cur, perpetual slave, blacker than ugliness."

"It was," Muhidin said, "the grunt of evil that blames its victim for existing in the first place."

Munira listened.

Muhidin said, "Being human is a rare art; it is not given to all equally." Muhidin then rubbed at the sweat and stickiness of the blue shirt clinging to his skin. His voice was suddenly gruff as he answered an unknown question. "Aren't we also men? Don't we also know something of honor?" His left hand clenched and unclenched.

For an interval, they just listened to the earth's simple sounds outside: birds, ocean, a woman singing, children playing and giggling, and the flow of tides. Muhidin said, "I noticed that the ants are carrying food into their nests."

"Storm?" Munira asked.

"Likely."

She said, "May it come. May it purge this evil." Then: "I like your voice. Even in fury it bears kindness."

He glanced up at her, startled. She smiled. He froze. The thick heat and humidity invoked lassitude, slowed down their futile hunt for solutions to heal existential uncertainty. The heat collected and stored the wind-borne smell of rotting mangoes and decrepitude—something of the essence of the liquids of death. Munira rose. "Must fetch herbs." She groaned again, covering her face. "Why don't they just immolate themselves in their slimy shit-pits?"

Muhidin wanted to assure her it would all go away. He reached out, but withdrew his hand before it touched her skin. He scratched his beard. Finger tapping the table, Muhidin cleared his throat and said, "We'll save Ayaana."

"How?"

"We'll rescue her from the burden of God."

Munira's response was cold and hard: "Muhidin Mlingoti, you shall only point my daughter to eternal possibilities. She was not born for limits."

"The risk—" he had cried, intending to argue his case.

"Fix it," Munira interrupted, nostrils flaring. "That's what fathers do."

Confused, annoyed, and also cheered by the word "father," Muhidin had meekly answered, "I'll try." He had gulped down his coffee, burning his tongue and throat, and stood erect to stretch his back, easing the tightness in his belly. As he released a breath, he said, "I'll rest now."

Munira had walked him to the door. But when he stepped into the hazy day, she had grabbed his forearm. A crack in her façade. She had asked, "What if there's nothing to hold on to?"

He had surprised himself by tucking away a stray lock of hair on her head, touching her eyebrows, and saying nothing, because he had no guarantees to sell.

[15]

Later, within the dim shadows of a dull afternoon light, Muhidin sat across his table from Ayaana, clutching a waterlogged dark green book. Brows meeting, he watched her, as she, hand to jaw, watched his mouth open and close.

Ayaana's laughter skipped around inside the room. "You look like . . . like a big fish!"

Abrupt. "Abeerah?"

"Mhh?" she answered.

Muhidin's fingers tapped a tattoo on the tabletop. "Abeerah," he repeated. "Some cursed toads from craven realms dream of drinking our blood. They are, of course, possessed." He pointed to his head.

Ayaana cradled her head. A mosquito whined. Muhidin leaned forward to add, "They are idolaters. They are stone-cold infidels."

She added, "And . . . aposto . . . apostorate."

"Apostates."

Ayaana's head went up and down.

Muhidin said, "Correct."

Remembering the previous application of "apostate," she whispered, "And you?"

"Me? Only a humble heretic."

"Me, too." She was emphatic. "Like you."

Muhidin grasped the tabletop. Some things were no longer a joke. Lest Munira hear about it, he hastened to correct her. "Er . . . only untethered . . . er . . . *men* are that."

Watching him, Ayaana decided she would also be untethered, whatever that was. Muhidin tried again. "There are malaria mosquitoes, which need to bite. They carry and spread sickness and diseases. So, too, do some people."

Ayaana's eyes studied Muhidin. "Why?" she asked, not understanding his words. Outside, a crow cawed. The sun's light changed, and it imbued objects in the room with a halo.

Muhidin's mind turned on its pivot. He propped up his jaw. "Can't explain humans." Muhidin stopped. He realized that he could not prevent some unpredicted horror from robbing Ayaana of her joy, some tragedy from stealing her life. He made a fist, despising his helplessness. She drew circles on the tabletop with her fingers and waited for him to render her world safe again. She whispered, "*Atarudi?*"—Will he return?

"No," Muhidin answered, little knowing that an invading alien army was already on its way, the fallout from Fazul that would deform their destinies. Muhidin paused. "Should anyone ever approach you as that one did, run. Just run." Muhidin's eyes bulged before turning red. "Promise?" His voice broke.

Muhidin's tears struck Ayaana's heart. She leaned over to wipe his eyes. "The bad man won't come again. I am happy."

Muhidin took Ayaana by her face, squeezing it. His voice was intense: "Why do you love the sea?" Muhidin trembled.

She half frowned.

He prompted, "The feeling of the sea outside and inside you, yes?"

She nodded.

"That feeling . . . that is truth, that is how the Almighty speaks." What more could he add? Beauty? He seized both Ayaana's hands. "Basmallah!" he exclaimed.

Remembering, she intoned, "*Bismillah ir-Rahman ir-Rahim . . .*"

He pleaded, "Slow-slow."

She repeated it.

Muhidin said, "That's it! That is it!" Muhidin then stroked Ayaana's hair and retied her mismatched ribbons. She did not need to know yet that other types of ugly soul-traders existed, hollowed-out entities that would also seek to gorge themselves on her body, mind, heart; memories, blood, soul; her will, her dreams, her desires. Not yet. Not yet. So Muhidin breathed upon Ayaana's head. He was willing Ayaana eternal safety. He wanted to take a whip to the disordered world and clean it up for her, to find all the Fazuls that still existed and break their necks. Muhidin breathed, and his voice was cracked: "Abeerah, render Basmallah in color blue, green, yellow, and red. Colors pink and orange."

"And purple," Ayaana added.

"And purple."

"Abeerah," Muhidin said, "this book"—he indicated the lumpy book she was kneeling on; Ayaana did not move—"is yours." She blinked at the strange title. "*The Poetry of Rabi'a al-Adawiyya.* I've marked some lines for you. Stay close to Rabi'a. She'll take care of you."

He prayed.

Over the days, weeks, months, and, later, into the years, on a wooden desk that Muhidin had carried from his house into her room—a desk that would turn into an untidy shrine for her accumulated treasures, including her calligraphy pens and books—Ayaana refined her Basmallah calligraphy. As the seasons flowed, she learned how to turn to the musty green poetry book to find a word or phrase or line and hear from Rabi'a before she ended her day. Almost at once, Ayaana started murmuring prayers again—speaking of easy things, such as asking for the protection of her mother and Muhidin, the father who was standing in for the father who was still lost. One day, she retrieved an old photograph of her mother to place on her table. She then went to Muhidin to demand one of him. He gave her one of him looking out toward the ocean from a ship's deck. She pasted these onto the table surface and covered them with plastic, these sentinels of her rest and her days. Yet, during some nights, Fazul's ravings inserted themselves into her dreams to breathe death, fire, and delusion. Sometimes she would scrabble out of sleep and hide under her bed. Sometimes, partway there, she remembered that she had Muhidin and that he was stronger than Fazul. She would return to her bed and fall back asleep.

~

After Fazul, Munira wanted Ayaana close to her. When the awful soldiers landed, men who disrupted her work and scattered her bounty—sweaty, loathsome, unmannered men—she needed Ayaana to be within calling distance. Ayaana joined in her mother's work and listened to the play of other children outside with jealous longing. Over the weekends, the heat, color, and voices of so many females cleansing, purging, massaging, coloring, oiling, adorning, incensing, and transforming themselves under her mother's watch filled the house; Ayaana, bored, now eavesdropped on their thoughts, sentiments, and experiences.

Ayaana helped blend the henna with lime, molasses, and black tea. She watched her mother spoon henna paste into small cones of assorted sizes, and draw a lacy pattern into a woman's scrubbed skin. Ayaana was soon permitted to add ingredients to her mother's herb blends, including lavender and clove, to store in a dark vessel for later use. Munira supervised her as, with pride, she first mixed the entrancing *singo* for a bride named Asha: perfect portions of ylang-ylang, jasmine, *kilua*, and many rose petals, cloves, sandalwood, and Munira's *marashi*, including her rose water, which was so distinct that women traveled from as far away as Tanga to buy up her stock. Women had earlier gathered in the house to exfoliate Asha's skin. They whispered to the bride-to-be about the many, many ways of being a woman. Other women sent Ayaana away on assorted fool's errands to stop her from prematurely hearing arcane woman-words. Ayaana tried to listen anyway. What did the florid words made of double-entendres mean? Why were these accompanied by outbursts of dissonant cackles by wrinkled beauties, the most eager arrivals when a bride was being prepared? Munira caught Ayaana lurking in the preparation room. "*Lulu*. Go fill those buckets with water from the *djabia*. If you see those foreign ghosts prowling, run back. Later, tend to the jasmine on the roof. Are you sulking? *Eh?* Keep testing me. I'll give you something to stretch your lips over. You can stay and listen on the day you acquire good-sized breasts. Now go! Don't dally. Just let the sun evaporate my elixir and you *will* hear from me!"

Off Ayaana went, fantasizing about the day when it would be her turn to be touched with beauty and scent and told secrets in wild, laughing words that would be her entry into this community of women. She also rubbed her chest to see if breasts had started to grow. Nothing there yet.

[16]

Earth dips. Another showing of a basket-shaped white moon. A boat was gliding into the channel. In it was a man, a surviving twin who had been taken off the island with his brother, Tawfiq, when they were six years old. Like all children of seafaring parents, he and his brother used to watch the waters for the return of their father, Muhidin. Too soon, the boys found themselves at this same jetty in February 1969, with an auntie they had not met before, setting off to join their mother in Yemen. They landed there to discover new relations: a sister, another father, and a tutor who would stuff new memories into their hearts. On this warm November day of a year in which rage had brought down two towers far from here, red strings dangled from the mast of a *dau* that returned an emaciated, bespectacled, thirty-eight-year-old Ziriyab Raamis to Pate's shore. His clothes stank of stale smoke, and his shaggy, soft hair was uncombed. His eyes were two doorways to a tomb. He muttered to himself, "The ocean is an old country." In their new life, everything should have ended well. It had not.

Ziriyab adjusted his glasses, his gold ring with its ruby strip glinting in the light. Fire hauntings. Then ash. Then darkness. Then nothing. *The ocean is an old country.* When he could get out from under an earth that had tried to bury him whole, bloodied and bruised, Ziriyab, moving on adrenaline alone, had needed to hide. *The ocean is an old country.* First, like most fugitives, he had made use of shadows, hollows, and holes, lurking in bushes, hiding in culverts, stealing a burka to wear over his clothes so he could walk among men, seeking a way out. Instinct led him to lesser-known ports and temporary landing spots along the extended coastline that deep-ocean travelers know. He had traveled boat by boat until Mocha, south of Hodeida. There, he skulked around until he found a night-moving, off-register, motorized fisherman's boat that was headed southward. Its *nahodha* had shrugged: he chased the winds. Ziriyab would abandon that boat at Kismaayo. Fortunately, at that port city he was already among his own—he could have swum to his destination if there had been no sharks lurking. *This ocean is an old country.* Boat chatter. Ziriyab listened. The seamen and seafarers were deriding some "boots" that had swarmed onto the island. Screeching men, commanding this and commanding that, their screams brewed in some abyss.

"The Terrorized"—the name given to them by the islanders—had leapt from helicopters whose winds blew the roof off a mosque. They proceeded to board boats and *madau* and seize people on the basis of a name and the shape of a beard. They searched as ferrets would. They scavenged women's cupboards to hunt shadows. Ziriyab listened to the low-toned murmurs. It looked as if the Terrorized had learned that their zeal had created resentments where none had existed before. They were attempting seduction now. The navigator said, "Monitor lizards posing as voluptuous sirens." Laughter on board. The boots' aims were to win hearts, claim souls, and change minds. They had announced that, really, they had come to help the islanders. They had taken it upon themselves to sink a well.

Now all the people on that boat were, as one, seized by tear-causing gales of laughter. They knew the punch line; Ziriyab did not. Huddling into his coat, he waited to hear it. He leaned over to whisper to the seaman nearest to him, "What's so funny?"

"*Duu!* You are a visitor?"

"Yes . . . er . . . from . . . from . . . Turkey," he improvised.

"Uturuki? How are our people there? Anyway . . ." Paroxysms of giggles engulfed the man. In between hoots, the seaman told Ziriyab how the boots had proceeded to dig a well without asking or being asked to. It took six months—more elaborate wells had been built elsewhere in eight days—and as they were building it, they surrounded it with a large metal fence, guarded by four large square-headed men wielding guns and looking fierce. When the well was ready, which was eight months ago, they had launched it with halfhearted song and speeches in assorted English accents in front of delegations from the rest of the world. A garrulous military man, whose coat had more metal than fabric, had then led the ambassador to cut a large red bow stuck at the entrance to the well with blunt scissors. And when the first water was drawn from the well and offered to the ambassador to drink, he imbibed it, and truth dawned on him. His pained smile informed the islanders that he, too, had discovered what centuries of Pate Island dwellers already knew: Pate's underground water was foul, concentrated salt, and had been so for almost three hundred years. After that day, this new well was not referred to again. However, the boots were planning a new heart-soul-mind-winning project that would help Pate islanders help themselves. They were building a pit latrine where no pit latrine had ever been built before. Surrounding them was a landscape containing ruins of seven-hundred-year-old wastewater channels and sewerage pits. The boat captain snorted. On board, more resigned, disbelieving laughter. The return of barbarous hordes had not been expected. It had been generations since a people completely oblivious to the codes of human hospitality had crossed

Pate thresholds. A perplexed silence saturated the boat until someone muttered, "They'll be weaving our fishnets soon."

The boat rocked with their amusement.

"And sewing our robes."

Guffaws.

Frail-toned, Ziriyab Raamis asked, "And where are they now?"

"The kaffirs in Nairobi have given Manda over to them," a disgruntled voice snarled. Silence again. This one created from the wounds of betrayals: first by Fazul the Egyptian, but the second, more serious one was that of the covenant of belonging and protection broken by the state of Kenya, which had willfully laid the island bare to the murderous alien hordes. Still, Ziriyab's relief was immediate. *Manda. Not here.* That is all he needed to know. Now he could permit the hunger, fear, grief, and exhaustion to take him over. Their boat limped into the mangrove channel, and long shadows flickered over Ziriyab's brittle heart. Choppy water. There were rocks beneath the surface of the sea; millennia of sunken boats rotted down there. He recalled stories told at night of shipwrecks, of ghost boats that emerged in storms to attempt to reconnect with shattered journeys. Then he saw children crab hunting among the mangroves. He shivered. This was the farthest place on earth that he knew to go. He could render himself invisible here.

~

There were essences Muhidin Mlingoti could blend, and supplications he could make; there was food he could chew and regurgitate to feed his returned son. There were invocations he recited daily; they included all of Hafiz's words that he knew. He could even give up his bed. But still the anguished, invisible world his son inhabited eluded his summons. His son would not speak. Ziriyab Raamis stared at his father empty-eyed; when he slept, a belligerent nightmare would have him clawing back into wakefulness with wild cries.

Muhidin stayed by his bed, looming like a mother ostrich, dabbing scent and blended herbs to pressure points, nerve points, and soul portals. He stroked Ziriyab's forehead, cajoled and consoled, addressed him as he would an infant. *Lala, mwanangu, lala*. There is a cure for every one of life's ailments. Muhidin's problem was an old one—discerning how and when to recognize the elixir when it offered itself.

Ayaana and Munira had kept away from Muhidin after the first commotion of encounter. Ziriyab had tumbled into the water from the boat at the jetty in a faint. Muhidin had ambled over to join some other men in hauling this stranger from the water. A man had pulled out and read a name from a drenched passport. And, hearing the name, Muhidin had found his son, upon whom he fell, whom he lifted and carried to his house, refusing all assistance, wailing, "Leave me my boy, leave me my son," to would-be helpers. Later, Muhidin had sent a note to Munira and Ayaana: "He needs time. I need time. We will look for you when we are ready."

A day, a week, Ayaana waited. She peeked into Muhidin's house from all available angles. She lurked beneath windows and tried to interpret the sounds and movements she heard. Munira pretended not to care. But, one day, she gave in to ask Ayaana, "What do you see? Did he say anything?"

In the middle of an evening in the third week, Ayaana dragged Munira to Muhidin's door; Munira let herself be dragged. Munira carried rose attar, her famed *halwaridi*, for Muhidin. When Muhidin opened his door, Ayaana at once shouted, "Even me, aren't I yours?"

Muhidin lifted her up and hid his face in her neck, recalling beautiful things—like songs in the sea—as Munira's eyes danced for him. He almost wept when Munira handed over the attar to him. He covered her hands over the vessel. "You took long enough," he said. "Come in."

Inside the house, Munira launched into cleaning, dusting, adjusting objects, rearranging furniture. "Ayaana! Water," she called.

Muhidin protested, "Let us sit, let us talk. How is the world coping without me?"

Munira said, "Better than usual." She giggled. Then she rubbed an already clean shelf. "Such dust." That way, she did not have to attend to a heart that was beating so hard, or to the unreliability of her emotions about this ungainly, hairy creature she had needed to see.

Ayaana produced a book of Hafiz's poetry she had taken off Muhidin's shelves. "Read," she said.

He rapped her head. "Say 'please.' "

"Nope," she answered.

"Nope?" Muhidin asked, his brows rising.

Ayaana glared. Muhidin took the book. "Let us see . . . Something about manners."

"Nope," Ayaana replied, "something about *disappearing*." She added defiantly, "And . . . and *forgetting*." Her voice shook on the word.

Muhidin bent to gaze into her eyes. He touched the side of her face. "I'm here." He picked a passage to read:

> *"Pour the red wine with control*
> *Like rose water into the bowl*
> *While fragrant breeze will roll . . ."*

Somewhere outside, a cock crowed; the muezzin summoned humanity to prayer; donkeys brayed; children giggled. The sea flowed with the sound of a storm passing elsewhere. Rain spattered. Inside, Muhidin pulled a window shut, enclosing them in their world, their love, their words, their Hafiz.

"How is he?" Munira whispered.

"His life's a wildfire. I gather soul ashes with my hands," Muhidin said despairingly. "My boy's dying." Ayaana rushed to wrap her arms around Muhidin's waist. He stroked her head. "Let's sit . . . for a little while. Tell me things of goodness. How are my girls?" His voice was brusque.

Upstairs, Ziriyab Raamis stirred. Soft voices were floating toward him. He did not yet have the power to open his eyes, but he could smell the salt of the sea, and a hint of jasmine and roses. Sounds he deciphered. A child's voice, awed, high-pitched: "The sea done bringed . . . uh . . . bring him?" A deep voice, now familiar, saying, "My son." A woman's breathy answer: "He's prettier than you." The deep voice repeating,

"My boy." Ziriyab clung to the resonance of that deep voice as he very, very slowly winched a way out of thick, black-mud dreams.

Five days later, a gale settled on the island. Driving, warm rain fell in broad sheets that flooded the land and whipped up the sea into a raging lather. Munira, Ayaana, and Muhidin sat on a reed mat in Muhidin's gallery with its sea-view balcony. They shared *halua*, and coffee flavored with ginger and rose water. Muhidin spun tales of sea monsters, his many ways of challenging storms. He explained that, when he had dared waves larger than mountains to swamp him and sweep him off the deck of his ship, they had, at the very last second, collapsed and retreated. He talked about the pleading cry of djinns that had fallen in love with him, their longing to grant him anything, if only he would grant them a glimpse of his face. In these stories, Muhidin never flinched. In his narrated battles, he never lost. In these encounters with strong, brave men, he was the stronger and braver, and for women of assorted beauty, he was always the prize. In the recklessness of that day, he went upstairs and returned with a yellow-brown parchment map in a book within a book.

What they saw: a dream poem in Kufic script.

نجمة. A star. A map. A road. A journey. A destination. Something. Muhidin told them—in half-word, half-song—how he had retrieved it from the inside drawer of an inside chest in a black cupboard within a crumbling house found at the bottom half of a doubling-back labyrinth. They stared at the fragment, willing it to speak. Munira then whispered about the fear of rusting in one place, of stagnating and of never traveling to experience other points of the world. She stroked the map. And outside: *Hooooooo!* howled the wind. *Whaaaaaa!* The ocean answered, and as night started to sneak in, they learned they were not yet ready to leave one another.

Ayaana cried, "Not yet."

So.

Muhidin roused himself, reached over, and dragged down one of the dangling soft blue cloths, which he draped around his body. Eyes rolling, body stiff, he attempted to rotate his hips. He began a growl that was soon deciphered by his hysterical audience to be Amr Diab's previously dulcet "Habibi":

> *"Habibi ya nour el-ain*
> *Ya sakin khayali*
> *A'ashek bakali sneen wala ghayrak bibali. . . ."*

They were giddy. Munira, feeling as she had not felt in nineteen years, arched her back as a child reading stars might, *taarab* melodies mixing and brewing within her. She seized Muhidin's idea of song, added the exaggerated warbles of a Zanzibari singer notorious for elongating vowels in music to make it wobble, wiggle, and hyperventilate. Munira sang:

> *"Ua langu silioni nani alolichukuwa?*
> *Ua langu lileteni moyo upate kupowa*
> *Ua langu la zamani ua lililo muruwa . . ."*

Even in mimicry, Munira's contralto blasted open recondite portals, revealed salted-and-preserved tragedies, and shook stability. As she sang, incandescence exploded to open pebbled-over lives. Muhidin ended his baying accompaniment. Ayaana lost her hysterical cackles. They simply listened, while portions of their beings fluttered over to the balcony to peer through mists into the wild blue-silver waves of a foaming ocean, searching for something they could not give a name to.

From his canopied bed in his room, Ziriyab Raamis also eavesdropped. A book of Tagore's poetry lay open against his perspiring head. His body, which had been shaking with fever, added fury to its vigor. Only later would he admit that he had been jealous about being left out, stranded in emptiness while life flowed on without him. From his pillow, he smelled *their* coffee, heard *their* laughter, *their* raucousness. A woman singing: her voice cut him up; he hated her. He grunted and thrashed around the bed. He tried to block his ears. He retched three times. Wrath lifted him off the bed.

. . .

Ziriyab Raamis seemed to materialize in the room. Sunken cheeks, long yellowish face, long lashes, almost hazel bloodshot eyes, and slender hands: he was a wraith. His sudden presence shocked Munira into silence. *With extra weight*, she thought, *this would be a most exquisite being*.

Ziriyab's face became distorted, as if a hooded entity lurked beneath his skin. Outside, thunder. Ziriyab's eyes moved across the three others. They perched on Munira. "Perverse leeches. Harlots!"

Lightning.

Munira scurried into her mask as a hermit crab would. How had she forgotten? How had she slipped into happiness? How had she lost the sense of foreboding that kept her alert? How could she forget the pursuing, bullying thing that always turned up to disrupt her tiniest joys? Here was its loathsome manifestation. How had she forgotten?

"So. A brothel?" Ziriyab's hand gesture took in the tableau. "After you've finished with him"—a chin jutted in the direction of Muhidin—"look to me. How much for your services?" He dipped a finger into his shirt pocket and dangled a foreign note. "Or will it cost more?" The money floated to the ground. Ziriyab Raamis's gaze crawled over Munira's body.

Munira reached down for her empty coffee cup and hurled it at him, clipping his ear as the cup bounced off his head. The coffee remains stained his *kikoi*. Then she was in his face, grabbing his throat, hands around his neck; her teeth bit his hand, and her voice was smoky with tears: "I've died before." She seized his hair. "Insult me, *mie langu jicho*, but in front of my child? You diseased *maggot*!" They grappled.

"Munira!" Muhidin grabbed her.

"*Ma-e!*" Ayaana kicked over the coffeepot to reach Munira.

Muhidin and Ayaana dragged Munira off Ziriyab. The outside storm was inside the room: Ziriyab's flaming eyes, a bruise on his jaw; Munira gulping air, hair unkempt. Muhidin dropped a firm arm around her shoulders and with the other drew Ayaana to his side. He glared at his son, his choice clear. Muhidin stared Ziriyab down. "*Mtupie Mungu kilio, sio binadamu mwenzi*," he snarled—Cry to God, what can a human being do? Suddenly still, they breathed, they waited, and they watched one another.

Munira wiped her sweating face; her voice shaking, she sniffed,

"*Ba* . . . now we leave. We'll borrow your umbrella. Come see us when you need to. Come, *lulu*."

Ayaana was hunched, watching Ziriyab with panicked eyes.

Outside, lightning. Muhidin said, "I'll go with you."

No one moved. Thunder. Lightning. Thunder. The outside storm was inside the room, and then, unexpectedly, it struck two hearts.

Glowing senses. Inner portals opened by a decision. Within Muhidin, newness sparkled like many diamonds set alight. He looked at the world light-headedly and looked through Ziriyab. Twinkling revelation, terror, and surprise. Muhidin then turned on his heel to gape at Munira, startled by his own breathlessness, his racing heart. He reached for her, but stopped himself, readjusted his reaction. A sheen of perspiration was on his brow; his lips were dry, and blood rushed and swirled in his head. Thunder. Lightning. Thunder. Muhidin draped his large arms around Munira and Ayaana again, to lead them away.

Yet.

His feet hovered above the earth and its lucent light.

Munira, Munira, Munira.

Heartbeat. *Munira.*

Dizzy, bracing himself against a pillar, Ziriyab panted. Then he laughed, his voice cracking and rising. He frowned. His limbs were quivering, and his heart beat to the rhythm of his single-word thoughts: *That. Woman. That. Woman.* Nothing could offend him now, not even his grief. Euphoria surfaced as a slow-burning buzz on his body. He garbled "Thank you" for the voice, song, scent, temper, skin, and eyes of a woman, *that* woman.

When Ziriyab first entered the room, Munira had just flung out her arms. Her face tilted backward toward him, and a light hovered near her head. Her face: 53 freckles. Though he had spat at her, he was bemused. Beyond his distress at his father's rebuff, he knew yearning. Ziriyab's suddenly gleaming world was made out of an effusion of fragrances and emotions: rose, jasmine, vanilla, earth, water, salt, hurt, fury, and desolation. He read her look of sorrow, for it came from a book of wounds he had known. He had wanted to cry to Munira, *Let's start again*, as if he were speaking to his original self. He decided he would be her scapegoat, her fool. He would earn her mercy. He would plead with her heart until she recognized that she was his restart. As the house returned to its groan-, creak-, thump-filled, in-between existence, Ziriyab knelt down to retrieve the money he had scattered. He limped over to the balcony, and dropped it over the balustrade. A wind swooped down on it. He reached for a cloth and knelt on the ground to wipe the spilled coffee.

Heavy footsteps coming up the stairs.

Ziriyab waited.

Muhidin reached the gallery, eyes popping and mouth open. But before he could pronounce a word, Ziriyab fell prostrate before him, arms stretched above his head, supplicating, words breaking off, starting again, returning, repeating themselves, so that when these came together, minutes later, he had wept. "Today I shamed you . . . offended your people . . . I beg you . . . forgive me. Please, let me stay. I'll change, I promise. Mercy. Forgive me."

He punctured Muhidin's ferocity.

A brief silence before Muhidin offered his son the smallest of nods and helped him up. He looked into his son's face and understood. For less than the length of a sigh, the deep fingerprint of loss poked into Muhidin's spine, and he might have stumbled. He knew. From the new will-to-live shine in his son's eyes, he knew.

Little by little, his son's consumptive shadows disappeared in tender-voiced *tell-me-about-her*—Munira—requests that made his eyes sparkle. "I dreamed that we danced last night," Ziriyab confided as he guzzled down milk and juice and herbal blends. *Tell me what she wore today*. Muhidin struggled to forget Munira's manners, her beginnings, her perfumes, her garden, and her scattered, silken, low laughter. Every detail he offered his son was as a eulogy. Verbal amputations from one unexpected love that had surfaced and changed the geography of his soul forever, far more than the seas could ever do, to feed another unexpected love. Muhidin was dying. Muhidin was giving life again.

[17]

As soon as his body could stay up, Ziriyab had shuffled over to Munira's house, wearing Muhidin's best *kanzu*, shaven and elegant, carrying a basket of household supplies. He stood outside Munira's house, afraid to knock. When she opened the door and saw him there, she slammed it shut again.

He stood outside to wait.

Ayaana opened the door almost an hour later. She studied him, wide-eyed. "You're the bad man?" she said.

"Yes."

"What are you carrying?"

"Food and an apology."

"Can I see it?"

"It's for your glorious mother, that perfumed queen, enchantress of my heart. I, a prisoner of her song, throw my tormented heart beneath her beloved and merciful heel."

Ayaana giggled.

Munira re-emerged, glared, dragged her daughter in, and slammed the door.

In the soft orange light of dusk, he was still there, seated as a Buddha might be, with his basket of offerings close to his feet, his pensive focus on Munira's door. From time to time, Ayaana peeped through the window to stick out her tongue at him.

"Stop humiliating yourself, fool," hissed Suleiman's mother, Bi Amina Mahmoud, to Ziriyab on her way to shop for fabric and pasta. "Why beg for what's offered free? Grow some testicles!"

Ziriyab did not react. He reflected on the sound of placid waves and an arcane stillness that persisted on Pate, now hearing the rustling of night leaves and smelling the wavering scents of dill, rosemary, mint, and sage, until close to midnight, when Munira stepped out with a glass of rose-scented coconut water for him.

He reached for it with both hands, enclosing hers in the act. "I was jealous . . ." he began. She dragged her hands from his.

She said, "I accept your apology. Now go away."

He jumped up, stretching cramped legs. "Please, take these, my Huma, and . . ."

She turned away.

He called, "Marry me then?"

Munira fled. Ziriyab heard the door slam again. Sipping the juice, he thought, *My Munira, my Buthayna, my Ghazalah, my own soaring Huma.* He glided back to Muhidin's, leaving his basket behind, grinning at night stars and cradling the glass as if it were a jewel.

Weeks later, Munira, in a pleasant tone, informed Ziriyab, who was dogging her footsteps among the fishermen as she sought to buy fish, "You're an ox and an indulged donkey." Munira added, "Your ears are the shape of shark fins, and you are rude, thin, and ignorant. You bite your nails and chew gum like a masticating cow." Ziriyab agreed with her. He told her of other flaws she did not know about: his bullfrog snores, sleeping with his mouth wide open while saliva drooled, and that, even though he was trying to be a fisherman now and scraping off the accountant's skin, he was unable to bear the floundering of fish in nets, gasping for breath and screaming in silence, big golden eyes pleading for mercy, so he let them go. And then he called her his Munira, his Buthayna, his Ghazalah, his own soaring Huma.

Munira stopped mid-hunt. Her eyes shot spears at him. "Now you decide to starve me and my child of fish!" She flounced away.

Ziriyab's head dropped. *What?* He did not know whether to laugh or to cry. He turned purple instead.

The next afternoon, he showed up with a carton-load of fish for Munira. He also apologized to her for every wounding word she had endured. He told her that he himself had clouted every fish on the head and enjoyed it.

Munira glowered at him. "You killed these helpless fish? What did they ever do to you?" Her door slammed.

Ziriyab's eyes popped. His mouth dropped open, imitating the look of the fish in his leaking carton. He kicked the box.

Persistent, Ziriyab bombarded Munira with crustaceans, songs, and sugary poems, the songs in styles borrowed from Indian, Turkish, and Egyptian movies. On one occasion, he hired cheap part-time minstrels to sing her these songs, two of which he had composed in what he hoped was the manner of the poetry of Tagore. These ghastly, rhythmless pieces compared Munira to a hibiscus and found the hibiscus wanting.

When it rained, Ziriyab sought Munira out with an umbrella to escort her wherever she sought to go. When she shopped, he showed up to carry her goods. He waited on her steps when she attended to clients, inhaling assorted scents.

In quiet moments close to her night sea, Munira contemplated this turn of events in her life: to be sought after and pursued, to be desired, and gazed upon as if she were priceless, so that even her insults were deemed poetry. She had tried to hide, but, in secret, her thirsty heart imbibed this, stealing its nectar, even as she waited for the return of the usual chill and sting.

And. Qualms.

In a word,

Muhidin.

Now.

His presence. His silence.

A riddle.

Her palms sweating, her knees trembling as she crossed paths to go to Muhidin's house.

"Hujambo?"

"Sijambo."

A split-second glimpse of truth; a brief unveiling. They stood close together, eyes averted.

Munira asked, "You approve?"

"Gives the boy new life."

"You approve?"

"He dreams of you."

"You approve?"

Muhidin never looked at her.

Munira stood unmoving, diffident.

Something else, aching to be expressed between them, palpitated.

Muhidin explained, "Before he saw you, he had willed himself to die."

She asked, "And so?"

"He's my son," he said, and his voice was sad.

She asked, "You approve?"

Muhidin turned to pretend to reach for an item on his clutter-filled table. "He needs you . . . to live . . . He's still so young . . . He's mine."

Silence.

Then she murmured, "*Mpenzi,*" testing the sound for herself, not for him. Beloved. Muhidin should not have heard it, but when he thought he did, he should have asked what she meant. He did not. Munira veiled her face. She walked out of Muhidin's coral house.

Four days after Idd-ul-Fitr, on a misty night, Munira relented. Sleepless Ziriyab had taken to standing vigil close to her door at night. He had seen her leave the house and had trailed her during her deferred night wandering. From a safe distance, he watched her as she walked the shoreline. But when she crumbled into hacking tears, he took slow steps toward her. He did not speak. She grieved. He reached over and helped her up. She did not react to the shame of being found unmasked, even though he was part of the provocation for these recent tears. But, to her surprise, she also realized that she was not frightened of Ziriyab seeing her desolation.

They stood shoulder touching shoulder. They wondered if the dawn would come. When it appeared, it was as a backlit gold-and-violet streak in the sky, refulgent. Ziriyab then spoke, and his voice was old, tormented, and deep. "I try to tear off my skin. I try to hide from myself." He said madness was a refuge that smelled of rust. Then he told Munira that something had happened in October, almost a year back. A foreign naval carrier had been bombed in his hometown.

Ziriyab said, "One of the . . . ones . . . who did it . . . I know him. His name is . . . was . . . Tawfiq." He paused. "My brother. The other one of me."

Stillness. A sliver of dread. Munira shuddered.

Ziriyab continued: "A scholar, Munira. A good man. Better than me. A good brother." His voice was serrated, and his tone sank into jarring grooves. "Didn't see the change." Tears as his body rocked. "A good brother. A professor. Microbiology. He was cleverer than me."

A man's useless, helpless, hated, unwanted tears. Mucus dripped down Ziriyab's face, contorting it. His hands gesturing skyward, he whispered, "Why?"

And the morning sky turned light blue, and dew settled around them.

As Munira and Ziriyab listened to the bustling of joyful birds. Ziriyab said, "Tawfiq protected even cockroaches. 'Allah created life to praise Him,' he would say. 'These little ones complete our song.'" Ziriyab now coughed into his hands. The cough became a dry heaving. Munira leaned into him. She listened to his voiceless weeping. Much later, Ziriyab continued: "When Tawfiq died with those others, when we found out . . . we couldn't stay. We left our home."

Avoiding a dragnet, a week later, the extended family left in a four-car convoy heading south. Ziriyab was driving the station wagon that carried his wife; his rich mother-in-law; his sister-in-law, Tawfiq's wife; and six children. They drove nonstop through day and night. Two days later, Ziriyab stopped. They were less than an hour and a half from the village that would be their hideout. He needed to urinate, he said.

But he had just needed breathing space from the incessant and suffocating put-downs of his mother-in-law, who, as with everything else, knew better than he how to drive, how to see the road ahead. This was interspersed with assorted insults against Tawfiq: his shame, dishonor, and unworthiness. If Ziriyab had not stopped, he said, he would have turned to choke her to death in front of the children. In the fresh evening air, in the cool, cool breeze, Ziriyab had lingered in an overgrown wild coffee thicket, gulping down air. The drivers of the other cars were gunning their engines, impatient to continue. He was doing up his fly when he heard what he imagined was a swarm of bees.

"There was humming, humming, humming. Then the air exploded." An angry, fiery, large, and hot thing had tumbled from the sky and obliterated all life within a twelve-meter radius, with a whoosh.

"Oh," Munira cried out.

"The inferno. Then nothing. But, me, I only wondered if *shaitan*, that mother-in-law, could actually evaporate."

Munira and Ziriyab begin to laugh. "My shame," Ziriyab says. They hold on to their stomachs, guffawing. Then they cling to each other. "My shame," repeats Ziriyab. Then they are sobbing, cheek to cheek, and Ziriyab murmurs names: Noor, Jibril, Issa, his children; Atiya, Seif, Umi, their cousins; his wife, Durriyah. "You would've been friends," Ziriyab says. "Perfect friends."

Munira, inside the tight circle of Ziriyab's arms, replies, "I'll marry you."

[18]

They were sieving orange-blossom water, straining out vagrant florets. They were softening water that would later be scattered over a woman's body when Munira told Ayaana, "I'll be marrying Ziriyab."

Ayaana had known. She had sensed the meaning of Muhidin's new silences, his lowered gaze, the sad wrinkle above his lips, his distraction, and his refusal to say her mother's name. Ayaana studied her hands in the scented water.

Munira glanced at Ayaana. "A 'real' father for you."

"No," Ayaana said.

"What?" Munira asked. A terse question.

Ayaana floated her hands in the water. Her voice was neutral. "I have a father."

There were eighty things Munira wanted to shriek. Words jumbled up. "You could try, *lulu*," she whispered.

"No," replied Ayaana.

Scented silence.

Two weeks later, on a Thursday, a short, lisping, nerdy *kadhi* married Munira and Ziriyab in a small, stark *nikah* ceremony in a corner of the Riyadha al-Jana Mosque in Lamu. An extremely distant uncle of Munira's, a long-distance truck driver of indifferent reputation, had played *wakil* and given permission for the nuptials, sight unseen. The idea of the marriage had amused him. Before the ceremony, Munira, Ziriyab, Ayaana, and Muhidin had stopped at the shrine of the saint Ali Habib Swaleh to invite blessings. Later, a mosque attendant, Ayaana, and Muhidin, who walked in step with one another, witnessed the nuptials. Stories are malleable within a person's feelings: they can be squeezed to acquire the shape of truth. And so Ayaana and Muhidin wandered the island with the intoxicated pair, almost convinced of their own happiness, too.

Ziriyab Raamis's spirited pursuit of Munira would eventually reach and be retold in Kismaayo sea enclaves as poetry to mock the lovelorn.

Ayaana called Ziriyab "Ziriyab."

Muhidin remained "*babangu*"—my father.

Ayaana made a point of pointing out things Muhidin could already see just so that she could repeat "*babangu.*"

Munira's mouth tightened.

Ziriyab remained oblivious.

Muhidin suppressed a laugh, even though his look remained troubled.

"You continue to defy me in this matter," Munira accosted her daughter one day in their kitchen.

Washing a pile of dishes, Ayaana let the banging of the pans speak for her.

Munira asked, "Why?"

"I already have a father," replied Ayaana.

Yapitayo hayageukani; yajayo hayaelimiki.

The past cannot be changed; the future cannot be known.

[19]

The tide went out, way out, so very quickly. Calm. Alluring. The water disappeared, and suddenly his boat, which had been in the deep sea, was marooned on black-brown sand. A few sparkling fish of splendid form flopped about within arm's reach. Enchanting. If he had been a fisherman longer, he would not have been mesmerized. He would have known to read the action of fish that had abandoned their feeding grounds that day. He would not have tried to read or wrestle with the whirling, potent current coming in. The secret things of the sea revealed would not have transfixed him. He might have turned his body and boat to face the incoming, speeding, giant waves. He might have understood that he could not make it back to shore in time. He might even have heard the echoes of 250,000 people screaming from the shores along this ocean, as they were swallowed up in five seconds, and he would have heard the howl of broken people trying to hold on to them. Like Ziriyab Raamis, many had forgotten how to decipher the habits of animals that, before dawn, had, in a rush, sought to hide. The second wave caught his boat sideways, and splintered it. He was breathing in water, being whirled in and swept out, and swept in and out and in again. He ached for just one glimpse of Munira, his wife of eighteen months, the wife of his life, his Buthayna, his Ghazalah, his own soaring Huma.

On that Boxing Day Sunday of 2004, a mad, mad current, on an uninhabited atoll where sometimes, once a season, fishermen stopped, vomited Ziriyab Raamis out. He was battered, naked, nameless, and boatless. And after a minute of nothing, he inhaled, he exhaled, he vomited out seawater. And his senses were on fire. And he heard a woman singing. Her voice poured out a name. He remembered that the name was his. And the song was his wife crying him home. Ziriyab Raamis took to swimming out to sea. He thought he and the sea might find and follow the song of his Buthayna, his Ghazalah, his own soaring Huma. And he drank rain water from a puddle and ate raw fish. He had honed a spear-stick with which to hunt and pierce eels. He ate a midsized crab and dreamed of a garlic sauce with which to season it. Eight and a half days later, mid-morning, six fishermen in a skiff from Mogadishu saw, in the distance, a figure thrashing about in the waters. They approached the specter. It turned into a nude human being making incoherent sounds and waving his arms.

"*Salaam aleikum*," the men's captain called.

"*Alhamdulillah!*" Ziriyab groaned. He laughed in small bursts.

The men in the boat studied the madman. "What brings you this far?" the skiff captain asked.

Ziriyab croaked, "An idiot current mistook this for my grave."

Knowing what had happened, a man threw Ziriyab a rope, and another of the men jumped into the water to help push him into the small boat, where other hands reached for him. "So—how's life?" deadpanned the fisherman who had dragged him in and covered his body with a stained green *kikoi*. "Is the fishing any good here?"

"With or without clothes?" Ziriyab Raamis answered.

A thunderclap of mirth riddled the boat. They told Ziriyab what had happened to the ocean: "Tsunami." The word was not rousing enough for him, not after all he had experienced of its effects. So he said, "*Dhoruba.*"

"*Dhoruba*," they agreed, was the finest of the fathomless words that spoke best of the convulsion of an ocean on one December day. Ziriyab and his rescuers fished all afternoon, throwing nets in arcs that shimmered in the water. Driven by a chill wind, and still jumpy about the waters, they turned sail and set off on a blue, stirring sea in the direction of Pate.

Ziriyab heard a woman sing. Her voice poured out his name. It sounded like his wife crying him home.

. . .

She was waiting for him in the water—as she had been doing for all the hours that he had been away. From the minute the sea had surged and covered the black beach, and fishermen who returned had told her that a wave the size of a hill had grabbed Ziriyab and swept him and his boat away, Munira had gone to the water to hurl prayers into its depths. She pleaded with the sea, parading within its waves. She had insulted those who attempted to haul her in. The islanders confirmed that Munira was unhinged, that her madness had started long ago.

Muhidin and Ayaana had, at first, stood by the shoreline, keeping Munira within their sights. They watched the sea swirl around her hips. Thick lines wrote themselves into Muhidin's forehead. His eyes were bloodshot.

"The ocean is me," he murmured to Ayaana. "How can it consume my son?"

Muhidin studied the clouds, watched the rocks, scrutinized the water; he had already searched the ocean with fishermen and returned empty.

Munira called for Ziriyab in a howling-keening chant. Ayaana's heart pounded; her armpits dampened. She wished that her mother's habits did not have to mean such humiliation in their lives. Her eyes watered. Here was their nothingness exposed. There was the world, disgusted by it. She shut her eyes tight. Why wouldn't her mother be like other mothers? She turned to Muhidin. "Make her leave the water."

Muhidin just stared.

Munira turned. She looked straight through Muhidin and Ayaana.

Ayaana had turned to flee and hide in Muhidin's house. "I need to leave, I need to leave, I need to leave. I need to leave," she repeated to herself.

Muhidin waited. He was praying to Munira's will; he trusted in its power to resurrect the dead. It was midnight. Some of the island now slept, while Muhidin and Munira stood guard over the sea.

In the darkness of her Bombay cupboard, Ayaana's thoughts allowed an image to emerge out of the components of Ziriyab's absence. In the secret of her dark shelter, Ayaana allowed herself to feel relieved over Ziriyab's disappearance.

105

. . .

Days later, Muhidin and Ayaana watched the blackened sea from his blue balcony. They huddled into the shawl of their fears. And inside Ayaana, whisperings of a strange hope—perhaps Ziriyab had really gone away. Perhaps *her* sea had purged him from their lives.

At sunset, a skiff negotiated hidden black rocks to an island. A woman howled out a name. Its command lifted Ziriyab out of the boat and propelled him into his wife's arms. And amid the rejoicing, a chill wind brought to Muhidin and Ayaana a man's song: "My Munira, my Buthayna, my Ghazalah, my own soaring Huma."

"Nothing bad can happen after this," Munira sobbed into Ziriyab's sunburned chest that night. "Nothing evil will ever touch us again. We have conquered death."

She was wrong.

Dunia mti mkavu, kiumbe usiuelemee.

The world is a withered tree; rest not your weight upon it.

[20]

Ayaana was racing back to the house, carrying a packet of lentil flour, the contents of which would be made into paste for a pore-cleansing face mask. Her thin limbs jutted out, and she was heavyhearted, still wounded by a snide comment her mother had made about the music she had put on permanent replay. Ayaana sighed. She was plowing through years in which she seemed to do nothing right, and the world, apart from the ocean, had become alien. The days were suffocating her, and everything felt like an obstacle course. No sooner would she take a step outside than somebody would appear to scold, exhort, chastise, warn, reprove her and deliver one more rule or habit she was to acquire:

Don't speak too loudly.

Cover your legs, your arms, your face.

Don't run.

Hurry.

Walk slowly.

Don't let your nail polish chip.

Perfume your body.

Cover your mouth when you laugh.

She walked, skirting the sea when there was light, because spying eyes had multiplied, ready to accuse her of some wrongdoing.

Her restlessness was mirrored in the lives of her peers, but they, unlike her, acted loud, and confident. They rapped modern songs in words she did not have access to. Ayaana had returned to school so that she might register for her standard eight exams. Muhidin's lessons had given her advantages over the whole class and made her a much-sought lesson companion especially in English and math. She relished this space of belonging among her peers even though she knew it would not last.

Her body grew and stretched and curved and developed bumps and smelled of otherness, and tasted of salt and something else, and wanted invisible, impossible things; her body was now the target of so many restrictions and bindings and shroudings, incited such a complexity of looks, an array of snide smiles and extra commands for decorum. The women in her mother's house pinched her body's various parts; they called her a young woman now. Her body was a puzzle, her thoughts a protest. A legion of unfamiliar shadows had emerged to scare her. Her dreams rearranged themselves and, to her embarrassment, invited in the image of the awful Suleiman, so that every day Ayaana's heart softened at the idea of him.

She noticed his height, and how he outraced everybody. She began to show up at the scene of the boys' evening football game just so that she could gaze at him. She was not surprised that he served as coach, referee, captain, and goalkeeper.

Ayaana now edited her conversations with Munira, because, despite her best intentions, these twisted into arguments.

Now racing toward the path that would lead to her house, she heard a scraping noise. Ayaana fixed her eyes on the bald-headed man from China, Mzee Kitwana Kipifit.

Squinting from under her veil, Ayaana spied the man sitting still and solid, next to the island's dome-shaped tombs. *What was he doing?*

"Ayaaaana!" A husky summons from a darkened doorway interrupted her musings. Amina "Mama Suleiman" Mahmoud, who weeks ago had returned from her tenth pilgrimage to Mecca and hosted a party to celebrate that milestone. Now she smoldered in the doorway like a Turkish soap opera diva, eyes fierce, head angled, a voluptuous, concentrated object of craving. Breasts thrust forward, everything about her promised indulgence, suggesting that, with her, no human hungers would be left unfulfilled. Seductive in her loftiness, she was married, but it was not clear to whom, or in which of the realms of earth her husband lived. Mama Suleiman was wealthy, with six commercial *jahazi*s sailing northward to Oman carrying smuggled cloves from Pemba, to return laden with contraband goods, including duty-free pasta, which wound up in Zanzibar and Mombasa shops. In the underground chambers of her grand house, she traded in gold and jewels, outside the purview of the Kenya Revenue Authority. It was also murmured that she was a tributary in a supply chain of girls sent to Saudi Arabia, to which she went twice a year. Her body poured out its jewel-adorned flesh. She was always incensed, perfumed, and painted. Today her hair was in a topknot, and she channeled something arcane, bewitching, and decomposing from the innards of the land, giving it voice and chilling pale brown eyes.

Mama Suleiman often sought out Ayaana in order to predict bleakness in her future—an ongoing proxy war against Munira, whom Amina Mahmoud had despised from the time their childhood friendship had broken up in a squabble over dolls. Mama Suleiman would tell Ayaana, "I see the future, little girl, and when I contemplate yours I am terrified." Or mock her fatherlessness: "How tall you are. I think, *mami*, your real father must be a Maasai." A cold titter. Their last encounter: "Too thin. Eat more, small girl. People will say you're sick with *ukimwi*." Dulcet toned, "Do you know your status?"

Her loathing for Ayaana was entrenched after the primary-school examination results listed Ayaana's as the best in the district. Ayaana had outshone her son, Suleiman. "*Ajidhaniye amesimama, aangalie asianguke*," she had cautioned Ayaana—Beware those who stand tall, lest they fall.

Mama Suleiman's specialty was seeding conflict by twisting stories—she displaced characters and spread innuendo that guaranteed, after she had finished her telling, that a quarter of the island would stop talking to another quarter, while the rest dithered over truth and illusion. It continued this way until someone, a week later, asked the dissenting parties to recite the Ayat al-Kursi. This dissolved vitriol—no one wanted to be accused of idolizing the human temperament over God's omnipotence—though sediments of suspicion lingered in the storehouse of human hearts.

Ayaana, strangely enough, saw in the contorted femininity of Mama Suleiman something she wanted, an invitation to become more like fire.

Mama Suleiman now cooed, "Ayaan-oo!"

Ayaana cringed, caught between fear and the regret of her near escape. She shuffled over and stuttered, "*Shi-Shikamoo?*" An excess of Bint El Sudan perfume attacked her nose as Mama Suleiman stretched out a hand, wiggling her fingers for Ayaana to kiss. Ayaana bent over the scented limb and imagined slobbering over it.

Mama Suleiman demanded, "Ayaana, idle insect, do *I*, a busy, busy woman, have all day to wait for you? Answer me."

Within Ayaana a spasmodic pang of terror: had Mama Suleiman seen her in the ocean last night? Ayaana had succumbed to the tug of the quarter-moon and sneaked out after midnight to jump into the sea. She curled her arms around her stomach and scowled at the woman's hennaed feet. Lacelike whorls, as from a peacock's tail feathers, feathered curves—Ayaana's own work. She should have painted snake fangs.

Mama Suleiman's kohled eyes glowered. "Time squanderer. Time is money. What am I saying? Money is not something you know, time squanderer." She uncovered her hennaed arms. *"Chokochoko mchokoe pweza, binadamu hutamweza"*—Provoke an octopus, you can't handle me. "Look at my limbs. Are these lotuses?"

Ayaana's heart convulsed, and she clamped down on her retort. *Oh, beastliness,* she thought. She mumbled so that it sounded like an incoherent apology. She knew that her mother's services depended on the supercilious goodwill of women such as these. Mama Suleiman now informed the skies, seas, and seasons that she had wanted the Lotus of the Nile design, the specific purpose for which she had bought expensive Yemeni henna, which Ayaana had spilled on her like saliva.

Lotuses! Ayaana rolled her eyes. The foolish squid wouldn't know a lotus from a catfish. Though Ayaana averted her gaze, she also wondered why she had ignored an instinct to add extra lavender oil or clove buds to this woman's henna. When she had touched Mama Suleiman's clammy skin, the tips of her fingers had felt the skin's indents and imperceptible bumps, and when she touched these, Mama Suleiman's eyes had flickered open to reveal, for a split second, a petrified sadness. Ayaana had *known* she should boost the henna with the oils. But in front of Mama Suleiman's omniscient commands, her ever-evolving expectations, and the exaggerated value of her henna from Yemen, Ayaana had doubted her intuition. Now Mama Suleiman bayed, "Tell your mother I won't pay for fifth-rate efforts. I'm not an experiment. From now on, she alone may touch my body. I gave you a chance, but you failed. Failed. Leave me now." Mama

Suleiman huffed and swung her voluptuous being away, gesticulating so the gold bangles on her arms glittered and clanged in the light of this lush and restive season.

Ayaana stood as still as stone, waiting for the waves of shame to settle in her middle, where other deformed feelings collected and turned into a stomachache. Why hadn't she added the oils? She knew what to do, so why hadn't she done it? She then allowed herself a second of longing for hips and bosoms as remarkable as Mama Suleiman's. Passersby glanced at her; some laughed. A hurrying man pushing a cart almost bumped her, and as she leapt away, the package of lentil flour dropped and split open. Ayaana gathered her niqab to her face, wanting to disappear, tearful, wishing she could retreat into the safe darkness of her Bombay cupboard.

Would Muhidin be awake?

He had taken to extending the hours of his afternoon siestas. She chewed on her finger. Muhidin worried her. His skin was dry; his thoughts were scattered. He always had a smile for her, but it was such a lonely smile. She kicked the heap of spilled lentil flour.

The truth.

Both she and Muhidin had lost their moorings to the ongoing fixation between Munira and Ziriyab. Ever since Ziriyab had returned from the storm, he and Munira were never apart. They cooked together, and Munira often went fishing with Ziriyab on his boat. Ayaana knew, to her disgust, that they even bathed together. Their unguarded eroticism was confusing for Ayaana, distancing and embarassing, especially when she realized how much it paralyzed Muhidin. She faked indifference, but every day, before she slept, she muttered imprecations over Ziriyab's name.

Yet. *Was this the meaning of man and woman together?* She chewed on her lips. There were questions she was suddenly shy about asking Muhidin. Now, when they sat together, they rarely spoke. They read books or listened to music or focused on the sea.

Cawing crows.

The lentil flour was unsalvageable. Ayaana stepped over it. She dragged her feet, mind churning, heart burning, and new tears of annoyance in her eyes.

Footsteps. Ayaana stepped aside to let their owner pass.

"Hallo, hallo." Mzee Kitwana Kipifit.

Startled, Ayaana rubbed her eyes. He did the same, then chortled and stretched out his right palm to show her a dried pink rose petal. She stared at the fragile, beautiful thing. He raised his palm, as if he would let the petal fall to the dust. She cupped open both hands, and the petal fell into them. The man's laugh was so tender that Ayaana looked upward at him, eyes wide and searching. Eyes on her, eyes like hers, and for a fleeting moment something familiar settled within her as a sweet sensation, as if fate had unexpectedly revealed its secret hand before restoring the world to old order. Ayaana did not realize she was crying until she pivoted to watch the old man stroll away. He was shimmering. She decided to trail him, wanting to ask him questions she had not yet formulated. Years later, looking out into another sea, she wondered if something of destiny had been transferred in a rose petal falling from a stranger's hands into hers.

Pate Island had seeped into Mzee Kitwana Kipifit's soul. Now he was struggling with the question of leaving Pate. Every day he honored the needs of the ghost sailors he now felt were his own. When he was not fishing, he tended to the tombs that he now suspected dated from the Tang dynasty era, not just the Ming. An older legacy. His shadow community. Looking after the tombs allowed him to believe he was atoning for the lost phantoms he had created through his previous work. Another time, another world. And every day he found another reason to linger. But he knew his self-distancing from China was not as complete as it could have been. With the violent arrival of crude military interlopers, he was stirred to act. In Pate, he thought, perhaps there was a way to secure a heritage of rightful belonging. His mind raced.

Much later, in a formal letter home to a high-level party man, titled "Belt and Road, Culture and Opportunity," he spelled out all he had known and seen on Pate Island. He alluded to crescent tombs, energy, and gem prospectors from other nations who reaped where the empire had historically sown. He wrote of Admiral Zheng He, referring to uncompleted voyages. "Our emissaries are here," he added. Then he signed his name. Days later, he took a slow boat to Lamu, where he mailed the letter himself.

Beginnings. Life had splintered in Beijing for this man at exactly three o'clock, one Friday afternoon in 1997, Year of the Ox. He was a specialist in sleep deprivation and simulated drowning methods, a fine artist of human pain thresholds. Though he was a good employee, he also accumulated toxins from the melancholy created by his delivery of suffering to others. He was also entrusted with profound secrets he could no longer endure. On that day, a Hui teenager, connected with an offender against the state, was brought to him, and the administration of electricity caused his unintended death. In the tedium of filling out forms to explain yet another fatality in custody that should have been unremarkable, everything short-circuited within the man. He had glanced out of his office window at the autumn foliage and recognized his own ephemerality. In the next instant, as papers fluttered about him, and his black chair twirled on its fulcrum, he fled from his room, howling at his comrades. His retirement plans were expedited, and by that evening his work as an interrogator for the party's *shuanggui* ended.

He did not go home, bewildered as he was by the distorted images of his life: a most enterprising wife in the export business, a concubine who tolerated him, a grown-up son who spoke to him only in complete, grammatically correct sentences. Unyoking himself, he hurried away from everything he knew, including himself. He traveled to Wuhan, in Hubei. Intensely crowded there among so many bodies, close to the Yangtze, he thought he might render himself invisible. And this portion of the world became his monastery. Among struggling humans mesmerized by their needs, he sought to barter his guilt for solitude. A broken Hui boy, and the 118 men and 13 women whose lives he had ripped apart, could gaze upon him with pity. Stillness. Those who might have searched for him were reassured by his new habits, the performance of insanity—the sustenance of silence. Any alley aunties with roving eyes and quick tongues would have confirmed this to their handlers. He did not need the money; he sought only to salvage life. Wherever he was, he studied human gestures and habits. During the night, he wept. A year went by.

One overcast morning, the seeker stepped off a bus and stubbed his toe on a rock. He stooped to look. It was an imitation stone, a discarded, ubiquitous "Made in China" thing made for tourists. He was about to hurl it away when he saw what had been etched into it.

We have traversed more than 100,000 li of immense water spaces and have beheld in the ocean huge waves like mountains rising in the sky . . .

"We." He knew who "we" were. The commander of the Ghost Fleet, the immense Admiral Zheng He. The man interpreted this as a message. So he sought out libraries and museums where he could pore over old images and chronicles. He read journeys and seaways. He studied maps of destinations with tongue-turning names: Palembang, Malacca, Samudera, Mogadishu, Malindi, Ganbali, and Calicut. A thought acquired shape. He would undertake a recovery voyage and create a soul-harmonizing postscript for the great admiral's disastrous seventh voyage, in which a third of the fleet was lost to East African storms. He would go to stand in a different place in the world. Two months later, with a new name—one of five he had set aside for himself—and dodgy papers, he stepped onto a plane to Kenya, East Africa. Destination: Pate Island.

Dunia ni maji ya utumbwi.

The world is like water in the canoe.

[21]

One morning, two years after the tsunami, as *matlai* dragonflies were on tiptoes waiting to catch the tail end of the *kaskazi* on which to cross the ocean, they took Ziriyab Raamis away. Three of them had leapt from beneath waves—beings in black. They seized him from the boat he had launched for an early fisherman's jaunt. Ziriyab had been humming old songs with contentment, rowing his reconditioned boat, feeling the new power of his body. He experienced his muscles' strain as he hauled in fish and grappled with the ocean—the tussle of a new friendship. Life sparkled. Some days, he just allowed the boat to drift so he could watch the world, and imagine his Munira, his Buthayna, his Ghazalah, his soaring Huma. He would reach for shores in the delectable knowledge that all his dreams were real, and were waiting for him scented with jasmine and *oudhi*, as was his ring with the ruby strip, which he usually left in the house whenever he went fishing in uncertain weather, and which his wife solemnly slipped on his finger every night, as if choosing him again.

However, today black-clad beings twisted his limbs, tied them up, covered his head with a black cloth, and threw him into a waiting launch that would ply waves heading to far-off giant foot-shaped Diego Garcia, in the Chagos Archipelago—where the Chagossian people used to live before the War of Contempt dispossessed them. They would take him there to smash up his body without opening skin, and to drown him to the point just before death so they could resurrect him, to begin the drowning again, until his soul might break, until he could, with his own voice, accuse and rename himself "terrorist." The invasion was intimate and brutal and so sudden that Ziriyab did not have time to wonder what had happened to him. He did not even cry out. They took Ziriyab Raamis away. They also sank his boat, with its fine fishing gear acquired from the one and only All Goods Supplies Store in Mombasa with money scrupulously saved from the proceeds of fishing and moonlight accounting, and from credit. What they left behind was decay and a void filled with grim clouds of suspicion and sadness, which swirled into the lives of a small makeshift family.

[22]

Neighbors sometimes heard the family weeping. Some understood. Most suppressed their reactions: the distressed looks and angry words that could be interpreted as betrayal or sympathy. The old days were over, when sorrow could be sheltered by the empathy of the many, confronted by imported rage, a most foreign beast at war with a human emotion—terror. The invaders, such angry strangers steeped in madness, paraded the island as if they were its new and infernal overlords. How fathomless was Fazul the Egyptian's betrayal of Pate and its people. The amorphous war he had stimulated cascaded over so many simple lives. It seized the best of Pate's men, implicated in this sickness only because they were the best of men. Most of the taken would never return, not even as corpses. Those they left behind were forced to learn the languages of eternal hauntedness and silence. The shadows of a thousand thousand nonexistences changed Pate again: new boundaries, new walls, new forts of the heart. So, when Pate saw Muhidin race from his house and break down and weep by the old jetty, it quietly cast its fate to God and waited for sky light to see.

The island was not to know that Muhidin had just been informed of the fate of his son Tawfiq, Ziriyab's brother, which was why he had a new reason to be afraid about Ziriyab's fate. Munira had told him how Tawfiq and his and Ziriyab's families, including Muhidin's unmet grandchildren, had been obliterated.

"He didn't tell me," Muhidin had bleated several times.

Munira had yelled back, "*He wanted to forget.*"

"He told you," Muhidin had accused.

Munira had shouted, "I am his forgetting."

Ayaana, who had just walked in, heard Muhidin cry, "Aren't I a person, too?," as he poked a finger at Munira's forehead. "You owe me a son," he had cried as he tore out of the house.

But Pate Island had never, ever kept its secrets as neat, secure packages. A serpentine coven of informants with grudges emerged, willing to hawk untruths. "*Haki ya Mungu*," some vowed, Ziriyab, the incompetent fisherman, had drowned at sea. "As God is my witness," insinuated others, Ziriyab was a thief who had died on the streets of Mombasa, victim of mob justice. A retired minor intelligence officer turned jeweler whispered to Ayaana to urge Muhidin to forget Ziriyab, because he had joined the *mujahidin* in Afghanistan, in Pakistan, in Iraq . . . somewhere. Ayaana had wondered, "How do you know?" She said nothing to Muhidin. The tailor later told her that "someone" had spotted Ziriyab in Cairo as he crossed the Qasr el Nil Street: "He was in a hurry." Stealthy encounters. Intrusions in the lives of those who lived with the void of their "missing." Unwanted intimacies with the incompetent, indifferent, and ill-informed state when the desperate went to search mortuaries, hospitals, mosques, police stations for their misplaced loved ones. They discovered unbending strangers with inflexible questions, a parade of uniformed idiots from assorted nations, the terrorist seekers: "When was the last time you saw him?" "Where did he sleep?" "Where did he pray?" "Who were his friends?" "Is he a terrorist?" As if the missing were guilty of future fratricide. Aspersions. "And you, are you really Kenyan?" Two men, former civil servants, had advised Munira, Muhidin, and Ayaana one humid evening that, in the matter of Ziriyab Raamis, a secret quest was the best approach. "Camouflage your inquiries. Imagine the world as a salt road, and yourselves as slugs crossing it," one whispered.

Munira told everyone that Ziriyab would return. She insisted on it. With feral intent, she held up the previous world order, keeping it familiar for Ziriyab, so that nothing would be out of place, not even the weather, when he returned. She wore his ring. She still dressed up and perfumed herself, her clothes, and their bed. She carried out her beauty work. What had changed was her appetite: she would drink sugarless but spiced coffee, rice with a sprinkle of coconut and *mchicha*, and nothing else. Exactly two months after Ziriyab's disappearance, Ayaana saw her mother sink to the ground in her kitchen, eyes staring. Giving in to gravity. With a cry, Ayaana flew to lift her up. But Munira abruptly rose before she reached her. "I stumbled," she said. "I'm fine. A shower, maybe?" An hour and a half later, Ayaana had to go in to retrieve her mother from the stall, where she huddled in a corner, naked and cold, as water rained upon her.

Ayaana held conversations in her head, first with Munira and then Muhidin. She picked up the threads of ideas from eavesdropping. She spoke to an imaginary Tawfiq to ask him what sort of stupidity caused a man to shred skin, sinew, and the lives of everyone he loved. Life-blow-up. Why would a human being willfully destroy his life?

Munira had receded into her bedroom, where she sat amid Ziriyab's shoes, clothes, shirt, books, CDs, and two cell phones. She moved nothing. Now she did not move.

Ayaana woke up with the taste of lingering silence. Senseless noise, scattered emotions. She watched Munira and Muhidin become more and more like mere impressions on an unpolished surface. Everyone tiptoed around words. When the imam came to commiserate and exclaimed, "*Mungu amlaze mahali pema . . . Inalilahi Wainailahi Rajiun . . .*"—May the Lord rest his soul—before he could continue, Muhidin had lifted him up and, shaking him, growled, "Swallow those words! Don't speak death. My son lives!" Ayaana dreaded the moments when skirmishes spilled over into public places, the public gaze. And time was memorialized as Before Ziriyab Disappeared, After Ziriyab Disappeared. Anguish was a buzzard circling them. Decomposition. Some words found shape in previously unimagined squabbles. Some were over drink: Munira informed Muhidin that she needed a tonic to help her sleep. Muhidin clung to his small bottles, refusing to share. Ayaana listened to them, huddling and petrified.

Waiting.

No rescuer had materialized to deliver them. And the island, stupefied, it seemed, by Muhidin's daze particularly—he was the closest they had to an oracle—struggled with a grammar for this time of its existence; too much history had fallen over their lives all at once. But it took solace in its daily routines and the reassuring rhythm of its tides.

Muhidin and Munira secured Ziriyab Raamis's place through silences. To those who commiserated, they offered a courteous lie:

"*Tumeshapoa.*"

We have healed.

A corrosive rumor: Ziriyab had freed himself from Munira and her spells and fled for dear life. Mama Suleiman started and fueled this fire. She had turned up in the middle of a windstorm, adorned in gold and emerald, to announce that Ziriyab Raamis had taken up with a *good* and *holy* woman from a fine family from Vanga. She said he had gone because a son had been born to them. The woman, whose name was Nadhifa Waseema, was a real lady, with a sweet voice, who lived in Tudor, near the docks in Mombasa. Munira, intoxicated by the details, chartered a leaky boat to Lamu the next afternoon. From there she took a bus to Mombasa.

Munira returned ten days later, to prowl the island, her lips thin, her eyes mean. She found Mama Suleiman holding forth on how to tell real from fake Bint El Sudan with Hudhaifa. Munira slapped Mama Suleiman.

Mama Suleiman touched her burning face. Motionless. Then: "Travel well?" A laugh. "I swear, peasant, one day I'll crush your pathetic corpse under my foot. Watch your back, dear."

Munira replied, "Make it soon."

She strode home, ignoring the stares. Munira entered her house and slumped over a table. On her face, a look of resignation.

Muhidin dressed up in a never-before-seen gray suit. He told Ayaana and Munira that he was going to Mombasa to make inquiries. When he landed in Mombasa's old harbor, he did not go to the police station. He went into Old Town to look for and hire a private investigator. In the evening, he proceeded to Malindi, to hire an inquirer of and negotiator with timeless spirit worlds. Both men guaranteed that they would locate Ziriyab, dead or alive. When Muhidin returned to Pate Island, four days later, he was eerily triumphant. But days and nights turned into months without tangible results from the pair, whose updates seemed to draw from the same nebulous source: "We are getting closer and closer to a vision of the target, who has advanced beyond an immense wall made out of a thicket of shadows." And then there was nothing. Nothing. Muhidin's phone calls to them always encountered a busy signal.

Ayaana had to become an emissary between worlds for the heart-wounded. Twice in a day she lifted Muhidin's unshaven face from his vomit, cleaned the mess on the table, and wiped his mouth. His eyes skimmed over everything. He stank of booze—light, as if it had been sprayed on skin. When he was not lost in thoughts, he tinkered with his electronics: fixing them, pulling apart components, and fixing them again. At night they all listened for the unexpected sounds a returning human might make: a knock, a creak, a crash, a scrape, a bump, anything to suggest the return of Ziriyab.

Ayaana organized her guardians' businesses. She dispensed their blends to needy clients. She sold Muhidin's books and suggested healing words, most of which she improvised from Hafiz's poetry. She calmed Munira's overwrought females, as she touched them with hands warmed by sweet jasmine oil and created, with henna, symbols that spelled hope, on feet, backs, and hands. Ayaana also found in some of these people the unexpected ways of human tenderness—the extra payments, food wrapped up and left behind, muttered prayers, and hands that blessed.

Thunder, lightning, two days of rain.

Ayaana jumped over rain puddles. An unusual blue mist covered part of the island, adorning it with a damned sort of beauty. She hurried across the island, looking over her shoulder, scratchiness in her throat, cold in her spine, surrounded by the miasma of the Thing of Fear that sometimes spoke to her in the sibilant whispers of Fazul the Egyptian. Creeping guilt, as if she had something to do with these disappearances. Yes, she had prayed for Ziriyab Raamis to get lost so she and Muhidin would have Munira again, as before. It was not as if she had *known* her prayers would be answered. In communal conversation they had become "the family of the missing Ziriyab." Ayaana pretended there was an end to "missing." Those who approached the family spoke deliberately of other things— the weather, fishing news, arrivals, births, and news from Palestine, which before the "War on Terror" had not occupied the islanders' imaginings.

Ayaana read. She inhabited characters' lives so that she might escape her world. She studied their words. She carried a moth-damaged copy of *The Story of Layla and Majnun* by Nizam that she had taken off Muhidin's bookshelf. In it she read of desire and need not unlike her mother's, and anguishes that surpassed Muhidin's. The words introduced her to new questions without answer. Later, Ayaana lay under the stars—the house was oppressive—listening to the night wind. This was the first of the nights when she heard the crying of the djinns in those high notes that sometimes ascend from the bottom of the sea. Listening to them, breath by breath, that night, she also found a cell of silence, a soft capsule that separated her from the rest of the world. The sea stirred. Moon on water. Mahtabi. Akmar.

. . .

Otherworlds. Betterworlds.

Ayaana hid from the daylight so she would not have to conjure up answers for the inquisitive.

She lifted up her arms to the night sky. She imagined she was throwing out feelers across life's uneven contours, reaching for the sense of Ziriyab Raamis. Up and down the coast Ayaana walked, combing the beach, crossing dunes, poking into crevices, immersed in sound, renouncing her secret sin, those jealous prayers uttered to God to take Ziriyab away. Now his absence was desolation; she was praying him back home. *Come back*. Below, waves spattered themselves against rocks. High-whistle winds. In the splintering of light on black water, for the second time, she heard the sigh of djinns. Joining them, she wailed out a longing to be swept into the soul of a storm so she might be fearless, formless, and strong.

She dared.

She dived.

The sea was liquid charcoal spattered with the innards of moonlight. She tumbled into the seduction of the deep, craving its feel. Pulsing water. No gaps in the ocean, no distances between beings. She sank deeper, losing the sense of up or down. The sea. Its iridescent layers. A creature burning an inner fire floated past. Her ears popped in the cooler waters below. Water citizens of many shapes and hues swam around her, an eel-like translucent being, round eyes on her, a shoal of tiny silver fish nibbling at her bare feet, tickling her skin. Soft, serene sinking, and familiar calmness oozed into her, dissolving time and trouble. The ocean pressed hard against her lungs, but she had borrowed enough air from the surface not to mind. She settled into the arms of her ocean. Cocooned stillness. It was easier to drop than it was to ascend. Homecoming. The murmur of djinns. She remembered then to twist her body to propel it back to the surface, kicking the water, tears melting into the sea, just as light had done before her. Bursting for breath, almost swallowing water. She surfaced. She let her body choose its direction. Drifting. Every day was the same day, every night the same color of nothing. Ayaana discovered that "nowhere" was also an inhabited space.

Somehow, a year slipped by.

[23]

Muhidin had decided to do the one thing he had imagined he would never do again: he left Pate Island. Muhidin showed up at Munira's door when Ayaana was at school. He muttered that he was going to Nairobi to settle the truth once and for all; he did not know when he would be back. Munira retreated into pride. She would not beg him to stay. Did not say that she was afraid, that she had run out of money. That Ziriyab's debt was 73,080 shillings, without adding interest. Munira said, "Fine," in a high voice. "Go."

Muhidin stood waiting, as if for something more.

He then pulled out a note he had written for Ayaana—he had chosen to leave while she was in class. He left Munira his house keys. "For Ayaana." He said, "The house and everything in it." The keys clanged between them. "In case . . ."

You do not return, Munira thought, and nodded quickly.

Muhidin left.

Munira unsealed the note Muhidin had left for Ayaana. She read it through a lens of tears. "Abeerah, I've gone to find our Ziriyab. I shall return. Be brave. Protect your mother. Study hard. It is I who am your father, Muhidin."

Ayaana watched green water churn in the pan. *Mwarubaini.* Neem, the malaria deterrent, which also treated thirty-nine other ailments. She boiled its leaves, its bark, and seed. The bitter elixir healed most anything. However, it could not cure grief.

Mtupie Mungu kilio, sio binadamu mwenzi.

Cry out to God; what can a human being do?

[24]

Ayaana suffered a midnight asthma attack in March, after Munira explained to her that there was no extra money to cover the fees for her second term at school. Wheezing under blankets, her frame supported by Munira, steam rising, heavy breathing.

"I'll find a way," Munira said.

They breathed in aromatic steam—inhale, exhale—absorbing shades of shame, of fear. "I'll read every day," Ayaana gasped. She coughed. "But I will help you with the work."

Twice a day, Ayaana sat and waited on Muhidin's stone step.

She dialed his phone number: *"Mteja hapatikani kwa sasa."*

The subscriber is unavailable.

The year flowed.

The year went.

Another New Year's morning.

Twice a day, Ayaana sat on Muhidin's stone step.

She dialed his phone number: *"Mteja hapatikani kwa sasa."*

The subscriber is unavailable.

Kaskazi season.

Two unexpected visitors showed up and stepped out of a small white-and-Egyptian-blue yacht named *Bathsheba* moored at the decrepit jetty, attended to by unspeaking uniformed crew members in navy blue and white. The pair smelled of new leather, gold, and a perfume with the freshness of crisp banknotes. Signs of casual wealth adorned their being: embossed sleeves, crafted ties, engraved rings, and monogrammed shirts. "Wa Mashriq." That is what the island called them, although they might have come from another place.

Five days later. In clipped and whispery English, one of the men drawled, "It is true, so true . . ." Munira's feet faltered on the dirt track. She could see her house a distance away. "The women here . . ." The man inhaled, shutting his eyes, pursing his lips, simulating ecstasy. "We heard. We came to see for ourselves. We are collectors. What do we find?" He smiled.

Munira frowned. Ignored the tickle of pleasure: were the words for her? Mild irritation. No place for blandishments in her life. Forward step.

The man called again. "We must talk. You and I. In seriousness."

She turned to squint at him. Saw scars crisscrossing his face, intricate, and elegant on skin the color of golden syrup. Deliberate, as if the man had chosen the patterns himself. Even teeth, almost yellow eyes, like a contented predator, manicured hands folded over each other, resting near his heart. He said, "Beauty such as this is meant to be beheld."

Munira rolled her eyes, flung her head back, and resumed her walk.

He said, "We really must talk, Madame Munira."

She stumbled when she heard her name. Over her shoulder, she snapped, "You know my name?"

"In matters of lucrative commerce, it is a requirement, madame," he said, holding her gaze. "What am I offering?"

Munira looked him up and down. "What do you know of what I need?"

The man bared his teeth—a sly grin. He ticked off the options on his fingers. "One, never having to work for anything or anyone in your life ever again. Two, paying for the dreams of those you love. Three, going where you wish to, how you want, and when, first-class all the way. Four," he lowered his voice, "fill in your blanks."

Munira's external look was steadfast, but inwardly she trembled. Disbelief. Huge goose bumps appeared like welts on her body.

The man continued. "A fee for a first meeting. Paid up front, no questions. At the end of the meeting, the same amount. Call it a 'sitting allowance.'" A teensy tinkle of a laugh. "If the deal goes through successfully, you receive a 'You Fill In the Blanks' check. Write up to one-point-five million. American. Larger sums create noise here. We don't like noise." Another tinkle laugh, like a happy shop bell.

Munira's eyes narrowed; her mind was in a whirl. What was this? Was it true? All her debts to society paid? All her struggles coming to an end? Could she finally leave Pate? She had a vision of herself landing in Zanzibar with an entourage looking for her family. She could shop in Paris, London. Even Tunis. She could start again. What did he want? She twisted her lips. What did most men want of women?

"How old are you?" Munira asked the man.

"Forty." He smiled.

She smiled back. They smiled at each other. Then the man sighed. "The arrangement is not for me. Ah, but if I could, I would." He smiled.

She smiled.

"I am a messenger," he continued. "Jibril making delicate arrangements for God."

She laughed.

He laughed.

She straightened her body. She asked, "In this matter, Jibril, God is . . ."

"You'll meet him soon. You've seen him, no doubt."

Munira vaguely recalled a bulbous being panting at the heels of this debonair matchmaker. She shrugged. Her eyelids fluttered: "So?"

The man rearranged his posture to hold Munira's gaze. His voice dropped four degrees colder. "We are collectors, I said. We hunt for masterpieces. We find these even if they are covered with dust."

Munira waited. The sea churned. The sun was hot on her skin.

"So now . . ." the man said. "So let us talk about your daughter."

Munira's heart withered. And then it began to hammer against her ribs.

"Ayaana," the man added.

Munira jumped.

He said, "She." Stillness. "Her."

Breath trapped in her throat, Munira stared.

The man said, "She evokes phantasmic worlds. Conjures dreams. Transfiguring, she transfigures. We saw her. He must have her. We will clean her up. Restore her. Adorn her. Position her where she can best be seen, enjoyed, experienced. She is a virgin? Virginity is important to him. Stamp of authenticity. He must have her."

A black torrent crashed over Munira's head. It gripped her heart. It turned electric inside her body, burning down her gullet and sending cold-hot-cold streaks of red lightning into her soul. And, for a millisecond, it was as if she had been shoved, stark naked, out of her illusory plane to Paris. First rage; then her face colored. "My daughter?" she spluttered.

"She." The man said. "Iconic." Holding Munira's eyes with his. "Her." Tilt of head. "Whoever did you think I was referring to all this time?" Toying with her. "We are perfectionists, you see." His teeth gleamed, glittered, and dazzled.

Munira's face flushed, and she struggled to breathe. The wind grabbed at their clothes. A cock crowed. The man said, "Boutiques! You open these in any city of the world. Your work is . . . fascinating. One of our factories could turn your concoctions into products. The industry worldwide is worth over a trillion. American. You must have a share. We'll package you. Women will wear you. It is all possible."

Munira's fingers locking and unlocking, thoughts roiling, head lowered, voice trembling: "For my d-daughter?"

"Yes." The man examined his nails.

Waiting.

Ayaana. Munira imagined her daughter. *Ayaana.* She imagined how the worlds of this creature would mark the . . . child. She also thought of Ayaana being secured for life. She imagined paying workmen to repair and expand the house, adorning it with the beautiful things she had wanted. She saw herself paying for an investigative process that would find Ziriyab. *Ayaana.* Their triumphant escape.

Ayaana. They could outdistance shadows that killed hope. *Ayaana*. Freedom. Munira whispered. "My baby, my daughter. A child?"

The man said, "Most humbly, I disagree." His tone was low and intense and reasonable. "A good painting is a painting, large or small. Art"—he looked upward—"it is without time or age. She. Untouched. Beauty lit from within. We have watched her . . . Such grace . . . like a deep-water bird. Little bones. She will flower with a gentle touch. He craves the beautiful." The man gestured. "To sip its light." He engaged Munira's eyes. "So tell me, dear one, when is a girl not a woman?" He grinned. "He is besotted. You understand."

Munira was breathless. "Art?"

"An original."

Munira moved her veil to cover her face. She looked around. Soft-feathered white-and-black birds near her feet, two tomcats yowling, an old lame rooster with long spurs—was it now ten years old?—gave her a quizzical look, as if she might be food. She asked, "You do this often?"

"What?"

"Collect girls?"

The man frowned. "We are connoisseurs. We like beauty. What's wrong with that?"

"What about the girls?"

Distaste twisted the man's lips. "No complaints so far. Certainly not from them. They can fly first-class to Dubai, Rome, or Istanbul." Tinkle laugh. Copperish gleam in the eye. "My dear, dear, how do you decide?"

Munira whispered, "I need time." Her body shook.

The man clucked. "How unfortunate. Time—the one commodity we cannot spare." Munira gasped. "You are surprised," the man said.

Munira gritted her teeth. "When I woke up this morning, I didn't know it was the day I would meet those who control time and fate. Is it true your kind are also excused from death?"

The man hooded his lids, clenched and unclenched his jaw, before forcing geniality. "Sarcasm, heh-heh. Luxury for *your* kind. Well done. But, still, you decide. You are a mother. I shall give you five minutes. If the arrangement is unsuitable, we leave tonight." Shop-bell laugh. "When he decides on something he wants, it is only that and nothing else. Counterfeits breed discontentment. He is always certain about his first choice. First choices have made him wealthy. He does not think in Option B's. But he never forces his will. The decision is in your power."

Munira's mouth was agape.

"You would have three days to prepare the girl." The man swung some keys he had retrieved from his pocket. As they jangled, he said, "Dress her up. Scrape out the mud. He loves that rose scent. Yours? It drew him to her. Delicate. Such an inspiration. He must have her."

Munira glowered. "Do you have an opinion?"

He raised one brow. "Yes, his."

In the stillness, a formless void seemed to emerge from beneath the earth under Munira's feet. The man added, "We would meet at your house. It is discreet. Thursday evening for our first meeting?" He leaned into his shirt pocket and pulled out a fat wad of notes. "Seventy-five thousand shillings. For your preparations. Sufficient to cover a lost husband's debt? You are shocked, heh-heh; we do our research. We are not insensitive to ordinary human concerns."

When Munira moaned, the man smirked. "Most businesses plan to fail when they disregard due diligence. The context bewilders them. We have never failed." High laugh. "Dress the girl in softness. Pastels. Mother-of-pearl?" He leaned forward. "Satin on female skin . . ." He kissed his fingers.

Magnetized, Munira's eyes were locked on the cash. Silence was a presence, a being between them, and it obliterated even the sounds of the sea. Munira watched. She waited. Four minutes. Emotions swirling. Terror. Clamped down on a scream. *Flee!* She saw herself running, but her feet were glued to her portion of soil. *Seventy-five thousand shillings*. She could even scent the rust residue of her old buried dreams, could see the envy in the eyes of those who had mocked her, felt herself rise, become the woman she had meant herself to be. Three minutes. *The cost of her child?* Stillness. Murmurings of her unrequited hungerings in her inner ear. They waited. Neither moved.

"Two minutes," said the man.

Munira cried, "What's your other name?"

A half-smile. "Really? Is that necessary?"

Munira pleaded, "I *beg* for time."

Silence. One minute. Munira spun to walk away.

She did not see the astonishment in the man's eyes, did not notice the relief that sagged his shoulders. Would not have recognized the glee flickering across his face as if he had seized a secret victory. If she had, she would have reconsidered looking back to say: "Thursday. Six-thirty. My house. As you suggest. I'll make the snacks. Or don't your kind eat food? She'll be readied." Munira lifted her nose. She pressed the veil to her face. She heard a bell-tinkle laugh chase after her and understood that Ibilisi might use a similar sound.

[25]

In that same hour, Ayaana, who had haggled with fishermen for fish—*dagaa* and *chole* for dinner—was meandering along the waterfront, eavesdropping and unaware of a glint of light reflecting off powerful binoculars trained on her from the yacht. Beachcombing, not so much needing to know the nature of objects as wanting to imagine where they came from and how they had traveled, so she could touch them. Messengers. She made up messages: Driftwood, the shape was the story. Dead eels were dead eels. Blue plastic turtle: a child setting his toy free to wander and gather tales from the world. In her imagination, she rode on the back of the plastic turtle and sailed to ports of the world where she was fêted, loved, and was able to retrieve Ziriyab from his hiding place, so that, at last, Muhidin would return. In her mind, Pate was not being leached of its people, and there were no new forms of darkness in night windows where flickering lanterns and candlelight shadows once affirmed life and presence.

Ayaana crouched, fingers in sand, wondering and not able to reach her inside pocket for *Dona Flor and Her Two Husbands* by Amado, which she wondered if she should be reading, but was reading anyway. Something strange had happened that morning. An angular, drawling, bushy-haired Suleiman had accosted Ayaana where she was washing clothes.

"Ayaana!" he had cooed, adopting a casual stance in his self-designed hip-hop getup. He wore his hair in a large, thick Afro now.

Ayaana had sniffed as she scrubbed a collar, dipping that portion into the soapy bucket.

Suleiman stood opposite her. "I've seen you."

Ayaana sniffed again. "I'm busy." The loss of a future through study had hit her hard, caused her dread; in front of her peers, she shrank.

"I've seen you swim in the sea," Suleiman said.

Ayaana dropped her washing. Her heart thumped. Suleiman, even though his presence caused her body to feel awkward and her palms to sweat, was a loudmouth.

"You are good," he said, "but I am better."

An upward gaze. "You won't tell?" A plea in her voice. She resented the sound of it.

Suleiman pursed his lips. He had wanted to see her get into even more trouble, but he needed to out-swim her and confirm to himself that he was better. In the secret murmurings of adolescent peers, Ayaana had become the subject of lewd teenage fantasy, not because of anything poetic but because of her illicit origins, which made her forbidden fruit. There was a bet among the boys as to who would secure the prize. At one point, Suleiman was certain that he was in the running for her attention. But when he approached her, she usually took off in another direction. Something about her made him want to bruise her. If she were a butterfly, he would have peeled off her wings in small strips. Ayaana's dropping out of school had left Suleiman at the top of his secondary class. He had obtained a great exam grade.

Now he tilted his head, quietly gloating. "I have excellent news." He studied her face for a reaction. "I'm going to the University of Sharjah. In the Emirates," he said. "As you know, my marks were the best in the district. I need a place that will grow my intelligence." He waited. "Kenya is too small for me."

Ayaana wanted to cry aloud. It was not fair. She was the better student. But then she lowered her head. Who was she fooling?

Suleiman then asked, "What will *you* do with your life?"

"Do?" she asked, her voice cracking.

"Yes."

Ayaana shifted her body and looked toward the sea. Tear-shine. Accusing life. Unfair. One person's life horizonless with opportunities, and hers contained in a leaking red bucket. She shrugged in answer. Suleiman rocked from side to side. Her shoulders hunched, and shadows deepened on her face. She asked him, "What are you going to study?" Her tone was so wistful.

"Industrial engineering and management. B. Science." He sounded as if he had already obtained the degree.

She nodded. "Now I need to finish the washing."

"Ayaana," Suleiman said, "I could tell people that you swim alone in the sea." He was smirking. She shrugged but her heart pounded. "But I like you."

She pivoted to stare at Suleiman. They were the same height, but he was bulkier. The sheen of wealth was on him. It was a scent; airy, textured. He grabbed her damp right hand, wiped it with his warm, soft one, and then pressed a cream-colored square of cloth in it, on which he had placed a marble-sized pale-pink pearl, from a necklace his mother used to wear.

Paralyzed, Ayaana gaped at the objects in her hand. Suleiman then lifted her wrist to his mouth, to suck on the skin. "You must wait for me to come back," he was saying as she closed her eyes, believing she could disappear into Suleiman's certainties for a second. He would have tried to kiss her had she not bent her head to conceal her confusion. He might have tried again, so that he could announce a victory to his peers, if his mother had not shrieked from some spot, "Suleiman!"

Suleiman dropped Ayaana's hand as if it were a stonefish and took off.

Ayaana called after him: "Suleiman?" He looked over his shoulder at her. She kissed her hand and waved it at him. Suleiman whooped.

Ayaana's heart did not calm down. She washed the rest of the clothes in a daze.

Now.

Beachcombing with wind, sea, and birds. A cock crowed. With the crunch of sand beneath her feet, Ayaana suddenly remembered time. She took off, veil flying, fishes in hand. She ducked her head to avoid the whirling dust that discomfited all creatures, including the goats, which bleated incessantly. Partly blind, Ayaana slammed into a body that huffed.

"*Samahani!*" she stuttered—Forgive me. Ayaana squinted at a bald-headed man from China, Mzee Kitwana Kipifit. His hand had stopped her momentum.

. . .

"*Mingyun,*" he said. Destiny.

They looked at each other, and for no reason other than the experience of the moment, they both started to laugh. Ayaana *suddenly* remembered a dry rose petal folded into a Persian calligraphy book. Mzee Kipifit patted her head and winked.

Stooping, he dodged the wind as though dancing, heading for his leaky fisherman's shack near the mangrove beach, where he also cooked seaweed and fish and tended to wounded birds, plants, cats, insects, and the other living things that were now seeking him out. *Mingyun,* Ayaana whispered to herself in the same high tone the wind was using. She retrieved the fish from the ground, wiping dust off them. What a day. And what exactly had Suleiman promised her? She clutched the single pearl as she walked home.

[26]

Ayaana circled her mother. Munira was unbalanced. Happy, then sad; delirious, then depressed; hugging her, then pushing her away. Speaking in riddles and preoccupied with the fate of women. Munira told her, "When clever women see options, they seize them."

They were washing dishes. Ayaana considered the words as she played with the soapsuds. "I'll go to school. I'll do well, you know . . . and then university."

"Where do I get the money to pay for this?" snapped Munira.

"I can . . ."

"What? Help me decorate women? Teach English to fishermen? Marry that drunkard who drives trucks? Become a servant in Saudi Arabia, from where you will return to us as a corpse? Why not marry the elderly camel-trader? The toothless bachelor from Kismaayo? Is that the life you want?" Munira's voice rose in fury, and Ayaana frowned at her.

After dinner, Munira sat on a floor mat and called Ayaana to her side. She started to brush her daughter's hair. Ayaana leaned in to her and said, "I can be an engineer. I will see the world." Munira listened as she teased out Ayaana's black curls. Ayaana dreamed. "I'll study business. I can start a business, *Ma-e*. I'll pay for you to live in a big house. In Mombasa."

Munira said, "Mombasa is too small for us, *lulu*." A pause. "Today I wash your body. *Singo*. You like that, my heart?"

Ayaana's eyes glimmered. She gasped. A bride's treat! Jasmine, turmeric, ylang-ylang, cloves, sandalwood, and rose petals in rose water on her body. The fragrance that lingered also offered a soft and gentle sleep. "Who is the groom?"

Munira did not laugh. She said, "Then I show you how to make and apply . . . secrets . . . so no man will ever leave you." Munira's words faltered. "Ah well," she muttered.

Ayaana turned to her mother and became aware of something murky hovering in the room around them. "*Ma-e?*" Uneasy. "Why are you crying?"

Munira rubbed her eyes. "Chili on my fingers! Silly me. Rubbed my eyes with it." She laughed. Her eyes were red as she worked on her daughter's body. She painted Ayaana's toes with red polish after giving her a clove pedicure. She covered Ayaana's arms and back with henna whorls. Skin, contact, touch, intimacy, mother, daughter, two women. Timeless space. What with the sky that day—an overcast dark blue—and the tang of lemon, mint, and cinnamon, and the low moan of a wind that caused the sea to churn with churlish intensity, Ayaana thought they might remain forever like this. Blurred beingness infused with fine scents and sumptuous meals. Ayaana forgot to miss Muhidin. Munira, reveling in the moment, forgot its aim and she started to sing:

"Ewe ua la peponi
Waridi lisilo miba . . ."

Ayaana turned to her mother, and her mother was luminous and other, and hers, and there was nothing in existence that she could love more. Ayaana reached out to move a hair strand that was hovering over Munira's eyes. Munira rubbed her own forehead as if scrubbing away a stain. *The heart is elastic*, she told herself. It could learn to love anything. This she hoped. She herself had once craved the fire, and it had taken years, but it came through Ziriyab, and she had known, for a season, that desire existed to be fulfilled. She had devoured every drop of pleasure. Now, even though haunted by temporality, she wanted more. "Love is a two-faced beast," she told Ayaana. She was about to say that desire and suffering were of the same substance, but then she clammed up and focused on making sure her daughter's skin would glow.

Cock-crowing relay on a bright Thursday morning.

Munira called, "Ayaana?"

Ayaana emerged from under her bedsheet. A geography textbook she had been reading the previous evening slipped from the end of the bed and fell to the ground with a thud. Munira flinched. Then she said, "Rest today. Sleep. I'll return in the afternoon."

At midday, Munira walked into Ayaana's room and unwrapped something that caused Ayaana to jump off her bed and whirl her mother about. Ayaana stared at the frothy pale fabric, tight-fitting floatiness.

She looked at her mother, eyes bright and wide. "For me?"

"Visitors." Munira said. She tightened her lips. "Wake up. They're coming to see you."

"Me? Why? Who?" Ayaana's mind whirred. "You told them about school?"

Munira rubbed a spot on the door. "I'll dress you up. Make up your face. They will explain."

"Make up my face? *Ma-e*, what do they want?"

Munira wiped another nonspot off the wall. "To discuss your future."

Munira coughed.

"*Ma-e!* Shall I bring my test papers? They will see my results are good."

Munira was silent.

"Ma?"

"If you want."

Ayaana skipped into the bathroom, shouting: "You have my school reports? I *must* pin my calligraphy to the wall. When they see, they *will* ask, *Who did that?* You *must* say, *It is Ayaana*."

Munira remained silent, rubbing the part of her chest where her heart beat, burned, and broke.

[27]

Salmon-colored chiffon cloth scraps. The dress Ayaana had worn lay shredded in the corner. Two streaked faces, one convulsing body. Cooling water on the floor—unwashable stain on cement, unwashable stain in partly desecrated flesh. The hot, sticky sugar water soaked a meal that had been spread on the table. It seeped into and eroded Ayaana's former childhood and became a mirror of origins she knew nothing about.

Munira, who had been led out of the house by the smooth assistant, and directed toward a corner of her garden where transplanted wild roses grew, strode with her head held unnaturally high. Lavender and rosemary scented the air as bees buzzed. A quick glance at nearby tombs, a trance-smashing question from the suddenly pensive matchmaker: "Rot and perfume in a single crucible," the man said as he saw a cream rose petal fall. "Decomposing beauty. Still desirable." He looked around him, inhaling the air, before turning to Munira, who was plucking at her veil. "Did you know that the word 'desire' is taken from the Latin, '*desiderare*,' which means, 'to await what the stars will bring'?"

Jauza, Munira remembered, a name in the stars she had summoned for two souls.

They walked. Sweat beaded her forehead. He sniffed the air again. "A whiff of desire blended with blood, smoke, shadows and—what is that?"—his voice was strangely ragged—"grief?"

A strangled sound from the direction of the house. It was cut off. Munira spun to look and then turned back to him. Cold curiosity was etched across his face. "Desire! Dreams!" he leaned over to whisper at her. And then Munira cried out, pivoted and tore back to her house. She burst through the door, hair disarranged, shrieking, *"Ah! Maskini!,"* in time to witness thick gold-ringed fingers on her daughter's body, twisting it this way and that, as the man breathed heavily in an attempt to mount Ayaana, a thick hand blocking a low-grunting scream that emerged from her daughter's mouth. The creature had already torn up the frothy dress that the child had delighted in.

Munira's hand went to the stove to seize a *sufuria* full of sugar water that she had left simmering on the stove. The caramel would have been used to peel hairs off Munira's clients' bodies. Now bare-handed and scalded, but unfeeling, automated, Munira poured the almost caramel liquid on the fat man's body, the back of his head, his back, and he had the grace to groan, to stiffen, to recognize what she had done to him, to see that she was waiting for him to refuse to move so that she could crush his head with the saucepan. Some of the syrup had also spattered on her daughter's thigh. She would forever carry burn marks, together with bite marks from an ugly rich man's mouth.

The bulky Wa Mashriq, after the first grunt of surprise and hurt, slithered out without uttering another sound. Even as his body burned, he did not flinch. Munira watched. She had scored him. He had proved to her that he was not the same kind of human as she was. The man studied Ayaana, her fallen, crumpled self rolled in the ball of her torn frothing dress, long thin limbs curved in, bare-breasted—her breasts had emerged at last—her makeup running, hair disheveled, more fragile than he had first believed.

Shattered.

He had grinned at Munira.

She read the message in his face as if he had spoken it: *I may have yielded the endgame, but you have lost your only child. Your loss is the more terrible one.* The man dropped a bundle of notes on his way out.

"American," he murmured.

He abandoned Munira and Ayaana to their silence in caramel-scented steam. Outside, restless winds lashed at waves, and the waves laved the shore.

"Get up," Munira told Ayaana, rather than *I'm sorry*. "I'll burn the dress," she said, rather than *I'm sorry*. She said, "You can't afford tears," rather than *I'm sorry*. "Go and clean yourself. I'll wipe this room. Have some milk. There's more on the stove." She said all this rather than *I'm sorry*.

Ayaana said, "Yes."

Obedient, sad, older, and wiser now.

They would both pretend that there had been no Thursday evening. Even though the shadow of the caramel-water stain on the floor marked the site as a gravestone does. Purgative options, a way through anguish: seven tablespoons of clove oil, three teaspoons of lemongrass stirred into a bucket of steaming bathwater. A promontory and the sea below it: the temptation to jump.

And.

Strangling sounds inside the solidity of nights. If the mute and nauseated Ayaana had cared to look, she might have seen her mother lying sleepless in bed, terrified of what she had almost been willing to sacrifice in order to snatch at a buried dream.

Munira stood up to listen to her daughter sob inside her room. She counted the shuddering pauses between Ayaana's breathing, her head resting against the closed door. She reached for the handle. Fingers curved over the metal. Would have pushed it open if she had been sure she would not fall into the chasm of her own making. Munira pivoted from Ayaana's door.

Ayaana watched the skies. Dark moon. No moon. A promontory and the sea below it: the temptation to jump. Munira watched out for her distant shape from the doorway of their house, her heart riven.

Seven days later, under the cover of an early-morning storm and a violet-blue sky, a shrouded, stooping Ayaana stepped out of a home stained by the cold shadows of a scarred conscience. She walked through a landscape now streaked with her humiliation. Sprinkles of water drenched her. Fresh, clean water. She paused to watch massive waves submerge fishermen's boats, listened to the tumult, the howling wind, a rumble of thunder disheveling frantic people. She made her way blindly over stones, past creaking shrubs, toward Fundi Mehdi's boat-repair cove, relying on smell and mood to sense a way. Hearing him carving away at something, she stopped under a grand coconut tree within which a giant cobweb hovered, with its resident victims and a single midsized brown predator. She watched the trap for a while before swiping it to nothing with her bare fists. When she appeared in front of Mehdi, she stooped, waiting for him to condemn her. He glanced at her. She saw the seven new "war on terror" wounds crisscrossing his face. He glanced at her, said nothing, and resumed his work.

So Ayaana took catlike steps toward the old stranded *dau*. She climbed into it. There she sat, cradled by namelessness, not crying out as she needed to, not examining the weals and violet bruises on her limbs as she wanted to, emptying herself to let in the sense of the sea and its splendid voice. With her head back, and without intending to, her eyes followed the flight of a brown raptor playing amid storm-carrying air currents. Ayaana's ghosts receded. In the background, a radio meteorologist's voice lamented the state of the tides.

Elsewhere.

Munira.

She glanced at the morning star at dawn and saw blood. She went to pluck the pale roses, pricked her thumb, and saw blood. Munira saw blood on the water when the dim orange sun set over the storm-purged ocean. When she soaked her wood shavings in pungent oils and purgative spices to make *oudhi*, even so, she smelled only blood.

~

Today. Making rose oil so that the light-etched perfume will exorcise the stench from the desecrated body, heart, soul, and blood. You intended the aromas to digest sorrow and then restore your child to you in this season of unquenchable loneliness. You wandered toward the fringes of your island at a desolate dawn, and crouched where threshold wild roses grow, to pick petals before the morning dew dried up. You gathered these in a woven reed basket and ignored the blood from the places on your hand pierced by thorns. You used your fingers to press tears back into your eyes. You then hurried through your land, ignoring, once again, the double glances sent your way by your people, who were now confirmed in their belief of your cursedness. You accepted it now. In your kitchen, you washed the rose petals in soft water and wept unutterable prayers. Your rose oil was famed for its truthfulness. Few knew how you first stroked the aura of the heart of rose to beg forgiveness for needing to shred its life. You offered the petals the tenderness you would offer your daughter if you could. Soon you would blend your oils—olive, coconut, grape seed—in the proportions that deepened their being. You had to bruise the rose petals. You did so with regret as you dropped them into the blended oils in dark-brown jars, which you carried to your rooftop wrapped in heated cloth. These would sit in clay pots that you would replenish with hot water. You would place these along shelves on your decaying rooftop, next to the pile of *oudhi*-making wood parings, where jasmine, lemongrass, and orange blossoms also bled in distilled water beneath the Pate sun, under the Pate moon, fringed by the Pate sea. Today you would stand in stillness to watch the hours of the day cook your rose oil. At night you would retrieve the rose-hip-oil-scented water you had prepared for your daughter. Yes, your *marashi mawaradi* was renowned, and your rose attar, the *halwaridi*, sold out before any could be stored. Now you took the rose water. You sprinkled it around your house while night birds stuttered. The scent infused your private hearse of pain as you heard your daughter moan in her room. In your memory, the curse "*ki-don-da*" resounded. Later, you would hear from the usual gossips that you and your child should be aware that the powerful-in-heat were never thwarted, that they had paid hungry stonemasons to reap for them what they could not harvest. You raced from island nook to island cranny, mapping spaces where your daughter could not hide.

[28]

Time flowed through Ayaana and proposed forgetfulness. She felt she was no longer visible to herself. She had lost the sense of a future to lean upon, lost the old sense of the safety of "mother." She had learned new eyes to use to look upon Munira.

Munira spoke to Ayaana. She said, "We must be careful." She said, "They want revenge." Ayaana stared at her mother, numb and dumb. Munira said, "They did not get all they wanted." Her head was bowed. *Paid for*, she remembered. She shivered.

If Muhidin . . . Ayaana began the thought before extracting it and rubbing it out. It lurked anyway inside her heart.

Days re-emerged with less and less of Ayaana as presence, as person. When her name came up again, it was now as a prospective bride for thirteen others, ranging in age from thirty to eighty, and cultures from Somali to Indian. There was a convert from Gujarat who wanted a fourth bride from the East African coast in order to consolidate his Indian Ocean connection. Names, names, names offered by emissaries. Her suitability as spouse was underlined by four ideas: she was young, female, and tainted with just enough scandal to be interesting and only slightly spoiled. Names, names, names that proposed forgetting and forgetfulness. Names that were a temptation because they were a way into something other, away from herself.

Almost two months later, Ayaana came face-to-face with Suleiman again. She had been avoiding people after the Thursday incident. She was heading toward the mangrove swamp ignoring looks that were also lewd questions. The keys to Muhidin's house clanked in her pockets. She intended to later sit in the Bombay cupboard. Ayaana stopped. Four bright green suitcases blocked the path. Mama Suleiman was ending a phone conversation with someone. Her other arm was locked around her trimmed, clean, blue-suited son. "You're leaving?" Ayaana exclaimed without thinking.

Without turning to Ayaana, Mama Suleiman said, "Go away.

You're cluttering our view. Suleiman, stop brooding; you're not a bird. Ayaana, there are jobs for maids in Saudi Arabia. They pay well, my girl." She smiled. "You'll need neither to solicit favors from strangers nor to sell your intimate treasures to the lowest bidder. Move, girl." She glared.

An exchange of furies in one glance. Ayaana clenched her fists, angry and hopeless. Mama Suleiman smirked. Suleiman guffawed.

Ayaana shriveled. By her will alone, no tears fell. Suleiman's braying pummeled Ayaana's heart.

He winked at her. "Hey, hey . . . Ayaana, do you still see the ghost of your ugly cat?" He pretended to rub tears from his eyes.

Right there, Ayaana learned unalloyed hatred. The sound that squeezed through her lips caused Suleiman to duck under his mother's arm. Bi Amina stepped forward: "*Esh*, girl! Don't you have tricks to learn? Go away. We are busy people . . . Suleiman, head up! Back straight. Are you malformed?" To Ayaana, "What? You bold thing. What? You are still here?"

Ayaana ran.

She reached the cove she did not yet know was also her mother's hiding place.

She tumbled on the sand.

Grieving, again, a dirty-gray kitten.

Time flowed through Ayaana. A seaweed, a rock shimmered from the fragments of so many dying hopes. There are lonelinesses that enter into a being in order to separate body from marrow.

Later, she knelt before her sea to bargain. *Take me away*. She glanced over her shoulder at the troublesome existences rushing at her. She turned to the sea. *Take me away*. A hungry plea. Straining toward the waters, needing to fall in. Yet she did not tumble. She breathed. She shrouded her body, a black-draped shadow with a quick, soft walk. Afterward, in the salt-drenched darkness that obscured her form and identity, she crept along the path that led to Muhidin's house. There she listened at the door, hoping to hear life stir within. She then unlocked the door and entered, and coughed at the cloying dust of absence. Heart. Pounding. Sudden flurry. Ayaana whirled. She swept the books off the shelves. She retrieved a kitchen knife with which to slash at fabrics and upholstery. She pierced the broken promises of men. She broke Muhidin's crockery. She then took the stairs, two at a time, to enter into Muhidin's bedroom. She aimed for and leapt on the bed, jumping up and down in her shoes, as if it were a tarpaulin, dirtying the covers, kicking down pillows. As she jumped, she felt her trajectory constrained by a hard object beneath. She jumped down and looked under the bed.

Muhidin's Lamu chest.

Minutes later, Ayaana had destroyed the padlock. Inside, assorted items, ship logs, ship tools. She found the dark brown book. Inside, the ephemeral yellow-brown memory parchment tucked in its middle pages. A parchment oozing *marashi:* scent of moon, promise of destinations. Her hands could not rip it.

Thresholds of hauntedness.

Then she saw it. Through tears. The memory of a storm-filled evening. A vision of fire lit up the parchment, and she read it now as a promise. There was music. There was music. And it was a feeling. Her tears dried up and the light and song on the page faded. Yet the hope remained. She tore a scrap of paper to craft a ransom note to Muhidin, which she left inside the chest. She left the house with the book and its parchment. She also knew what she had to do.

~

The next day, Ayaana raced across the island to the fence that delineated the boundaries of her old school. She waited all day under the tree for Mwalimu Juma to emerge. In the evening, he locked the single large classroom. He was crossing the compound before he saw her. She got up.

"You!" he exclaimed.

"Yes."

"What do you want?"

"Teacher," she said, "I need to do my form-four exams."

Mwalimu Juma considered her for a minute. "Exams save you from foolishness?"

Tears ran down Ayaana's face.

"Answer. Can exams save you?"

No reply.

"Today you look for Mwalimu Juma? *Today* he is clever?"

Ayaana's body heaved, every hidden hope carried in a word. "P-please, teacher."

Mwalimu Juma cleared his throat. Wretchedness irritated him. He was curt. "Listen, can't ready you myself. But you are intelligent. Will get you some past papers. Practice, practice."

She sobbed. He conceded some more. "You have—what?—five, six months? Quick. Go register in Lamu as a private candidate. How many subjects?" Ayaana rubbed her face. "Number of subjects?" He recited, keeping time by knocking on the door, "English, Kiswahili, mathematics . . ."

Ayaana continued: "Biology, chemistry, geography, art and design, business studies."

"Not art and design; do agriculture. What you want is to pass well. Eight subjects, five thousand shillings. You have it?"

An image of money tumbling to the floor. She studied the ground, saying nothing. Mwalimu Juma's voice was softer. "Find that money, girl. Then come back. Quick. Quick."

That evening, Ayaana approached Munira. "I need five thousand shillings."

Munira did not ask why. She went into her room to count out seven thousand.

Five months later, over the course of two weeks, Ayaana took her exams along with twelve other candidates, including a sixty-five-year-old widow, inside the Lamu Museum building. Ayaana could have gone on writing and drawing cell membranes and filling in the details of the human eyes and calculating angles and writing even more compositions for examiners. The following February, when the national exam results were announced, Ayaana huddled in her bed as she heard the announcement repeated in the morning news. Four hours later, Ayaana's taped-together cell phone, her mother's old one, burred.

The results.

Munira would not ask Ayaana about her results; she had lost the strength to endure another disappointment.

. . .

Later that evening, Ayaana carried the phone to the cove close to Mehdi's shipyard. Under the shelter of sea and wind and humid air, she pressed the "open" button. A light revealed her results: Two A's, three A–'s, two B+'s, and one B–. Ayaana lifted her arms and gave a sound-emptied scream. Then she whirled and whirled and fell to the ground, staring at the stars and laughing at last. Nobody saw her. Nobody heard her. Because the district education officer, located a distance away, at Faza, was on leave, no one in Kenya ever asked who the third-in-her-district "Ayaana Abeerah Mlingoti" was.

Munira watched the night for her daughter's return. The dark cloud from that Thursday happening continued to pursue them. Threats muttered, promises of vengeance. The bark of drunkards, but she had gone to the sheikh for advice. He had counseled prayer. She had suggested that she might have to appeal to the government for help. The man had counseled patience and told her that other protective eyes watched over them. Still, Munira waited for her daughter's return. Munira saw a slender figure skipping along the path. It took her several moments to realize it was her child. So she covered her mouth, hiding both her fear and her hope. She retreated into her bedroom, where she huddled amid the lingering scent of unanswered prayers. She peeped through her door to watch her daughter bounce into the house. Munira almost allowed herself a smile.

At dawn the next day, Ayaana sat among the herbs and flowers in her mother's garden. She dug around the jasmine bower close to the shadow of a pawpaw tree. She whispered her news to the ghost of her kitten. On top of stones from ruined shelters, bright-eyed, hungry crows watched her. They cawed. A donkey brayed. The ringing of a bicycle bell, the muezzin's summons. A man carrying a fishing net approached the area. He had paused at the tombs of ancient compatriots, as he did every morning and evening. He saw the morning light shroud Ayaana, who in that moment looked like a transplant from Zhaoqing.

Lipunguze omo tanga, kuna kusi la hatari.

Lower the sails; the fierce southeasterly blows.

[29]

The *kusi* bombarded the shoreline before easing up to reveal eleven new arrivals, visitors who beamed and bowed as they landed on Pate Island. They had traveled to the southwest coast, to Pate Town, where they stretched out hands in overeager friendship. Mzee Kitwana Kipifit, sun-browned and nervous lest his actions be interpreted as dishonorable by the island to which his fate was bound, shifted as he waited for the visitors. Mzee Kitwana prepared to present the guests to the local member of Parliament, the district administrator, the tall, attenuated, and eternally lugubrious police inspector, and select imams and sheikhs from Faza, Siyu, and Pate Town. A tinge of pride, because he could play host, extend the Pate codes of hospitality as if he were a *mwenyeji*, a person who belonged. He even introduced himself to these guests as "Mzee Kitwana Kipifit," much to their bemusement. He replied to their queries in the florid Kipate he had acquired from the island's epics he studied.

The visitors crossed thresholds and the full force of the island's hospitality codes came into effect. They shared family meals. Slept in family homes. They were listened to. They laughed in the right places. They had brought with them so many red-wrapped gifts. They spoke often of their desire to harmonize the past; they spoke of a debt of gratitude. It was not clear whose burden the debt was; guest or host. They stood by the domed graves, where they shed a few polite tears. They listened keenly to Mzee Kitwana's explanations in Mandarin. They spoke often of Haji Mahmud Shamsuddin, the one they also called Zheng He.

. . .

One of the retired Pate civil servants spoke as if the admiral were alive and the events outlined were of recent memory: "Was he not a military man whose role was to grow an empire? Was he not in our waters for the purpose of extracting tribute? Did he not threaten our people? Were not our people forced to deliver what he demanded, or risk war? Is this the one to whom you refer?" A fly buzzed in the ensuing silence. One of the visitors, blushing because he had to deviate from a whitewashed official script, ventured, "A different age, a different way." His companions then resumed their spiel to speak of ports like Taicang, of navigation and cartographers, of ancestral sailors, currents, trade winds, and memories.

Later, they would ask to be allowed to see inherited pots, pans, plates, and cups in some of the island homes. In the evenings, they sat down with the men to hear faltering recitations of genealogical epics, listening for the sound of familiar names. Days later, four of the men went out fishing with morning fishermen, arranged by their hosts. They startled these by stripping off their clothes. On board, they watched fishing styles, helped haul nets in, wondered about the preparation and cooking of fish, and distributed more small red-wrapped gifts. If there was any disappointment in the quality and character of the gifts bestowed, the hosts did not say. Two of the visitors had joined the island's men for prayers at the mosque. Even there, given an opportunity to speak of themselves, they spoke only of Haji Mahmud Shamsuddin. The guests photographed everything. Then, one day, just when Pate had become accustomed to their ways, the guests announced their departure.

Three months later, six of these visitors returned to Pate ahead of the *matlai* season and its birds and dragonflies. They were in the company of the staff of the Kenya National Museum, an upcountry woman who drank bottled water all the time and three men—one of whom spoke in full paragraphs. Heritage experts. These came to explain "DNA" to islanders, and why they had come to collect it.

. . .

The past. After a giant ocean storm, six hundred years ago, capsized an admiral's junks and drowned at least six thousand of his men, some of the survivors floated onto Pate's mangroves and dark sand beach, crossing thresholds. Years later, a few boarded *kusi*-powered vessels to return to China. However, most stayed on, having pronounced Shahada and taken the purgative bath. They had re-emerged in white garments under new names, with new wives and a covenanted allegiance to Pate alone. It is said they conceded to the past by naming their living zone "Shanghai," their place of memory and ghosts. Time, decay, and Pate abbreviated this to "Shanga," a necklace or a yoke; unrequited memory can be an adornment or a prison.

[30]

On Pate Island, wind flurries and news carriers brought word of odd happenings in Arab lands: the smell of revolution. People clustered around battery-driven television sets and radios, picking out tales, not so much to be inspired as to understand. Elsewhere, DNA test results confirmed some of the intimate "lines" of connection that linked Pate to China. The visitors announced that they were looking for someone to walk the space between the past and the present, so that the future could be shared. They sought someone to bring home the spirit of those who had "entered the dark room" far from home, these *xunnan*, these *kesi* who had waited six hundred years for this day. At the mosque, one of the men spoke. He said they sought a *houyi*, a "Descendant."

A quartet converged on Munira and Ayaana's house. They bore gifts—a porcelain set, two cell phones, silk fabric, a large sealed red envelope, and a long rectangular wooden box containing twenty-six herbal blends and sandalwood essences in slender glass pipettes, the one item that told Munira that these strangers, like those others, had scoured something of her life to know it. Munira held her tongue. They were two men and a woman from China, and a man from Nairobi—a Ministry of Foreign Affairs person who had never before ventured closer than Mtito Andei, more than five hundred kilometers away, who, finding himself on Pate, was pop-eyed at the idea that this, too, was Kenya.

Elaborate pleasantries were exchanged.

"You honor us . . ."

". . . an honor for us."

Much was made of Munira, the mother. She was wary. What did they want? But she urged them to sit as she retreated to prepare and serve her rose-water-infused tea. She would listen to them. Again, at some point in the encounter, the quartet, in a chorus led by a round, bespectacled, solemn-faced Beijing bureaucrat, intoned as if rehearsed:

"You honor us . . ."

". . . an honor for us."

"Yes."

"We honor you . . ."

"We do."

"We have a favor to ask . . ."

". . . a favor . . ."

"A gesture . . ."

"Yes, a gesture."

". . . a fragrant flower of Kenya . . ."

"An emissary to China . . ."

". . . a bridge . . ."

"Our friend . . ."

"We desire her presence . . ."

". . . a Descendant . . ."

"Yes."

". . . our Descendant . . ."

"An ambassador . . ."

"From the good-willed people of Kenya . . ."

"To the good-willed people of China."

"Yes."

"Bearing the treasure of a neglected past."

"Yes."

"She'll find friendship . . ."

"Yes."

". . . and kindness."

"Kindness."

"An eternal sea unites our people," concluded the intoning man. "Because of the water, we are one destiny. The string of destiny binds our feet."

"Yes," echoed the Nairobi man.

"'String of destiny'?" Munira frowned.

The woman spoke slowly: "China is in your blood." And she looked at Munira as if she were a dear relative.

Munira waved her hand, wondering what this meant. What did these people want from her? "Thank you. As you can see on this island all the world's blood flows. It is Pate."

The man from Beijing leaned forward. "Yet fate has chosen this moment to invite us . . . and you . . . into a duty to history." His Nairobi counterpart blinked, his face and expression not dissimilar to that of a happy sheep. "Fate," repeated the man from Beijing.

"Fate," echoed the Nairobi man.

Munira faced the Kenyan, gaze intent. She spoke in rapid Kiswahili: "Who are these people? What do they want?"

The man replied in kind, "Take what they offer. It is free."

"Nothing is free," Munira retorted.

The Kenyan official said, "Just listen to them."

"Your daughter," said the Beijing man.

"Yes?" Munira said, ready to attack.

"China. To travel. To study. To share the memory."

Her daughter? Again?

And when she might have launched a physical attack, she saw clearly how she would escape Wa Mashriq's pollution. Deflating, she cupped her chin; her face was burning. Unseasoned hope.

"Ayaana?" she asked.

"Ayaana," the four intoned.

And then she laughed. "This fate of yours, it seems, must take from me all my people."

Munira started to cry.

The quartet waited.

Ayaana had run to Fundi Mehdi's workshop the moment whispers had touched her. From her mangrove hideout, she had seen the quartet disembark at the jetty. She had seen them wander, get lost, and then seek a way to her mother's house. "Munira-Ayaana-Munira-Ayaana!" Whispers spread across the town. Ayaana had fled. In the shipyard, she glanced about her. Fearful, push-pull emotions. Like her peers, she looked seaward for a larger, truer, fuller self—for life. Could this be their escape from the stench of that Thursday that was a burn mark on her inner thigh, escape from waiting for Ziriyab and Muhidin and a father who had never shown up, escape from herself?

When Mama Suleiman discovered that it was Ayaana who had been chosen to travel to China as "the Descendant," her body twitched, her skin itched, and her face was blotched with fury. She wept until her eyes turned red. If her son Suleiman had been here, he would have benefited from this honor. He *was* "the Descendant." In a snit, she hurried to complain to Hudhaifa. "No more! I refuse to even look at 'Made in China' anything. You may not stock or show me any low-grade, cheap, and *bandia* things. Do you understand?"

News of the selection spread. Mama Suleiman returned to Hudhaifa. "It's not as if she's better than us." Her pointing finger wagged in all directions. "*Mamake ni mchawi*"—Her mother's a witch. "'*Angenda juu kipungu hafikilii mbinguni.*' Even me. I have Chinese blood—you see my eyes? Can you see?" She pulled at her eyelids.

Hudhaifa leaned forward to look.

The surprise of the Arab Spring lost out to Pate's wonder over "the Descendant."

"Food!" Mama Suleiman exploded to Hudhaifa on another of her comfort-shopping missions. "I'd be going myself if it weren't for their food. Did you know they make rice from plastic?"

"Tell me . . ." urged Hudhaifa.

"And vegetables from tinted paper and plastic. Disgusting!" Bi Amina Mahmoud grunted.

The island rumor mills now churned with Mama Suleiman's

insights. Ayaana would have to eat dogs, cats, donkeys; pig and pork; pig balls and feet; sow ears and sharks; cow and goat udders; rabbit heads. Things that move and things that should not move: stones, scorpions, rats, foxes, snakes, spiders, and crickets.

"Frogs!"

"Roasted giant roaches that chirp."

Mama Suleiman expanded her wishlist for Ayaana. Ayaana, she announced, would be sullied by a people who worshipped rhinoceros horns, elephant tusks, and leopard gall, consulted astrologers, and built shrines for their cars. And they would sell Ayaana for her body parts. "*Aliye juu, mgoje chini*"—Whoever climbs must come down—Mama Suleiman concluded, and she felt much better. She remembered something else: "That girl will also eat cats and gnaw on tiger bones." She then ordered a freshly made juice blend of avocado, lemon, and ginger from the fruit vendor next door.

Hudhaifa's eyes glittered.

What a delicious turn. As much as he relished the triumph of underdogs, he preferred the titillation of twisted bloody endings. Such a spectacle! He giggled. Moreover, when Mama Suleiman was unhappy, she bought reams and reams of cloth. He had better stock up.

[31]

That evening, Munira stood close to Ayaana, wanting to tug at her cheek. *Poor child, so thin.* What was *that* she was wearing? Munira's faded, patched maroon A-line dress. Munira said, "*Bahati haina hodi.* This is your luck. In China you will become anything you want to be." Munira's tone was wistful. She touched Ayaana's hand—its rough palms, uneven nails. "Let's go to Mombasa," Munira suddenly said. "Let's buy a new dress for you."

Ayaana's head jerked back.

Only then did Munira remember the pungent smoke from the last new dress Ayaana had had. She backed away.

Later that night, Munira, her heart roiling with the forces of everything that had happened to their family, the strange, strange twists of fate, rose from her bed and relit a lantern to venture into Ayaana's room. There she was, her little girl. Munira stared at Ayaana. The flickering light shed a warm orange upon Ayaana's face. Mother-tenderness flowed for the splayed, sleeping young woman, whose right leg dangled off the end of the bed. Munira gathered bedclothes to cover Ayaana. She bent over her and inhaled orange blossom and jasmine suggestiveness, bergamot, patchouli bitterness, ylang-ylang dreams, and the seductive venom of oleander—the fragrances of expectation. She kissed her daughter's forehead, lips to skin. *Poor child.* Munira remembered another woman whom she had banished from her thoughts.

A flurry of images from the past: a restless, ridiculous, giddy creature who was cosseted by grown-ups and sure of her belovedness and belonging, who waltzed through the world gilded by her father's influence, money, and indulgence, his confidence in her, as if she were immortal. The young woman had once spurned this mangrove-fringed island to risk everything for the savor of *more*. Imbibing life, its banquets, pouring faith into the world's glittering promises, and that of the best-looking man she and her hooky-playing girlfriends had ever met.

They had all been in a bridging-year computer college, and would dodge their network of busybody guardians. She was the beautiful one, the best dressed of them all. She was the outrageous, jeweled one, the boldest, bravest, and most intelligent. On a dare by her friends, she had gone up to greet the tall, sleek, black-haired man, with his square jawline, wide forehead, and high cheekbones, dressed in a beige linen suit.

Head tilted, her breathy "*Salaam*, sir, what time is it?"

He had turned. Eyes crinkling at the corners, gleaming, finding hers. "I saw you," he had answered. Gentle-spoken. She had to lean toward him to hear his words. "Please, share a cup of tea with me; I have been lonely for beauty."

She followed him. She sat next to him, in awe of this splendid being with his tender voice and sad eyes, flattered but not surprised that he had noticed her.

He talked. Said he had moved to Mombasa two years ago. He worked in the mining sector, linked to a firm on the South Coast.

"The time," he said.

"What?"

"You'd asked about the time?"

She lowered her head, covered her mouth, laughing.

"I did."

He moved next to her so that they could read his watch together.

"Four thirty-eight p.m.," he whispered into her ear.

Just as she had seen the females do in the films she loved, and even though she felt she was melting, she looked into his eyes; acting, she asked, "Really?" Feeling very grown-up.

They met every day after that. He blessed her every thought, her beauty, which she knew about, but not in the way he described it, how it colored his dreams, how he could not think without invoking her as an angel for his moments.

He asked her to walk and twirl for him. She was a gazelle. Had she ever thought of modeling?

Her father would never agree, she had explained.

He had nodded. "We must honor fathers. We must obey their love." Then he remembered that he needed to go and pray.

Later, he told her about Paris, London, Dakar, New York, Kuala Lumpur, Ankara, and Beirut. The next day, he showed her the label on his suit, Hugo Boss. The following day, he bought her a silk scarf and perfume, Opium.

His sentiments. She would show the scarf off to her friends. He said he needed to know her better. He said he could not sleep because she possessed his thoughts. He had blushed as if embarrassed by his own words. He had apologized with a stutter. She basked in his glow. Another day, he lit a cigarette and shared it with her. When the Nadi Ikhwan Safaa *taarab* music group came from Zanzibar, he escorted her to a private performance at a wealthy trader-friend's house.

"Be careful," one of her friends warned her.

Jealousy, she thought. She began to avoid her college friends, impatient with their provincialism, their contentment with small things. She was irritated by their lack of curiosity, their unwillingness to hear her bore them with the virtues of her catch.

The man introduced her to his business partners: loud, sharp-suited men who called him "Chief" and conceded to his arguments, which seemed to leave them all tongue-tied.

She was proud of him. His partners envied him her company. "Such a beautiful thing; where did you find her?" He liked it that other men envied him. He wanted her to think in broader terms about her education. He was willing, he said, to go to her father and convince him to let her study in Singapore. He also said he had something even more important to talk to her father about.

She went coy. He must mean marriage. She had wanted more time to experience the world, but such was destiny. Their children would be beautiful. He said he would always protect her, said life in Singapore or Malaysia was very different from anything she had imagined—richer, better, faster, fuller.

One night, returning late from a film followed by a party, he suggested that she crash in his apartment rather than drive across the town to her small room.

She did.

It was so simple.

He had only one bed—his own.

That is where she slept. It was not as if she had a choice, she had informed her heart.

A chaste rest.

After that, it became easier and easier to sleep in his arms, his safe and securing arms. He always talked about prayer and lulled her into sleep.

It wasn't rape.

She could never argue that he had forced his body into hers and made her bleed without her consent. But neither could he claim her consent when she woke up suffocating, to find that he had pinned her arms above her head, and had dragged her nightdress up to her neck, so that she did not fight back, or scream, or scratch, or kick, or punch him, or mark him with her manicured, painted nails.

After he had finished, with an extended grunt mingled with expletives and prayer words, he had rolled off her body and asked a logical question to her silent sobs: "If you didn't want this, what were you doing in my bed?"

Not like this, she had thought, cleaning up her body, collecting her clothes. Eyes dry.

"Stay," he said. "We're married by deed now. Come, the second time is better."

Six weeks later, when she told him she was pregnant, he had held her face between his hands and said, "As God wills."

Subject to his whim, thought, intent, her life depended entirely on his choice. He knew it. She prayed for goodness. He used her desperation by turning her into his maid: Do this, do that, go here, there, everywhere. So she started to dream of walking through the doors of women who vacuumed out unwanted presences. The word they had whispered behind scandalized hands at school: "flushing." Flushed. Gone. And she would make her way back home, purged, cleansed, and forgetting.

Yet.

Perhaps the unseen thing inside her body did lurch at her thoughts. Perhaps she really did feel a small warm hand cup her face. Perhaps she imagined it, just as she was imagining everything else.

She waited for the man's next move. Two months later, he said. "We'll fix things. I finish with my employer in three weeks, four at most. I get the money. We see your family. We marry, on Pate?"

"No," she had answered, so deeply relieved her voice was shaking, "here, Mombasa."

"Done."

She had then fallen on her knees. "Don't leave me here."

Hands in his pockets, he had looked at her. "You look foolish like that. Why don't you trust me?"

"I'm afraid." She had wept.

He had said, "When you are sniveling, you're a bore. A boring black prostitute."

She had heard him. She had wiped her voice. She rose from her knees and shut up.

He left.

Three months later, he had still not returned. The Bohra landlord came to collect his rent. She said, "He's been delayed. We're getting married soon."

"Good for you," the landlord answered. "Six months I wait. Six months I'm patient. Six months no rent."

The things she did not know.

Six months' rent-free living.

Munira had collapsed to the floor, retching and yet paralyzed.

. . .

Later, she waddled to their room and dug through her handbag to retrieve all the money she had. Her handbag lay on a glossy black table on which a large, shining television presided. It took an hour. She returned to the waiting landlord with an inventory of household goods on a sheet of paper with a forged signature, and her own as witness: leather couch, washing machine, thirty-two-inch television, entertainment unit, dishwasher, stainless-steel pots and pans, bedroom ensembles, and two business suits that he could hold as collateral, or sell for the outstanding rent. That afternoon, she took the ferry to the South Coast and journeyed the distance to the new mining territories to look for the man.

"Oh, him," the company people said. "Was he the geology consultant who was here with us a year ago? Absconded from duty, even though he had been paid in full. Pity! Had come well recommended. Where's he now?"

The things she did not know.

Despair.

On the road, on the ferry, on the road again, she wanted the journey never to stop; she did not want to have to reach a destination and make a decision.

But she did.

In the apartment, she called her father, her cherished father. She said she needed more money to finish an extra finance course. He teased her, said he would send a relative to fetch her—was she plotting to take over his businesses?

No! She pretended to laugh. She said she wanted to learn how money worked.

"You're my pride," her father said, "my smile."

"I miss you," she said. Quiet tears.

"Come home soon," her father urged.

He wired her the money, and extra, at once, and she dropped out of college. She filled a bag with things from the apartment—not a big bag, just things she would need in rented one-room servant's quarters with a shower/toilet in Ganjoni. Her new landlady was an upcountry woman who operated a clandestine bar/brothel/beauty parlor in her spacious compound, who wanted her rent on time, and tenants who minded their own business. Munira returned for more soft things from the apartment—sheets, towels, and perfumes—and then she disappeared from herself, friends, and family.

The baby grew, and when Munira wasn't vomiting, she was inundated by cravings for fresh juice and vegetables and fried fish. Her emotions seesawing, she struggled with knowing what to do. She spent some money on a burka, through which she could stare at the world. She went out in the late evenings, traversing nights, hoping to be attacked by night trolls who would offer her an excuse that would lift from her the burden of responsibility.

Not my fault.

Nothing happened to her; nobody approached her. Sometimes she went to the apartment to see if any light had come back on. It never, ever did. Most of the day, she sat on her mattress, retching into a blue bucket, knotted up inside, surviving on spiced tea, listening to radio chatter, *taarab* music, her thoughts suspended, and she cried because she needed her mother. But her mother would tell her father, and her father's heart would die, and that she could not live with.

Taarab music from the dingy bar six doors away.

A woman sang in the voice of wounded longing:

> *"Ewe ua la peponi*
> *Waridi lisilo miba*
> *Kwenu kakutoa nani kwenye maskani yako . . ."*

The melody halted Munira's progress. She listened until the song was done. When it was done, it let her go.

Nightmares.

One cold morning, she woke up soaked in sweat and dread. The terror stayed with her all day long, so that in despair, in the evening, she bought herbicides and rat poison. She would evacuate the thing inside her. Instead, she almost died, she drifted into another nothing, suspended on the edge of a cord that she was tangled in. There she saw images of her family and her father, and how her dying would eat him up. She vomited everything out. Two weeks later, tired of being afraid of everything, she drank down a jar of anti-malaria tablets. This precipitated labor pains. *At last*, she thought.

She had prepared for the horror. Water, basins, scissors, towels, bandages, plastic garbage bags. She moved with the waves, shoving the thing from her body, clamping down her lips, not making a sound.

The mess—blood, sweat, shit, and chaos. The twenty-eight-hour travail. At 2:00 a.m., as students in a far nation were unveiling the *Goddess of Democracy* statue on Tiananmen Square, a shriveled thing resembling a clod of pale beige clay popped out of Munira's body. It lay unmoving. Panting, Munira seized scissors to hack off the flesh cord that still bound them to each other. To do that, she had to touch the still-warm, bloodied creature, and when she felt it, something feeble fluttered, and the fluttering turned into a stabbing explosive light inside her soul, and she became as big as the cosmos, so that in pure awareness she was breathing into the child, sucking out the mucus, purring and chirping until her child could breathe on its own, until her baby coughed and opened her large eyes, and then lifted tiny hands toward her.

Munira had sobbed. "Oh, you! It is you? Ayaana," she had cried "Oh, Ayaana." And she clutched the child to her body.

Minutes later, as the baby suckled, Munira stared, transfixed, thoughts dropping like small bricks. It did not matter, then, what anybody would think about her. Anything could happen to her now. She did not care. She loved. That was all. She could endure anything—go anywhere, do whatever she needed to do—to live for Ayaana.

For Ayaana, Munira risked the contempt of her landlady.

She went to beg to learn how to plait hair, do facials, manicures, pedicures, and massages. Munira started by sweeping the cut-off, rubbed-off, flaking-off human pieces from the floor—hair, nails, skin. She learned touch, acquired its language. She washed hair. She was allowed to do pedicures, then manicures, then henna, and then everything else. She worked on commission. She learned how to ward off the leering attention of the men who came to get their hair cut and, to her shock, their nails done. They learned to ask for her. She learned to offer a soft touch, a sideways look, a small laugh that preserved fragile egos and camouflaged her aversion.

Munira used the money she earned to buy baby formula and secure some postnatal services. Inside a *buibui*, her dress was shabby. A steel will denied her the indulgence of dreaming of Pate's sea and her home.

Munira worked five more months, until an unbearable pressure in her skull, the inability to wait anymore, made her wrap up her daughter and walk out of her single room. She left the door wide open. She walked all the way to the Old Harbor, where she found a fisherman willing to sail to Pate Island if she would help out with the cooking on board. For Ayaana she would do anything.

And she did.

Here she was. *Ayaana*. Now almost twenty-one years old, gangly and deep in sleep. Munira watched her. Doubts turned into certainty. The things a mother had to do. No one ever spoke about the bittersweetness of this beyond-feeling pain, of realms beyond limits, of having to pull away from the most beloved thing. Women never spoke of such things, of secrets etched into desolate absences. Giving birth was an unending journey, and sometimes the character of its harrowing only deepened with time. The choices a mother had to make.

Munira left the room.

She left to seek the sea.

The vanquished do sing.

One song. A tribute. Munira breathed from a fathomless corner of yearning. She sang for daughters. She, too, had been someone's daughter. She sang for her father, her long-dead mother. She sang most for Ziriyab and Muhidin. And then she sang for Ayaana.

> "*Ewe ua la peponi*
> *Waridi lisilo miba . . .*
> *Mabanati wa peponi hao ndio fani yako . . .*"

Munira stopped.

The booming of waves. Hissing stars. Muted night sounds. Was this not life, to allow for anything? Munira covered her head and stepped into the shadows snaking along the shoreline.

. . .

Munira did not see Muhidin, who had been waiting out the night near Mehdi's cove. She did not hear his choking gasp. He had heard from whispers, on this evening of a quiet return on a fisherman's boat, that Ayaana would be leaving home.

~

Munira barged into Ayaana's room at dawn. "Go, *lulu*! Leave this place. Do not look back." Ayaana gaped at her mother, whose hair was disheveled, her eyes wild. Munira breathed hard, and her hands fluttered. "We must go to Mombasa for your passport. You are lucky. Others here receive only a death certificate from Kenya." She panted, leaning against the wall. And suddenly, for Ayaana, four weeks was a lifetime away.

Later that afternoon, Ayaana crept over to Mehdi's again. She was unused to her new popularity: exuberant greetings, invitations to ceaseless cups of tea and meals, photographs. In all this, the unchanging constant was Mehdi. He had become accustomed to Ayaana's sudden appearances and soliloquies. These were not unlike the daily news of the tide that he received. "I'm to go to China," she announced from her old perch in the abandoned *dau* as Mehdi fired a plank.

Mehdi lifted the wood. The tiny radio was providing weather reports. The ocean was in flow. It said that low tide would begin at 1743 hours.

Mehdi muttered, "Muhidin. He has returned, hasn't he?"

Ayaana stared.

He nodded.

She lay in the broken boat and stared at the sky.

~

It was night. Ayaana stood outside Muhidin's house, pounding on his door. Sitting on a low stool, staring at the screen of his old color television, Muhidin clutched one of his books. He had inserted the note she had left him after trashing his house: "You left me," it said. It leached sorrow. He crumpled the note.

He heard Ayaana pounding on his door. "Do you want your stupid map back?"

Muhidin's fingers tingled where they connected with the note.

Ayaana sat on Muhidin's stone step and dialed his phone number.

"Mteja hapatikani kwa sasa." No reply.

Ayaana shouted in Kipate, "Did you find Ziriyab?"

Muhidin was still.

Outside, Ayaana rubbed her face. *"Chal chal chal mere haathi . . ."* She sang it as a question.

No reply.

"When you went away, the bad people came." She dropped her head to her arm.

She waited for the moon to move to the lower sky before she set off for her mother's house. Inside the room, Muhidin wiped his bloody mouth, winced at the cut on the tongue, where he had bitten into it.

When her voice had faded, the first echo of a child's *"Nitakupenda"* reached for him. *Abeerah.* Muhidin went to his door and hauled it open. Looking out, expecting to see a girl and her kitten, he saw only moon-daubed darkness.

[32]

Muhidin fought through dawn's riptides into a black day made so by a sky pouring out torrents of stormy rain. The wind flapped his coat, which he huddled into, as he waded in the flowing water of already submerged pathways. He knocked on Munira's door, ready to tell the truth, to ask for the truth. The doorknob turned. She stood there, her unveiled hair in a single long plait, holding a needle, a thread, and the orange dress she was repairing. As she broke the string with her teeth, she said, without looking, *"Naam?"*—Yes?

Muhidin said, “Munira.”

Her head snapped up.

She dropped her sewing, and it fell in a heap around her feet.

Muhidin saw widening eyes that got squeezed in by a hard frown; flaring nostrils; she licked her lips. He observed slender hands that trembled as they touched her right cheek. She gulped in air and said, “You?”

He answered, “I couldn’t call.”

He was a wall, she thought, and behind chasmic eyes, some painful witness, some injury. She waited. He repeated, “I couldn’t call.”

She asked, “Should I have noticed?”

He bent under the rain in the dismal light. Swirling emotions, an eddy of rage. He had heard of curious visits: Wa Mashriq. The Chinese. Nairobi. Eddies of yearning: straining not to grab the one pined for, not to squeeze body, soul, and heart into her so that he could taste of life again, assuage new thirsts like the homesickness wrought by being at home. Impeded by invisible barriers, he scowled. “Ayaana.”

Munira was ice. “My daughter.”

He tried again. “I wanted to come home.”

“Your wish is now fulfilled.”

“I am told there were strangers. I want to hear it from you.”

Munira looked him up and down, and her upper lip was a twist. She scoffed. “As who?”

A struggle. The fresh scars he carried on his body and soul stung. Through gritted teeth, Muhidin asked, “What are you doing?” Disappointment.

Still. This face. *This beauty*. Within new folds, lines, and hardnesses, sadness’s fresh residues. Still, *I can find your face even in the grime of the world.*

Munira’s eyes slipped away from Muhidin’s gaze. Guilt-bitten. She focused on Muhidin’s body’s rough, sinewy urgency, how beaten it looked. Haggard in its stooping. She accused him before he could accuse her: “So now, when it is too late, you come.”

He pleaded, “China?” The fall of water from high roofs drenching him, Munira’s disgust oppressing him: “China, Munira?”

She gestured. “What do you know of what you don’t know?”

Even though their tones were civilized, and they stood as close as those mist-shrouded portraits of lovers, their guardedness alone, its undetonated presence, caused passersby to make detours.

Muhidin said, "Ziriyab . . . you understand . . . I had to . . ."

Munira intervened, "As now I must. For *my* child." Fake smile. "It is good that you understand."

"Abeerah . . ."

Lightning spiked across the sky.

Munira huffed, "Ayaana?"

Muhidin reached for Munira's arm. "You are . . ."

Munira was polite as she slapped his hand away. "You're good at leaving, my beloved; we learned to manage without you. *Nenda zako!*"—Get lost.

The soft slap lacerated Muhidin's heart. After twenty seconds, after he had restrained his fists from smashing in Munira's face, he turned to hobble away, his gait bent so that he would not fall to the ground; he tumbled once, but picked himself up. He hurried on, a man whose chest was burning. He was an old man who, single-handedly, had succeeded in losing everyone who had ever tried to love him. Behind him, a door slammed so hard he felt its reverberations beneath his feet.

Four weeks later, a village gathered for prayers and blessings that would lead Ayaana off the island into her destiny. They prepared her for journeys they had only dreamed about: exhortations, directions, things to do, things not to do, the invocation of God. Ayaana listened to these with a sense of distance. She thought of the district administrator, who often threatened the mostly indifferent islanders that one day he would "wipe the dust of this island off his feet." Now, if Ayaana had been brave enough, she would have informed Pate of her intent to scour its dust off her existence. She would have cursed its rumor-mongering strandedness, and its previous contempt for her and her mother. She was delirious about removing herself from the land's griefs, quarrels, ghosts, presences, and absences.

Ayaana carried little: her mother's prayer mat, her calligraphy pens and some ink, two packs of henna from Sudan; three dresses, a pair of jeans, two *leso*s, a *kikoi*, two *buibui*s, some jewelry, Mehdi's compass, and Muhidin's map, into which she had attached Mzee Kitwana's dry rose petal. She left Suleiman's pearl on her table. Munira added her gold bracelets to her daughter's collection. She also wrapped five small brown plastic bottles: rose essence, rose-hip-seed oil, orange-blossom attar, jasmine oil, and thick clove cream. She added two sets of *leso*s, printed with the aphorism "*Siri ya maisha ni ujasiri*"—Courage is the secret of life. They stored these things in a tightly packed medium-sized dark blue cloth suitcase, "Made in China."

They were two hours late and attempting to outrace the wind and take advantage of the incoming tide. Munira was already waiting aboard the white motorboat with Ayaana's luggage, her robes flapping, stately in her bearing—the mother of "the Descendant." This was her hour of triumph. She and Ayaana would be spending a night in Lamu, from where Ayaana would depart with an appointed chaperone for the harbor in Mombasa where her ship waited.

Ayaana, who had been delayed by the formal introductions to her escort, a Chinese woman from the embassy, was being hurried toward the old wharf when, from amid the milling crowd, Muhidin emerged.

"Abeeraah!" he hurled, as the wind swept away his *barghashia*.

Ayaana twisted away from the woman just as Muhidin reached her. "Where is my map?" he shouted, embracing Ayaana, clutching her to him.

She sobbed, "I'll tear it. Half for you, half for me."

"How?"

"We share," she said.

He grabbed her shoulders. "Abeerah . . ." he pleaded. He shook her. "You soiled my home; you stole my treasures."

Her eyes were fire. "Where were you?" she howled.

Reacting to her suffering, Muhidin recoiled. Ayaana said, "The bad thing . . . he came. You were not here." She hit his arms. Her head now against his chest, she reverted to childhood cadences: "I do not find you."

The wind tossed her black veil this way and that. Muhidin was growling. *Run*, he thought. He remembered Munira. And Ziriyab.

He recalled his recent entanglement with "Kenya." He peered into the future and saw nothing of substance left for any of them. *Run!* His eyes grieved, his heart broke. *Run, child!* "I am here," he said. "I am here now."

Muhidin had gone to Nairobi, a citizen asking authorities simply to explain his lost son. Instead, he had been forced to prove he was "not al-Shabaab," "not al-Qaeda"—that he was not a part of things he had not known. There had been nobody to speak up for him when he was robbed, stripped, accused, charged, and remanded, no one to protest his detention. No voice was raised as a lament against the abuse of his person and the desecration of his dignity, history, profession, and people, the rubbing away of his "Kenyan" identity by those who had the least right to lay claim to its story, who could not even locate Pate on a map of Kenya. No one came to explain to his tormentors that Muhidin's two-year stunned silence was not evidence of guilt. It was not that he had "something to hide"; he was just oppressed by meaninglessness.

To escape, he had to sell values he did not know he had. He had no valuables to give or provide access to, no one to call lest this visit trouble on someone's head. He, and others with whom he shared a charge sheet, had co-opted avarice to assuage the barking leprosy in the hearts of their guards. Money. There were six others in the cells with him, Kenyan Somalis. They had shared court sessions. They connected with Muhidin's name. They treated him as a brother. They had raised his share of the bribe—seven thousand shillings, the price of a nation's shriveling soul. Sated, their guards had one visiting day, left their cell doors open. A twelve-minute window was sufficient for the seven remandees to change clothes, walk out of their cells, mingle with guests, and leave the prison. The others then gave Muhidin another four thousand shillings to cover the cost of a ride back to the coast in the cabin of a cargo truck.

Even now Muhidin still felt putrid, as if a stinking carcass of ugliness, a Kenya-specific demon, clung to his soul. Now, as the wind disheveled their clothes, Muhidin looked at Ayaana, her awkward posture, her hopeful heart-in-eyes. *His daughter.* He preferred to surrender her to a future that was a dice roll so that she could make deeper, truer, and richer choices. In an uneven tone, he said, "I've been to China." He lied, "You will be so happy there."

Two fat tears in her eyes. Afraid she was reading abandonment in his words, Muhidin lied again. "I *shall* find you, you know that; I always find you."

She hiccupped. "I have a passport." She dug into her new green handbag and pulled out the blue object. She opened it for him to read "Ayaana Abeerah Mlingoti wa Jauza."

She said, "Now it is written. You *are* my father."

Muhidin kissed the document. He cleared his throat. "I am sorry I went away. I left you and your mother undefended. Forgive me . . ." His voice shook.

Ayaana touched his wind-mauled face. "*You* mustn't cry."

She cupped his face as she used to when she was little. Then Muhidin wanted to warn Ayaana: *Destinations are ephemeral. Nothing lasts, only the voices of the heart and gut count.* Instead, he said, "Listen, listen, the most important things are concealed in the unseen; the most essential truths inhabit only the unspoken." And then he recited, "Greet Yourself / In your thousand other forms / As you mount the hidden tide and travel / Back home . . ."

Muhidin paused his invocation of Hafiz. He murmured, "You know, my own, I *shall* love you."

Ayaana's official escort succeeded in unclamping Ayaana's convulsive grip on Muhidin's body. Firm and irritated, the escort snapped, "We so late."

"Your passport!" Muhidin handed Ayaana her document as her escort dragged her toward the idling speedboat.

Muhidin tore out his watch. "Abeerah, take this." He squashed it into Ayaana's hand.

"You *will* find me?" Ayaana cried.

If he did promise, it was lost in the clamor of Ayaana's departure and the high tide's wind. The chattering crowd parted for Ayaana, her mother, and her escort. They boarded the boat. Muhidin's gaze caught Munira's. She turned her back on him. She focused on steadying Ayaana, leading her to a corner seat. The captain gunned the boat's engine.

"*Abeeraaah!*" Muhidin howled.

Ayaana kept him in sight until the boat took a sharp left turn. She heard Muhidin yodel: "*Chal chal chal mere haathi, o mere saathi . . . Hai hai oho ho . . .*" And soon there was only the rumble of a speedboat pushing hard against a muscular neap tide.

Pweza kwambira ngisi
Wapitao kimarsi marsi
Tutwafutwao ni sisi.

The octopus told the calamari,
When you see them [humans] churn the waters
It is us they seek.

[33]

One day in 1995, as a dirty blue fog enshrouded China's Kinmen Islands, under the watch of a cold moon bleeding borrowed light over Fujian's waters, a thin man with a bandaged face towered over most of his compatriots as he faced the sea. Hands trembling, Lai Jin had removed his cracked sunglasses to rub out the salt-spray stains from the lenses. Thin-legged birds with drooping brown wings browsed by the shore. Buffeted by yowling winds, here was the should-have-been scion of the Lai family, the only son of the third son (who, in a village scandal, had married a much older, free-spirited part-Uighur, part-Japanese ceramicist named Nara) of the first son of the second wife from the branch with distant, obscured, and unfortunate Japanese roots in the courts of the third emperor.

Lai Jin had just returned from Meizhou Island, where he had followed pilgrims heading to the Temple of Mazu, patroness of the sea, awarder of bounty, turner of tides. She who read the stars and waters was also a bestower of healing. He was not a man given to faith in anything, nor did he wish it for himself. But something had happened when he wandered into the dark, older section of the shrine to retreat from the many Mazu venerators who had gathered to belch their bad spirits away. While he was lurking inside, an unforeseen balm-like softness had seeped into and traveled from his heart and into his thoughts, stilling their restlessness. When he left the temple, hours later, he did so as one startled by a strange gift he was compelled to bear. Now he felt not so much peace as resolution. The fervid desire to drive and drive without stopping, as he had been doing for two and a half months now, had just simply disappeared. Listening to the ebbing tide and the waves that heaved in solemn interludes along a beige-and-white stone-and-pebble shore, he discovered that his recurring fantasy of entering into the ebbing tides and sinking into the deep had also lost its seductive edge.

Foghorns.

Heralds of a fate that would bind Lai Jin to a still-distant land. His memory and sadness flowed toward the three phantom hulks, rust-and-gray ships heading elsewhere as the cold wind drowned itself in the harbor.

Foghorns.

Lai Jin rubbed his arms, warming them. There were a few new things about living that Lai Jin had discovered: that the earth still shuffled from west to east; that life did not stop to lament the elephant-foot weight crushing a man's chest; that existence is disordered, neither symmetric nor harmonious, but woven out of infinite textures and shapes of nothingness that change at whim.

In the beginning, there was fire.

This has been said by others before. In Lai Jin's second beginning, there was an ordinary fire. A New Year's conflagration had turned an exclusive, festive Beijing restaurant into charcoal and ash, and in the process had charred Lai Jin's soul. When the fire and 258 howling escapees were done, there was silence, and what had once been six men and seven women, some of the glittering, youthful icons of China's "*gaige kaifang*" epoch, including Lai Jin's beauteous wife, Mei Xing, were grotesque, smoke-spewing black sculptures, lying on their backs with arms and legs curved upward, their mouths frozen in the grimaces of last words, the extreme opposite of breath.

The fire had destroyed both Lai Jin's appetite for the feasts offered by the new dispensation and his calling as a member of the society of New China aristocrats. Lai Jin had been late to the celebrations in the restaurant; he had been attending to a needy but wealthy likely investor in a commercial space launch scheme he had been dreaming up. When news of the explosion reached him by phone, he had headed for the site at once. Reaching it, he had crashed through the steel barrier around the steaming restaurant with superhuman strength. Ignoring the cloying smell of too many roasted things, he had dashed to and fro, turning over fire-charred objects, looking for Mei Xing. He had called out to her. He reminded her of thrusting needs, kaleidoscopic desire, ten thousand soft, soft touches, the enchantment of last night's slow, sucking kisses. He had hunted through the crumbs and plotted to force Mei Xing back to him, now with words and then by will alone. He reminded her of their children, the ones that still needed to be born. He had ended up kneeling on ash and scratching the surface of the gutted space. Lai Jin had fallen into a soot puddle. Inside, he had seen a bleached skull. Reaching for it, he had touched his own reflection. Stygian water had scalded his skin, and Lai Jin buckled on smoldering steel. The fire had burned through his clothes, into flesh, and carbonized his spirit. The back of his left arm, half his back. Crackle and spark. Then he felt Mei Xing's heart beating inside him. Then he heard himself cry, the voice of Mei Xing's sadness. Two fire-stained men had dragged him out. Lai Jin had been mostly dead—eyes fixed, body limp.

When Lai Jin had sufficiently recovered from second-degree burns and smoke inhalation, he returned to the site, three months later. He found repair works almost complete as if the fire had been a mere interlude. An overwhelming taste of meaninglessness filled him. Trying to escape the sensation, he sought and found members of his old clique. They had migrated to even shinier places, to party harder than before. "To be rich is to be glorious!" a voice intoned to him from the karaoke bar into which he had ventured. He had imagined he might just resume his life from where he had left it and shake off the despair. So he drank. And vomited. Drank. And vomited, and tried to sing with the friends, and wear the faces that suited their ceaseless nows, and tried to forget that not one of these, the gilded ones, had come to visit him in the hospital. Nausea. And the scene had tunneled into a horrific sewer in which the music turned into his wife's howls and every glittering dream was ash. He recalled the communal grave where anything that was determined to be human content from the fire had been buried. And he looked around and realized he had become a life member of a noisome asylum that was, at its core, a void.

Lai Jin had staggered home, stinking, sick, and lost. The next day, he went to his office and immediately offloaded the coveted prime land in Shenzhen where he and his wife had intended to design, build, and rent to rich foreigners compact luxury homes. He destroyed the blueprints for his rocket-assembly plant. He sold all the businesses and the apartment, along with most of everything these contained. Through Mei Xing's party connections and her diligent festival "gifts" to the influential, they had acquired significant rights to one of the lesser-known of the many islands of distant Shengsi county, just south of Shanghai. Speculative purposes, they had imagined. Land banking. He would try to get rid of that, too—eventually. Lai Jin retained most of the artwork he had collected, all his Zao Wou-Ki collection, and loaned these out to a small gallery with an eccentric owner, without specifying a return date. Lai Jin then set out in the red Audi sports car he had bought for Mei Xing's last birthday, intending to drive himself to death. But when he reached Xiamen's Tong'an Qu two and a half months later, he had stalled.

Now.

Fifteen years later, landfall made his stomach heave. Almost a day away from Kilindini Harbor, Mombasa, aboard the merchant vessel *Qingrui*, its captain, Lai Jin, stood scowling at the black-and-chrome satellite phone. A Voice had co-opted the powers of politics, history, cultural studies, philosophy, and geography to commandeer his ship. The inflection-free Shanghai Accent was as delicately tuned as a four-string lute, and just as precise. Now it asked him, "How will you transport two pairs of giraffes?"

Lai Jin clenched his jaws at these red-tape conversations. Although he was saying yes, yes, yes to Shanghai Accent, he was also sifting inner words for a self-preserving way to say "fuck off." He found himself listening to the man, stunned. Shanghai Accent explained how Lai Jin's present itinerary not only mirrored the year, season, and moment of an ancient calamitous journey, but also coincided with the discovery and salvaging of wreckage from a Ming master ship, one of the few that had broken up in a storm off the western ocean six hundred years ago. "When fate throws a dagger at you, there are only two ways to catch it: by blade, or by handle," Shanghai Accent quoted to Lai Jin. He went on to congratulate him for the convenience of his ship's presence and the wisdom of his employer, who, understanding destiny's convergence, had agreed to the use of ship as a "bridge" for the realization of a symbolic journey-memorial for the blighted Western Ocean voyage of the once-again great Admiral Zheng He.

"There have been findings of import," Shanghai Accent added. Relics from the lost ship, timber, crockery, jade pieces. "Including"—quiet—"a representative *houyi*!"

Pause.

Lai Jin understood that Shanghai Accent had hoped to hear him gasp, reflect excitement. Instead, his head ached and his thoughts remained stuck with the vision of tall, thick-lashed, spotted brown animals galloping aboard his commodities-bearing ship. Shanghai Accent spoke again. Did Lai Jin realize the honor of being the one chosen to return fragmented portions of Admiral Zheng He's expedition—broken Ming crockery taken from East Africa back to the people of China?

Lai Jin's migraine turned into a buffeting squall. He tore at his pockets, digging for painkillers, as he cleared his throat, attempting resistance. "Might this auspicious re-enactment, sir, not unfold in a vessel, sir, that is more suitably outfitted—given that we shall, as previously arranged, sir, be also"—he improvised—"traveling with passengers? Didn't the employer explain this? No? Ah! Perhaps this prestigious undertaking belongs to a grander vessel, sir, and should involve a far worthier personage than myself, sir?"

Shanghai Accent sounded cross. "Of course *I* will be in Xiamen to meet the ship *Qingrui*." A pause. "*Qingrui?*" An irritated sound. "That is not an adequate name."

Lai Jin held his tongue, squirming. He could not depend on his employer for anything. They would sacrifice him to shrimp gods if it meant profit and prestige. He listened to Shanghai Accent lifting metaphors from vats of misty legend—dragons, mulberry trees, tigers, persimmon fruits, jade wheels, and nine drops of smoke. Lai

Jin pinched his brows. *Giraffes?* His head throbbed. His ship juddered. What would he tell his crew? That history had called them? Would they merely snort, or would they topple over, consumed by guffaws?

Lai Jin grunted. Now that he had lied about it, he was obliged to find passengers to present as evidence of the inconvenience of this proposition. What a mess. The MV *Qingrui* was a cargo ship, a bulk carrier. If he, Lai Jin, had wanted to carry passengers, he would have worked on a cruise ship. He hadn't. He had needed to be left alone with his thoughts and his sea. He had fought to gain the sea: Shanghai Maritime University, a stint in Singapore, working his way up to ship captaincy. He liked his cargo. Cargo neither spoke nor required entertainment. Cargo was simple. He rubbed the band of sweat on his forehead. It stimulated a perverse impulse. "What's the extra pay?" He already knew the answer. It was confirmed by the silence emanating from the other end of the phone, exuding disapproval and disappointment.

Waiting. Which silence would outlast the other? Lai Jin, now a cog in a wheel, crumbled first. He asked about "the Descendant" and its expected needs.

Her, corrected Shanghai Accent. Underlined. "Our *houyi*."

Lai Jin choked. Crushed, he asked, "The giraffes?"

Shanghai Accent seemed to have forgotten about these. "The . . . *giraffes*?"

A compromise to water deities. No giraffes, and he would take on the human. He thought of his ship and its layout. Spartan and steel. A solitary man's stark realm. Where would he insert a "Descendant"?

The MV *Qingrui* was an even ship. White with red stripes, fifty-four meters, her name painted in black. Today she was also flying the Kenyan flag, a tribute to her target harbor. She was the main reason he stayed on this job. She was his lucky ship, a container-carrying box with a single-decker hold. With her hard-coated bottom tanks, she had been imagined by the ocean and for the ocean. Since the advent of slow steaming—lower fuel costs—she traveled at twenty-three knots at her fastest. Lai Jin preferred slow travel. His employers did not. Though he was not a man subject to fantasies, Lai Jin was sure that his ship was imbued with a playful and courageous spirit. She met colossal waves by anticipating the ocean's next moves. She protected her crew and cargo. She always made her destination. If Lai Jin could love anything now in this world, it was the MV *Qingrui.*

Foghorns at dawn. Mombasa presented itself as a gold-orange sprawl, witness to the long history of human arrivals and exits. Lai Jin slowed down his approach. Trepidation swirled inside him. His memories suffered on land; his nightmares were elemental and more defined. They revealed a Lai Jin who was a prisoner to unending longing. They emerged from abysses that lured him with illusions of a still-living Mei Xing, so that waking also ripped open old scars of anguish. In most ports, if he did not remain on his ship, he would wander the streets at night, hunting for the other shapes of solitude, drinks and food. With the light, he repaired to whatever lodgings he had in time for breakfast. Later, he would lie still in bed waiting for dusk. The night blurred everything. At night, he could dissolve into breath.

[34]

A tugboat that would escort the MV *Qingrui* to harbor offloaded a pilot whose eyes were half closed as he led the MV *Qingrui* into Kilindini Harbor. When the ship had anchored, her gangway and ladder were lowered to the quay on the starboard side. Soon a group of men—immigration officials, as well as bureaucrats from the Embassy of the People's Republic of China in the Republic of Kenya—stepped on board with the ship's agent, a monosyllabic man whom Lai Jin recognized from his previous year. His crew were in good hands.

Lai Jin breathed in. Each port had a distinctive smell, as if the sea distilled the climate, hopes, and experiences of each place into a unique essence. Kilindini. Top note, earth, fire, moon flowers, and blood; middle note, salt, putrefying seaweed, and rust; bottom note, wood, twilight's sun warmth, sweat. Fresh cadences, whirling emotions, a temple bell sprinkling high sounds, laughter from somewhere, and the call and response of at least seven different bird species. Containers, cranes, ships. The voices of stevedores. Lai Jin looked past these as the old burn wounds on his body stung like clotted memories being poked at. He looked to the cloud patterns. Mombasa's heat seeped into him. Even though there was a salty, cooling breeze, Lai Jin was already sweating. He straightened his back and prepared to meet his hosts and exchange courtesies.

Movement.

Clang and clash of heavy cargo moving. Screamed-out warnings—"*Kaa chonjo!*" Exhortations—"*Shime wenzangu!*" Chant. A day and a half later, the wheat aboard the MV *Qingrui* was offloaded. Lai Jin waited for the consignment of tea and scrap iron that would much later be loaded for his return trip. Perhaps he might venture out in the day to slurp and savor black pekoe, the best of which formed the bulk of his return load. Curiosity. His country, the home of tea, sought tea's great-great-grandchildren from distant places. He tasted teas to test how the flavor evolved after it left China.

By two o'clock the next afternoon, an all-Chinese work team, supervised by an embassy official and a construction-company owner who was fluent in Kiswahili, took over the MV *Qingrui*. Lai Jin packed an attaché case and a clothes bag and slunk out of sight. In his anxiety to limit contact with the bureaucrats and builders, he only just remembered to let an officer in the harbor master's office know that he urgently needed passengers.

"How many?"

"Four, five. What they pay—keep fifty percent. No questions."

The man's smile—when it emerged, it glowed.

Lai Jin resurfaced at the Nyali Beach Hotel. With a fountain pen filled with thick black ink, he attempted to summon the essence of Mei Xing, his beloved. On rice paper, lines, words, ink smudges, and tears. He waiting for a feeling, an image, a signpost to the chasm into which his wife and life had fallen. Sweat drops in in-between spaces. She had been the second person in life not to treat him as an aberration from the unspoken Han ideal. The first had been his mother, the ceramicist Nara, who had then given herself over to madness.

Lai Jin was born in Tianjin, after two aborted girls. His father had wanted a son: it would boost his name and party standing. A son would compensate for an artistic wife who could neither serve the party diligently as a worker in its numerous agricultural schemes nor cook well. For Lai Jin, growing up meant living in the shadow company of his dead sisters and their devastated nonlives—ghosts to whom his mother increasingly deferred as she illicitly wove exquisite clay vessels to contain their always spilling souls. Until, one day, when he returned home from school, his mother was not there, and his father's only comment to him was "Now she is gone." Within a year, another woman, so much younger than his mother, entered their household. A skittish and dazzling being, she was kind to Lai Jin in public, but pinched him when they were alone. She inserted herself between Lai Jin and his father, so that she became the primary interpreter between them. To survive her, Lai Jin immersed himself in his studies, choosing to excel when he was not losing himself in imagining another life inside the ruins of his vanished mother's clay-making kingdom—a creaking wheel, its crumbling kiln, half-done pottery. There he could retreat to a bright-blue imaginary sea of goodness, love, and beauty. When Lai Jin was twelve, to his dismay, the family moved to Guangzhou in Guangdong. His stepmother let him know often that his father's promotion to a higher party position was blocked because he, Lai Jin—an interloper, like his mother—existed. She called him "Nikkei." It wounded his heart: because of his looks and height, his identity was often questioned. The woman told him to return to Japan by jumping from a bridge. "Kamikaze, save your father," she goaded. He focused on doing really well in his exams. His father sent him first to Hong Kong, to acquire English and an initial degree, and then to Montreal, Canada, to secure the world and a Western passport. But he was so homesick that he returned after only four months. On his plane home, he met Mei Xing, who would, in the space of three weeks, become his wife. She was from Beijing, but had lived in Canada for seven years with her mother, who had fled there on the tail end of a scandal. This, the imagined dishonor such an alliance brought to the Lai name, coupled with the fact of a new three-year-old son positioned as heir by the stepmother, broke the already fragile filial cords between Lai Jin and his parental home.

Now.

Sweat drops on a page, and a wild orange dusk in Mombasa. Three black crows cawing at his window peered at him as if they were relatives he should recognize. He watched them and they watched him. He blinked first.

[35]

Eleven days after his Mombasa arrival, Lai Jin returned dockside and made his way along the quay. He halted, and stared at the hulk in front of him for a long, long time. There was his ship. Slowly, his fingers rose to prop his chin. He was unaware that his skin had reddened and his eyes glowed. Perhaps half an hour later, the harbor master's deputy sidled up to study the vessel with him. After five minutes, the man cleared his throat. "Captain, sir, pardon me."

Lai Jin turned and bowed to the short, round brown man. "Captain," the man said in a confiding tone and tapped a finger at pictograms on an official seeming stamped sheet of paper, "is 清瑞 the same as 国龙?"

Lai Jin glanced at the paper, and back at his ship. What could he say? He reread his ship's new name. 国龙, *Guolong: Dragon of the Nation*, framed against dark clouds. He reflected on the man's question, flirted with the truth. Retreated. He could take refuge in dissembling—*I do not understand*, he might say. For harmony's sake, to reduce the bureaucratic quibbling, he would slash and burn a version of English. Code-switch camouflage—when convenient, conform to others' uncertainties about you.

Lai Jin answered, "Many names, same names, same heart, same

emotion." He looked at the man and nodded. "Same ship." But he sighed inwardly. *Guolong?* Really? Was there no other stereotype of China to amplify? Dragon of the Nation? His light-spirited ship? A tic pulsed above Lai Jin's eye. He hoped the idiots involved had also taken care of the paperwork.

Golden sun-fringed storm clouds spread over the harbor. "Rain," noted the harbor master's deputy.

"Yes," replied Lai Jin.

"I'll see you before you go?"

"Yes," said Lai Jin, wondering about the voyage ahead, and the name—was it auspicious?—imposed upon his ship. The official shuffled away, frowning at the documents. Lai Jin stared at his renamed ship in dismay.

They would be leaving Mombasa in two weeks. Aboard, Lai Jin paced. His stateroom, as stark as a monk's cell—with the main color provided by an untitled Zao Wou-Ki print, before which he paused often—remained untouched. He had offered to surrender his captaincy if his cabin was interfered with. Lai Jin expected to be chastised at some point for this act of noncooperation. He wandered over to the cabin renovated for the Descendant, the cabin formerly designated to the chief engineer. He flinched in front of a bureaucrat's interpretation of contemporary Taoism blended with further China-clichés. If the intent was to depress the cabin's inhabitant with an excess of China-isms, it would be successful.

There were red dragons on one wall, supplemented by art prints of mountain landscapes—sunrise and magnolias—and everyday life scenes—fishing, pouring tea. A seventeenth-century woodblock print depicting Admiral Zheng He's treasure ships, and a photograph of a statue of Zheng He himself. Lai Jin informed the image. "*Zhe shi wo de chuan*," he said—This is *my* ship. He adjusted his shirt and strode out. His footsteps echoed on the steel floor. *Guolong*? He still mused, watching unknown birds soar and dive. Here he was again, asking for a thousand paths, and always being returned to one—waiting. Always waiting. *For what?* Storm front rushing in. Black-ink skies. Lai Jin waited.

Kupoteya njia ndiyo kujua njia.

By getting lost, you learn the way.

[36]

Only one passenger had booked a passage on the MV *Qingrui/Guolong*, not the five Captain Lai Jin had hoped to parade as impediments to a bureaucrat's schemes. Still, one was better than none. Three others who came on board as registered passengers were all linked to the bureaucrats' plans. Lai Jin studied the passenger manifest and wondered what destinies had brought them there.

~

Shu Ruolan had never boarded a ship in her life. She concealed her trepidation and adorned herself in her new role as chaperone to the Descendant. She was a fragile-looking creature, unusually doe-eyed, with pale skin, and silken black hair styled to allow tendrils to frame a perfectly heart-shaped face. A polyglot, she stumbled over only a few English words, in an accent with a hint of the BBC, a staple of her childhood. Her mother had insisted. While her peers aped Michael Jackson's songs, she pored over Shakespeare and Austen. After the university, she became a translator, hostess, and English teacher for high-echelon bureaucrats. Everything would have been fine for "Teacher Ruolan" had she not become the object of competitive yearning among four officials, one of whom bought her an engagement ring on impulse; this caused her to be promptly relocated to faraway English-speaking East Africa. Shu had sat before her mother, trembling. "What is Africa?"

She left for Kenya accompanied by what the World Wide Web had suggested to her as necessary Africa travel literature: works by Paul

Theroux, Ryszard Kapuściński, and V. S. Naipaul. In these she found the writings of lucid adventuring solitaries who brandished cutting adjectives, who were unfazed by the aggressive overtures of hostile beings whose guttural cries—as conveyed in the books—suggested the intent to cannibalize. When Shu Ruolan's plane landed at the Jomo Kenyatta International Airport in Nairobi, the first Kenyan customs official she met immediately dismayed her. Not his sable shade, or the brownness of his uneven teeth—that was to be expected. It was his English, handled as if he had grown up frolicking in a gnome-dotted Sussex garden. Immersed as she was in the anthropology of bureaucrats, she recognized a ubiquitous specimen. But eight months later, Shu was on the MV *Qingrui/Guolong*, heading back to China. A high-ranking official with a Shanghai accent had persecuted the embassy into releasing a female to chaperone a young traveler, known as "the Descendant," and instruct her on China basics. Shu was the easiest to sacrifice. She was only just getting comfortable walking through a river of dark-hued bodies, in which she was a minority soul.

Nioreg Marie Ngobila was listed as a passenger. Wide forehead, cleft-chinned, black-marble-toned, with close-cropped hair, a baobab-trunk neck, and a barrel chest, bow-legged, six foot four. This fifty-year-old man, originally from the Democratic Republic of the Congo, carried multiple passports—flags of convenience. He had driven into the port in a large green tropicalized 4x4 with Mozambican license plates, which he abandoned in the parking lot. Few people bothered him: His size. His demeanor. Courteous. Distant. He had been linked to guerrilla squads in Angola; he was now a freelancer loosely attached to a "special services" company. They had assigned him this ship duty, his fourth ocean-based project. Upward glance. The ship was smaller than he had imagined. He hefted a leather barrel bag and a canvas rucksack and headed for the docks, then paused to see, really to take in, the sight of a bird—green, blue, white, and orange—slender, long-beaked, chatting to the world as it scoured for insects. It is the bird that prevented him from running, right then, into the being who would divert the course of his life.

. . .

The first thing that people noticed about Delaksha Tarangini Sudhamsu was the broken trapeze-shaped plum-colored wine stain beneath her left ear. Today, they would also see a blood-streaked bandaged hand. This five-foot-five woman, whose fluffy black hair with five gray streaks now hung as limp strands around her face, wore oversized dark brown sunglasses that were two hues darker than her blotchy skin. They covered the blue-red of a healing right-eye-shutting bruise. "Rubenesque" was how she described her figure on her good days. Twice she had turned around, but then returned. As she approached the harbor master's office, she straightened up, tightened her lips, and burst through the door.

Her clipped English had a lachrymose quality to it that complemented her overly bright, brittle smile. "Good afternoon, my name is Ms. Delaksha Tarangini . . ." Words failed her. She tried again. "I'm trying not to cry," she explained to the suddenly nervous man at the desk. "I was reading a book a few days ago, a South American author . . . Well, he has his character enter a tavern and go up to a tavern keeper and request a *solicitud de asilo*—lovely word—'solicitude,' it evokes protectiveness. So may I bother you and make a request for shelter?" In her mind's eye, a vision of a simple white-sheeted bed, a breeze blowing through wide windows, voices on the street. She added, "I need to go home to my mother." She opened a pouch and showed two passports. "Which one? I beg you, which one will take me back to Kerala?"

The man, bombarded by sound, color, and words he had never heard strung together like that, cleared his throat before speaking in the "Be reasonable," long-suffering manner of old Kenyan bureaucrats. "Now, madame—now, madame—listen, madame, there are procedures we must follow, the rules are . . ."

She wilted before him and blubbered. Her tears made the kohl run down her face, streaking it black. "Please . . . please . . ."

Desperate, the man shuffled papers. Emotion was not his forte. "What can I do? See . . . madame . . . Kerala?" Where was Kerala? Seizing straws: "Madame, if you have . . . do you have fifty-two thousand shillings for a cabin in a cargo ship? China. From China maybe you can . . . uh . . . uh . . . Kerala?"

Delaksha dug into her handbag and drew out all the Kenyan shillings she carried, even the coins. The man counted 74,793 shillings. She said, "If there was more, I'd give it to you. Take it all."

The stupefied man watched her carefully. She had materialized from nothing. She shifted shape. She leaked. She flowed in multiple directions with unexpected consequences for him. He looked at his tabletop, studying his Bic pen. He would fill in the form for her; it would make her go away quickly. "Your hand, madame," he muttered, "is bleeding."

She said, "Yes. I had an epiphany." It was better for him, the man realized too late, not to speak. Delaksha was frowning at her bandaged hand. "Pontius bit me." She told the man. "He's a Doberman-Alsatian."

The man worked extra carefully on Delaksha's form.

"The dog pities me," she told the man.

It was good news, the man understood, that this woman was leaving Kenya. "Kerala?" he asked. "You will be happy there."

"Thank you for saying that. I could kiss you."

"Please, no, madame." He froze, not daring to move lest it encourage her. "Please." He was firm about that. When Delaksha left, he made himself a cup of hot tea.

Apart from Captain Lai Jin and the officer of the watch, there was a first mate and nine other crew members: an able-bodied seaman, and an engineering team led by a barrel of a man. A bland chronicler of this voyage who had been dispatched from Shanghai, wielding a computer and camera, whom the captain had breathed terror into, daring him to interfere with the smooth flow of things, was also on board and assigned crew quarters. Another man who may or may not have been South African, endowed with a rugby forward's protuberant forehead, was second engineer. Two deckhands, and a wizened, tattooed tree-trunk-like Malaysian whose spread of duties included chef and steward, rounded out the souls on board.

Creaking chains, the clunking of solids. Floodlights lit up the hold, and cranes like slender giants presided over the cargo. Much of the ship's cargo was Kenyan tea, and high-quality coffee whose aroma escaped tight seals and roamed portions of the ship, blending with the smell of sea and giving birth to a temporary pungent headiness. A whole section of rust-colored containers contained scrap metal for export.

The captain was an imposing sentry in the dawn when Ayaana approached his ship. Daybreak's light had framed him so that, for a second, he seemed to be half in and half out of existence. Morning crows cawed as Ayaana started across the space that divided her old world from the new. She started to hyperventilate. Inundated by the ship's otherness, bigness, hard corners, steel, and echoes, dwarfed by machinery, some with chains and rims that were the size of large motorcycles, by the tiers of containers, mostly rust-colored, that dominated the view just before the blue ocean. A world of blue-and-white steel, narrow corridors, and small staircases leading to windowless heights. Fire extinguishers, monster ropes, life buoys, life rafts, mysterious things that hummed, bubbled, beeped, groaned, and grunted. Pipes like giant black millipedes leading to and into holes in the wall. Yellow cranes pointing skyward, funnels, and a rotary device that spun around and around before which paused quick-moving men in beige overalls and matching hard hats—the crew, some of whom wielded extra large tools. The ship spat out foaming water from hidden orifices and strained its anchor, anxious to leave with her, and suddenly she felt in her bowels the sense of her own absence from Pate, from Kenya, and from her old self.

Teacher Ruolan had seized Ayaana's elbow then, and in a firm yet reverent tone had said, "*Chuan zhang.*" Then she had shaped Ayaana's body into the proper posture. Teacher enunciated, "Honorable ship leader, Captain Lai Jin."

Ayaana had scrutinized the square-shouldered, sad-aura man with faraway eyes on a face that was a convergence of symmetry, scars, angles, and smoothness set off by close-cropped black hair. He stood in a space that could have been the center of the world. "We are friends from long ago." Soft words collapsing into one another. Ayaana stared. The right side of his face was written out in smoothed welts. Unthinking, she exclaimed, "How did the fire write you?"

Then two strangers' eyes met. His sense of presence was as an avalanche rushing at her, crowding her. Next, dissonance. Fleeting glimpse of time's essence. She deeply felt her clumsiness and a mouth filled with out-of-control words. Even with her eyes closed, she was seared by the memory of this man's no-smile face and his presence, which evoked a desolate, horizonless wasteland. No hills, no crevices, no trees. No end in his look. He seemed exasperated by the proximity of disordered things, which she was. Surfing the silence. Ayaana waited for an interpretation of this, the stillness. The question circled them, and Ayaana's stomach churned. Her palms were wet.

Lai Jin shut his eyes for half a second, breathing in rose, the citrus in rose, the musk in rose, the rawness of rose and its transmuting presence. *What a question*, he thought.

Teacher Ruolan blushed crimson after Ayaana's question. Teacher Ruolan nudged Ayaana, whispering in hard words, "You talk last. Last!" Ayaana bent her head to see her red-painted toes showing at the tips of her new maroon cork-heeled sandals, strapped above the hems of stonewashed jeans, beneath a black *buibui*. No words. If Teacher had not lifted her head, Ayaana would have continued to watch her toe colors merge into the steel of the ship.

Then, from the gangway, lumbering footsteps, shrill laughter. Other voices. A phalanx of men and women in suits. This was Ayaana's official send-off party.

The Kenyan and Chinese bureaucrats lined up for endless photographs with Ayaana. Soon they were caught up in a rhapsody of self-congratulation. The senior Kenyan diplomat gave Ayaana a gift to present to the people of China from the people of Kenya—an ocean-rescued bit of Chinese porcelain, a relic from a just-recovered junk. It was wrapped in "Made in China" red felt and contained in a black-and-gold woodlike box of smooth texture crafted in Makueni. The package would be secured in the ship leader's stateroom.

After the speeches, followed by early-morning ritual libations that went down throats, and caused red spots on some faces, and slurred words on other tongues, Lai Jin retreated. More photographs with

Ayaana. Her veil slipped farther and farther away from her face, the better to allow her escorts to capture the slant of "almond-shaped eyes," the genetic-puzzle single-skin eyelids on dark golden brown skin. A mêlée. More speeches. A mirthful official from the embassy assured Ayaana of the greatness of China. Ayaana thought of six-hundred-year-old dead seamen, who would not have imagined this postscript to the story of their fate.

Another frantic thought. She turned her body toward the gangway. When she might have given in to the impulse to escape, a hand touched her wrist. She gasped.

It was the captain. He shook his head. Then he smiled. Pressure on her wrist; she followed its leading. An alcovelike cranny temporarily separated them from the party. Ayaana clutched the gift with one hand and readjusted her veil with the other. Together they watched the impromptu party fizzle to an end. They waited a minute longer there. Then the man sighed.

"Now," he said.

Ayaana followed the captain out so that they could stand in final ceremony as the bureaucrats wished them a safe journey. The merrymakers disembarked in undulating descent, careful to support one another, and demonstrating proof of the power of cheap champagne to forge loving connections between two uneven countries.

Teacher Ruolan, who had been conferring with her embassy boss, had lost sight of Ayaana. She was scanning the deck when she saw Ayaana emerge with the captain by her side. She hurried to interpose herself between them. After the bureaucrats had gone, she directed Ayaana up steel steps and down a narrow corridor, their footsteps punctuating the steel. They squeezed past a woman whom Ayaana towered over, whose wind-churned hair matched her "Where am I?" pose. The woman's flowing white dress was stained; her eyes were hidden behind extra-large sunglasses. A turquoise necklace with its tigereye pendant hung in her décolletage, beneath which large breasts strained. She was patting an indigo-colored bag as if it were a sentient being; a thin white unlit cigarette hung between her teeth, in spite of the "No Smoking" signs.

Twenty souls left on board MV *Qingrui/Guolong* as she sailed out of Kilindini Harbor, Mombasa, with the mid-morning's high tide, despite big waves and a cool wind that breathed into the harbor's mouth. A harbor pilot escorted them away from Kenya's shores. Other ships sounded farewell horns. The *Dragon of the Nation* foghorned back. At the horizon, the morning star. In international waters, a deckhand lowered the red, green, black, and white Kenyan flag.

[37]

On the first evening aboard the creaking, thrumming, vibrating vessel with its smell of diesel and oil, while the other passengers lumbered into an indifferent mess furnished with a melting plastic object that was supposed to represent a lily, Teacher Ruolan escorted Ayaana into the captain's mess, with its many plaques and pictures of ships. Her emotions darting like a bird unable to perch on anything, Ayaana focused on Teacher Ruolan's hand on her arm. As they sat down, Ayaana stared at a stain on the table that was raised like a wart. Place settings for a single serving: a cup, a bowl on a dish, chopsticks on a holder, a ceramic spoon.

Ayaana glanced at the food at the center.

No one moved until the captain gestured. "Please," he said.

Assailed by the cadences of English, tonal variations she had not ever imagined, Ayaana was suddenly uncertain about her grasp of the language. She started to panic about acquiring another language as well. Listening closely, trying not to miss anything, Ayaana also studied Teacher Ruolan from beneath her thick lashes, observing and envying her gracefulness. The woman turned to attend to Ayaana, showing her the thin black sticks with which she would eat from now on. Ayaana slowly picked up hers, and in so doing somehow managed to drop the ceramic soupspoon. It tumbled to the floor.

Ayaana froze.

Nobody seemed to notice except for Teacher Ruolan, who skewered her with a hard look as she pointed out the food: "Roast-duck noodles with green pepper, century eggs with ginger . . . for you . . ." Ayaana's eyes widened—those black, vile-looking things with green centers emitting unholy fumes were eggs? "Boiled peanuts with soy sauce, cucumber-stick pickles, and, especially for you, honored guest, duck leg."

Ayaana informed herself that, should she give in to the impulse to cry, she would betray her island, and her nation. She was hungry. She studied the meal. Lai Jin thought that describing its meaning would help. He said, "Century eggs—*pidan.* Duck. Prepared for months."

Words. They had the strength to shut doors that would never be opened in this lifetime. Ayaana stared at the eggs, half expecting them to detonate. Lai Jin turned from her to dip his chopsticks into his bowl and in one movement captured a portion of an egg and brought it to his mouth. Ayaana wielded her chopsticks as a pitchfork. Lai Jin watched Ayaana's impending battle with the meal, eyes gleaming. Ayaana glanced at him. Their eyes locked, and for half a moment she was again a little girl on the edge of the mangroves, in awe of homecomers. On childish impulse, she waited for the captain to look away first. He was again surprised by the familiarity of her otherness—complex, balanced, like the scents of pear and wood. Like her cryptic rose scent. He blinked. Was that his mind calling forth fragrances? He grimaced.

Ayaana's hands hovered above the bowl. Her stomach rumbled. She wanted to plow fingers into the bowl to pick out its substance. Ayaana watched Teacher Ruolan's dainty consumption of the duck, her chopsticks working like knitting needles, with not a peep from her mouth: no slurping, not even the sound of chewing. The steward then brought the bowl of steaming dumpling soup with even more noodles. Ayaana despaired. So it was for this that the spoon she had dropped was intended. Ayaana turned to tackle her bowl. She speared a piece of duck and rushed it into her mouth. New textures. Soft. What flavors. She tried with the noodles, but they successfully wriggled away from her chopsticks. Ayaana rested her chopsticks against her plate and watched her soup. She reached for the enemy chopsticks again, aiming them at the vegetables. She tried to use the wooden sticks as mini-shovels. Peanuts, pickles—sweet-sour, hot-cold, bitter-sour reached her mouth in whiffs, not substance. She glowered at the food.

"Perhaps a fork? And, yes, another spoon." The ship leader gestured to the steward. Teacher Ruolan fluttered her pretty eyes at the ship leader, moved by his consideration. In seconds, the cutlery was delivered. Ayaana turned to the captain. "Thank you," she said. Now he held her look, and she was the first to look away. He smiled when he turned to his bowl.

[38]

Zar: The murmuring cry made by djinns at night. Past the engine roar, with the stench of diesel clinging to the nostrils, the straining of metal above and beyond, the creaking shadows, and the toil of unseen men, she heard the warbles from beneath the water. Now, if Ayaana were to carve these in the new language she was being asked to inhabit, it would emerge as "memory": 记忆.

Shu Ruolan was implementing a curriculum to prepare Ayaana for her "auspicious arrival." In forty days, the Descendant should have knowledge of at least fifty characters. That first morning, Teacher Ruolan smiled at Ayaana, her neat teeth showing. "Now I show you."

The ideogram: 非洲.

Sound: *Fei zhou.*

Teacher Ruolan formed 非洲. She broke it down for Ayaana: *Fei:* nothing, wrong, lacking, ugly, not. *Zhou:* being, state, country. Put together: Not Existing. A teensy giggle bubbled forth. "Oh dear." A pause. "We continue." A bold sequence of strokes produced 中国. Zhōngguó. "China!" she exclaimed. "Middle Kingdom. True. Beautiful."

Ayaana watched. Ayaana listened. She imaged "Teacher" in Kipate: *Ujinamizi.* Nightmare. Noun.

Spattering raindrops created small, furious streams in metal furrows: above, the slate-gray sea; below, white-topped waves. Dissipating mist and *Zar:* The sobbing of djinns before dawn. Ship bump and creaks. Footsteps echo. Movement shadows. Used to the life of restless shadows from her island, Ayaana did not react to the ship's inexplicable sounds, or to the strange silhouettes it spawned, which traveled down narrow corridors unaccompanied. Light tread, restless traveling within small spaces. Footsteps below the deck. Ayaana ducked, nervous about being caught. She was supposed to be memorizing new ideograms. She leaned over and saw the ship leader prowling, hands behind his back, eyes on the water. His crew danced in wide circles around him. He never shouted orders. He showed up as an apparition, and left before the certainty of his presence had registered. Ayaana thought about the fire marks on his face. They were like etchings, a message carved into skin. Ayaana backed away from the railing. Walking backward, she slipped down the corridor to her cabin door. She slid it open and disappeared inside.

Ping!

Muhidin's watch.

Ayaana stiffened.

Footsteps receded.

Inscrutable seas. In the morning, the passengers found that the crew had woven coils of razor wire all around the weather deck: a precautionary public performance of a ship's defense against pirates. "Safety Measure" was all the sign said. The passengers were obliged to undertake a fire-and-lifeboats drill that afternoon. When the alarms went off, all souls on board rushed to their meeting point to rehearse survival. They wore bright orange life jackets armed with whistles and lights. Flying fish soared out of the sea, glistening with reflected sunlight, then fell back with small splashes. They distracted Ayaana. Swallows roosted on the containers, to rest before resuming their migratory journeys. Halcyon moments. Disaster was far from Ayaana's mind. Teacher Ruolan and Ayaana were assigned the same lifeboat. They stood close together. A different alarm clanged to prepare them for a "man overboard" exercise. The buxom woman, who was in pink mules, huffed and offered for consideration the phrase "woman overboard." No one paid attention. The instructing crew member recited by rote: "To survive, you must guard each other's lives." The drill ended. The passengers scattered and returned to their private cocoons.

On that second night, after dinner, passengers were told to secure themselves in their rooms for their own safety while "an operational check" was being advanced. No one asked why. They would dutifully wait for the "all clear" alarm. After passengers retreated into their cabins, when the MV *Qingrui/Guolong* had slowed down to virtual stillness, Ayaana listened to the sounds, trying to build a picture of what was happening. She heard the growl of fast engines, muted voices, and the *clung, clung* of items being dragged on board. Above the clamor of the ship's engines, and the creak of its machinery, she also heard the suddenness of human silences. Soon after, she felt the MV *Qingrui/Guolong* recover its previous speed. What was happening? No one spoke. The absence of chatter on board mirrored the solitude of the iceberg captain. His aloofness was reassuring, as if everything were in the hand of an unmoving and unmoved deity.

Now. *Ping!* Ayaana was inside her cabin for the *dhuhr* prayers. She processed her impressions and clung to the robe of God-still-on-Pate. She breathed out the afternoon and her confusion. Head to cabin floor, head on her mother's prayer mat, rubbing her face in the scent of this, its rose scents, and the unresolved thing lurking between them.

When Munira shook Ayaana awake on their last evening together, on Lamu, the night had been on her mother's skin. Munira had hugged her, rocking her. "Become big, *lulu*." Ayaana's fingers had pressed into Munira's skin. Feeling the shame of that Thursday evening. Ayaana then spoke into her mother's ear: "Paint me."

"Now?" Munira had asked.

Ayaana had dragged off her nightshirt, baring breast and back.

Munira had rushed for her henna. She had blended in herbs and added rose attar. It would have to do. She returned to stroke small, intricate patterns on her daughter's body. Munira at last touched those Thursday-evening burn marks for the first time. Tears, as she painted brown lace into her daughter's skin. They had cried together.

Ayaana lifted herself off the mat and touched the mother-made whorls on her skin. These were words. Glancing through a porthole, Ayaana glimpsed the arrival of an impressive flock of small chattering brown-and-white spotted birds, which settled on the ship's cranes, rails, and radar. Visiting flowers. Outside her cabin, a mincing tread like emphatic little commas on a steel sheet. Teacher Ruolan. Ayaana braced herself for a fresh litany of complaints. Recent ones. Ayaana was *too* loud, gestured *too* much. Her *borrowed* eyes often bulged like a frog's. Ayaana frowned. A lady never frowned. Her skin was the color of burned pork. Her man-voice would not help much. Ladies did not emit such pungent smells. She, Ayaana, was undereducated. Teacher said that when her Chinese relatives saw her they would be ashamed. Teacher, clever Teacher, packaged offense in polite questions: "Is it not barbaric to write on skin?" Teacher attempting thoughtfulness: "What kind of soap can freshen your body?" Political Teacher: "The achievements of your country are few and invisible. Are you ashamed?" Teacher the philanthropist: "You are very familiar with hunger?" Teacher the philosopher: "There are *houyi*s and there are *houyi*s." Aesthetics lessons: "Why, you are taller than a man, but not as good-looking." Introduction to the Orient: "When I see you, I think, 'Hundun.' "

Pause. "Hundun. I tell you what it means?" Teacher Ruolan asked. She was smiling. "Okay, I tell you." The word described primordial chaos, she said, a manifestation of disorder arising out of abysmal darkness. "It is a particular madness." Teacher clapped her hands and studied Ayaana's reaction.

Ayaana shrank inside. Her gaze became hunted. An unspoken battle declaration, but Teacher Ruolan had the advantage; she was the bestower of words. Like "Hundun." Ayaana could not unsee words. Picture words. Reforming the silhouettes of her own world. "Prayer," she informed Teacher Ruolan, adjusting her veil to cover her face. She fled her desk to retreat into her cabin to breathe. Teacher Ruolan read about "Africa"—the better to understand Ayaana. Today it was Ryszard Kapuściński: *The Shadow of the Sun*.

. . .

Late lunch gong.

Ayaana stared at the steward's dragon-and-skull tattoos on an exposed upper arm as he delicately laid out dishes for the passengers, who received the food in silence. Steamed fish with rice, a plate of sautéed greens decorated with peppers cut into flower shapes. A fishy broth. Rice: Ayaana's new torment. Naturally, she sighed inwardly, there were rules for eating these as well. Teacher Ruolan: "Eat rice with bowl up, and do not make a noise." Her little nose wrinkled at even the thought of noise. A speck of rice dangled at the end of Ayaana's black chopsticks, waiting for her to try to lead it into her mouth. Halfway there, it escaped.

Teacher huffed. She squeezed Ayaana's fingers into the chopsticks, refusing her cutlery, and slapping her hand when she tried to sneak some food into her mouth with her fingers. "We don't have time," Teacher hissed.

"I need to eat," Ayaana said.

"Learn or starve."

Waves rocked the boat. Captain Lai Jin strolled into the mess. He paused and bowed to the passengers, murmured something to the buxom woman in a neon-green dress. She was still wearing her sunglasses and picking at her plate. The captain glanced over at Ayaana's table. *Chuan zhang*, Ayaana remembered, bargaining with her meal, summoning a pictogram—船长—ship leader, remembering last night. Ayaana had stepped out of her cabin to experience the night sea. When she looked upward, she had glimpsed the captain on his watch, face forward, gaze fixed on the water, body straight and tall and still. The call of the deep: she watched a man whom the sea transmuted.

[39]

From his armchair, Ship Leader Lai Jin folded and refolded a white napkin. On its blankness, he projected a reflection of a blurred image.

Before the girl boarded his ship, he had practiced saying, "We are friends from long ago," as Shanghai Accent had instructed him while communicating the sense of pride, grandeur, and cosmic continuity that was China. It had meant nothing to him. Shanghai Accent had inserted, "This is your duty to history." "We are friends from long ago," Lai Jin had dutifully repeated to himself until he had worked the resentment out.

When the Descendant had approached his ship—shrouded in black, emerging from the gangway as if from hazy memory—her fragrance, a multilayered scent of rose, had reached him before she had. A black-and-silver *buibui* with silver trimmings covered her, molding itself to her body contours. Her half-veiled eyes scanned the world. Her presence: its distance. He noticed the single slim gold bracelet and a clunky man's watch on one wrist. Her other was bare. Both arms were marked with lacelike shapes and lines that gleamed red, brown, and orange under light. He thought of the *xi geng qiang wei*—slender stalked rose nurtured by secret solitudes. Then she had stopped before him. She reached his chin. He had stooped and forgotten to speak. He had sought out eyes framed by black cloth, and though he had been prepared, he was startled to find China's gaze tilted back at him. There was an enigmatic wistfulness written in her pale brown eyes; this surged toward him like a wave, before eddying back. He looked at her for four seconds too long, and a distant gong went off. He had wanted to exclaim, *What are you?* Then he remembered to declare in haste, "We are friends from long ago."

Her gaze had lingered on the scarred portion of his face, which others pretended not to see. Her mouth opened. He had to blink twice to hear her question: "How did the fire write you?" Before he could reply, she had remembered where she was. Had remembered they were strangers. A dark flush stained her skin. Her fingers fluttered, and she bent her head. She stuttered something, and then a weighted silence waylaid them. He had at once told himself she was the most foreign object he had ever encountered. To have to engage her in English he was not certain he still had full control over amplified their distance. He had shifted, now critical. She was far too slender, too much a drooping branch on a weeping willow, an unfinished twig.

She did not matter. He had angled his neck as if to dismiss her presence. But then the wind had caused her veil to slide off her face, and he had been transfixed by a translucent, unmarred visage, with high cheekbones, a pointed chin, thick, curled lashes, a pert nose, full lips on a small mouth, creating a bud, a perfect set of teeth, and warm-toned, golden brown skin.

Later, from a niche that had kept him safe from merrymaking bureaucrats, he had watched her turn this way and that from officials, as if she were a snared deer. He recognized the second when her body tilted toward escape. Unthinking, he had stepped out to reach for her and brought her into his hiding place. From there, they watched civil servants in full frolic, and he heard her beating heart. He felt his cohere with the rhythm of hers. And he was suffused with scents of other worlds, of a youthful femininity he had not often thought about, of sudden fear, because, in spite of his choices, and his ascetic dedication to a liturgy of the seas, she fascinated him. It would not take them long to reach Xiamen, he had reassured himself then, and he reassured himself now.

A clatter of plates. Lai Jin started as the steward set out his meal. The food was the same as the other passengers' but in larger portions. He transferred his gaze to the broth and noted its color and density, pulling himself together.

~

The night djinns sobbed. Prickling of spine hair. Spot of heat on her back. Shadow in the shape of a person using light borrowed from the dark night's shimmer. She did not turn to look. Lai Jin leaned against the guardrail. They listened to the sea. That shrouded moon.

He had heard her weeping.

He said, "*Ni hao*"—Hello. To his surprise, it emerged as a longing-laden whisper, not the lighthearted teasing he had intended.

She remained silent.

He watched the sea with her. The things they shared: pretense of choice, its illusory veneer of celebration, human will set against fate's forces, and role-playing. She a fate-commandeered girl ambassador, moving as she was told to; he ship leader of a commandeered voyage. *Ni shi shei?* the ocean asked.

Later that night, in his stark stateroom, Lai Jin dreamed of fire. He woke up. He switched on a lamp, and used its light to look at his Zao Wou-Ki, seeing oranges, rust, and red ink—blood colors. He did not return to sleep.

[40]

Thump! Thump! Thump! Tra-ta-ta! The sound of automatic weapons split the 2:00 a.m. sea. Lai Jin had just folded himself under the sheets in his bunk when the chief officer on navigation watch pounded on his door. Lai Jin leapt out of his bunk, threw on a shirt, and pulled on trousers as he sped out, asking, "How many?"

"Eight, sir."

The fire hoses were already hooked up and shooting over the sides, and lights blazed on board. The crew's two-way radios cackled, hissed, and sputtered strategies and secrets. Though, in moments like these, everything did become clear and defined, and Lai Jin even heard the drip of water in an open faucet in some cabin, and his body was open and ready and unafraid. *Eight pirate speedboats.* He did not mind; he was indifferent to dying or living. But he was now responsible for other lives. Irritation. Lai Jin had not been expecting an attack, certainly not in the time of the southerly monsoon.

Boom!

Lai Jin suspected a rocket-propelled grenade. But the ship was prepared. His crew knew the drill. Some of them would have roused all passengers and guided them to the below-deck passage into a safe room. Another set would implement the ship's other arrangements.

. . .

Shouts and pounding outside her cabin door. Ayaana woke up from a dream in which she had been running after the poet and mystic Rabi'a. She stumbled to the door, a bedsheet wrapped around her body, but when she slid it open she did not recognize the shouting man on the other side. He grabbed her wrist, saying, "Emergency! Come with me now." Ayaana heard foghorns, a loudspeaker, a woman somewhere saying, "Oh, for fuck's sake." With a clumsy lurch, sweating, bewildered Ayaana allowed herself to be dragged in the direction of the ship's engine rooms. Numb. Barefoot. She stubbed her small toe on something and cried out. "Hurry, miss," was all the man said.

Dark green metal door. Hole in the steel wall, weak lights within. Crouching, Ayaana entered. She felt the blood on her foot. Buttons and lights from equipment blinked on and off in the long room. Shelves laden with food, water, first-aid items, more blankets. As three crew members prepared to drag the thick steel door shut, a full-figured woman tumbled in. The men triple-bolted the lock.

Trembling, the woman Delaksha looked around the room. She was in a knee-length glittering black body-fitting nightgown, a fashionably oversized silk Pink Camellia dressing gown, and incongruous peep-toe heels. The white bandage around her hand looked like a fashion accessory. There were tears on her face. In the turmoil of the rush for safety, Delaksha had been rooted to the spot by the vision of a man apart—visible, it seemed, only to her. Detached from the chaos, he had crouched as might an old, giant boulder in a blustery river. A rifle rested by his foot. It wasn't the surprise of this or his camouflage-pattern bulletproof vest that caused Delaksha to gasp; it was the sight of a small fluttering bird in his hand, over which he chirped in tenderness. She spied on him. He might have seen her, for he shut his door at once. But in that moment, all her dread subsided. Just then, another set of humans rushing for the safe room pulled her along with them.

. . .

A young voice spoke to her: "Don't be afraid."

Whiff of jasmine mixed with rose. Delaksha turned her neck to look, nose to Ayaana's skin. She found and clasped Ayaana's hand. In a half-sob she whispered, "A giant just kissed a little broken birdling."

Ayaana held her hand. Touch, like the soul, cannot lie. It is an anchor in uncertainty, like some of the sounds that words make: Giant. Kiss. Birdling. Ayaana waited. Delaksha wiped her eyes. To Ayaana: "Sit with me, you lovely creature."

Ayaana moved.

Teacher Ruolan sat on the other side of Delaksha in a red nightgown, lips slightly parted on a pale, powdered face. Ayaana clutched her bedsheet, aching for her mother, Muhidin, and Pate with such vehemence she almost vomited. Her blood-sticky toe throbbed.

"My name is Delaksha Tarangini," the woman told Ayaana, "and this must be Miz Rio Lin—sounds Brazilian. You two are as thick as baobabs, aren't you? Your heads always in a huddle." She reached for Ayaana's hand.

Touch. It anesthetized the fear, distracted them from the thumps coming from the outside world. Time disappeared.

Ayaana's voice was soft. "What's happening?"

"Pirates, probably," Delaksha said.

"They kill?" Shu Ruolan asked.

Delaksha adjusted her nightgown. She started to braid Ayaana's hair as she mused: "We have too much to *try* to do . . . right? Would be wrong to exit the world now. It is necessary to *demand* good things of life. I have informed God . . . Am I talking too much? Always do when I'm nervous, ha-ha. What a kerfuffle. Would make a Carthusian scream. Terribly exciting, horribly frightening. The pirates—they don't *want* to kill hostages, just require them as fund-raisers. Very corporate." Delaksha's voice faltered. She imagined her husband being contacted for her ransom. He would pay only so that he could emerge as a hero, complete with photographs. "I'd rather die," Delaksha said to herself.

Ayaana turned to Delaksha, whose thoughts had flitted in the direction of the giant she had seen. Such a presence did not suffer terrors. She could believe in him. He had saved a bird from its fears. Delaksha lifted her face to sniff Ayaana's shoulder. Her scent. "Gulab Jal?"

"What?"

"Who is the scent by?"

"My mother." Ayaana needed to say the name, use it as a talisman. "Munira." Relief. Mother as talisman.

"Must get some for myself. Why're you going to China?"

"Study," answered Ayaana.

"Fascinating."

Teacher Ruolan rubbed her nose and eyes.

The interminable jabbering of this *zhutou*, the sow, was squeezing her skull. Teacher Ruolan ached for decorum, delicacy, and harmony. She longed for order. She ached for her home, her two Siamese cats, the firmness of earth, and her mother. Wouldn't this woman just stop talking? She adjusted herself to jab an elbow into Delaksha, as if in error, and murmured a fake apology. She jabbed Delaksha again. The ship lurched.

"The proverbial tight spot, heh-heh, isn't it?" Delaksha shifted. "Life and people shouldn't be forced into small holes. But here we are. Dying would be a bore. I'd be very cross. Death should be elegant; don't you think?"

Shu Ruolan had to ask, even though it wounded her to direct the question to Delaksha: "Do they hurt women?"

Delaksha tilted her head. "Hadn't thought of *that*." She turned to Ayaana. "S'pose you know 'bout the itty-bits of life, dear—birds, bees, and other beasts? You are Muslim. Ought to help. They don't rape Muslims . . . unless you are the wrong kind of Muslim"—she peered into Ayaana's face—"which you may be, poor dear. Stay close to me. I wore my Louboutins. Sturdy creatures. They will be good for at least four broken pirate balls."

A fresh wave of fear; its pungent stench. The ghosts of things undone. Delaksha touched Ayaana's hair. "How do you say your name?"

Ayaana wanted to say "Abeerah." Here she could be the other Ayaana. A pause. "Ayaana. Abeerah," she said.

Delaksha said, "I *loove* your voice. Makes one invoke traveling and coffee. Oh, stop! Don't cry. We *shall not* be harmed. I have told God that I shall not die here. And neither will you. I intend to die in my bed: satin sheets, and very warm. What do you think? God is *such* a gentleman. He *has* to keep his end of the deal." Delaksha stretched her legs out, flexing her toes. "Do you like my shoes?" A cracking sound from stressed joints.

Suddenly Ayaana began to giggle.

Delaksha turned to her. "Hysteria, darling, is really *not* healthy at a time like this."

Ayaana tried to stop, but she sputtered, and more laughter spilled out. So *this* was life? At first, Teacher Ruolan ground her teeth, an audible sound. Then her rage dissipated as she heard Ayaana's high, ringing laugh, which was as young and fresh as September rain. A smile appeared on Teacher Ruolan's mouth. Ayaana saw it. Both women's eyes widened. A glimmer of warmth passed from one to the other. The moment lingered, then dissipated. Teacher Ruolan retreated into herself, remembering to sulk. She frowned. She would have to have a word with the ship leader about unruly passengers—she speared Delaksha with a look—a bad egg who could influence an already complicated assignment with the rather dense Descendant. Destruction in this Western Ocean? She shuddered. Destiny as mirror—a poetic ending. Please, no. She turned to focus on the attending two-man crew, who were watching the safe-room door as if expecting an alien to materialize.

The last time the MV *Qingrui/Guolong* had been swarmed, off the Bab al-Mandab Strait, an Iranian missile frigate had responded to the ship's distress call. When it showed up, alarms blaring and guns showing, the pirates had withdrawn. It had been a good-humored stand-down. Whooping, shrieks, and amused insults: "*Nabadgelyo, safar wanaagsan*"—Farewell, travel well. A promise to meet again, God willing. Lai Jin could not publicly admit his admiration for the men who had redefined the world's maritime rules, and whose boldness had brought back adventure to these waters. The courage of seemingly small men who were able to cause all the world's great navies to scramble around the Indian Ocean hoping to stop them. Lai Jin had stood at the rail in subtle salute to the sea rogues in their small, fast boats, watched their frothy water trail, and wondered, for a moment, what it would be like to be one of them.

Now.

Game on.

Like jogging along a precipice. God willing. Or not. Captain Lai Jin had, of course, officially "not seen" any of the weaponry his second engineer and team had hauled in and assembled on board. The night when the chief officer reduced the ship's speed to "allow an engine check," a skulking dark green speedboat was able to catch up with the cargo ship. On board, and off the record, was a four-man crew, whose baggage included rocket-propelled grenades and automatic rifles. The ship's crew operated as the pirates did—out of jurisdiction, disguised, armed, and sailing under false pretenses. The crew were occasional fishermen, one of them an avid sports fisherman who had netted a record-sized marlin off the Pemba Channel. The men stood rigid before the second engineer, who was the most public senior face of a private security company that had focused its services on Indian Ocean maritime needs, made lucrative by pirates, whose well-being and growth he prayed for every day and night. Pirates had made all of them very wealthy.

The passenger Nioreg Marie Ngobila was linked to the same outfit through offshore companies, but was loaned to the ship courtesy of an older, longer-established band of brother soldiers who sought or created wars for the pleasure of battle and for cash or kind. "Kind" now included crude-laden oil tankers, mining concessions, and shares in Fortune 500 companies.

If such a matter should ever come to hazy public light, captains like Lai Jin could legitimately deny any knowledge of the *actual* existence of security people aboard their ships.

Code yellow.

Lai Jin sounded the foghorn, increased his speed to 20.2 knots, and radioed ships in the vicinity about the "threat of pirate attack." The pursuing speedboats were on his tail, moving at almost 27 knots. *Code yellow.* The air crackled. A sardonic thought struck Lai Jin: Admiral Zheng He would approve. Show strength. Give room to the human inclination for self-preservation. Say little. Choose harmony. Lai Jin blinked. An image wafted into his mind, like the scent of night jasmine—the Descendant.

Sudden irritation. He was being *obliged* to succeed. He was now *forced* to act, by fate, pirates, and stupid bureaucrats. Choicelessness. In danger, with danger, through danger, life was fluid, clear, and tangible. He preferred spending his life with ghost memories and companion shadows. Lai Jin loved his sea as a recluse loved his hermitage. Stripped bare-to-minimum rules, single-hearted focus, simplicity; but life on the sea was subject to mystery, and, because he was captain, he chose the way. He was king of a crag. His life had felt so well defined. Blood flooded the surface of his skin. He was remembering Shanghai Accent and the rose-scented consequences of his whims. After this voyage, he promised himself, he would find another path—something that further limited his interactions with people.

Thump!

The on-board RPG lit up the night. A round of ammunition battled the noise of sea waves, scattering fire into the darkness like giant deadly fireflies. *Thump!* The eight pursuing boats slowed down, accompanied by a flurry of shouts. Insults? Then the first boat spun around, away from the ship, followed by the others. There was no laughter that night, no mock farewell. Apart from the waves and the creatures of darkness, everything turned rather quiet. Outside, a deep-violet sky, a smattering of stars. Lai Jin watched these from his bridge. Feeling the pulse and flow of the ocean's current, like a giant serpent beneath his feet. Feeling this other hunger-desire of his: an ache to be possessed by this wilder face of life, this ravenous friend who pushed him out of commonplace shadows. Lai Jin increased his ship's speed, but then eased back. He had lost the pirates. By the time the ship was back on course, the weapons and accessories, such as night goggles, that had been on display had disappeared from sight. The men would also retrieve rocket-propelled grappling hooks and ladders, evidence of the pirates' attempt to board. The evidence would end up, with the weapons, at the bottom of the deep blue sea. Less paperwork. When they reached the Gulf of Aden, they could depend on the protection of any one of the many world navies that continuously lurked there.

Word would pass to the pirate mother ship, and then up and down other pirate groups, that the *Qingrui/Guolong* was armed. The MV *Qingrui/Guolong* would not be bothered again. Lai Jin assumed an air of normalcy.

His passengers! Lai Jin grunted. "*Chengke.*" He made the command to proceed sound offensive. His chief officer flinched as he took the helm.

Captain Lai Jin descended to the deck to consult with the gathered crew. Half an hour later, the occupants of the safe room heard a knock in code on the steel door. The crew unhinged and dragged the steel door aside. Bright lights drenched the ship. The exiting passengers rubbed their eyes, hands shading their faces, as Captain Lai Jin apologized for inconveniencing them. He said they had needed to assess an uncertain situation lest it risk the passengers' safety. Thankfully a false alarm, he added.

Teacher Ruolan observed the stateliness of the ship leader, his harmonious strength and cultivated manners. She admired unobtrusive leadership, a sign of inner courage. Just then, Delaksha, who was pressing her groin with her fist, announced, "I must pee-pee." Teacher Ruolan glowered at this unsalvageable barbarian.

Buzzing in Ayaana's ears, throb of foot, an uncommon high. She looked back at the safe room. It had shattered boundaries. The wind grabbed her curls and wrapped them around her face, and her sheet floated around her body. Firm hand at her elbow: Teacher Ruolan. Ayaana turned toward the sea, wanting to see the world anew. Captain Lai Jin's look got in her way. He held her look. The world divided: their world, the others' world. His eyes stopped on her hennaed left arm. She retracted it as if touched. He said something. She did not understand. Teacher Ruolan dragged her forward. Uneven steps. Ayaana stumbled into her cabin, pulling her arm away from Teacher Ruolan.

[41]

Echoes of images from last night's mercurial world: a shattering of existential guarantees. There was a short woman of many curves and many words, there was her teacher's smile; there was a captain with his question-in-the-eyes look. She had sat in a steel room waiting to know if she might live or die. Ayaana sat on her bed, head on her knees. When she started awake, the ocean was still murmuring, *Ni shi shei?* She crawled into her bunk to try to sleep.

. . .

Last night's happening had reduced the passengers' reserve toward one another. They chatted together around the breakfast table, with dim sum, and green tea in glasses, savoring food born from a makeshift steward's blend of experiences, as they all expressed doubt at the captain's denials.

"I know what I saw," declared Delaksha.

Ayaana listened, fascinated by how Delaksha oozed into spaces, places, and others' opinions. Shu Ruolan had tried to say that it was better to believe the ship leader for the sake of harmony. Delaksha replied, "Capital Bull and Shit." That was when the bulk of Nioreg filled the entrance. He sauntered in and sat at his usual brown table for two facing the entrance. As he adjusted his body to the too-small chair, he tucked a napkin into his blue-black Mobutu shirt. The steward brought him his breakfast tray.

Delaksha had stopped mid-flow. She was silent. Her spoon hovered above her plate. Then her fingers tapped a tattoo on the table. She inhaled before she swiveled to stare directly at Nioreg. "Come and sit with us," she said.

Nioreg looked toward the door. Delaksha said, "You weren't with us in the safe room last night."

"*Non*," he said without turning his head.

"Exempted from the drill?"

"I prefer sleep." Nioreg chewed his food.

"With all the noise?"

Nioreg popped a dim sum into his mouth. Delaksha sniffed her aromatic green tea. Sensing a tempest brewing, trying to distract her, Ayaana told Delaksha, "I like your dress." It was a silky mauve floral-print dress with an orchid motif. But Delaksha's mouth puckered as if she were about to cry. She gave Ayaana a look of such emptiness that Ayaana gasped. Delaksha turned to Nioreg, her voice urgent. "I saw you."

No reply.

Teacher Ruolan then pushed back from the table and tilted her head meaningfully at Ayaana, who leapt from her seat, scrubbing her mouth. Ayaana set off, her limp noticeable. She crossed the threshold, into a view of the dark blue sea, dark blue clouds, waves that were rounded smooth and filled up, not breaking. Ayaana's heart eased.

"How is the wee bird?" she heard Delaksha demand of her prey. "Answer me that at least."

"*Non*," replied the man.

That night, after the passengers and crew had consumed portions of snow peas and garlic, chicken in soy sauce, and stir-fried beef with spring onions, and savored conversations and sweet-and-sour after-dinner intimacies, the morning squall brewed and stirred by Delaksha broke. Captain Lai Jin, whose presence might have prevented the detonation, was absent.

"What kind of bird is it?" Delaksha called to Nioreg, her voice shrill. Nioreg stared unmoving at his water glass. "Just tell me the name of the bird you saved," she insisted.

The others looked from Nioreg to Delaksha and wondered, *Bird?* Nioreg pushed back his chair and stood up. He threw down his napkin and gave them all a curt nod. Delaksha reared up and moved to block his way. "You will talk to me."

They stood at the door as if carved from the floor, uneven-sized pugilists, scowling at each other. Nioreg moved close. Delaksha stood strong. Nioreg lowered his head. He tilted Delaksha toward him, his hand on the back of her neck, her feet off the floor. Nioreg kissed her on her mouth. One, two, three . . . nine seconds. He returned her to the ground. Smoothed her hair. Bowed. Stepped to her right and walked out of the mess.

Delaksha froze. Then hand to mouth. Hair strands floating. Tears. Mucus slid down her hands. Melting from within. Ayaana watched, discomposed. She turned to Teacher Ruolan, who, seeing her look, poked at her fish, then glanced at the woman in her sheath lemon dress sobbing alone at the door. "*Chi doufu*," she muttered.

No one else spoke.

The passengers and crew left the mess, tiptoeing around Delaksha. Ayaana hovered, fingers fluttering. When it was her turn to leave, her steps were slow. She touched Delaksha's arm on her way out.

[42]

Steam shower. The henna lines her mother had painted into Ayaana's body were beginning to fade. Ayaana touched flesh, its softness, and bones—her scrawniness. Touched her mouth, wondered what lips meant to a body: *to taste being?* The fluttering thing, the confused thing, the stuttering yearning thing inside a woman's life. She returned to her room, changed into nightclothes. Lay on the bed, her hands beneath her head. She turned and glimpsed the niche her suitcase was latched into. She got up to drag it down.

Ayaana found Delaksha leaning against a wall, staring at the sea, hugging her body. She went and stood near her. "Henna?" Ayaana asked. "I can do it for you here."

Delaksha turned to her. "I *know* what I saw."

Ayaana then gave her a small dark brown bottle half full of rose attar. Shyly: "Please, take it."

"Your mother's?"

Ayaana nodded as she knelt down. She started to spread out the basics: a plastic-looking bag shaped like a cone; yogurt-textured green paste, black in the silver evening light.

Delaksha crouched next to her. "Honey, I couldn't."

Ayaana looked at her. "Keep it." She laid out her henna kit. "Sit," she said, surprised by how lucid her voice was.

Delaksha sat down in front of her. Ayaana sat cross-legged. This was her first practice without having her mother nearby. "I start with your feet." She tapped Delaksha's foot. Delaksha shifted. Ayaana tugged off the black heels and settled the right foot on her own thigh. "The stem of a vine," Ayaana said, using the henna paste in a thin cone to draw a finger line on the ankle. "Jasmine petals. First I wipe your feet. Mother's *halwaridi*." They settled into silence, and the scent of wild roses suffused the space for a moment, overwhelming the smell of oil and diesel.

Almost two hours later, Nioreg appeared, white shirt flapping, half swallowed by the night. Stillness. Waves, wind, lusterless quarter-moon in a black sky. He cleared his throat. "Miss. I allowed myself to be provoked. I am sorry. I beg your forgiveness."

Women's silence—a capacity to be and act as if nothing has been said or heard. Ayaana colored in whorls on the vine that circumnavigated Delaksha's feet like a dervish dance weaving a spell; in that possessed, cramped corner of the cargo ship, its fulcrum was ocean, wind, and Ayaana's hands.

Nioreg waited, his head bent.

Delaksha smiled.

Ayaana saw the smile and wondered. She then leaned forward to blow on both Delaksha's ankles. "Don't move. Let it dry," she whispered.

Delaksha said, "Oh, honey. Oh, *honey*." She meant "thank you."

Ayaana gathered her things.

"I *am* sorry," Nioreg repeated.

"Are you? *I* am not," Delaksha replied.

White froth on the sea's surface. Sea drops spattered them, a sprinkling of cold. Nioreg's low, rumbling pitch: "Ortolan bunting. *Hortulanus*."

Delaksha asked, "Otto who?"

"The bird," Nioreg said. "Ortolan bunting." Quiet. "Must have bolted from someone's net." Tense body stance, as if suppressing fury. "Lost its bearings." Silence. "She found us." A soft, cool wind wafted over them. An unseen creature's screech sawed into the night, then faded out. Delaksha got up, shook her cramped legs. She interlaced her fingers and raised her arms above her head, palms facing upward. "Storm in a few days," Nioreg said, watching the dim light glance off the woman's bare feet.

She asked, "How can you tell?"

"Wind on waves."

She smirked. "Sooo . . . weapons are now allowed aboard freighters?" Nioreg gave her a death stare. Delaksha blinked. "The truth, dear, can help me unsee everything . . . except for the Otto-thing bird."

Ayaana, who had been sidling away, faltered. She was curious about the crackling atmosphere as Nioreg and Delaksha circled each other.

The tension grew.

Nioreg submitted, "I work in security."

"For the ship?"

"That, too."

Delaksha then said, "Thank you."

"For what?" he asked.

"The truth."

Nioreg corrected her. "*A* truth."

"It suffices," Delaksha said.

"I can rely on your discretion, miss?"

"Naturally. And . . . Delaksha. My name."

A curt nod. "Then *bonsoir*."

"No, not yet," Delaksha said quickly. "Thank you for saving the birdling." Nioreg frowned. She explained. "Your look . . . that touch. Wanted it for myself. I *ached* to be the bird in your hands."

Stupefied, Nioreg said, "I must go."

Delaksha at once leaned over to slip her hand into Nioreg's. She swung their intertwined hands. Nioreg was wary. Flight- or fight-ready.

She flows, Ayaana observed, her eyes large. *She pours into life. She flows through every "no" and makes it her "yes."*

Delaksha said, "I'm married."

"I apologize again," Nioreg answered.

She continued, not sure about her desperate sense of urgency, as if she had to speak, as if she were the small bird in a big man's gentle hands. "However, I've run away from home."

"I see." A tiny smile, eyes transfixed by their clasped hands.

She said, "You don't. Not yet. The dog bit me." She turned their joint hands to show her bruise. "I'm that cliché spouse who keeps 'running into doors, windows, and other hard objects' . . . until the dog bit me. His name is Pontius. The dog, I mean."

Nioreg waited.

She said, "Heard it."

"What?"

"Your thunder. Sensation in soul, dread before an assault." Nioreg's hands closed over Delaksha's. Experimentation. She said, "I'm shuffling words. Truth is, I'm embarrassed about a truth."

"Which?"

"My sadness."

Quiet.

He was inundated. Transfixed by this tangled yarn. How did he get cast into Delaksha's skein of messy veracity? He was as vigilant as a besieged sentinel. She frowned. Ocean swells. A temporary red hue stained the night skies. A spot of light was the only lingering memory of a day that had disappeared. She asked, "You married?"

"Long ago."

"What happened?"

Nioreg stiffened.

"You can tell me now, or tell me later, but you *will* tell me."

Hoping to silence her, grasping for lies, tempted to lose his masks, he almost laughed. He would scare her. "All dead when I found them." He waited for her reaction.

She looked back at him. "Them?"

"Wife, four children—three sons, little girl, Annick . . ." He stopped.

Delaksha burrowed her face into Nioreg's arm. Eyes wet. A muffled "You poor, poor man. You poor, lovely man. What, for fuck's sake, happened?"

"War." Puzzled. "Poor"? "Lovely"? "The twenty-first century battle frontiers now include homes and dining rooms." Stiffening. Clambering for control. "Excuse me, madame."

She sighed. "You brave soul. What a horrible, horrible thing to experience."

And, for the first time since that night of horror, he remembered the stench and the death of grief. It had been a different season. Returning the veil over memory. Returning to amnesia. The ocean, its surging. This woman, her madness. A school of small fish leapt in synchrony out of the water. The waves called, the wind responded. He needed to escape.

"Good night."

Delaksha said, "If the storm kills this ship, we'll be the ones that others come home to and find dead, new immigrants in the never-go-back-again kingdom."

Hard silence. "It is getting late. Now I must go and rest."

Her voice was gentle. "You are a soldier."

"Yes."

"Because of what happened to them?"

Nioreg shut his eyes. "Became a different soldier."

Splash in the water—something anonymous and large. Then Delaksha said, "Ask me anything." Pause. "Ask me about beginnings."

"Why?"

"This is one."

"What?"

"Beginning."

"Yes?"

"Us."

"Us?"

"Yes."

"C'est une chose à laquelle je n'avais pas pensé."

"You think too much."

"Yes."

" 'Us' is unthinkable."

"Us?" Bemused.

"Yes."

"What is 'us'?"

"Woman, man, curiosity . . . desire. So ask me about beginnings."

"*D'accord.* How did you meet your husband?"

She groaned. "Why him?"

"Phantoms are interesting. He is handsome, no doubt?"

"Rather."

Delaksha had nicknamed him "The Adversary," as a joke, when they met in the cloisters of the Social Sciences Division at Oxford University in England, and loathed each other at first hearing during a debate on "Usury and Third World Debt." One late-spring evening, in a shared tutorial, they found each other again, and immediately took up opposite positions in a discussion of "Fiduciary Stewardship and the World Bank."After the session, they had continued their snarling down streets, and into a discreet restaurant, where they ate, argued, drank wine, argued about who should settle the bill—until they were politely ushered out by management. They had carried on their argument into Delaksha's dodgy rented digs, where, mildly drunk, they agreed that they both intended to change the world, but differently. The argument turned to methodology, doctrine, and a frenzied stripping of clothes, a ferocious mating.

Delaksha told Nioreg, "A malignant magnetism." She made a face. "With flowing black curly hair, thick red lips, an intricate mind, and Kama Sutra lusciousness, I wielded a deft upper hand." She laughed. "So I thought. We got married a year later, in Grisons. A civil ceremony conducted in Romansh, witnessed by bored Swiss strangers."

"Felicitations," drawled Nioreg.

"Fuck you," replied Delaksha.

Titters.

A rumble like thunder followed by a streak of bright-purple light in remote skies. Another rumble. Delaksha shuddered.

"Work took us to Kenya. Supposed to be for a year." The wind on the water. "But we fit. The husband, the country, and I. I had the children there. They also fit." The wind whipped Delaksha's hair around her face. *Why am I blabbing so much?*

"Is it true," Delaksha asked Nioreg, the stranger-confessor, "that there are bats that can suck your blood as you sleep, and all you might feel of the draining is a sweet-sweetness, and only when you wake up do you realize how grievously mutilated you are?"

They shivered. Delaksha murmured, "We adapt, you see."

In Nioreg's head, a sudden headache-giving hammering. Listening in spite of his inner terror. *What am I letting myself be dragged into?*

Delaksha's mind dipped into her past: when she had flitted from person to person in a large, well-lit room with chattering fervor. That night, a harassed-looking woman whose lipstick had run onto her neck had grabbed Delaksha by the arm and croaked, "What is your secret? Tell me how to be happy." The question had almost dissolved the gilded pressure cooker in which Delaksha lived. Steel-willed, she had kissed the woman's cheek before swirling away, her dark blue gown rustling and glinting in the light. Now Delaksha moved away from Nioreg and reached for the guardrail.

Ayaana's openmouthed paralysis, her intense listening and a new fear of life, its mysteries, and how it lived in a woman. Delaksha spoke to the darkness. "Gross protoplasmic suckiness consuming every good as it shrouds itself with a veil of lofty worthiness. It makes itself the 'Author of Right,' to preside over others' life and death." Tears reached Delaksha's jaw. She bit her nails. "Imagine *needing* to screw that." Delaksha swung toward Nioreg. She pounded the rails. She wiped her face.

Nioreg watched the woman's uneven silhouette shift inside the empyrean rose-colored foreshadowing of dawn, or was it a retrospective? The wind grabbed her hair and tossed it around. She was maskless. *Et ecce mulier.* A sigh. He felt the breaking of his mask. Not because of this odd woman exposing her naked soul to him, but because he was quite suddenly weary of the human games in life. Nioreg rubbed an area that chafed within his chest. *Cela aussi passera.* Waves slapped the side of their ship, keeping time, dipping him into memories of the women in his life. Waves and the chorus of sea creatures, the ship in movement, and in the shadows, thinking she was unseen, the young Kenyan girl now as enmeshed as he was by the wild rubric that was a mystifying woman's life. Falling out of time. It was a dark and sultry night; the perfect setting for fallen and falling creatures to meet.

Delaksha leaned over the rails, and then Nioreg was reaching for her, imagining himself as a hero preventing a death rather than delivering it. But she was merely angling for a better view of the ship's frothy wake. His arms were hard around her body, and she tilted her head up at him.

"I'm your bird." She laughed, and then she asked, "Share with me a cigar."

Nioreg raised a brow. He suddenly shook his head. He rocked back and forth, prelude to a huge, soundless laugh. His sides ached. *Who is she?*

Delaksha retreated to retrieve portions of her story. "Nothing can purge the core where horror broods. Do you understand?"

Nioreg grunted, "I do."

"My children are ashamed of me," Delaksha added. "So I left." She watched Nioreg, expecting judgment. Nothing. Her children had been unimpressed by her drunken tottering, extravagant, and loud proclamations. Delaksha said, "Now I'm going home to Mummy." A dry laugh. A thought: *I'll walk to the place where the waters end.* Where had she read that? Her lips trembled. "She will be most surprised to see her prodigal return."

Ayaana imbibing words, hearing resonances of her poet guides—Hafiz, Rabi'a—seeing herself looking out into the world, prayerless. Ayaana saw Delaksha's words, her story pieces, codes, gestures, lines, silences, as clues in an emerging map of life. Ayaana watched two battle-worn humans reach for each other, their look naked, and so horribly raw that she had to turn away, but not before she saw space adjust itself to contain them. Nioreg had lifted Delaksha's hands to the dim light. The stone in her wedding ring glittered.

Nioreg touched the ring. "What's your hope?" he asked Delaksha.

"Deliverance."

"How?"

"Via purgatory. I need fire."

Nioreg stroked the swollen part of her hand. "Limbo is better." He blew on her painful hand. "No expectations." She winced. "This husband—if you desire, I'll return for him." Nioreg stooped to taste Delaksha's mouth.

She asked, "And pain will dissolve?"

"It can be balanced, no?"

"Ah, my dear." She pulled down Nioreg's face to hers. "It is 'delete' and 'restart' I desire."

Nioreg nodded. He took her hand to pull off her ring. Delaksha's fingers curled ever so lightly before she stretched out her fingers again. When he had the ring in his hand, he dropped it into her hand.

Ayaana watched Delaksha turn toward the sea to hurl her ring into it. They all watched it rise and fall. Stillness.

Nioreg engulfed Delaksha.

Nioreg said, "Your ortolan bunting . . ."

"Yes?"

"It is pursued by demons, too."

"What?"

"French chefs, for example."

"Tell me." A laugh and a catch in Delaksha's voice.

Ayaana would next hear about a sumptuous songbird—a chatty bird with orange, brown, gray, and olive feathers whose journeys into Africa got hijacked by men who raised nets on behalf of a cult of chefs who sought to imprison this little bird and store it in a blackened cage. She heard how some of these villains plucked out the bird's eyes so it would perceive an endless night, which would provoke it to eat even more. Ayaana then heard how the bird would be force-fed until it was ready to burst. This was the signal that it was ready for drowning alive in a vat of Armagnac. After it was killed, it was plucked, roasted, and served whole, with its bones intact. The bird would be gobbled down by one of a select group of gluttons, who would cover their heads with a white cloth, the better to absorb aromas arising from the spiced and liquored suffering of a small creature, the easier to evade the gaze of disgusted holy angels.

Ayaana bit into her inner lip, straining to stop the flow of sudden tears. Her hands clamped over her henna bag. Nauseated, she felt as helpless as the bird. She was being suffocated by an excessively perfumed man with cardamom-and-cloves-fed breath. Delaksha's shoulders heaved against Nioreg's chest as she cried. Nioreg soothed her: "Some ortolan buntings escape their cages and do find their way home."

[43]

Disarrayed. Intoxicated by hope. Fear. Grief. Want. Ache. Doubt, doubt, doubt, *what-does-it-mean* doubt. The dissolution of trust in absolutes, including the structures and strictures of life—she had been betrayed by ephemerality, had run full-tilt into this wall. Jumbled imageless dreams poured foreign emotions into her heart and created holes in her stomach. In her cabin bed, Ayaana rolled about as if she were fluff. *Abeerah*. Not a voice, not a sound. Breathing like dry wind, and it filled her world with questions. Something that was also of Ayaana's being eased from its confines to flutter before her in defiance. When she opened her eyes, it was long after the hour for *Fajr*. She found that she had lost her appetite for prayer. For the first time in a long time, Ayaana stayed under the covers in the hour of prayer, waiting for her rebellion either to subside or to be discovered. Nothing happened. Lost in the silences of immensities she had taken for granted. So what was life? The words 生活. *Sheng huo*. To live. *Kuishi*.

Ayaana got out of her bunk bed and padded over to the shower. She washed her hair, its black tendrils sticking to her as the water sprayed her body. Disarrayed. Fear and exhilaration: there were no predetermined paths. There were no guarantees. She pinched her scarred thigh, and stroked her face under the water. Feeling. She turned off the water, stepped out, and dried her body. She splashed on the rose water she had made from her mother's rose attar. She pulled on jeans and a white T-shirt. She seized her *buibui* to roll and throw toward the low cabin ceiling. She watched as it tumbled back to the floor. She moved her mother's mat to the side of the cabin. She jogged within the confined space, twisting her fingers. She inhaled and strode into the day.

Elastic time.

Crossing timelines.

Ayaana twisted her hair as she strolled in the direction of the bridge. The captain was on the watch, eyes forward. Ayaana gaped. The man inhabited his solitude fully, and everything else was extraneous: he and his ship and his sea. In that second, if Ayaana had ever craved anything in her life, it was this: to be of this replete mosaic as an elemental component.

"Come."

Ayaana turned.

A crew member, a giant with brutal scars, beckoned to her. He opened a large umbrella. She ducked under it. She followed him up narrow steel stairs to the bridge. Teacher Ruolan was already there. When she saw Ayaana, she narrowed her eyes and looked through her. Ayaana glanced at the equipment coughing out reams of paper with minuscule details: consoles and computers sputtering. Maps, living things that shimmered and beeped and signaled. A uniformed man nodded at her. Lai Jin turned to watch the seas. The giant pointed out the Global Positioning System consoles to Ayaana. Crackling voices from a radio handset, English words, some of which she could make out, transfixed her. *Over. Over.* Whisperings from beyond-ordinary realms, keys to so many destinations. Knobs and buttons and blinking lights. An electric sense of rightness filled Ayaana. There was the expanse of sea. There was the sky. Here was how to traverse both, the power in the human hand. Clouds hung low in the sky and seemed reachable. Her mouth was dry. Her heart pounded. The 180-degree ocean view, the red-and-orange cargo casing. She whirled and glimpsed the giant compass set in the middle of the room like a hallowed object. She tiptoed toward it, stifling an outpouring of questions. When she again spun around, she saw and leaned over the chart table to look over the positioning systems. "Where are we now?"

The giant man, amused by her wonderment, now showed her distances that seemed to be the length of her forefinger. He then led Ayaana to the console, where Captain Lai Jin presided over beeping, purring, crackling tools and screens and a multi-spotted radar screen that blinked lights and coordinates.

Ayaana stood next to the captain, watching the sea. Two birds of prey preened on the cranes as the ship rose and plunged on a swell. A pod of dolphins acted like ship guides, leaping in and out of the waves before they disappeared. Cormorantlike birds roamed the area, staying close to the vessel. Flying fish. The saltwater worlds were replete with life. In a reverie, Ayaana slipped into ship-think, anticipating sea troughs, and for a moment could see the tracks in the sea as clear as light, moving with the boat as if she were guiding its way. She glimpsed the descent of the sun and the first sprinkle of stars. She saw the constellations and forgot to breathe. Silent journeying. Traveling white-and-beige birds descended to roost on the ship's masthead. Mist on the water, mist in her eyes, until it was fifteen minutes later and darkness had tainted the waters.

Lai Jin then whispered into her ear, "*Ni huxi*. Breathe."

Ayaana turned to him, bereft of words.

"I know," he said, smiling at the water.

He said, "Starboard: *youxian*."

"*Youxian*," she repeated.

"Weather forecast: *tianqi yubao*."

Ayaana repeated, "*Tianqi yubao*."

Watching them from the corner of her eye, Teacher Ruolan was filled with a weighty sense of unease. She walked over, tutting in Mandarin, "You have so much to read." Her hands clamped over Ayaana's shoulders. She told the captain, "Thank you for your kindness." Her lips were rigid.

Panic and then resignation replaced revelation in Ayaana's eyes. Her head swiveled to take in the bridge consoles as Teacher Ruolan hustled her out. The raised portion of the upper deck met the ocean head-on. *Jingyu*—a whale—a giant blue beauty breached on the port side of the ship.

[44]

The morning had turned dark, and the sky dense and leaden. Ayaana woke up restless. What was that destination she had sensed from the captain's bridge? She could reimagine herself. The ship dipped and rocked. Ayaana slid open her cabin door. She watched ocean birds roost on the ship's masts. She heard the pounding of ocean waves. She heard voices and laughter and smelled a rich, earthy scent of what she would later discover was cigar smoke. Yes. She would claim this day for herself.

The monsoon squall raced toward the ship. Ashen-faced, Lai Jin walked along the rain-flecked deck. He had not been able to sleep. Before first light, he had sat in front of his Zao Wou-Ki print, waiting for a vision, a thought, a feeling. He had found a fragrance for this Zao Wou-Ki. It was made of secret roses—musk, warm, sweet, with fluid moods. He watched the sea. Fading orange-red lines in the sky as livid as a healing scar. Distant thunder, a menacing drumroll. The storm had concealed itself from the gadgets of false prophets, those uninspired weathermen. If they had not depended on their own sense of water, the storm might have ambushed them. The chief officer was monitoring its approach. They had started a discussion on how to deal with it. Nothing was certain. He wanted to sneak behind it rather than meet it head-on and ride it out. Lai Jin turned starboard and saw a flash of pink—a flying scarf followed by a *ping!* There was Ayaana, her body stretching upward toward five thousand fluttering golden dragonflies, soaring, falling, stooping into minuscule pools of water. Her movements were a morning dance, and her face shone. Her contagious laughter swept Lai Jin into the memory of a barefoot boy flying a mad, high-soaring homemade blue dragon kite, chasing and learning wind currents with pure joy. He had chased his dragon kite hill after hill, until he had got lost. He had learned how intoxicating life could be. The shard of a pang: how had he forgotten? Lai Jin watched as an ocean wave reached up to splash Ayaana.

Ping! She ducked with a giggle, still reaching for the dragonflies, unaware of the danger. A rogue wave could drag her to her death. But a bubble of light had lit up Lai Jin's mouth. Instead of warning Ayaana, he backed away. Heart-warmed. It was auspicious that sojourning dragonflies had taken refuge on his ship together with the birds. Nature had confidence in him. Whatever his decision, it would be the right one. The jocund bubble on his mouth spread across his body. With nobody in sight, he allowed himself a pivot. He looked around. Nobody had seen him. He straightened his spine.

[45]

Lightning with jagged edges connected sky to water. Storm scent: a pungent tartness in the air. Cresting swells. Churning froth on blue water; baying, yowling winds that shattered the life of day; the lurching, rolling ship; sky-suffocating clouds. The ship's bow dipped into the tumult, then rose. The men at the helm engaged the storm head-on. Fog and fifty-five-knot winds, twenty-five-foot waves. The lightning hit the water again. They did not know yet that Ayaana was pinned between pipes in the deck head without a life jacket. When she leaned above-deck to peer at the pipes below, Muhidin's watch had eased off her wrist and tumbled to the bottom. Without thinking, against the regulations, she had climbed down to retrieve it. She searched for her watch amid a snarl of pipes and tubes. She crawled on the steel floor, becoming more frantic in her search, as if losing this watch were the same as losing home. She could not let that happen.

The wind bayed at Ayaana like a pack of hyenas, encircling her. She looked with awe at the storm. In it was the specter of the loneliness that had hounded her soul in her mother's house; in it were all the hungers. She scampered upward, abandoning Muhidin's watch. A three-story wave crashed on the ship. She was soaked, and aware of her smallness. Here was a hunting angel, a grand presence; here was immensity; and she was inside it, and all she could do was wait until the metal pipes among which she was lodged gave way. But they held on. Her open mouth was at once filled with seawater, which she spat out, snatching breath, waiting, her body tilting this way and that with the groaning ship. In that moment there were no prayer words—the moment was the prayer, and then she lost the will to try. The sting of the sea on her skin was new. Its chill was new. And the more she sought to live, the more she understood she would not. The louder she tried to cry, the greater her knowledge that nothing would ever hear her again. The more she knew these things, the more she tried to live and cry. Her hands glued themselves to the pipes. Grief, at the passing of her life. Time slipped into her and roosted, as did outrage at her powerlessness before the eyes of fate.

Hands on the black-painted pipe. Chipped pink nail polish on low-cut nails—rounded, not squarish, as her mother liked hers. Plunged into stillness and silence, beyond desolation, beyond the clamor and power of the storm waves clobbering her body. Then. Nothing.

[46]

He was in a brilliant yellow heavy-duty waterproof jacket, a bib and a brace over a life jacket. He was stumbling through darkness, screaming, "*Haiyan! Haiyan!*" He was calling the girl. There was no answer. *Not again. He could not be struck with the loss of another human. Not death again.* His shouting turned into a bargaining plea. Panicking. He had not asked to be responsible for a human being; it had been imposed on him. An inner retort; but he was the captain. *Haiyan!* he called. Blurring of rules: a captain should not leave his bridge in a time of crisis, not when the air was thick with electricity and smelled of burning. But as the ship's prow had plowed into sea troughs, out of the depths a wraith wreathed in fire had emerged with a blood-curdling howl that had penetrated his bones and still echoed in his head. He had seized a life jacket as he handed over the helm to his chief officer and taken off, following the sound, which was Mei Xing. Slipping past time. He reached the lowest deck and saw a pink scarf on the ground. *Haiyan!*

. . .

He saw a huddling lump. He had found her. His torch shed its light on her form. He knew that she was dead, that the storm had crushed her. She was bleeding, the crimson seeping through clothes that stuck to her skin. He dropped the torch and offered the sea his back. Rule: a seaman must never turn his back on the sea. But he used his body to shield hers. Unbeknownst to him, he stopped a wave that had formed itself into a giant receptacle from sucking her into the sea. The seawater battered his body. When he looked over his shoulder at the water, the sea, in revenge, showed him again the departure of a beloved. He watched the silver ghost of his wife recede into the night waves, and in an infinite moment of insanity he perceived that it was she the sea had come to take. The wind howled. He howled back, and his sorrow stirred the girl his body protected, and for another second, he imagined that if he let the sea have her it would return to him his wife. Yet, when he should have let Ayaana go, he could not pry open the arms he had locked around her. Rule: a ship's captain must be sane and lucid at all times. Existential dread calcified in Lai Jin's fathomless being. Everything hurt, and cried, and mourned in this watery darkness. He thought he might allow both their bodies to slip over the edge. But Ayaana shivered and coughed, and her eyes opened slightly, and when she saw him, he imagined her smile. Fear twisted his being, as if hope could kill. He lowered his mouth close to hers to give her breath. Praying away the blood on her face. Bargaining with the conflation of despair and, now, desire. Life, life, life. Never again. Never another death under his watch. Heart palpitations, so he unzipped his jacket. He would cover her.

Ayaana turned toward the warmth of the presence anchoring her to life. Her extremities had contracted. The ship heaved. Whisperings in a mysterious language wrought by the sea. Ayaana heard from the sea and from a man. She clung to them—all their new promises. Around them the clamorous, wild grandeur of existence, the threat of death as the storm's waves tried other ways to dislodge and dissolve the sheltering bodies. It pummeled them, one into the other, until there was, as always, only waiting.

The wind speed dropped to twenty-eight knots, and the storm eased an hour before daybreak. Searching crewmen would find Ayaana and their captain more than two hours later, crushed, drenched, and dying of cold. Lai Jin was slurring incoherent words. The chief officer said, "Your clothes, sir." Lai Jin listened. "They are wet."

Exceptional insight, Lai Jin thought, suspended in hoped-for sleep.

The chief officer continued, "You are shivering. Your lips are blue. You might die. Do you hear me?"

Is she safe?

Darkness.

In Captain Lai Jin's cabin, the only one large enough to accommodate more than two people at a time, a temporary infirmary had been established. Two souls wrapped in thermal blankets, recovered from a tempest. Bandaged. Nothing was broken, it seemed. Through half-closed eyes, Lai Jin watched his men blunder like misdirected ants. He heard Teacher Ruolan's sharp phrases sniped at the men. *A cross cat*, he thought. She wanted to sit guard over Ayaana. The chief officer wanted distance from her.

A chronic shivering had seized Ayaana's body and separated her into three Ayaanas: one was reversing the sea-travel route to look for her mother, another occupied the present brokenness as a refugee might a borrowed shack, and a third, called into being by the storm, was squeezing out of her to step into the world with a keen intent to drink of shadows, to soar in its mists.

Hands on her—hard, rough, worried hands—and more whisperings. Headache. Warm liquid. A cloth rubbing her body. A woman's low-pitched question. A man's absolute "*Bù.*" An ideogram tumbled in her mind. It floated with sluggish suspense inside her skull: 不. Her teeth chattered as someone cleaned wounds that stung. Slipping into sleep worlds where everything was possible, and nothing stayed hidden, and loneliness was only a temporary guest. She met unmet ancestors: grandfather, grandmother, aunties, and uncles who led her through a closed door. She lifted her fist to push it open, because she knew that her birth father stood behind it. The door fell, and Wa Mashriq and Fazul the Egyptian lunged at her. She struggled into wakefulness, summoning, for this fight, the fury of Muhidin.

~

Captain Lai Jin swayed with his pitching ship, ignoring the ache of his strained and bruised back, the weakened arm, the throbbing of the fire scar on his face. The Descendant tossed in his bunk bed, and he was wondering in gloom about the beyondness of life. He turned to the girl; the many small cuts on her body were no longer bleeding. She would heal. Light filtered into the space. The roundest, heaviest, bloodiest-shaded moon daubed everything a luminous red; his fate rested on the recovery of a young stranger.

~

Under the command of the chief officer, the MV *Qingrui/Guolong* returned to its course. Visibility on the high seas improved after eighteen hours. The chief officer corrected the ship to its easterly course, traveling at twelve knots, avoiding the tangle of human disorder around him, stealing time for his captain—he would claim fuel management—needing Lai Jin to take charge of the ship before their arrival. The captain's malady, even though storm-created, would be read as a blight on an impeccable record. The officers declined to summon airborne help.

. . .

A storm-battered ship. Dents, broken components, straining metal, the silence of threatened humans. Memory as a telescope. In the flotsam on the sea, assorted metaphors to explain the debris of human breaking, of human changing.

[47]

Drifting slowly to the surface, past soupy murkiness pressing into her chest and tickling her dry throat. Fighting for breath. Arms pulled her out of the thickness. And when she opened her eyes, the ship captain was grabbing her shoulders, shaking her as she gasped for air. A voice: "You must breathe!" She frowned. She murmured the question she had first asked him: "How did the fire write you?" and then, "What?"

"Absence," he whispered his reply.

"Oh," she said, recalling a storm, and what it had tried to tell her. Her head dropped onto the pillow, and she returned to the deepest of sleeps. For a long, long time, he stood to watch, willing her never to stop breathing.

It was raining nonstop. Unmoving in the captain's bunk bed, Ayaana spent hours just looking through a porthole. Lai Jin watched from a camp bed on the other end of the cabin. When she opened her eyes, he was still watching her. She turned to him. That was how they learned each other—through a gaze. Their silence subsumed Teacher Ruolan's interminable clucking outside the closed door. She still wanted Ayaana to be moved to her cabin.

The thing about falling into the crevices of near death is that veneers and baggage fall away. The shoulds and should-nots are transfigured. Long after midnight, Lai Jin asked Ayaana an odd question, given where they were: "Will you," he asked, "tell me about your sea?" It was sound he sought, words as a rope to bind this other to life. From behind the inner stone tomb which had been his sanctuary with the ghost of Mei Xing, a slab had smashed and forced fresh air in. The storm had entered the gap and deposited this foreign creature there. Lai Jin contemplated the girl. She was studying him, eyes lit from within. And, oddly, he wanted to be seen by her. When she tried to speak, she suffocated. So he leapt over to prop her up and thump her back until she could breathe again.

In the dawn, when they opened their eyes in their respective ends of the cabin, they saw the traveling golden skimmer dragonflies that had taken refuge on the ship.

"*Qingting*"—Dragonflies—Lai Jin said.

Listening. She would remember this. "From India," he added, needing her to talk.

Her eyes wandered into the future. "They won't stay." Words in borrowed languages. "*Qingting*," she echoed, completing the circuit.

The silence sizzled. Lai Jin focused on the fading henna lines and whorls on her skin. He had touched that skin already, first to clean and seal and heal its wounds, second to follow the whorls and lines. "They will come back," he promised.

Words as alchemy: if he said it, they would stay.

She turned to him. In her eyes, the pity that comes from older knowledge.

The golden skimmers left just before sunset.

Ayaana's searching gaze had found Lai Jin's untitled Zao Wou-Ki. He followed her look. He asked, "What do you see?"

Ayaana stared at the print.

Lai Jin approached the work, tilting his head at it, touching the part of his face that had been burned.

Her voice: "Does it hurt?"

"The painting?"

"The fire on your skin."

Outside, a sea wind's high-pitched shriek—it scrambled thought. He answered her: "When I remember."

Morning. The room was under the spell of pointillist pale light. Ayaana's eyes were on the Zao Wou-Ki. She saw a figure inside gauzelike red brushstrokes. Ayaana watched it until the sun flooded the room and overpowered the view of the painting. In the painting, she imagined she could give meaning to the shock of being drawn to this man, this person so alien to anything she had known or wanted before.

Lai Jin said, "Shadow picture." When she looked at him, the storm was prowling in her eyes. Lai Jin's voice broke as he said, "A copy." He moved closer to her. He looked down at her. He then turned to the Zao Wou-Ki print reading emotion in color. Lai Jin asked Ayaana, "You see?"

Ayaana read the violent blue, red, and black brushstroke signals like colored scars on an immense page of light. World and memory cartographies, like those now invisible strokes left on her body by the storm—that she could endure—and a stranger's brutish touch, which had also marked her soul. Reading wounds. Darkness had insinuated itself inside her. It would not be painted over, even by silence. But she understood now that there was not yet a complete language for shame, as if it was the consequence of some failed test of existence.

She blinked.

There! In a streak of yellow-white light on canvas, she saw again the conjuring of the life-offering dance that Delaksha had summoned out of Nioreg. In those colors she was invited in as witness of a sublime revelation.

Ayaana blinked, turning away from the print to look again at the images from a Thursday evening.

Hands kneaded her body, a large booze-tinted breath mouth intending to tear, bite, and eat her, fat limbs trying to force openings for an obscene invasion. Her mother had known. That was the sorrow. Munira had known the meaning of the fleshy, perfumed body waiting for her daughter like a vulture, had known why a grown man would whine, "*Je veux le bijou.*" Her mother's touch had pre-softened, pre-scented, and scrubbed her skin—soft touch breaking the eggshell of trust. *There!* Now she could touch fractured portions of self, sullied and fallen, later blending with the salt of the sea. Now she could taste the flotsam of betrayed bits retrieved from a buxom woman's life story. She was the fluttering in the heart of an ortolan bunting; she was the pursued. That was what an artist's multi-shaded, fragmented brushstrokes whispered. That was what she found in the fire etching on a ship captain's face. That was what the storm had come to explain to her.

It was past midnight again. The ship was pitching. Foam on the water. In stowage, containers shuddered, banged, and groaned like many suffering beasts. The girl's breath was on Lai Jin's face—not stale, not anything, just warm. She was awake, listening to this and other storms in a self-contained place of dark formlessness. Breach. What had he dared? He had told himself it was to stop her thrashing about lest she hurt herself. He had stooped over her. Then he was curious. Not the otherness but the feminine, the woman-ness. The opposite of him. Then her body in his arms had been soft and malleable and cold. So he had thought to warm her up with his. He was still holding her to him and remembering how it was to press one body against his own. She was as awake as he was, listening to heartbeats as he was. Molded and waiting in stillness, just as he was, and all the hungers Lai Jin had cut up and thrown into the sea emerged now from fathomless depths like a prehistoric entity to stain his skin and set his belly aflame. Rusty whirr of memories of intense, eternal, fleeting bliss. The caress—her hand on the burned side of his face—had reshaped, retextured, and short-circuited his previous intentions. He had planned to maintain a distance. Slow arousal. Sudden fear. Not about the girl, but about the danger of losing again. *Gray ghost.* He mocked himself. *Fungus phantom.* Lai Jin told himself, *She is young,* even as her fingers touched his ears, his jaw, and his mouth. Gathering details. He, too. This skin, this look. She smelled of water, of salt, of elsewhere; she smelled of dust and earth. She smelled of softness and rose, and he learned that the chains to which he had bound his needs had broken.

Ayaana's hands, on their independent journey, traversed Lai Jin's face—sacrilege, this trespassing. The benefit of laws or the arbitration of prophets, all erased by their post-storm universe—no stockades, no intermediaries. Body possessed, she tasted the texture of this man's fire scars in a muffled ocean night, suspended in the immensity of her *where*s, taking refuge in intimate anonymity. Her body arched into him, grasping for something. And she was startled by the liquid rush of wanting, wanting. Her body unknown. Retreat and curiosity. *Who is this?* Her, him. And so her questions leapt like crickets from one brush to another. "How do you pray?" she asked, but she had tilted her face to his.

"I don't," he answered. He kissed her mouth.

"Where is your home?" she moaned.

He said, "I carry my home."

His lips were warm.

"Tell me about *your* sea," she gasped, heated and sweating and thrashing.

His eyes were dark and unblinking and said one thing; his mouth, almost touching her skin again, another. Then he raised himself from her, with an almost smile. "The best is deep water . . . or you float like a plastic duck moved by currents." Lai Jin became silent. Cold fires in memory: "Life"—he retreated to some inside horizon—"nobody knows where it lives." He glanced down at her, shifted. "Maybe you find out." He settled beside her, wrestling with his strength. "She is young," he muttered to himself.

She was still watching him. Lai Jin leaned back, struggling to rein back what the storm had unshackled within him. "January 1992, in Pacific Ocean, twenty-nine thousand yellow ducks fall from a container ship. Plastic ducks. They float away. They travel across the world." He added, "Inside the box were also toy frogs and turtles. But the ducks"—here a big laugh—"they go their separate ways." Her laugh was a reward. So he continued: "Sometimes, on the water, I see things other ships have lost; one day I saw a car, a Volvo . . . on a floating island in the middle of ocean. Like a crazy ghost." Another smile.

Crazy ghost.

"Ziriyab Raamis," Ayaana eventually said. "One day the tide came and took him away."

Lai Jin nodded just as if he, too, knew Ziriyab Raamis.

Inside the storm-created world that separated her from reality, Ayaana could now contemplate her mother's and Muhidin's pursuit of apparitions, recall messages in dreams, the human tumbling and groping, the eclipse that had become Ziriyab, and how it took over their habits and caused other infernal creatures, such as Wa Mashriq, to emerge. Suffocation. Rising from the dead, yet still scalded by her mother's hot water. Holding her breath, diving freely into silence, drifting with the green-blue warm undertow of memory. Underwater, she did not need to label things in order to contain them. Feeling, sensing, experiencing—that was knowledge. There, in that stillness, its colors evoked for Ayaana a green-feathered, song-bearing creature destined to be stuffed with life's dense flavors so it could be consumed in darkness in a human's single bite. Her mother was an ocean, roiling in gales that life delivers, surging as a sea mountain, unsettled and given over to rubbing out boundaries, even the necessary ones. Her mother was one of the storms that existence delivered to the earth, and she loved, yes she loved, but it was a love that singed. And she . . . Ayaana hesitated, chewing on her lower lip, thinking. Thinking. And she . . . yes, she had to embrace the fullness of this mother.

"You know the ortolan bunting bird?" she asked Lai Jin.

"No," he answered. Puzzle pieces: *Ziriyab Raamis, ortolan bunting.* Lai Jin gathered the words as if they were rare visitors from an invisible world.

The ocean's night entered the captain's cabin through its open door. Lai Jin had bent his head to kiss her forehead. And then his mouth hovered over hers. *In dreams,* she thinks, *I travel inside stars, on stars.* Her arms slipped around Lai Jin's neck. *In dreams I am a tunnel made of darkness, and I know the way. I'm not alone, even when there is nobody with me.* She should have known dread, but in the solitude of this uncertain eternity, there was, now, only peace. "Tell me about the sea," she said.

Conversion.

"The sea," he gasped, "cannot be spoken."

She rubbed the backs of her hands against his mouth, his lips, struggling with herself, the draw of the shape and feel of his mouth on her skin. There was another scar there, beneath his lower lip. Roaming thoughts, cascading emotions; fearful forebodings, too. It occurred to Lai Jin then that he could be executed for this choice. But tonight he could live—a smile—with that. The substance was this: a sudden aching-craving-yearning, to decipher the mystery of a woman's gold-brown body, the shape and feel of breasts, the tumbling dark curls that half veiled her face, the hint-of-rose smell of her, to feel again her weightlessness against his body. From inside the cage of his mind, he heard Mei Xing's mocking cackle: "Fake, you are a mere man." "I am," he answered himself. And the grimness dissipated from his mood. Now he bent to kiss her again and again as he told himself that, should anyone ask, he would say he was helping her breathe. Light sips, tentative tasting, lips, mouth, teeth, tongue, lips again. *I need to know*, he told himself, and his fingers were on her face, her shoulders, her small waist, and then, so very gently, her breasts. His hands moved lower, to her thighs.

She waited.

It was like this whenever she let her body sink in seawater, in pursuit of a summons to experience what inhabited the depths, seeking to press it to herself, feel it on her skin, etching the unreachable into her dreams.

He watched her. She watched him. Head throb, and then a rush of loneliness, and it covered her body with a chill.

Lai Jin slipped from the bed. He crossed the room to double-lock the cabin door, leaning against it, refusing to clear his head. He looked across the room at Ayaana. Outside, the ship and the sea; inside, only the present. He crossed the room and squeezed in next to the girl. Breach. Acclimating to woman again. Grappling with his own ache to pierce, penetrate, disappear into, and remember the past and its addictions, lose the world, its fetters, its woundedness. This, he thought, this was what he had left behind at the Temple of Mazu the sea goddess. The girl's bare legs were wrapped around his. He was slipping. Negotiating compromises with himself. He dragged off his shirt. Her fingers were on his chest. Sculpting desire. He could define its limits.

She is young, he groaned to himself. A word. A word. "I . . . youn . . ." he uttered.

Restless waves rocked the ship, and night creatures stilled their wails. Two souls lying in a dark cabin—the rhythm of the sea became of their bodies. He was thinking that he would drape her body around his and let the ocean move them. Moon-carved intimacy. The night was their empire. She was drifting in sensation while a hand reached over to drive her toward an elsewhere that she had suspected exists. She was in the current, with the current, yielding; his hands directed her way, and then she was gasping. But he stopped. He waited until they found a normal rhyme of breathing, and when they did, he started again.

This was now her body, her feeling, and her wanting. This writhing, twisting, seeking, this was also who she was, and feelings spilling out provoked by this man's touch, and she saw what had possessed Wa Mashriq in the restraints this man imposed on himself as he moved her body and cried and then pulled away from her and listened for her return to stillness. Lai Jin then arranged her so she was on top of his partially clothed body, and he gripped her, pressing her to him, surrendered to sensation. He vowed he would do nothing more, absolutely nothing more. Savoring now. This he could offer himself, plundering hope. Hours to daylight; they did not yet have to mull over the meanings and words in and of the world.

[48]

The captain's argument with Teacher Ruolan, who was waving her curriculum notes, had been brief and in terse English.

Intense and carefully enunciated: "We are slow." He stared at Teacher Ruolan.

"Only seventeen words," she said. "Very slow."

"She's unwell. Weak," the captain said.

"She hears, she can learn. No time." She waved the papers. "Also"—she indicated the cabin—"now she can stay with me."

Lai Jin stiffened.

Shu Ruolan looked him in the eye. "Your cabin, ship leader? It is not proper."

"I can watch her."

"Where do you sleep?"

"My bed."

Teacher Ruolan said in a soft voice, "Ship leader, you are a man."

Lai Jin recoiled, acting offended. "Teacher Ruolan, in what swamp does your mind dwell?" Shu stuttered. Her face turned red. "Teacher Ruolan, remember you are a guest on *my* ship."

"I must report this."

Lai Jin nodded. "I shall help you with the story."

Teacher Ruolan studied the captain's face for sarcasm. Nothing. She muttered at her notes before turning to him. "When she is ready?"

He shrugged.

Resigned, she said, "I wait in class."

Lai Jin walked away. *Theater of pretense.* If he had not crossed a thousand boundaries last evening, Ayaana would be learning Mandarin nouns today. He paused. *What is the matter with me?* He leaned against the railing, shielding his eyes from the sun's light. Thinking about—what was the expression?—"quenching his thirst with poisoned wine." Sea sprays sprinkled his shirt. He watched the sea. His sea. It rubbed out lines—shadows, light, darkness, passages . . . and words. On the seas, he was the law. There were no aphorisms to explain the fate of those who had stared into the eyes of death together. He turned away, heading for his cabin. On the way back, he informed the galley cook to leave the food tray outside the cabin; he would bring it in himself.

In the hour before dawn, Lai Jin, with a simple sarong around his waist, and Ayaana, in a floaty flowered nightgown that belonged to

Delaksha, sat on a chair to look at the Zao Wou-Ki. Lai Jin had placed Ayaana on his lap and wrapped his arms around her; his nose was on her skin, finding faint traces of her rose scent. Connecting with skin, to feel curves again, to touch the slenderness of a woman's waist. He looked at his hands on her body, how strong and big they looked. His nose was in her hair.

Ayaana said, "When stars fall near water, they turn into sand."

Lai Jin grasped her hand. "I've seen stars fall."

"Why do they fall?" she asked.

He bent her head with his, and leaned close to whisper into her ear the words for "red," "white," "black," "blue," and "orange" in Mandarin: "*Hong se, bai se, hei se, lan se, cheng se.*" He rocked both their bodies in rhythm with the ocean; his hands gripping her hips, fingers digging into flesh, he repeated the words until he could no longer speak.

Later in the day, Ayaana memorized these colors. She drew pictograms on scraps of paper: 红色, 白色, 黑色, 蓝色, 橙色. Lai Jin oversaw her refinement of the lines on the 橙色."蜻蜓," he added, leaning over her, breathing into her ear. "This is how to write 'dragonfly.'" *Qingting*. She remembered.

~

"*Deng yixia*," Lai Jin said. *Wait.*

Ayaana had said, "Today I return to my space."

Lai Jin had choked, "*Deng yixia.*"

Ayaana hovered close to the door. His right hand was on the small of her back. She leaned back into him. "*Deng yixia*," she murmured to herself.

The steward delivered an early dinner tray to the cabin door. There was a special jug of custard-apple juice. After dinner, Lai Jin and Ayaana lay in the cabin bed, spooned, skin to skin, warmed bodies, not thinking. Lai Jin's pale skin, Ayaana's brown one. She rubbed her body against his, nipping at skin, surprised by the ceaselessness of human craving, all its variety. Cutting binds and bonds. She should have worried. She did not—not in the capsule she had stepped into. *You are young,* Lai Jin told himself. *I'm only passing by.* She felt the warning in her spirit, and a hollow ache formed within her belly. *I cannot stay.* He was retreating to a refuge of remoteness. *My only wife is the sea, is in the sea.*

[49]

Before dawn, when the djinns should have started their wailing, another Ayaana opened the captain's cabin door to make sense of the world. New moods in the freshness of the morning; she was engulfed by sensations, the spirit of change, the sense of pain of a different sort of leave-taking. She inhaled the air and watched the passing morning birds. She leaned over the railings to peer at the thin strip of light from the approaching day.

Ni shi shei? The sea reached up to touch her. Ayaana wandered along the deck and smelled rich tobacco wafting in the air, then heard Delaksha laugh from inside Nioreg's cabin. She passed Teacher Ruolan's corner to reach her room. She turned the door handle. Nothing. Locked. When she turned, Lai Jin was there. "Your key," he said.

She took it.

He waited fifteen seconds before turning away. The opened cage. She stepped into the room, and noticed the crowdedness of its China images. She looked at the likeness of Admiral Zheng He. She stooped over her mother's prayer mat. Everything in the room was exactly as it had been before the storm.

She wasn't.

That evening, Ayaana returned to Lai Jin's cabin, henna kit in hand. She had spent the day in her cabin, painting her feet, washing her body and hair with her Pate Island oils.

Henna was the preserve of women.

But.

On her knees now, Ayaana stroked the naked, supple body of a man in the golden light of a sea evening. Lai Jin rested his head on his arms as she touched the burned portions of his skin and told Lai Jin the stories of Pate that she had lived, and that she had heard. She was drawing on the parts of his body that clothes would later shield from the outsider's gaze: his back, his front, the top part of his thighs. She spoke. "My town lives inside the ghost of a city that was the center of the world," she said. "Many come to stay." She spoke of Muhidin. "I chose my father. His name is Muhidin." Traversing scars. "Munira, my mother, is the best singer in Lamu Island, except nobody knows but her and me." She covered Lai Jin's body from below the neck with lotuses and whorls. He listened to her; felt the tickle of Ayaana's brush and the cold liquid on his fire-smoothed skin. She inscribed Pate there with her voice. Transferring memory. "Wings," she said, "like dragonflies." When she finished, she leaned over Lai Jin to kiss the scars on the side of his face. She stroked his head and told him to remain where he was for at least an hour before washing off the excess. Then she gathered what was hers and left the cabin.

Ayaana opened the door of her cabin at dawn.

Zar. It was turning to light when she heard the djinns sob.

She is young, Lai Jin told himself, his eyes watering. *Her destiny is her own*.

Maji hufuata mkondo.

Water follows the current.

[50]

Ayaana left her cabin at nine in the morning. She wore a flowing white blouse with stonewashed jeans. She was barefoot. Her hair was in a topknot. She skipped breakfast. She carried her lesson books and went to wait for Teacher Ruolan in the lesson room. As was her habit, Teacher Ruolan showed up on time. She found Ayaana seated. She stiffened, did not comment on the girl's bare feet. She recovered. Fingers trembling, she turned the pages of a reference book. She said, "In our last lesson, we learned about China stars; our Tou Mou, empress star. It never sets." Ayaana picked up a blue pen with which to take notes. She remembered again, that sometimes, when stars fall, they become sea sand.

Captain Lai Jin resumed his place at the bridge. He was as competent as always. He acted as if the storm had not happened.

Delaksha leapt at Ayaana as they met on their way to dinner. Oozing a heavy dose of rose fragrance, she grabbed Ayaana in a tight hug and exclaimed, "You! Silly, silly thing! What were you thinking, wandering about in a bloody storm? You were rather dead when they found you, lady. Scared the shit out of me!"

Ayaana touched Delaksha's face. *Ortolan bunting*, she thought. Delaksha squinted at Ayaana. "Oh, my dear, dear!" Delaksha called out to Nioreg. "Nio, look! Here! Our migrant bird has reincarnated."

Nioreg nodded at Ayaana, his look enigmatic. "*Bonsoir.* You're well. Good."

Delaksha said, "Nio, darling, so effusive."

Nioreg kissed Delaksha on her forehead.

Ayaana smiled. "Where is the bird?"

Delaksha answered amid the clatter of cutlery and crockery in the mess and galley: "The sweet wretch. After feasting and drinking with us, and enjoying asylum as we processed its visa, no sooner did the storm cease than she flew away. She did offer us a backward glance, didn't she, Nio?" Laughter. "Odd being." Pause. "Do tell, little Ayaana," Delaksha continued, "what is our lofty captain like at close quarters? He was soooo protective of you—took your almost death rather badly. Not as if you wanted to kill yourself to spite him. Had to tell him so."

Ayaana's stomach did a flip. She blanked her face to look at Delaksha. Camouflage. "Nice," Ayaana said.

Delaksha sighed. "By 'nice' you mean inarticulate bore. Oh well! Come! Let's eat dumplings. I swear I'll never eat another dumpling in my life after this. Nio was telling me about the *Maersk Dubai*. Ever hear about the evil ship? Diabolical captain. Disgusting. Chinese."

"Taiwanese," Nioreg corrected.

"Same difference," continued Delaksha. "Demonic. Had to get Nio to guarantee that our captain did not feed you to the piranhas. Didn't I, Nio?"

"Yes," sighed Nioreg. He turned to Ayaana. "She was in good hands."

Ayaana coughed. "Yes."

Nioreg added, "Delaksha, the sea does not have piranhas."

"I'm sure they exist; humans have just not spotted them yet," Delaksha replied.

They reached the table. The soup was already steaming in a large bowl. Delaksha brayed, "Ooh, look! Green squiggles gasping for breath in our soup. Hurry, Nioreg! Rescue them." Delaksha was gurgling. "Darling girl, sit next to me."

Ayaana observed this Delaksha, in her bright gowns, her unmade-up face with its bright, clear eyes, her disheveled hair, and her glee. Her thorniness had vanished, as had her aura of suffering. Ayaana tilted her head to study Nioreg covertly. He seemed as unchanged as an old rock in the sea, but his equally bemused and amused gaze turned often to Delaksha. Ayaana turned to her soup and in it glimpsed a fragment of the Zao Wou-Ki, which had leached into her senses.

Clang of heavy machinery, and the shouts of crew attending to invisible tasks. Inside the mess, at the table, Delaksha was speaking of purgatory again. Nioreg had spoken of security contracting—war profiteering, Delaksha had corrected him—in the world's conflict arenas. He suggested that the truth of what humans had done in the world's new wars would one day emerge; his look bereft and bleak, he swore that on that day human beings would conceal their faces from one another in existential shame. He would not explain what he meant.

In the pause, Ayaana asked, "Why?"

Nioreg said, "Make no mistake, little Ayaana, 'man is a wolf to man'; there are no 'good guys.'" His voice was dry when he added, "But the wolf is far more honorable; it hunts under a moral code." Nioreg's eyes had turned inward, bright and desperate. He murmured, "I am afraid we have bequeathed a wrecked world to your generation."

Delaksha punched Nioreg's forearm. "You are not to scare her, Nio—you must not."

"Delaksha, *chérie*. It is good for her to lose her illusions now, here, with us."

Delaksha turned to Ayaana. "Years ago, I was in Rome with the beastie I married. I wandered out and happened upon a building with a white façade sandwiched between orange and brown edifices. It was a church." Nioreg grunted. Delaksha pinched his hand. "Church of the Sacred Heart of the Suffrage." Her voice lowered: "Dedicated to purgatory and its fires."

"What is . . . ?" Ayaana started to ask.

Delaksha cut in, "After-death space of purification and atonement . . . like a spa that uses fire as its only ingredient." She glared at Nioreg, who had scoffed. "Purifies human rot and stains." Ayaana leaned forward to listen. Delaksha continued, "The *museo del purgatorio*. Inside the church is a shrine to the stained who reach back to the earth with limbs of fire."

Nioreg's sardonic "Ha!"

Ayaana asked, "Why look back?"

Delaksha cupped Ayaana's face. "*Souls*"—she turned to glare at

Nioreg—"require the help of the living—yes, Nioreg—to help them realize their eternity. They return to let us know—yes, Nioreg—that there is more to life than what we see." Delaksha continued: "In that place, I understood that life is crafted from the foundation of second chances."

Nioreg grunted, "Delaksha, there's no superlife, no afterlife, no . . ."

She snapped, "Death?"

"So what?" It was a bellow.

Delaksha said, "Do you dare explain death?"

"I *know* it annihilates life, Delaksha. I *am* an actor in our hideous human wars. There is no answer for the *fire* that turns a brother into a headless, roasted, bleeding meat chunk . . . Yes?"

Delaksha rolled her eyes, unsympathetic. "What you mean is, you have not yet dreamed up a convenient mathematical formula to explain meaninglessness." She turned back to Ayaana. "Women from our worlds have clearer, deeper, other senses. Keep yours, sweetheart, so that you will still see the message within shadows, darling. It is a power." A pause. "Now let us eat and talk of other things . . . Nio, I'm not through with you yet . . . Look, Ayaana, noodles!"

Ayaana smiled, but her thoughts were awhirr with new words to mull over. *Purgatory*. She stared at her soup with its wriggly green vegetable. Delaksha seemed to intuit her thoughts. She leaned over to whisper, " 'Love,' honey, is mostly purgatory. It is one of the many versions of darkness." Ayaana gave her a startled look. Delaksha smiled. "Tell me, sweetheart, what do you love best in the world right now?"

Ayaana deflected: "Pate."

Delaksha said, "Never made it there. A pity."

Nioreg asked, "What's to love?"

The ideal of home, which distance amplified. Ayaana tuned into a vision of home as if she were a home-comer. Her face softened as she clothed her island in her mother's scents and the Almighty's stars. In Ayaana's grammar, her listeners glimpsed Muhidin and Munira, witnessed the surge of Pate's moonlit seas from a sand dune, and smelled a jasmine-infused night. Ayaana's Pate was an antidote to desecrated worlds, so that, when Ayaana finished her remembering, there was silence. She picked up the chopsticks as the ocean whooshed answerless questions. Nioreg's tough-man mask slipped. "Miss Ayaana, we shall visit your home, yes?" He turned to his meal.

Delaksha took Ayaana's hand. "Don't let the world change you." Delaksha was addressing both Ayaana and Pate.

[51]

He battled a sudden desire to abandon everything he knew to follow after the uncertainty of his untrustworthy emotions. Vague fears. Hanging on to the hermit-crab-shell scraps of life he had created for himself. The captain addressed his passengers in English: "We reach Xiamen in five days." No emotion in his voice. He saw that Ayaana lowered her head. He turned away.

Lai Jin approached her. "Walk with me."

They strode along the deck in silence. Then he said, "China will find China in you; you will also find your China self."

Exposed. Another rush of tears. *Cuttlefish!* she evoked desperately. Couldn't she change shape and color and disappear into the scenery?

Lai Jin said, "You will forget this?"

"Yes," she said, defying herself.

They turned the corner, down a tight corridor, and he seized her there, hands wrapped in her thick hair, pushing his body against hers. She flinched in pain. She shuddered, reaching in to him, for him, swallowing fear.

She was satin-skinned and young; she was tall and soft; and her eyes were inside his storm-shaken soul. He buried his head in her neck. Breathing hard. Her fingers found a way to his chest, down to his stomach, past it. For a minute, Lai Jin could hold her; he could hold on to her for sixty seconds. He breathed into her. "The world is waiting for you . . . and I . . ."

Hurrying footsteps on the steel deck. They pulled away from each other. He quickly adjusted his clothes and hers. She stared into the pitiless moment, its facelessness, the way it scalded the deep-withins. Here were memories made out of a stinging scalp. *What have I done?* Lai Jin asked himself. Ayaana might have asked the same of herself.

Maji hayakosi wimbi.

Water always has waves.

[52]

The cargo was bleeding. The stench of rotting blood pervaded the ship. The night had been terrifying. Waves like towers—the ship had pitched. But now that it was almost calm, the cargo seemed to be bleeding. The chief officer dispatched a crew member to look. The man, a rough-looking unshaven giant, re-emerged half an hour later, looking wan. He spoke to the chief officer. The chief officer went straight to the bridge and asked to speak to the captain.

Everyone gathered at the top deck in the rain and was looking down at the contents of three split containers. Five hundred death grimaces of African beings: lions, leopards, pangolins, zebras, and gazelles. Ayaana counted and recounted the elephant tusks. Not the giant ones, but the small, unformed ivory of young elephants. Some of the pangolin bodies moved—not yet dead—and that was the most distressing of all. There were things she had not known she believed in, had not imagined she might feel for. Had not understood she might ever weep for this, the evidence, of the wasteful plunder of the treasures of her homeland. Heaving, she battled to keep her breakfast in.

The MV *Qingrui/Guolong* had slowed down to five knots. Delaksha started up the steps to the bridge, howling. Nioreg restrained her as she hurled, "You horrible, horrible, greedy little fascists. Murdering everything. Beauty-eating barbarians. Why don't you die? Let me go!" she screamed at Nioreg, who was dragging her back. "Let me slaughter these shits. Original thieves! Is there nothing you would not desecrate? *Ahh!* Nioreg, stop protecting them!"

Inside a mess, Captain Lai Jin heard echoes of Delaksha's insults as he studied the cargo manifest for the fiftieth time. He paused to remind himself why, in normal circumstances, he never, ever traveled with passengers. Adjusting the papers in his hand, he observed again that the containers in question were listed under the tag "Scrap Metal." Lai Jin focused on the name attached to the cargo list. It was an investment-and-trading company, and if public rumor served him right, it was linked to the powerful functionary Shanghai Accent. The man of prearranged sound bites that camouflaged intention.

Outside, Nioreg clamped both his arms around Delaksha. Delaksha yelled, "Assassins!" She twisted her body. "Where's that woman?" She was looking for Shu Ruolan, and spotted her standing next to the guardrail. "Explain this, you supercilious self-righteous bitch!"

"Delaksha!" Nioreg scolded.

"What, Nio? What? Everything is negotiable for you, is it?"

"Be reasonable."

"Why?"

"It's not their fault."

"They exist, don't they?" She then slumped on Nioreg, arms hanging loose, drained.

When Lai Jin made his way past the passengers, he avoided all eyes, but his steps were firm. Ayaana watched him, stricken. His steps slowed down. What could he say? That they had been used? His senior crew advised that they seal the container as best they could and sail on. They could endure the stench for a few more days. But they had been used. They had been played, and this—the assumption of his dumb gullibility—wounded both his pride and his honor the most. He had gone to the sea in order to rewrite his life. But now malevolent humans had woven the grotesque into his destiny. Today, life lay heavy within him. It was not just about the bloody contraband on his ship; it was also about the potent uncertainties that had shaken him. What if he had resigned his commission on the day he heard Shanghai Accent? Too late. The chaos was in full flowering within and without. Lai Jin retreated to the helm. The boat set off on a faster course. No one spoke. It returned to being a ship of human silences offset by the groan of machines.

Lai Jin was expecting the knock on his cabin door. He slid it open. Her eyes were red. She had been crying. He lowered his head. "I apologize," he said.

Ayaana touched his arm.

Lai Jin straightened up slowly. Weary, weary eyes.

She sat on the edge of his bed. When he looked at her, it was with resignation.

He got up to stand before the Zao Wou-Ki print, addressing it as he rubbed the burned side of his face. "I am a plastic duck floating in current." Bitterness in the turn of his lips. He turned to study her. "Go to sleep, *Haiyan.* Tomorrow I will do something." His fingers touched hers. "You believe me?" His voice was cold.

Ayaana stared at him before muttering, "I need air."

She left.

Lai Jin straightened his cuffs and stepped out to return to the bridge and relieve the night command.

When the morning came, Captain Lai Jin was in dress uniform. He had never fully exercised the legal authority that his command of sea vessels gave him. Dared to walk a precipice. Playing with fear, playing with fire. A gamble. First he summoned the entire crew and apologized for jeopardizing their jobs by not anticipating the deception that had allowed globally condemned illegal shipments aboard their ship. His apology contained a subtle warning; it was in their interests never to be linked to this sort of contraband if they wanted a future in shipping. He said he had come to a decision about the cargo, the responsibility of which was his alone to bear. He informed his crew that in the night, he had received orders to meet another ship in the high seas in order to transfer this particular cargo. He added that he intended to ignore it. He demanded the cooperation of his crew.

Ayaana's lessons with Teacher Ruolan that day were a return to the basics:

"What is your name?"
"Where will you live?"
"How do you know?"

The late-afternoon skies were violet and broody when the plan was executed. At the instigation of the usually taciturn captain, some key crew aboard the MV *Guolong* imagined a storm. What a storm it was, for it rendered the instruments that stored and conveyed data useless. Electronic failure. It caused the MV *Guolong* to "lose its bearings."

Lai Jin asked the chief officer, "What ships in the vicinity?"

"Three. Can't tell." He studied the radar. "Fishing boats."

"Let them pass," the captain said.

After three hours, the execution of an illusion.

"Rough seas."

"Massive waves."

"Rolling ship."

"Thirty-five-degree pitch?"

"Make it forty."

"Mortal danger."

The "threat" of the ship's capsizing forced the captain to select containers to dump overboard. His instructions were carried out. After three hours, six steel containers full of "scrap metal" were sinking out of sight. A necessary loss—it was thus recorded. Being "off course" after the "storm," the MV *Guolong* missed its rendezvous with the waiting ship. In addition to this, an uncommon static had been interfering with the MV *Guolong*'s communications system, and no messages were coming through. The MV *Guolong* went even farther off course. The ship's log recorded an unusually storm-haunted passage to Xiamen.

Order returned to the MV *Guolong*. There was the continued murmur of gentle seas dotted with many fishing boats that scrambled out of the way of the great, lumbering vessel.

[53]

Lai Jin walked into Ayaana's cabin with the Zao Wou-Ki print in a roll secured inside a plastic covering. He found her sitting cross-legged on her floor, looking at a map of China. She did not look up at him. He crouched next to her. His fingers stretched her curls, watching them spring back. He wanted to tell her about dumping the containers overboard. But he also knew that, the less the passengers knew, the better for all. Shanghai Accent was a powerful man, and not everybody on the ship could be relied on to maintain the silence. Someone would break. The fallout would bury him . . . He would not worry yet.

Ayaana examined her map. "How much longer?" she asked.

"Thirteen hours," he said, stroking her face. *Touch.*

Now she looked up at him, asking with caution, "I will not see you again?"

He gave her the Zao Wou-Ki print, not answering.

She took the print. "Something else," he said. He handed to her a wooden box lined with "Made in China" red felt. It was the ocean-rescued bit of Chinese porcelain, a relic from an admiral's junk, gift of the people of Kenya to the people of China. "Keep it safe," he told her. But he also had to wipe the tears from her face, using both his hands.

Silence engulfed them. Ayaana had then retrieved a wrapped package from her suitcase. In it was Fundi Mehdi's compass. She offered it to Lai Jin. She said, "Keep it; it is from *my* sea." He did not react. She repeated: "Take it."

What he did was tilt her head to watch her eyes, to watch them and then to kiss her, biting her lower lip. And then she was crying. Her hand rose. She scratched his face where the fire scar was. He winced, but then laughed and dragged her to her feet. They leaned in close to each other, clothes entangled, swaying, not really touching. He bent his head to inhale, as if for the last time, her scent. Like autumn's last apples. Like waiting for rain. Like the moment just before the Qiantang River plows into the East China Sea: scent of sea and life and earth and fear, rising skyward as a tidal bore. This was the smell of now and—as always—waiting. He murmured something into

Ayaana's lowered head. Whatever it was, it secured the spell. With his head touching hers, he said, "*Ni hui gudan.*" A pause. "It is the way of life, *Haiyan*. Loneliness is a country with a teacher's voice." He thought that he was being lucid, that the words he strung together made sense. "Also, *ruxiang suisu*"—Become that which you find at your destination. However, Ayaana heard only sounds that crashed over her head and racked her heart. He took the compass gift and marched, quick time, from her cabin. Lai Jin would stand outside for thirty seconds, touching his own face, the burned, scratched side, in lieu of goodbye. The storm that had unmoored him from his pathway should have subsided within him. It raged.

It was portentous that Ayaana's first glimpse of China would be through the filter of unshed tears, and a body quivering as if in the throes of malaria as it wrestled with a new inner sense, that of unrequited hauntedness.

Bahari itatufikisha popote.

The ocean leads anywhere.

[54]

The high-pitched screeching of Xiamen's emblematic egrets was supposed to herald auspicious arrivals. Today, because of the mist, they appeared as omens of disquiet. Lai Jin glanced over his shoulder at the sea. It was as troubled and hoary as he was. A cold wind blew in like a chill warning. Lai Jin had hoped for warmth. Unease was like an itch on his tongue. He tightened his lips. Whatever his fate, he would receive it.

The harbor. Mandarin: *gang kou*, Ayaana remembered. Teacher Ruolan had told her to imagine the things she would see from now on only in Mandarin. Ayaana's gaze was struck by the numerous cranes and containers, and a flotilla approaching the harbor. To the east was a smog-filtered Taiwan. She had found it on the map. She looked for it through her window and saw only Kinmen. Grand words blared a message that was echoed back from Xiamen. She would one day decipher what they meant. She saw the high white buildings and sweeping structures of a nation speeding toward its vision of progress. Swathes of green, and acres and acres of apartment buildings. Ayaana's eyes scanned the distant hills.

Destiny.

Ayaana had suddenly forgotten the Mandarin word for "destiny." Inside her cabin, a cramping knot in her stomach. From the deck, a cool wind. Scent of salt and spilled oil: a particular perfume of harbors. They would need to wait awhile before the tugboat and pilot that would escort the MV *Qingrui/Guolong* to harbor showed up.

Blaring foghorns. Was she home?

. . .

Sounds of arrival, the rumble of the anchor; the ship had become a thing alive. Vibrating, clanging machinery, mechanical groans, and grunts and whines. Raised voices, shouts, and commands. Lights. The mixed relief of arrival. Within the farewells, a reluctant wrenching of souls from the intense temporary universe they had inhabited, forced to re-emerge into a land-based reality. The struggle of separation, even though for many this was also a homecoming. Delaksha had been wandering around for hours, huddled in Nioreg's black jacket, and when she bumped into Ayaana, she had whispered conspirationally, "Here is life! Here is life."

Ayaana walked as one condemned. She ached for a return to life aboard the ship.

Ni shi shei? the sea still called out to her. *Who are you?* She ignored it.

Disjointed hours. Ayaana relinquished herself to the guiding hand of Teacher Ruolan. Delaksha had sought out Ayaana and smothered her in a tight, teary hug as Teacher Ruolan glared. "You thing, you lovely thing. I could eat you up. I most emphatically love you, child. We *will* come and see you—won't we, Nio? We shall travel to Pate with you—won't we, Nio? Nio, give her your number. It must serve as our address and means of contact for now."

On impulse, Ayaana turned to and cupped Delaksha's face to kiss her on her forehead, as Munira used to do to her. "Thank you," she said. Nioreg handed Ayaana a business card, with a single number on it. He nodded at her. "You have *your* people." He patted her shoulder.

Ayaana hugged him. Around them, amplified noises and voices. Their bodies swayed, as if the ship were still being buffeted by waves.

Assorted officials boarded the ship to scrutinize their documents. There was a further delay. A meeting of crew and ship captain with another set of officials had resulted in a terse shouting match. Yet another bunch of officials came on board the MV *Guolong*, one of whom was the square-jawed Shanghai Accent, who was wearing a dark brown hat. He glared at Captain Lai Jin, who stood before him at ease. They left together to survey the cargo hold. A few minutes later, shouting from below resounded on the ship. They all re-emerged almost an hour later. Shanghai Accent was waxen with distilled rage, his mouth a thin line. Captain Lai Jin was pale and uncommunicative, a red streak across his face. An indifferent smile was on his mouth, in his eyes, the resigned look of a pickpocket discovered and destined for some pain. "With evidence from the voyage weather report, you will be shot as a thief." Lai Jin did not react. The MV *Qingrui/Guolong*, even-keeled and loyal, already seemed diminished by her motionlessness, and wounded by what was to come.

[55]

Ayaana hovered at the threshold of a step that would lead her into China. Before she left her cabin, she had vomited her fear. Moving forward now, when everything within her screamed for retreat. The captain and some of his crew stood in line to say goodbye. When Ayaana reached Lai Jin, she lowered her head, as he did. No words. Teacher Ruolan and Ayaana were swathed in silence. After the officials left the boat, Teacher Ruolan was the first of those who had traveled from East Africa to disembark, with Ayaana at her heels. A porter carried their luggage. There was no retinue to welcome them, no elaborate speech makers, just a single black car to carry both of them away. Neither looked back.

Inside the car, Shu Ruolan exhaled. "Now we start again."

Ayaana nodded. Shu Ruolan bowed her head to look at her cell phone, which had suddenly clicked into life. Ayaana asked her, "Where will you go?"

Teacher Ruolan carried on with her clickety-click for a minute, before she turned to Ayaana. "I go back to work. Like you."

The car was on its way to Xiamen University, where Ayaana's China sojourn would unfold. They traveled on the widest roads Ayaana had ever seen, within view of the largest number of people she had ever seen using a single pavement. She gaped at the sight of all the floating bridges. Ayaana watched as though she were in front of a television screen. The sun was high and cool over the humid land. Amid inundating odors, she sniffed citrus in the air, and stared when she saw the first of the flame trees lit up with red flowers, transplanted exiles from her own world. She counted the flame trees and imagined them as family so she would not feel the bite of the loneliness that was already burrowing into her bones, then turned to watch the moving crowds, the density of numbers. She felt herself contract as their car raced along the roads and Shu Ruolan studied the messages on her phone.

[56]

Among the last to disembark from the MV *Qingrui/Guolong* were Nioreg and Delaksha. Delaksha had been forced to wait, because special paperwork had to be organized to allow her temporary entry into the People's Republic of China. To her giggling delight, on these documents, for ease of processing, she was listed as Nioreg's wife. Seventy-two hours later, halfway down the gangway, Delaksha pivoted to tease Nioreg, who was lugging their luggage behind her. Some mechanism groaned. The shouting of several men just as Delaksha pointed out to Nioreg the greenish tinge in the clouds hovering over the land. They were shaped like giant spacecraft.

[57]

Stranded by fate, his nerves on edge, Captain Lai Jin declined to leave his ship. On top of everything else, neither he nor his crew had been paid their wages. The crew at least had options, and people waiting for them. Lai Jin had only his ship, the MV *Qingrui*, and the shelter of his seas. He also had Shanghai Accent's ringing vow: "I will bleed you; I will boil your bones in my spit." Lai Jin had wanted to laugh at these imprecations, thus making the mistake of underestimating the depth of human malice.

Captain Lai Jin was made culpable for all the losses and tragedies now attached to the ship and its passage. The Powers used these to make the captain pay for the loss of their illicit cargo. Even though his crew confirmed his witness in their testimonies, he was still accused of incompetence and overreaching his mandate. The ship's owners were then slapped with a two-hundred-million-yuan penalty—which was far, far too much for lost scrap metal—which they ignored by declaring bankruptcy before the court orders could take effect. Overnight, the company dissipated into Xiamen's morning mists.

Lai Jin had been abandoned on his ship. His migraines had returned. The pain drilled into his head. He shut his eyes. And then, in the silence of that night, in the condemned, decrepit part of the harbor, to which he and his ship had been consigned, *ping!*

His eyes snapped open. He had waited. Another *ping*. And then the sound started to fill the ship and its emptinesses and the hole that had opened inside him, so that, hours later, wielding a torch, he set out to find the source. Focused, mind emptied of all other wanderings, he searched his ship, listening. He was in the engine room when the *ping* gave away its hiding place. Lai Jin retrieved the watch from within the nook of a tangled mess of pipes. For an elongated moment, elation. He rubbed the dust and oil spatter off the watch with his finger and stared at the ticking minute hand. In another extended moment, the sense of existential loss. He touched the leather straps, and fastened Muhidin's watch to his wrist.

Fuata mto uone bahari.

Follow the river to find the sea.

[58]

Falling leaves, a low-whistle wind. A permanent woolen cloud shrouded the skies. She walked with hesitant steps on pristine streets, wading through ineffable stories in a land that was not quite her own. She turned to the cloud, attempting to discern a glimpse of definitive sun, ignoring the cry of food vendors on the streets. The sun. She knew it was there, because her dress clung to her sweat-drenched skin. Her world was touched with fluorescent strangeness, and somewhere out there, in the mesmerizing dissonance, was the promise of happiness she was eager to discover. She heard her heart thumping as if she had been running. Her moving through Xiamen University Street caused heads to pivot. She heard voices, these other voices. Sounds, noises, words, strings of letters that dissipated around her, without meaning. Tuning in to the unspoken, unstated, to the contours that made up these other faces that she was supposed to be part of. Still she drifted. She counted the hills and trees and giant bridges and heard the birds and tried again and again to see the sea before her.

Dissolution.

Nothing had prepared her to imagine this place.

How was she to meet this gargantuan land with her pre-broken heart, shattered by absences, her soul resculpted by a stranger's hands? Ayaana hurried down a quieter alley, escaping the thick weekend crowd and the layers of novel scents, smells, faces, sounds, and whispers. Every way she turned, someone was watching her. Now she shrank, as if to become invisible. Futile: she was taller than most of the crowd. There were some tourists, too—Westerners, with the look of the perennially surprised. Her eyes scanned above heads as if self-programmed, scanning for images and any likeness of the familiar. She was mute in her hunt. When she looked at the signs above shops and the street signs, it was as if she were blind, and for the first time in her existence, she became conscious of the shade of her skin. All the phrases she had acquired on board the ship had scrambled; she walked with a dictionary even as the pictograms she had memorized metamorphosed into a single silent creature that ate even her speaking voice.

Perhaps that did not matter in this land drenched with noise, noise, and noise. The main dialect here was Minnan, not Mandarin. She crossed a wide street, looking left and right, expecting a wild car to rush at her and toss her off. But the cars stopped, obeying rules. This, too—this sight of rushing life coming to an obedient halt to let a person cross their street—this shocked her, and she reacted by sitting on a bus bench and thinking. An old woman wrapped in a sky-blue shawl sat down next to Ayaana and started to talk to her. She reached out and rubbed Ayaana's hair, then, immediately, pointed upward, her hands flapping. When Ayaana looked up, she saw two small birds with yellow-gold plumage gliding; one had its beak pointed downward, looking for something specific. The woman grinned at Ayaana, and said something in a dialect Ayaana was only just getting familiar with. The woman was ancient, and her eyes shone, and she rubbed at Ayaana's skin as if the color might bleed, chatting all the while. Ayaana leaned toward her speech, the cadences, looking for reassurance. Birds twittered. A reticulated bus appeared. The elder slowly got up and hobbled on board, still talking to Ayaana and gesturing.

Ayaana watched the bus leave. She glanced upward to orient herself, using the sky-scraping red-tiled roof of the university. Losing her voice—what was her language now? She walked until she stood outside the library at the Nanputuo Temple. And it was as if the air in her existence were squashed out of her and she had been cast adrift on a nameless, formless sea. Ayaana turned and fled. She tore through the streets, down the side roads, past the boulevards, and into the storied structure that was the student hostel, and into the elevator, and stairs that led to a numbered door—454—that opened into a small room, at present her sanctuary, before her hosts at last showed up with a plan and program for the rest of her life.

The seduction of places, their iridescent layers. Ayaana listened to the garbled Baidu Map instructions as she faked ease and meandered past Xiamen's rushing citizens. Inundated by bodies, discovering that a human could be alone in a crowd. She stumbled into and became negative space. The grandeur of this nation's dreams, its seething force, its giant machines—nothing had prepared her for the capacity of anything to imagine planning for and moving a billion people from one end of an infinite realm to another. Citizens of many shapes and colors managed to gawk at her mid-rush. She flinched when someone trod on her toes. Baidu Maps eventually led her to a massive tech-goods shop where she would buy a new phone.

Later, Ayaana phoned home. She heard her mother's "*Naam.*"

"*Shikamoo,*" Ayaana started, formal and shy.

"*Marahaba, mwanangu.*" Her mother laughed out loud. "What now, child?" Munira could not wait. "How is it? Tell me."

Ayaana only laughed. "It is big," she said. "Everything is big. So many people."

"You are happy, yes?"

A simple question, yet it disassembled Ayaana. Shadows within. Motionlessness before she switched the conversation: "How is my father?" Then an old piercing longing returned, as if a knife were lodged under her rib: her wait for an absent father who had not ever returned to look. "Muhidin," she clarified, for herself.

"Who knows?" Munira sounded indifferent and annoyed. "How are our people there?"

Ayaana's laugh was flat. But she started to regale her mother with the habits of her hosts. She suddenly needed to sustain the myth and mystery of other worlds for her mother. "Eh! They have buildings here that reach to and cover the sun."

"*Mashallah!*" A pause. "You look like them?"

No. "In some ways."

They talked some more. Ayaana recorded and stored her mother's voice in her memory, in her heart—its timbre. This was her map home. She listened with tears running down her face.

Munira said, "*Kenya ni Kosi.*"—Kenya is a goshawk. "*Halei kuku wa wana.*" It does not nurture the hen's chicks. "Nothing here . . . Marines, al-Shabaab . . . Now some are here drilling for oil." She scoffed. "They have chased our people away like goats. From their homes." Desperate-toned. "*Hekima, salama.*" Wisdom is safety. "Find a fresh path, *lulu.*"

"Yes," replied Ayaana.

"Try," Munira insisted.

They spoke until Ayaana's phone credit ran out. And then she sat, still holding the phone to her ear, listening to its nothing as if it were the wail of a shell dreaming of a different ocean.

Ayaana had to learn how to cycle. Every day there were Mandarin lessons to go to, and at night, she attached herself to earphones attached to a disk loaded with Mandarin phrases and their visual histories; she was downloading this into her dreams, where images were the language. The accompanying dictionary rested beneath her pillow, her hand in contact with it. Teacher Ruolan had seeded the ground well. *Ruxiang suisu*—Belong—she had insisted, as had everybody else. Language was the password, Ayaana imagined. Calligraphy—but it was the Basmallah she etched over and over again.

Ayaana retrieved the card Delaksha had told Nioreg to give her. She needed to understand how to heal a seeping heart. Mostly, she wanted to tell Delaksha that on the ship something had happened, and it had caused her to misplace herself. She dialed the number. The phone rang and rang. Nobody took her call. Nobody ever did in her early days in Xiamen. She tried every day. Much later, when she tried the number again, a foreign female's voice informed her, in the inflection of similar voices elsewhere, that the subscriber could not be reached.

Ayaana hovered outside the Xiamen Ferry Terminal, trying to peer at Gulangyu Island, also known as Piano Island, across the pale green water, past fifteen white boats tethered to the land. A place of artists, of musicians. She had thought she might give herself a break from falling as she learned to cycle. She needed to escape from the invasion of pictograms in her dreams. She wanted to watch people. She wanted to look back without averting her eyes. She wanted to extend her hosts the same courtesy of curiosity they extended to her. She needed the sense of human eyes gazing back at her.

In between language and Chinese-heritage classes, Ayaana did her "duty to history." She knew her language skills had improved when she realized she could follow a whispered debate between two professors who were arguing whether to classify her as *laowai*—old foreigner—or merely *heiren*—black person. In public she was "the Descendant" with the right kind of eyes. Her linguistic progress, though slow, was acknowledged, and her opinions of China and being Chinese were sought. On the few occasions when Ayaana spoke—swathed in Chinese dress, in a voice to which she was still a stranger—she spoke basic Putonghua.

She could now make a joke in basic Mandarin, and, on cue, a hall-full of five hundred people laughed, clapped, and beamed at her, and she felt temporarily lit up from within. The next time she spoke to audiences, it was near Taicang Port, fifty kilometers northwest of Shanghai, where Admiral Zheng He had embarked on his journeys into worlds that included her own. Ayaana used words she had carefully prepared and rehearsed. She referred to common sailor ancestors, to Tang and Ming dynasty ceramics, to distinctive crescent tombs. She spoke of a child stumbling home one night by the light of the moon and meeting an old man, her Yue Xia, the matchmaker who created connections between strangers. She said that she and other islanders called him Mzee Kitwana Kipifit. Her audience laughed. Ayaana added that fate had betrothed her small island to an immense nation. The audience applauded. They especially applauded Mzee Kitwana Kipifit, the man who had sacrificed his life to offer companionship to the ghosts of lost sailors. Later, Ayaana traveled inland, where many of the tens of thousands of Ming-dynasty sailors came from, places with names she promptly forgot. She watched a likely relation—there had been a DNA match of sorts, an uncle, presumably—hack and spit a gob of phlegm. It struck the earth. She stood with many possible relatives. They shared one another's perplexity. Four putative aunties touched her hair and rubbed her skin. With time and distance from official eyes, something meaningful could have evolved. *Duty to history*, she reminded herself, *and to our nations*, as she waited to be told what to do and where to go next.

"*Ni shi zhongguoren*"—You are Chinese.

Ayaana so badly wanted to feel it.

But the more she spoke, the more Pate pervaded her dreams, until she could no longer speak of Pate without weeping.

She was surrounded by new acquaintances. She offered them portions of her heart. She imagined she might belong. "Now you are Chinese," they said. And she imagined they were right. Then, four weeks later, she was invited by a classmate to a tea party to find thirty people waiting for her with cameras. Flashes of light, the forced selfies, the rubbed skin—made her recognize the mere novelty that she was, something to display to family and neighbors. This realization was like news of a death. It formed a new crack in a much-fragmenting heart.

Game face.

Ayaana's public smiles started to fray. The difficulties only increased when she went to Nanjing Province to visit Admiral Zheng

He's cenotaph. The nothingness of the cenotaph was as a confusing blow. Not even a stopover at the stark new museum dedicated to his honor could assuage her sense of drifting.

Thinking of the admiral: "Where did he go?" she asked her hosts.

It was assumed that her question was rhetorical.

When Ayaana returned to her hostel room, she would sleep and pray that the dawn would postpone its arrival. Drifting. Drifting in a place where industrial fumes and towering structures choked off the sun. How could she explain to her people in Kenya that there were places in the world where humans purchased fresh air, packaged it, and sold it in cans? She slept, restless, and had the first of her dreams in Mandarin.

"What does Rabi'a al-Adawiyya say?" That is what Muhidin asked her when she whispered to him over the phone, and only him, about her discontent.

Rabi'a would have said, "Listen."

Ayaana leaned over, the better to hear the question from the audience: "Will the bones of our ancestors on your island be returned to China?" Ayaana said, "No, they belong to Pate now." After that, no further questions were permitted. Ayaana was instructed to say, in future, "Everything in time." Two days later, a question from a different audience: "What does China mean for you?" Ayaana answered, "Everything in time."

Her China? It was frozen within a Zao Wou-Ki print, spoken in the tenor of a ship captain whose hands her skin knew. A smile. Self-mockery. Learning the art of concealment. To her mother she spoke of the colors, sounds, and senses of Xiamen as if she were Xiamen's tourism ambassador. No shadows. When Munira asked, "How is school?" Ayaana trained herself to say, "Fine."

She cut back on her nonofficial outings. Her circle of acquaintances diminished. It was made up of Chen Sheng, also called

Shalom—who was obsessed with the dead poet Hai Zi, and who practiced her English on Ayaana—and Sung-Hi, who was South Korean. These became Ayaana's mall-going, clothes-shopping, Korean-pop-music-listening, park-walking, study-sharing friends. They went into one another's rooms to boil water for tea and biscuits. The two other girls hoped that their destinies and future husbands lived in North America, where they would go to after Xiamen. Ayaana wondered what she belonged to, and then slipped into bookshops to binge-read. To improve her language knowledge, she bought several children's beginner stories—folktales with pictures. Having done that, she rewarded herself by going to the English-language shelf. She noticed a title, *The Book of Chameleons*, and picked it up, as her new friends tried to hurry her up.

As part of the Descendant's tour, her hosts had taken her to Xi'an, in Shaanxi Province, the point zero of the Silk Road, which was woven into the history of Ayaana's seas. Amid the songs of Islam, of prayers in mosques and muezzin utterances, when she glimpsed Islamic themes on prayer rugs for sale, she broke down for no reason. She ached for her mother so fiercely that she bent over. In the public event titled "Descendant of the Seventh Voyage," Ayaana counted headscarves on the heads of women, the range of shades and shapes of faces; the young were dressed exactly as she was, jeans and T-shirts, and when the food was placed before her, there was no pork on the menu. She was served a large bowl of beef-noodle soup. She swallowed her food unafraid.

Ayaana sometimes escaped her responsibilities by seeking out and hopping onto fast trains to experience movement and live out the illusion of traveling miles of earth in the shortest of times. She had been given a generous travel stipend. She would travel one way to find giant cities raised by human will alone. She traveled into and through the frenzy—of movement, of people, of growth and destruction, of starting again and again. She traveled to escape, to rest. When she went to Beijing, a fog entered her body and clamped down her throat. She choked. But she lingered, whirled by the vortex, the flurry, a city of the world, for all the world. She witnessed the trading, entertaining, performing, choosing, erupting, becoming; noise, colors, crowds, scents. Someone hawked phlegm, which spattered her shoes. No space or time to stop and exclaim. Ceaseless movement. Everything was on sale and seemingly for sale. There was nothing she could not buy if she wanted. She was losing breath. She took the slower train back to Shanghai, and then Xiamen. That way she could sleep on board and imagine she was on a ship. She returned to Siming the next day. At night, as stars tried to peer down from clouded skies, a confusion of yearnings made her wonder to what she belonged? In Guangzhou, which she later visited, a West African colony had taken root. There were so many who looked as she did, in-between children, so she was the one who searched out eyes with more than curiosity. Still, after nine months of performing "the Descendant," Ayaana began to dream she was hiding inside Muhidin's Bombay cupboard, and Muhidin was outside, staving off the assaults of phantoms. In the daylight, when she surfaced, she spluttered as if from a drowning.

Mtumi wa kunga haambiwi maana.

The carrier of a secret is not told its meaning.

[59]

A gibbous moon rose high in the northern skies like a veiled beacon, and shrouded the humidity of Siming District with pale light on a Tuesday evening in early February. Ayaana looked out of her fourteenth-floor hostel window at the remains of the Spring Festival, Chun Jie, the ghost of red lanterns strung across the streets, remembering overeating, looking at the car lights from the traffic below. High tide was a kilometer away, and boats on the bay bobbed. Haicang Bridge was like a skeletal scepter haunting the waters. Hokkien-speaking voices below—it was as if all the population of the Siming District had wandered out to exclaim at the night. Upstairs, Ayaana blew her congested nose and coughed. The days had been exceptionally cold. Strident screeches from outside blended with muffled scramblings from within the corridors of her hostel. Her flu headache throbbed. Now she was gasping for silence. She held her breath. She looked at the people below as if they were fish and she a diving bird. Stillness. Feelings and colors floated past a breathless place of her own making. She opened her mouth and gulped down air, letting in the noise again.

Through half-shut eyes, she traced the outline of the midnight moon, grasping at memory, unsettled by its changeability, how it deconstructed, like the egg she had tasted a month ago, which was served as blue foam and tasted of salted fish. "Egg," she was told, and had to trust the notion. Now. Disjointed life-images more and more interwoven with the Pate she had thought she had relinquished. Xiamen's potent history had engulfed her and then tossed her into its accents, colors, streets, shops, music, water parks, the botanical garden, shops, puppet shows, food, shops, voices, the architecture of a trading people, a conquered people, a people cohabiting with the cultures the sea brought to them. She had wanted to know, to become more of herself.

Here there were routes and means of travel to every destination on earth: by road, water, railroad, and air. She had been caught in that flurry of ceaseless movement and, for a season, entered into the rush to get things done. But her feelings short-circuited. She had scrambled for and found places into which to retreat: Piano Island and Xiamen Haicang Oil Painting Village; the everyday streets, where she watched workers at work, repairing roads, pipes, and lights; the night streets, with lights twinkling, shining, beaming, ghostly beckons in what should have been darkness. Subsumed by invitations to new sentiment, new sensibility, new smells, and new ways of hearing, tasting, seeing. Yes, dissolution. And new answerless questions echoing down the corridors of her being.

Large yellow moon. Ayaana watched her world as if from within a glass cage. She coughed again and dabbed her nose with a handkerchief. Disparate soundless word: "not." Another soundless word: "what." "What then?" Yesterday, daringly, boldly, as one who burns the single road behind her, she had decided to abscond from her "duty to history." Five weeks ago, at the event where she had eaten the deconstructed almost-egg, her hostess had declared to her, in a heartfelt speech: "There is one memory. Like blood. It is on your skin." Ayaana had wanted to protect her body parts. She had then counted the heads of those who now looked at her as if she were an heirloom. *One hundred and twenty-eight heads.* An heirloom, she had read in Mandarin, was an object of value belonging to a family that had been in existence for generations. So she stood next to cardboard cutouts of Admiral Zheng He. "We are old friends." This was spelled out in four languages: Cantonese, Mandarin, English, and Kiswahili. After yet another public outing, the word "family" replaced "friends." Oddly for her, because of the questions, she was forced to pore over a past she had not known to learn before. She retraced the admiral's African pathways to anticipate what she was supposed to become. The study of Kongzi, Confucius, suggested to her other ways of knowing and reading the world. Cohabiting with shadows—here was the weight of a culture with a hulking history now preparing itself to digest her continent; here she was, with something of this land already in her blood, being made into something of a conspirator, anointed with a sobriquet: "the Descendant."

~

A slender cloud drifted past the moon's big face. Shadow and light within and outside her window. As Ayaana tilted her head to scan curved roofs in silhouette, the headache adjusted the center of its pounding from the frontal lobe to the side of her skull. In daylight, the scene below would become mostly green amid flamboyant trees, imports from her East African universe, that had been carried as seedlings and then colonized the landscape to become a Xiamen emblem. Around these, giant palms, black swans, green benches, and slate-gray water edged by green forests, bicycles to borrow, and trees with huge roots that held up the world. Her cell phone rang from under her bed, where it had slipped. Ayaana withdrew her head from the window, chewing on her bottom lip. Documents of acceptance and admission to another university lay scattered on her bed, like rectangular white puzzle pieces. She fell on her knees, hands stretched to reach for the phone. It went off. She picked it up. Missed call: Shalom, her most consistent friend. She stared at the phone, into the dimension that was Pate, from which a choice-shaping call had come.

~

Country code 254.

Kenya.

Her mother's contralto, its delighted "Ayaana!" Words rushing into one another, backtracking, circling, craving, returning. Ayaana's words jostled with her mother's phrases, picking up images to offer, so she was now telling Munira about differences in the colors of light. "It is not the same moon here," she said.

"*Du!*" her mother exclaimed. Then she asked: "Are you eating? Do you have friends? How are your teachers? Do they like you? Are you warm? Will you become a lawyer?"

Ayaana recalled the acupuncture sessions in her Chinese-medicine class. *Lawyer? Ha!* She offered a noncommittal "Mhh."

More news from the island, the state of tides and fishing, the return of species that used to be hijacked by trawlers before the pirates secured the currents, the death of two fishermen—freak accident on the jetty—the heart attack and consequent death of the muezzin Abdulrauf. He was not going to be replaced.

Munira's voice deepened. She said, "I have important news."

"Yes?"

"Are you sitting down?"

Ayaana's heart faltered. Fear monsters filled the spaces of distance from her beloved ones, and circled Ayaana with morbid suggestions: Death. Disease. Loss.

Ayaana bit her nails as her mother said, "Something's happened."

Ayaana strained to hear.

Munira rushed, "*Lulu* . . . do not object . . . Now Muhidin, your father . . ." she said. "Well, Ayaana . . . we decided . . . What am I saying? We are to be together. We shall marry." Silence. "Ayaana?"

The ground had tilted.

Munira's words only coalesced inside Ayaana's mind after a minute. Ziriyab's omnipresent phantom gasped through her. Could the agonizing season of his absence simply be ended? How unfair life could be.

Something Delaksha had said niggled at Ayaana: *We adapt, you see.*

Ayaana said, "Muhidin?"

Munira said, "We were not expecting it, but then . . . well . . ."

Utter silence.

Munira added, "And . . . you know . . . it's been difficult in Pate, so . . . Ayaana, we are going to Pemba. Mozambique. There's work there for Muhidin. Oh, Ayaana, and, at last, we will go to Mecca together. Ayaana, are you there?" Munira stopped. "Ayaana? Hello? Hello?"

. . .

Ayaana had dropped her phone. She sat on the floor, staring at the wall and seeing nothing. Nothing. Ayaana retrieved the phone to call her mother back half an hour later.

She asked, "You are l-l-eaving Pate?"

"Yes."

"Put him on the line," Ayaana said.

"Ayaana . . ."

"Ma . . ." Her mind was racing. Hadn't she wanted this? So why was she horrified? She knew why. She wanted to be where they were, to have this adventure with them—to know that they were not proceeding with life without her. How could they leave home?

Muhidin's rasping voice came to the line. "Abee-hee-rah," he breathed.

Ayaana waited.

"Abeerah," Muhidin repeated, "you are happy?"

Silence. *Why leave?* she wanted to ask.

Muhidin said, "So, my girl, life happens. What do you have to say, hmm?"

Ayaana said nothing.

Muhidin laughed. "Shocked?"

And Ayaana understood then that her mother and Muhidin would proceed with their choice with or without her blessing. She asked, "When do you leave?"

"Maybe after two months."

Ayaana's heart pounded. Sweat beaded her brow. Muhidin said, "Pemba is not so far away."

Silence.

Muhidin asked, "How are you?"

"Fine," replied Ayaana.

"Boys bothering you? Remember what I taught you to give to fools? Kick the balls, punch the nose—*twa!*—break the bone." He cackled.

For a tiny second, as Muhidin spoke, the long shadow of Lai Jin flickered, and she thought, *There are those who steal in through the heart.* She laughed, but her soul was not in it. Her voice shook. "Will Pemba now be home?"

"It is on our sea; our sea is home. Pemba is just next door."

"Let me speak to Mother."

Muhidin said, "First teach me Chinese. How do you say, 'The sea is warm'?"

"In Mandarin, *Hai shi wennuan de*."

"*Hai shi wennuan de*, Abeerah." Muhidin cleared his throat.

They paused, as if touching heads, as if Ayaana were reading him through his eyes. Then Munira returned to the line.

"You are happy?" Ayaana asked her.

Munira did not answer.

Ayaana now understood something of the fear of unseen forces that hovered, waiting to consume hope. "I'm happy for you," Ayaana burst out, in defiance of greedy fates.

Munira's soft, soft laugh. Stillness. Until Ayaana suddenly whispered, "Who is my father? Where do I find him?"

Munira heard her. Munira ignored her. Munira said, "It is so late; soon we shall speak again. I leave you in God's hands."

Abandoned.

Haunted by transience of the one thing that should have been constant—home. It should not have mattered, since she had wanted to leave. But it did. It felt like betrayal. It made Ayaana's skin clammy and her body restless. A question hammered at Ayaana day and night, aggravating a headache and growing flu.

What was she?

What she was now certain about: *not* a Chinese-medicine practitioner.

Emboldened and confused by the change of direction in her mother's life, Ayaana thought to remake her own world. The sea. The only thing she was sure of was the sea. In the sea, there was always room for her. Just after the moon appeared, Ayaana had reached into her wide, three-level bookshelf and dragged out the first book: *Treatise on Cold Damage Disorders*. She carried it to her open window. Enough with the geography of Chinese bodies, and expectations that she master meridians and map energy flows, herbs, temperature, color, and harmony; no more struggling with qi, yin-yang, and qigong; no more Wu Xing—*mu*, *huo*, *tu*, *jin*, and *shui*—wood, fire, earth, metal, and water—to decipher inexplicable things. She liberated herself from Zhong yi. As the book flew out of her window, Ayaana also declared her independence from "duty to history . . . and to our nations."

[60]

After Ayaana left for China, Muhidin had suffered Munira's ignoring him, her sniping if he tried to talk to her. She tossed aphorisms at him—*"Huna mshipi, hu nangwe"*; *"Kuomoa tenga na nini?"* She would not engage. One evening, after Munira had for the third time in two months dumped rancid water on his head as he passed beneath her low balcony, and had exclaimed, again, *"Aliye kando haangukiwi mti"*—A tree does not fall on one who stands aside—Muhidin had finally snapped. Dripping water, he pounded Munira's door for at least half an hour, quite ready to destroy it.

Munira had finally flung open the door and started to say, "You drinking ass," when, without speaking, he herded her back into the confines of her kitchen and shoved her up against the table holding a bowl of rose water, so that her hand touched the vessel and it spilled over. *"Atekaye maji mtoni hatukani mamba,"* Muhidin breathed.

Munira wanted to scoff at his allusion to crocodiles again. Instead she breathed, "What do you want?"

"You, of course," Muhidin answered.

Blood rushed into Munira's head as Muhidin lowered his head to touch his mouth to the center of her neck. He continued, "Since I am a man of tradition—I no longer approve of adultery—we shall be married."

She responded by trying to scratch his skin. Her fingers tore off his shirt. A confluence of emotions. "You hyena!" she moaned.

Muhidin dragged her down to the floor with him. In urgent possessiveness, they tumbled together down their chasm of longing.

"I've needed you," Muhidin repeated to her. "I've needed you. I've needed you."

Crushing each other, now that there were no others to hide behind. Falling, falling into each other.

Just before dawn, they had sought out the night seas together. "This is where I first saw you," Muhidin said. There they spoke of hidden things.

Munira spoke of beginnings—"I don't believe in man," she said.

"You'll believe in me."

She told him of learning how to die every day. "You can't outrun your shadow," she added.

He asked, "Who decides?"

She answered, "Stop it. We *know* the truth. Even as we lie." She added, "We will speak of death before we dare to speak of our loneliness. *Dua la kuku halimpati mwewe.*" The prayer of a chicken does not move the hawk. "But I'm alive. Isn't that good?" Laughing at herself, bile in her voice.

Muhidin shook her. "Stop that!" Munira shivered. "I am here," Muhidin said. Munira was crying in a high voice. Muhidin said, "Who will hurt us now together like this?" Munira wanted to believe Muhidin.

One day, two months later, Muhidin told Munira, "We are leaving Pate."

Her eyes widened. Fear, and then a subtle thrill. "What's this, Muhidin?"

He did not answer at once.

Munira deflated. "Ah! You wish not to be seen with me." She pulled away.

Muhidin grabbed her by the shoulders. "Munira . . . listen . . . When I left . . . When I went"—he lowered his head—"to Nairobi to find out about Ziriyab . . . went to the CID . . . then, you see, they took me to prison. I was in prison. They held me there. You see, Munira?" Muhidin broke down.

"Why?" Munira whispered.

"They said I was a 'terrorist.'" Muhidin wiped his face. "No court. No judge. Every day, questions: What do I know, what do I think, what do I do? Where was I when this or that happened? Who is my God?" Silence. Then "What's this 'terrorist'?" Hard look. "My identity card—it is not mine. I stole it, they say." He laughed. "One day they'll come to look for me."

"Why?" Munira stroked his face.

Muhidin muttered, "*Pwani si Kenya*"—The coast is not Kenya.

Munira dropped her hand. "I hate politics."

"No, *mpenzi,* it is what Kenya says to me."

"You drink, Muhidin?"

Muhidin glared before growling, "Kenya cured me." He sighed and continued: "If I stay here, I'll become this thing. Then they'll kill me. They'll say, *We have our 'terrorist.'* And when I die, who will shield you?"

"So you will leave?"

"You will come with me."

"Why?"

"I won't leave you again."

"Ziriyab."

Muhidin blinked. "Yes."

"What do you say?"

"Nothing. You?"

Munira moved her hands to her neck to unclasp the gold chain that held Ziriyab's ring, the one with a ruby strip. She opened up Muhidin's palms to place the chain and ring in his hands. A tremor in her own hand.

Evaporating ghosts.

They shielded their affair from nosy eyes, and hid their plans. They whispered their expectations and fears only to each other.

"We're not young," Munira said more than once, her eyes wistful. "To start again . . . we're not young."

"We are alive," he insisted.

She asked, "How to live?"

"Let's go."

"Where?" She asked.

"Pemba . . ."

"Not Zanzibar, Muhidin, please," she spluttered.

"Mozambique, my dove. I've got people there."

Munira stared at Muhidin, soundless. She stretched out her hands toward him. He lifted them to cover his face.

Almost a week later, Munira phoned Ayaana to share their news with her.

[61]

Days after that phone call, unbeknown to her sponsors, Ayaana searched for and found a bachelor-of-science program in nautical science studies. With this, she disconnected herself from her role as the Descendant. Ayaana applied for a fall semester admission to Xiamen Maritime University. She invoked Admiral Zheng He in her letter as her motivator, reference, and inspiration. She wrote of practical legacy. She saw herself as a bridge, as ships are, between worlds and people. "The ocean is but a passageway," she wrote. "It needs navigators." She was offering her service to the sea. At first her requests were ignored. Then she was informed that she was jeopardizing her scholarship and her living allowance. Ayaana hesitated. The generous allowance meant that she could save properly for the first time in her life. But in her next public-encounter meeting, Ayaana spoke of her dreams of the ocean, invoking the esteemed admiral again. She spoke in simple Mandarin, dressed in a Chinese dress of vivid red, looking modest and humble and grateful. It was her best public performance. Her hosts could not refuse her dreams without losing face. Moreover, there had been no written contract covering the shape of this particular adventure. Her admission into the maritime school was accepted in bad humor by sponsors who had also grown bored of generating narratives and performances for their *houyi.*

Liwalo lolote, na liwe.

What will be will be.

[62]

There were seventeen others in her class in the nautical science studies program, and they represented different maritime countries. Chinese and Malaysians, two Indians, two Pakistanis, one from Singapore, two from the Philippines, one Turk, the rest from Indonesia. There were two other women, both Chinese, one of them from Hong Kong. Ayaana was the only Kenyan and African. With her "Descendant" tag, her lanky height—she was taller than most of the men—and her dark-skinned yet also familiarly Asiatic looks, she had to contend with extra curiosity. She shrugged this off, focused on her work, and passed her continuous assessment tests with good marks.

Ayaana was surveying the longest line on the globe's three-dimensional grid, the equator, the first line of latitude. Her special point zero, 40,075 kilometers long; 78.7 percent across water, 21.3 percent over land, zero degrees, all the Kenya equator places she had never imagined to claim as her own: Nanyuki, Mount Kenya. The invisible equator line crossed only thirteen countries—Kenya, Ecuador, Colombia, Brazil, São Tomé and Principe, Gabon, Republic of the Congo, Democratic Republic of the Congo, Uganda, Somalia, Maldives, Indonesia, and Kiribati—thirteen countries that were the center of the world, and hers was one of them. She vowed she would one day go and walk the spaces for herself.

Ayaana turned her gaze to the blue area on the globe, to the 78.7 percent of equator that she was supposed to reflect on.

Deluged, and at sea.

Far too many forces to contend with. Yesterday's celestial-navigation session had introduced her to quasars, those remote, energy-producing constants from which GPS devices framed their reference. The week before, the class had focused on active and passive sonars. The sea had many sources of noise, she had learned; she had been surprised that something so obvious was treated as news. Today Ayaana scowled at an enhanced image of the oceans. Earlier, the class had been reviewing electronic navigation systems while she had been daydreaming about Mehdi's and Muhidin's stars, or night boat rides from Pate to Lamu with a *nahodha* who watched skies, monitored winds, and read sea surfaces. She blinked and returned to the work at hand, disappointed to imagine that getting from point A to point Z now required so many beeping and burping units that governed the waters on behalf of real navigators. She was studying the data from her Geographic Information System readings and toying with other buttons to try to make a map of her own imagining of the seas. Ayaana moved the navigational computer's cursor before pushing a button that revealed the latitude and longitude of a longed-for waypoint: "Pate Island: 2.1000 ° S, 41.0500° E."

Ayaana would learn that there seemed to be no absolutes in the world, only codes and questions and a guarantee of storms. In realizing this, she excavated echoes of a childhood conversation: She had asked Muhidin, "What is good about water?" Muhidin had said, "Storms." She then asked, "What is bad about water?" He had answered, "Storms again." Now, in class, Ayaana stared miserably at her accumulation of the technical instruments with which she would analyze and eviscerate the unknowable sea.

She raised her hand.

She lowered it. What had she been about to ask? A matter of distances, the place of intimacy: *What was the story of a human being within the epic that was the sea?* She chewed on a finger and looked around and chose silence.

She would have to relinquish her feeling for water to the power of numbers, navigational compasses, Napier's Rules, coordinates, and geopolitics. She watched her lecturer. Could she propose that the sea sweats differently depending on the time and flavor of day and night? That there are doorways within the sea and portals in the wind? That she had heard the earth and moon and sea converge to sing as a single storm-borne wind, and these had called her to dance, and that she had danced at night with them under a fecund moon?

A secret grin.

She would be deported.

A shuffle of papers, a different image on the projector. The lecture on sea routes was proceeding with another elaboration of "the Belt and Road Initiative." They were reviewing the Five Principles of Peaceful Coexistence. Suddenly the lecturer called out Ayaana's name: "*Baadawi xiao jie.*" Ayaana jumped as the lecturer gestured. "Shared future destiny, yes?"

The class turned to gaze at Ayaana.

Ayaana shrank into her seat, focusing on the sound of the slogans: "Honor in trade, prosperity for all." The lecturer continued, "Our Western Ocean is our gateway to mutual greatness." In the retelling of the life of her sea, Ayaana saw that the Maritime Silk Road initiative had gobbled into Pate's place in the Global Monsoon Complex. By her very presence, Ayaana felt implicated, as if she were betraying her soul. She sank further into her seat, also overwhelmed by this infinite land of infinite armies and infinite words, and the machinery that at a signal could roll over skies, waters, and earth to reach her home and cause it to disappear. She had come to school wanting to enter into the language of the seas through a people she was to imagine were her own. Instead, she was learning how the world was reshaping itself and her sea with words that only meant energy, communications, infrastructure, and transportation. Storm warning. Neither Pate nor the Kenya she had rarely thought about had acquired a vast enough imagination to engulf the cosmos that was writing itself into their center. Ayaana suppressed a sigh and eavesdropped on the snipings of the other foreign students, who had resorted to petty territorial snipings that changed nothing, her thoughts in turmoil.

One hot and humid day, Ari, a student of marine engineering from India, observed that the Maritime Silk Road initiative subsumed the *Indian* Ocean—he had emphasized "Indian"—to "others." "It is not for nothing that the ocean is called Indian," he noted.

Ayaana retorted, "Ziwa Kuu?"

Ari turned to her. "Oogle Boogle?"

"Ziwa Kuu." Ayaana refused to cede territory.

Ari said, "We'll discuss that with your good self the day your country acquires a motorboat to start a navy."

Ayaana said, "Ziwa Kuu, and we have a navy."

"Doubtless its fish bounties are commendable, but what else?"

Titters.

"Ratnakara," said an Indonesian.

"*Indian* Ocean," emphasized Ari.

"Ziwa Kuu," repeated Ayaana.

"*Indian* Ocean."

Two Pakistani students chimed in: "Ziwa Kuu!"

The class slipped into an uproar that did not change Chinese foreign policy. The lecturer, who had watched the disintegration of order in his class in disbelief, his face becoming blotchy, at last screamed, "The Western Ocean! You are in China."

"Western Ocean," murmured Ayaana, looking at Ari from beneath her bangs as she doodled the words "Ziwa Kuu" on her notepad, thinking about a Kipate toponym, her heart pleased about the meaningless skirmish she had stirred. The lecturer was shouting out his points. Ayaana returned to jotting down notes of another nation's imagination for her sea. "One belt, one road," she wrote. She would have to ask Muhidin what the different Kipate names for her sea were.

The debate re-emerged outside, and more positions were taken, which then split into nation-states and cultural attachments. Ayaana was in the middle of the argument, standing on the shifting water of history, her memory, and the silences of men like Mehdi. She was still astounded by the delusions built over the debris of the lives of her people, stories razed and reacquired by others, the strangenesses—that, for example the *dau* belonged elsewhere. She did not have the lexicon, and she knew the fear of an inability to explain, reclaim, and possess. She tried to speak of the poetry of sea lives, of the ceaseless ebb and flow of her people to other worlds—as traders, seekers, and teachers; as navigators, shipbuilders, archivists, and explorers—and their return.

"Slaves," Ari added.

Ayaana glared at Ari. She had never spoken so much to her classmates. In slow-drip mischief, she told Ari, "We want our maharaja back." Ari gestured at her. "Sardar Singh of Jodhpur, Ari." Her voice was cool.

Ari spluttered.

Then, just as quickly as her ire had risen, Ayaana was overcome by the languageless-ness of the present, the silenced and ruined who inhabited the present, the terror that there would be nobody left to salvage the ocean's Kipate name.

She walked away.

What was the point?

In this country, they spoke of the sea's future in Mandarin and English, not in Kiswahili, or Gujarati or Malay or Kipate. Ayaana walked toward the shimmering water, scanning for patterns. Dark blue clouds in southwestern skies—a cold front was approaching. She strode past an older student, a man turned out in the latest Yohji Yamamato gear, who had taken to watching Ayaana, and to whom she was still oblivious. She was thinking of the charts she had not studied in preparation for the rough-seamanship sessions taking place on open water the next day.

[63]

The rain and mist had reduced visibility to zero when a vision rose from the smoke of an explosion that had just killed his ship. It had outlived its usefulness, Shanghai Accent had informed him, enjoying his pallor. Lai Jin had raised his voice in rage at the plan, and by doing so had inadvertently revealed a vulnerability point. Shanghai Accent would avenge the loss of his contraband. MV *Qingrui* would be scrapped. It had taken time for them to obtain all the documents for a legal scrapping. This coincided with the end of Lai Jin's prison term. Now what Lai Jin saw cut him. An explosion. He heard it. He saw it. He acknowledged it. It was intended, although it would be registered as an accident. Buffeted by a helplessness that his recent prison sojourn had underlined, Lai Jin watched his beloved companion, the MV *Qingrui*, die needlessly. And a grown man who had been unable to grieve his other losses bawled for an even-keeled, plucky vessel of the seas that had always brought her captain and her crew to harbor. He saluted her and wished death on the insensible world.

. . .

Captain Lai Jin had been arrested, charged, and judged guilty of negligence and obstruction, and of partial responsibility for the death of an unregistered passenger. Before he could protest, imagining this was a joke, to his shock, he had then been sentenced to prison for thirteen months. Losing face. Losing life. Losing self. Losing heart. He did not faint. He lost his voice. He had disembarked from his ship and re-entered his country in chains, his home a dormitory also occupied by murderers and embezzlers. They all worked the fields and roads. His only meaning was in routine. Rhythm, as if this were a version of sea waves—this and silences kept his mind ordered. He learned to become indifferent to his nightmares until they, too, lost their voices. A year and a month later, his sentence served, the prison authorities returned to him his earthly goods. These included Muhidin's watch.

Ping!

In the end, again, there was fire. This has been said before. In Lai Jin's end, there was a fire. If passersby wondered at the disheveled man peering seaward and stooping next to a temporary rubbish dump, they said nothing.

Ping!

The watch: marker of sentiments. It reminded him of her.

He would return the watch to her. Finish with the past. He was a product of his country and its habits of rewriting itself and always starting again.

Ping!

He had paid his debts.

He watched the minute hand of the watch as if it might go backward.

Ping!

There was only now.

Yellow fire, thick black-silver smoke, and the stench of dead dreams: in the beginning, there was fire. In the distance, five rust-and-gray ships drifted toward other elsewheres. He was standing before thresholds again. Lai Jin shuffled his feet, warming them. They pressed into a brittle object, which crunched and cracked. He bent and picked up a broken embossed vase, with an unusual red swallow fluttering over a motif of blue waves. It had a thin white glaze. There was nothing special about it.

The next explosion that rent the air disintegrated the former MV *Qingrui.* Black smoke. Lai Jin might have cried out again if her spirit had not descended from the fray and found him. *We shall sail again,* he might have promised her in English, which was the agreed-upon common language of the waters.

But everything fades.

Even promises.

Above the fire, dark sheeplike clouds trotted across the sky. Lai Jin watched. He heard seagulls cry, playing with airstreams and diving for fish.

Life.

What was his destination now? He looked at the glaze on the vase, reading its texture with the tips of his fingers. *How did the vase travel here?* The rain and sun and dust had left traces on these fragile portions. Churning heart. He stroked the shape of assorted brokenness, its bruises. *Where did it come from?* He looked around for its other parts, retrieved a discarded plastic bag, and started collecting ceramic shards. *To whom did it belong when it was whole?*

Memories. His mother, Nara, at her kiln.

She was weaving his tiny hands into the wet clay. Laughter. They laughed because they were not expected to. She was mad, he was told, and she laughed far too loudly, and she pulled odd beasts out of the soil with her hands and turned them into things that lived. "Vessels," she had whispered to him, when he was too young to understand, "they are for the storage of ghosts." They had laughed again before he was found and taken from her. But he knew that the night was for making things. He would crawl out of bed to find her at her wheel, then watch her until he fell asleep. He watched her because he was afraid *they* would make her leave him. They would. They did. They never told him. At night, before they dismantled Nara's wheel and brick kiln, he would still go to the wheel and will it to action. He would do this until the day he was also sent away from home—to study, they told him.

A landfill guardian appeared. He chased the former ship captain away, imagining him to be another decrepit entity, one among millions who scavenged for the scraps from life's table. Lai Jin hurried out with a supermarket bag over his shoulder. It was bulging with so many broken fragments.

[64]

Ayaana had swathed herself in the cocoon of night as one of Xiamen's many anonymous restless ones. Night pulsed with its particular beat. From a wooded enclosure where swans slumbered, close to the waterfront, Ayaana watched the flickering of human nightlights as if they were the stars she needed to sit under. Another landscape, one she preferred, emerged after midnight. Here she forgot about the day. Blurred objects. Blurred emotions. Blurred lines. A good night was if she managed four hours of sleep. Nothing worked. Since she did not bother with sleeping pills, she preferred to watch the night as if on a ship's bridge, navigating her vessel through dense currents, under the gaze of constant stars.

Stillness.

Then something stirred in the woods—a breaking twig, the mew of wind, salt smells, a lone bird's frantic cry. The scent of sea here was not the same as it was in Pate, nor were the silences. In the night, she could see into the edges of her heart and hear its silent hopes echo back. Soon a sense that she was not alone settled upon her.

One night—*ping!* As if Muhidin's watch and its lost time had found a way to her. She did not turn. She shut her eyes and remembered the indecipherable murmurs of the djinns at sea. Two days later, a delicately wrapped package was delivered to Ayaana. When she tore it open, she found Muhidin's watch. There was no return address. The watch pinged. A feeling grazed her heart. It was the same as that of being seen and known by a Zao Wou-Ki painting.

Munira called Ayaana. "Rumors in the wind. Suleiman has been lured by the Jabhat Tahrīr Sūriyā al-Islāmiyyah."

The Syrian Islamic Liberation Front.

Stunned silence.

"Amina Mahmoud parades the land, cursing the stars, demanding that God retrieve her son."

Ayaana shivered: the specter of Fazul the Egyptian. The memory of how her will had been bled by a ghoulish man with word, touch, and a look. She scratched her skin and looked over her shoulders. "*Ma-e*, have the dragonflies returned yet?"

"Soon. Why do you ask?"

"No reason." Ayaana missed the golden skimmers. She missed her anticipation of their arrival. She missed how they summoned the rain and the warm *matlai*. "No reason," she repeated to her mother. But, later, she would whisper to the Fujian night that the dragonflies would be landing on Pate Island, far away, that a boy she knew might have been seized by an abyss of hate.

Elsewhere.

After that infinity of watching his ship disintegrate, the man would take a year to cover a wide and large road back to one of the places that had been home for him. Guangzhou in Guangdong. The place from which he had departed to enter the world, leaving behind a career bureaucrat father and his fancy wife. Lai Jin had gone to Beijing to study business, physics, and visual arts before being dispatched by his father, first to Singapore, and then to Canada. Lai Jin would give up on his half-hearted efforts to keep in touch with the family that, he realized, had restarted life without him. He had focused on excelling in business, and, after he met Mei Xing, becoming the quality husband his father had not been for his mother, Nara. But now, wistful steps back. Emptied. He stopped to gape at the multipurpose complex that had replaced the apartment building where the family had lived.

Seeking work, Lai Jin looked up a former business associate. The man, a maker of kettles for export, offered Lai Jin the job of factory night watchman. Lai Jin tried to object. Tried to ask how the stain of a perceived disorder—his imprisonment—could erase the knowledge of his total being in the eyes of one whom he had imagined was an intimate. They had got drunk together, several times, at Lai Jin's expense. A single crack on the record of his life now prevented this person from seeing him as he had been, and still was. Hollow-eyed, cracked-lipped, he gathered his few things, those broken shards of glazed pot he had picked from the shipyard, and quietly walked away.

Shattered self, shattered illusions, scattered thoughts, and little more than the memory of a storm—how vital he had felt then—on a ship to keep him intact. He wandered, his collected shards tinkling in rhyme with his steps, not knowing whether he could stop this time. One dusk, looking down at the sea beyond a former fishing village that speculators with their concrete-edifice raising machinery had started to reclaim, with the last light shining in his eyes, he suddenly remembered Mei Xing's Hangzhou Bay property. He had every hope that it had slipped through an asset purge to which he had been subjected when he had lost his freedom.

[65]

Xinchun kuaile—Happy new spring! *Xinxiang shi cheng*—And may all your wishes come true. Nostalgia-tinged bonhomie. A young woman laughed in the crowded room, which already smelled of illicit smoke. A heady sense of simply being swirled within her, in time to the music. Everything had acquired extra depth. Life throbbed with such an intensity of possibility that an enchanted Ayaana had laid aside her ordinary caution. Someone replaced the same teeny voices, same song, same melody of ubiquitous Korean pop with the convoluted sitar riffs of an unknown male singer. Three wall-mounted television screens flickered. The creatures they portrayed gestured and gasped like drowning shadows. Nobody was attending to the broadcast. Scattered around the room lay the debris from an indifferent party with food specially prepared for Chun Jie, the New Year's celebration: dumplings filled with every type of meat, spring rolls, and *niangao; tangyuan* for family harmony and fish to increase prosperity. Ayaana had avoided the noodles. There were also fizzy drinks and juices, and smuggled-in alcohol, evident in the slurring conversations and familiar limb draping around unresponsive bodies. Round and golden citruses, red-and-gold-themed room décor. Voices and words in Mandarin, Cantonese, Hokkien, and English. The room was full of the refugees of the spring break—the outsiders who had no family nearby to retreat to.

A young woman swayed slightly as she watched the dancers, not knowing yet that she would become beguiled by an enigma. Koray Terzioğlu watched her. They were the only two who had not joined the general fray. The international students had clumped together to mark, not the occasion, but their homesickness. Surveying the room, Koray rubbed his cheekbone and nose with the nub of his brass ring. He leaned back on the fat purple cushion to contemplate the now laughing woman through his bangs. The students were performing a serpentine Bhangra conga, to music that, for him, was a sustained hyperventilation. The woman by the window seemed to know the lyrics; she was mouthing them. Koray had never paid attention to the contemporary music of India before, and he would try never to do so again.

One of the oldest students, Koray was muscled, hooded-eyed, and full-lipped. His thick, black, glossy, curly hair had its own Twitter hashtag. An earring dangled from the tip of his right earlobe—an experiment he would give up that night. Koray, something of an idol on campus, was one of the very few students who could afford to live in luxurious sea-view apartments. His English was proper; his family had paid for an English tutor. He was a catch, and he knew it. Captain of the basketball team, he had also created the institution's first sommelier club. He held the record for the best calculus grades, to the chagrin of his Chinese peers, until a young woman from an obscure African spot materialized and took the shine off him. He would learn that she was some sort of Chinese symbol. Curiosity piqued, he had sought her out and had become dry-mouthed when a slender being wafting some ineffable fragrance had glided past without seeing him. She had earphones on, and her eyes were cast low. She never saw him following her. This rankled the most. Koray decided to study her as he would a territory he intended to dominate.

A new song interrupted his thoughts. Hearing it, Koray seized his head. Was this not perhaps the same song he had heard a second ago, by the same croaker, who should never have been near a microphone in the first place? He watched Ayaana's mouth. Sure enough, it moved as it mouthed words to what was probably a song about a fat wading waterbird hunting for frogs with extraordinary success. Koray leaned forward to straighten the cuffs of his shirt. He retied the laces of his bespoke sneakers. He rose in one languid move. The action attracted the attention of some of his inebriated followers. "Koray, Koray!" They were inviting him to the dance floor. He ignored them. He sauntered over to a table laden with drinks. His eyes settled on a jug of cheap sake.

Koray had already downed a plastic mug half filled with the drink, and was topping up, when the hint of rose made him turn.

Ayaana was diluting a juice cocktail with ice water.

Koray greeted her. "Gong Xi Fa Cai!" His accent was flat. Ayaana turned. "Nonalcoholic?" He stepped into her space so she was forced to move back. Ayaana glanced up. Fathomless, scrutinizing gaze. She had to step away again from this presence. Of all the students on campus, he oozed a certain careless air, as if it did not matter to him whether he passed or failed. His eyes caressed Ayaana. "Your drink"—she looked at the pale orange liquid—"is diseased." She giggled.

"Good. I wanted you to laugh for me," he said. She tilted her head. "Tell me, from where did you acquire the words to these maledictions?"

Ayaana frowned. Koray gestured at the speakers. "I suspect you believe this to be 'music'?"

Ayaana's laugh exploded. "'Dilbara,' from *Dhoom*."

Koray raised a quizzical brow. "Why would an African know that?"

"Uh . . . Bollywood!" Ayaana suddenly felt awkward. How to explain the feeling that her world had became larger, more colorful, and musical because of her dips, with Muhidin, into Bollywood? She was turning away when he said, "I have wanted to meet you for a long time, Miss Ayaana."

Ayaana pivoted. Koray reached for her arm, mistaking the shine in her large, slanted eyes for interest. He enunciated his words. "We have much in common. China, classes, faith, history, the seas . . . destiny?" Half joking, he wagged a finger at her nose. "Don't ignore me." He stared her down.

She remembered to pull her arm from his hold.

Koray flushed. "Your calculus marks are unassailable. I am struggling to crush them. You irk me." He stooped to whisper into her ear, "I have never learned how to lose."

A challenge, a warning. Her confusion clashed with a most unexpected frisson. It was the combination of Koray's touch on her skin and his cologne, a blend of sea spray and metal. He had the girth and height that women often confuse with a guarantee of protective strength. She now blinked at Koray as a cat might.

"Koray," he said.

Ayaana gestured.

"My name, *canim*. Koray Terzioğlu."

She shrugged.

She was heading for the opposite end of the room when he called, "Miss Ayaana!" She turned. "I intend to seize and keep your heart for myself."

Her eyes widened. And then she laughed at him. And what a laugh it was: low, infectious, and uncontained. Those who heard it laughed, too. Koray also laughed, as the first of the interminable fireworks display began. He laughed for a different reason. His boredom had dissolved. He was in pursuit of quality game. He watched the other students drift over to the balcony to stare at the display.

Ayaana stared at the ephemeral beauty of the lit-up night, hearing again the daring intent of an odd man. She was tired of her inability to resolve her restlessness. She made a face. Something about the frivolous fireworks invited recklessness. She straightened her spine and looked back at Koray. She *had* seen him in one of her classes. His expectation of being worshipped had reminded her of Suleiman, her kitten's murderer, so she had ignored him. Now, there was Koray, with his clutch of adoring females and awed males. There he was, deflecting unabashed come-ons with meaningless phrases offered in bad Mandarin: "And you are flightless, my bird beak."

Ayaana smiled.

Koray caught Ayaana's look. He pointed upward, a vow. She turned away to see a Catherine wheel burn itself out.

. . .

"Excuse me." Ayaana squeezed past the female closest to Koray. Soft-voiced to Koray, "Good night." She glided out of the room, heading for her hostel.

Hurrying footsteps. Koray's voice: "I will escort you to your door."

Ayaana slipped her hands into her pockets. "I can find it on my own."

Koray said, "You are pretty."

"As you are," Ayaana returned.

"Sarcasm, Miss Africa, right?" Ayaana looked at the sky, saying nothing. Blue pin, and yellow Ferris-wheel fireworks. Koray added, "Far from home."

She sighed, "As you are."

Koray suggested, "Fireworks; splendid colors. Shall we talk? Why waste the night?"

"No," said, Ayaana. She hurried past other sky-watching clumps of people. Koray protested. "Slow down, girl." He caught up with her. "I live in Istanbul. Have you heard of Turkey?" She rolled her eyes. "You are studying navigation," he persisted.

She hastened her pace, now regretting her gamble. In the background, above the din of foghorns from the nearby seaport, the smell of phosphorus mingled with the usual scents of Xiamen. Ayaana breathed these in. Night clouds hovered just beyond the thousands of red lanterns hanging across the streets. From the south, a refreshing cold wind approached. Koray said, "Where did you learn your English?" Ayaana ground her teeth. Koray added, "You know we have Africans in Turkey. They come on boats to escape war and poverty. We are a sanctuary." His tone was solemn. "There are some whose families have been there for centuries. Who were their ancestors? Slaves?"

Ayaana suddenly halted. "How many countries are there in Africa?"

Koray waved his hands in casual dismissal.

Ever since she had landed in Xiamen, she had been subject to great obtuseness about her continent of birth. By virtue of her existence here, she was also expected to be the "Africa interpreter." She was obliged to research the continent to prepare for the inevitable idiot question. Questions brewed out of malice, she had at first assumed, until she understood that ignorance did have unfathomable dimensions, that the word "Africa" did trigger the release of some stupidity hormone, that when a physics professor wondered aloud to her why Africans ate Africans while there were lions around—why couldn't Africans eat lions?—he was interested, not insane. Ayaana had at first tried to counsel the foolishness, discovering a new voice within herself. But she had neared saturation point.

Slowly, as Mama Suleiman might, she noted the blobby earring on his earlobe. Her eyes narrowed. "Koray"—Ayaana's tone was cold and dry—"use your time here to get educated about the world. Right now you sound thicker than a baobab trunk." She looked up at a circular building with lights in scattered windows. "My hostel." She walked a few steps forward before looking over her shoulder. "Is that a bull's nose ring attached to your ear? Why would a human being do that to himself?"

Koray, gape-jawed, watched Ayaana vanish through a door. Had she just associated him with livestock? He touched his earring. *Thicker than a baobab trunk?* He started to walk away in slow steps, enraged. He rubbed his head and then allowed himself a cool chuckle.

I only wish to face the sea, with spring flowers blossoming.

—Hai Zi

[66]

Weaving clay. Tugging at the tides and drawing time inward. Feeling, touching, watering, molding new life, the vessels. There was age in the dust; there were memories, and ashes from the press of earth on souls. When he touched the clay, it was as prayer, and he knew the prayer was for life. It was either this or die. Weaving clay, sewing up the holes in his life. Kaolin stains on a man's overalls, his fingers wrapped around a roundish, moist gray lump of clay pressed to a rotating wheel head. His dampened hands slapped the clay, creating evenness. Squeeze, pull, cradle, shape. He moved his thumb, feeling his way into a center, pressing the lump down and inward. His right hand pressed the clay down. He dampened his hand. He was getting better and better at communing with the clay, knowing when to stretch it, smooth it, add water, and soothe it. He worked it up as the wheel turned and the hole widened. Right hand, fingers, both hands cradled the lump, giving it a form. His hands thinned the sides of the clay. The vessel had started to emerge, inside the neglected shelter he had reclaimed. Now he smoothed the mouth. He was starting with the basics, remembering the terse dreams of a silent mother. Like her then, he too had lost himself. Now, a repossession of meaning, memory by memory, while trimming the vessel he had created with a scalpel. Removing the extraneous things. He would be using a firing mound. This was his thirty-fifth attempt. If he were to be grateful for just one thing from his unfair prison sojourn, it was that the hand-roughening, soul-crushing labor on fields and roads had offered him a reacquaintance with soils.

[67]

Ayaana was hurrying from the small-town mosque, her head covered with a neon-pink scarf, and dissatisfaction marring her face. The overwhelming smell of street cooking made her retch. She covered her nose. She did not dare lower her veil. It hid the disastrous outcome of her first visit to a hairdresser who had at first gawked at her in terror, as if her hair might bite him. He had then permitted her to lean back over a basin, where he proceeded to scrub her hair for fifty minutes, muttering about its hardness in a ceaseless whine. Whatever he was incanting attracted a salon crowd that gathered around her head with dragon-slaying looks on their faces and exclamations in their voices. A few rubbed her skin, as if expecting her gold-brown to rub off.

She had endured it all. What she had ached for was to feel the warmth of human hands on her face and hair. She had wanted to be pampered and tended to and pummeled and kneaded until she would emerge streamlined and beautiful.

It was not to be.

In spite of the triumph of the hairdresser, who was confident he had achieved a look that approximated those of the Supremes, Ayaana wanted to chop off her head at the neck, not just her hair. She had stumbled into the light, and desperately sought a clothing shop. In a shop that sold faux-silk scarves in colors hitherto unseen on the earth, she bought one that seemed to be pink, without haggling. She immediately wrapped her head.

Weighted down by unnameable despair, she had ventured into the mosque she had not intended to go to. There a red-bearded imam explored sacred texts and spoke in elegant Mandarin, most of which she did not understand. But other people's prayers washed over her. She told herself that she needed to be grateful. She needed to feel lucky. She was enjoying her lessons. She was talking to her mother more. Her hair was a tangled shrub with the texture of steel wool.

She was scurrying out of the mosque when a voice called, "Good evening, Miss Ayaana."

Koray. He had been waiting for her. He said, "Thought it was you."

He looked at her with a brow tilted and a smile on his lips. "Observance is very attractive in a beautiful woman."

Ayaana did not want to talk to anybody.

She tightened her veil.

"*Ex Africa semper aliquid novi,*" Koray quoted. She turned. " 'Always something new out of Africa.' " He walked beside her.

Ayaana looked around the street. Its scents were less oppressive now. She wrinkled her nose. Other days, she reveled in the smells and mapped new journeys by the variety of aromas alone.

Koray leaned toward her. "Fifty-four sovereign states, two *de facto* with limited recognition, and ten alienated territories, including Réunion, Mayotte, and Lampedusa. Sixty-six states in total."

Ayaana sighed, "What?"

"Countries in Africa. I've also been researching Kenya." "Kinya," he pronounced it. "Your country." He sounded pleased with himself. "I am preparing myself to win all my arguments with you." The lunchtime crowd squashed them against the walls of a building. Koray was in full flow. "Amir Ali Bey . . . a Turk. Stayed in your islands, fought on your people's side against marauding Europeans." He grinned. "What connections we have, Descendant."

Ayaana looked dejected, her mouth turned down at the edges.

Koray's voice was soft as he looked at her. "However, we shall not argue today." She looked up at him. "No," he said, and his eyes sparkled. He murmured, "I intend to charm you." He touched her shoulder. "I think you need a laugh, and perhaps, if I may hope, a friend?"

A salty lump grew in her throat.

Koray gestured. "I get it."

She glanced up at him.

He stroked her cheek. "I know what it is to feel lost in someone else's vast dream. You are supposed to call China home, aren't you? You think you should belong. Yet this land guards its soul with a cold-hearted dragon that won't let you in. And for you, who look a little like them, watching from outside the gates is not enough."

Tears pebbled Ayaana's eyes. Then she tried to smile.

Encouraged, Koray tucked his arms into hers. "So what really upset you, *canim*?"

She looked at him from beneath her veil, and knotted her scarf, saying nothing. They walked a short distance before Koray asked,

"Tell me, can two not-such-strangers who share a history at least break bread together?"

Touch, warmth, banter, and she realized she was hungry.

"Yes?" urged Koray.

Ayaana nodded.

Koray laughed and squeezed her arm. "Then, if you allow me . . . may I show you a little place where they serve *qingzhen cai*, chicken and noodles? And, Miss Ayaana, they also have *halwa*."

Real tears.

They turned a corner. Ayaana exhaled and composed herself. "*Halua?*" she squawked, grateful for his uncanny understanding.

"*Halwa*," Koray intoned.

Her eyes became dreamy. "*Hal*wa?"

"Yes, Miss Ayaana, *halwa*." Koray nodded at her slowly. He pulled away to jog backward, bumping into passersby.

Ayaana followed. "The people . . ." she gasped.

". . . can avoid being run over. Hurry! *Halwa!*"

"*Hal*wa!" Ayaana now sang.

"*Halwa*," Koray shouted back as the crowd parted to accommodate the madness of two foreigners zigzagging through their country, looking for sweets.

~

The shadows from the outside lights seeped through the open windows of the dingy restaurant. Eleven p.m. found a young man and woman still skulking over a steaming pot, the remains of their earlier indulgence scattered around them—bones, skin, shells. They were drinking coffee from the same mug, wrapped in the micro-universe they had invoked, oblivious to the sounds of traffic, and citizens' footsteps on the pavement. From time to time, they would pause to listen to the music, which was nothing that they had heard before, and yet was somehow familiar. There were only two others left in the small restaurant, whose owner sat in a booth in the corner, watching the world and his guests.

. . .

The pair dived headlong into a maelstrom. The look-into-my-eyes game that would become a proposition. Koray lit a cigarette and offered it to Ayaana, who wrinkled her nose and turned away sharply. She started to cough. "Smoking is not your strength," Koray deadpanned as Ayaana choked.

Koray leaned over to pound her back. He murmured, "My ex chain-smoked. I hate the stench of nicotine."

"You are smoking," she pointed out.

"Testing you," replied Koray. He ground the lit cigarette out.

Eyes streaming, Ayaana stared. Before she could formulate a question, Koray had lifted her wrist up to his nose. "Damascus rose." He said. "From Turkey."

Touch. But smell was more intimate, like being breathed in. To disguise her sudden disorientation, she retorted, "Damascus is in Turkey, right?"

"This species of rose is." His teeth gleamed, and he bent forward to kiss Ayaana's forehead and nose. Before she could react, he had returned to his seat, laughing.

Ayaana's new pink scarf had fallen to the ground. Her uncovered hair confronted the world, a defiant, hardened bouffant, as she admitted to Koray her salon misadventure. He guffawed. She sighed. He told her that beauty was a permanent condition. They giggled over his word play. Ayaana's heart started to flutter; she had not known that a person could laugh like this with a stranger.

"What does being *houyi* mean?" Koray asked her, holding on to her wrists.

"Blood connections." She shrugged. "Maybe," she added.

He paused. "But you are from Af—from Kenya."

"We share a sea. A past."

"We share the sea, too, Cousin Houyi!"

Ayaana laughed.

Yet she also paused. Wondering. The chasms in her mother's words. *Who is my biological father?*

Koray watched her shiver. "Ghosts?" he asked. Her head snapped up. Koray continued, "Tell me everything."

"No," she said.

"I insist."

She stared at him, unmoved.

Koray shifted in his seat, and dug into the sugar bowl with his fingers. "I want to know you, Ayaana." His eyes darkened, his look an accusation. "I strip mysteries . . . naked"—he grinned—"and lap their souls."

Ayaana closed her eyes. He was the most unstudentlike of students. "Why are you in China?" she asked.

Koray raised his brows at Ayaana. "To learn it. China and I have no illusions about each other, *houyi*." He stretched across to hold her hands. "Don't tell anyone else, but the truth is, the family wanted me to be here in Xiamen. It is strategic for us."

Ayaana looked quizzical.

Koray explained. "China International Fair for Investment and Trade?"

Ayaana shook her head.

"In September. Talk of the cities." Koray reached over to pick at her food. "The world's trading future is designed there." He looked at her. "You ought to attend. Come as my guest."

She gave a noncommittal shrug.

Koray leaned back, watching her. "I am here primarily to set up networks, build relationships. Acquire language competence. Observe the habits of the natives. Much easier with a student visa."

A peculiar lassitude had floated in, to settle like a fog around them. Koray's fingers drummed the table. "Are you happy?"

She said, "I am happy to be here."

"Not the same question," he noted.

She flushed. In spite of herself, she said, "I miss home . . . even if . . ." The words coming out of her mouth these days bothered her. "On most maps of the world, my island does not exist."

Koray's eyes crinkled. "Behold! A phantom from the crevices of space and time. When I saw you, I knew it!"

Ayaana laughed out loud.

Silence.

Then Koray said, "Home is imagined, Miss Ayaana." Ayaana lifted her head. Koray continued: "We are another generation, a different people. We need a new imagination of and for life. Our home is anywhere and everywhere. Wherever we want it to be. The future is not a country, not for me, and not for you."

His words entranced Ayaana. Koray tilted his head to consider her. Something cold but also mischievous lurked in his gaze. The hairs on the back of Ayaana's neck rose. She looked away, making the mistake of imagining the chilling sensation spreading all over her for attraction.

Loaded silences. Echoes of seabird cries. A waiter brought a bowl of what might have been chili chicken wings.

Koray noticed. "Sad again, *sevgilim*?"

She touched the water glass. A half-smile. "Not really."

"Try me."

Eyes meet. She pointed at the wings. "So small." She remembered the ortolan buntings.

Koray's brow puckered. "Life is drenched in absurdities; it is even woven with the suffering of birds." Ayaana drew invisible lines on the tabletop. Koray used his fingers to seize a chicken wing and pop it into his mouth. "Mmm," he said.

Ayaana looked toward the wide-open doorway. She watched a woman with back-length hair swab the floor. Zhou Bichang's low-voiced mellow tunes wafted between them. They listened to their thoughts and to Koray's chewing. Ayaana turned to the rose lokum. She moved it with small pincerlike tongs next to the pistachio *halwa*. Her heart and mind were churning. Koray's dominant familiarity was not something she knew how to deal with. She had also stuffed herself with far too many sweets. She said, "We should go back."

"Already?"

Her elbows were on the table. "Class tomorrow?"

"Hardworking *xiao jie* Ayaana."

"Yes, *xiansheng* Koray."

He looked serious. "Friends?"

Her gaze swept up, and then down. She flushed as if he were asking for more. His look was hooded. "Ay*aa*na?" he breathed.

She tilted her head. As if on impulse, Koray seized her hand. "Don't say yes or no yet . . . but, please . . . for the August-September break, before the trade fair, come home to Turkey with me. You will *love* Istanbul. Your time, your space, our family's guest. Mother will enjoy your company. Your presence will assure her that I am not wallowing in debauched loneliness in a foreign land." He lifted his hand. "No, don't answer yet. Let it steep inside your delectable head. Now"—he jumped up—"we return to the cold world. I'll walk you to your door before retreating to my bed, where I will dream of . . . you . . . and your"—his eyes glowed—"invisible island."

Ayaana punched his arm.

Koray chuckled. "I punch the girls I like." He took Ayaana's arm. "And I like you, Miss Ayaana."

They took the most circuitous way home, playing catch with bright fragments they found, chasing random flying objects, running after each other, hopscotching past people, until they reached a place where Ayaana could twirl under the night sky and Koray watched her. How they laughed. They held hands afterward. They talked. They walked in silence, surprised by their ease with each other. Outside her door, Koray kissed Ayaana on her cheek. He kissed her twice.

The days were like the shadows of swooping eagles falling on the students on campus; there was the threat of grand tempests of assorted names, but what did appear were the winds that made the sea froth white. And for Ayaana, that was the backdrop against which Koray became fascinating, for he made sure he was often in her vicinity: a charming friend, an elegant fellow student who made it apparent to others that he preferred to be where she was. When she was in Koray's imposing presence, Ayaana wondered what "man" meant, and she noticed odd things—the gestures of indelicate hands, the downturn of his lower lip when he paused to think—and her arms tingled from the imprint of seemingly unconscious caresses. It was his habit to take her arm and invite her to walk with him. It was her habit now to agree.

Aingiaye baharini huogelea.

One who goes into the sea must swim.

[68]

From the air, the Bosporus Strait resembled a strip of turquoise ribbon pouring itself into the dark blue splodges on either side that were the Black Sea and the Sea of Marmara. "İstanbul Boğazı. Inside, an undersea river . . . would be the sixth largest river in the world. It feeds the seas," Koray informed Ayaana, whose eyes were fixed on the colors of the water. "Europe, there"—Koray pointed to one brown contour—"and here is Asia." He gestured toward another brown lump. "The separation of spaces and places by name alone."

There were some visions for which words did not exist. Ayaana leaned in to the window, her eyes scanning the ground. They had studied the Bosporus. It was a crucible of testing for navigators who had to contend with, in parts, forty-five- and eighty-degree course alterations while battling unpredictable currents, blindsiding bends, and heavy maritime traffic at the same time. Narrow waterways were notoriously challenging, and this strait was right up at the top with the worst. Heart-quickening. Ayaana knew she would adore the Bosporus. Their China Southern plane touched down. "Welcome to Turkey, Miss Ayaana." Koray was clutching Ayaana's hand. She leaned in to him. He nuzzled her hair. "You shall like it here," he decreed.

She imagined she would. When they stepped out into the warm evening, Koray inhaled, his head turned skyward. Citrus and mystery. Koray said, "My country."

Residues of histories pervaded the atmosphere and Ayaana's pores. This was indeed an old country. Ayaana watched worlds of people crisscross. This place had been enshrined in the poetry of her oceans in honor of those who had come to these lands, and then returned to repeat tales of the mysterious Bosporus, home of secret water-beasts. Buzz in the air, colors and voices. And, as a whisper barely heard, floating in to strike her heart and ears, resonances of the Adhan just uttered. Her heart stirred, thrilled in spite of uncertainties, Ayaana plunged into the seduction of this drama, what it might mean to belong to a place such as this, where she imagined she might find a deep echo of home.

Ayaana whirled into Koray. And then she laughed when Koray lifted her high and swung her around. She had already forgotten the first of her errors: when Koray had sought to make their travel arrangements, and asked for it, she had handed over her passport. Even as they checked in, he had wielded it and then pocketed it with his documents. Taking charge. She had not imagined she ought to ask him to return it to her then.

Outside the arrivals door, a dark blue Mercedes stopped for them—an illegal pause that no official authority came to contradict. Koray opened the car door while a man in a gray suit collected their luggage.

There is, it is true, a powerful underwater cosmos under the Bosporus, presided over by a dense, high-volume, thirty-five-meter-deep submarine river replete with tributaries, rapids, and waterfalls. It feeds secret denizens. It bears down with sediments of history and gold and oil, which it keeps invisible to the uninitiated gaze. As below, so above: gilt-edged shadow tentacles slithered over Ayaana, causing a sudden chill to travel up and down her spine, and, when she looked, she saw a darkness trespassing on Koray's gaze.

They drove up to the mostly white Terzioğlu villa in Istanbul, one of three the family owned in the country. In partial but acceptable decay, this was their most valuable property. It was a coveted venue in space-hungry Istanbul, with its three pristine acres of thick garden. Koray told Ayaana, "I grew up mostly here. They sent me to England to study when I was twelve." A pall had stolen over him.

Ayaana studied the house as she might an eerie, grand setting for a high-volume dream. Koray's hands pressed against the small of her back. She sniffed his cologne, then stepped back to lean against him, and wiped her face as if she had stumbled into a cobweb. Koray looked down at her and half smiled. Ayaana shivered.

The large doors flung apart to reveal a made-up woman with a jar-bought glowing face. Her perfume, an intensity of flowers, and some dark spice, impregnated the air. Her delicate hands made elongated gestures, as if in prelude to a dance. She moved in quick steps. A silklike robe draped her body and veiled a dress covered with white pearls. Her thick hair, held in a bun, was bleached blond. Her posture was that of a dancer; her coordinated hand-to-eye gestures those of a Kathak adept. Koray was sedate as he stepped forward to greet his mother and kiss her on either cheek as she exclaimed, "Let me look at you." Before she turned to Ayaana.

Koray said, "Mother, Ayaana."

Nehir scrutinized Ayaana, her head tilted. "She's doable, Korayğim," she concluded. To Ayaana, "Such a creature." Ayaana automatically performed a half-curtsy. Nehir took her hand. "Kiss me here." She presented her face.

Ayaana, who was taller than she, stooped to bestow the kiss.

Nehir continued, "We will get to know one another," then swung back to her son. "Koray!" she chastised. "This is *not* a small island bird in need of feeding. Your descriptions are lacking, dear!" She leaned close. Ayaana could smell the cardamom on her breath as she said, "My son takes up causes." Nehir laughed at a secret joke. The harsh laugh chilled Ayaana. Nehir added, "Follow me. I will show you to your room—far, far away from Koray's." She laughed again. Turning back to Koray, she said as if in jest, "This child is so deliciously unfinished—unadorned face, no lipstick—deliciously unfinished. What fun we shall have together."

Ayaana looked back, glaring at Koray. He winked at her. They walked past two cracked stone wolves that guarded either side of the entryway, and up some steps, and through a large door that smelled of rust.

They walked down a dimly lit corridor from which rooms branched off. Ayaana peeked through the open doors. There were books and maps everywhere. On a large bookshelf along the passageway were books from many ages, and all authored by one Terzioğlu or another. A thickness to the air; in Ayaana's imagining, they crossed into another realm. More paintings and tapestries with folktales woven in, hung on different walls, amplified by window-sized gilt-edged mirrors. Persian carpets on the floor, and Byzantine ceramics in discreet alcoves. Some rooms were hidden behind bolted, reinforced steel doors. Soft-footed servants ordered the Terzioğlu worlds with invisible efficiency, silence, and covert side glances at Ayaana. *Where am I?* Ayaana wondered.

[69]

Unbreakable routines marked the Terzioğlu hours. Sit-down breakfast, lunch, and dinner, and the dinner drinks served in a drawing room where a glossy black grand piano lay in wait, its top board exposed, as if it were a river crocodile faking death in the hope of an easy meal. Sometimes they talked; most of the time they listened to the musical offerings of either a devotional singer or an assortment of classical music selected for their elegiac melodies. The ritualized expressions of Terzioğlu hospitality, every gesture governed by a subtle rule Ayaana had to intuit. She was repeatedly welcomed, but in every gesture and word she felt herself being assessed, studied, observed. This made her twice as nervous and three times as sensitive to nuances in the air. Her China-gained confidence shriveled before a constant gaze that seemed to have the force to reshape even her dreams.

"So . . . your father is in boats?" Koray's mother asked Ayaana, her Indian-dancer eyes lifting up, then down, and sweeping sideways.

"Navigator," Ayaana stuttered, elevating Muhidin's career choice. "Retired," she added.

"Did he do well for himself?"

"Mother!" Koray protested.

"It is an important question," retorted Nehir. "Well, did he?"

"He did his best." Ayaana stared at her soup.

She kicked Koray under the table. *Did he tell his mother everything?* He smiled.

"What does your mother do?"

"Beauty."

"Cosmetologist?"

Ayaana did not know that word. "Yes," she said. *Whatever.*

"Ayaana is studying navigation," Koray drawled.

Mother and son exchanged a look. Nehir's gaze returned to Ayaana's face. "My son tells me that you are somewhat precious to the Chinese." Ayaana sputtered. "Yes? No?" Nehir demanded. "Who is Chinese in your family? Never mind. The Chinese, my dear, are very, very tricky. Possessed of terrible hungers, dear, *fa-thom-less* hungers," she emphasized. "But there you are, learning them—so necessary if we are to have a future."

Ayaana swallowed hard, suddenly wanting to defend China. *They are gracious.* Eyes darting. *They work hard. Their dreams are bigger than the world.* She thought Koray would intervene. Instead, he sat with hands folded across his chest, watching the interaction with a smug look. Nehir leaned toward Ayaana. "What does it mean to be a Chinese heirloom?" Koray gave a warning sound accompanied by a "cut-off" hand gesture. His mother then exclaimed, "Navigation!" as she sought black pepper to add to her soup. "I suppose your generation must experience *everything*. I suppose you *want* to have your own boat one day"—she gestured with her hands—"traverse great streams." She offered Ayaana a slow, sly smile. "Women need dreams . . . perhaps more than men do. Did Koray tell you we are in shipping? Seven ships and a tanker, four named for me. Emirhan, my spouse, indulges me . . . Eat, eat . . ." she said.

Fragrances of rose and mint in the clear soup. The aroma transported Ayaana to Munira's unadorned kitchen. An ache for home. She lifted her head to say something about Munira. Nehir exclaimed, "You are an odd beauty, dear child." She touched Ayaana's eyes. "I am *dee*-lighted. One cannot fault Koray's taste in women." She paused.

"I am not—" started Ayaana.

Nehir interrupted her. "Are you religious?"

Ayaana's spoon hovered, suspended between her plate and her mouth. How and what was she supposed to say now?

Koray offered a non sequitur. "Ayaana is at the top of the calculus class."

Nehir stared. "Girl, are you religious?"

"I . . ." Ayaana glanced at Koray for direction.

He crossed his eyes at her.

Nehir said, "You either are or aren't. Are you observant?"

"I am."

Nehir nodded, as if a box could now be ticked off. "Yet one must not overdo things—everything in moderation. The past adapts to time. One must remember this. Saves us from excesses. I suppose you'll be desiring to visit a mosque? Koray, inform Khaldi." Nehir turned to Ayaana. "Our chauffeur. He is at your disposal, dear."

This was not quite how Ayaana had imagined her first real holiday would unfold.

When Ayaana returned to the villa after a daylong encounter with Istanbul, its history, its scent of disquietude, its ruins, its disappointed hope for an unknown future, a nostalgic dereliction that caused even the ugliest modern structures to be covered with the colors of the past, she found that two new pink suitcases had replaced her red rucksack. Five pairs of Italian designer shoes—slingbacks, boots, ballet flats, peep-toes, and espadrille wedges—had replaced her sandals and scuffed sneakers. Another box contained a black silk nightgown. Her clothes had been replaced with Audrey Hepburn–style dresses in four colors—black, white, blue, and red—and an array of accessories, including shawls and handbags in black, white, and beige. Ayaana waited for dinner to begin. "Are my clothes in the laundry?"

"No, dear." Nehir spooned minestrone into her mouth.

Koray broke the bread and buttered it.

"Where are they . . . and my bag?"

"Please, don't slouch, dear. Isn't this selection far more suitable? I wanted to surprise you. Is that wrong? I want you to feel comfortable . . . and . . . and Koray was so *encouraging*." Ayaana almost swallowed her spoon. "Tomorrow," Nehir added, "I have prepared a treat for us. Chocolate tasting! You will adore it, adore it!" She patted Ayaana's cheek and tittered, "Heard all about your sweet tooth."

Ayaana's neck ached. Her head pounded. She was struggling for air.

. . .

Ayaana cornered Koray just after dinner. He tapped under her chin. "Love the outraged-kitten look on you, *canim*! Go on. Play along. She does mean well." Ayaana wondered if Koray were addressing her in hieroglyphics.

"I—"

Casually, Koray interrupted. "Among the Terzioğlus," he said, "there are no 'I's. We are *we*." Koray's smartphone rang then. He winked at Ayaana and snapped open his phone. She watched him as he spoke in rapid Turkish to someone. He gestured. Ayaana heard the word "Syria" repeated. He ended on a furious note before ending the call. Without turning to her, already moving, he announced, "Something's come up." He paused. Returned and stroked her head. "You will look extraordinary in those clothes." He kissed her head. "We like 'extraordinary.'"

Ayaana glared at his retreating back.

She had wanted to ask about going to Konya to visit Mawlana Rumi's tomb. She wanted to swim in the Bosporus. *Chocolate tasting?* Ayaana's sleep, though restless, was dreamless that night.

At dinner, the family would slip into and out of Turkish, English, French, and German. Even as Ayaana struggled to keep up, she was compelled by the performance of power and wealth, the sense of the unspoken predilections of those who knew they had created some of the rules that kept the world in turmoil. "Are you happy?" Koray asked her. The chocolate-tasting expedition that day had been a mystifying sequence of tasting, snapping, melting, and exclaiming, "Educating the taste buds." It was not an experience she wanted to repeat soon.

"Yes," she asserted to Koray.

Yet everything she had hoped for had been subsumed by whatever "being Terzioğlu" commanded. Koray spoke to her in a labored tone. Undercurrents. He had aged here. He was bigger, taller, harder. Cuff-linked and gray-suited, leathered (shoes, briefcase). Certainly not a "student." He prowled and simmered. Something of the force to which he belonged radiated as a magnetic, brutal, and seductive aura. Any light in him now seemed artificial or borrowed. This she had not expected: the mutability of human-being-ness. Beguiled, she made the mistake of conflating mercuriality with meaning, and in her fogging mind started to think she could better inhabit the world by this ceaseless reimagining of self. She started by trying to change her posture and the way her body moved in spaces. Smaller, tidy steps; straightened spine; smaller, tidier smiles. It was exhausting.

[70]

Ayaana sipped orange juice and looked through a newspaper after breakfast. Earlier, Koray's gaze had been stuck on the centerfold. The images: the face of a man in the water; bodies floating on the sea's surface; men, women, and children being hauled out of the water; white-costumed rescuers; a dead dark-skinned man still clutching a dead infant, a boy. This. She had never before recognized what placelessness looked like. Koray, watching her, said, "They gambled. They lost. No one is obliged to carry the weight of their failure."

She almost jumped out of her seat. "Failure?"

"It behooves them to survive, doesn't it?"

"How are they to blame, Koray?"

"Don't be so bloody naïve," Koray snapped before getting up. "And don't argue with me about things you will never understand." He seized the paper from her and left the room, slamming the door behind him.

Ayaana sat still, staring at a spot on the carpet for a long time.

"The most important things are concealed in the unseen; the most essential truths inhabit the unspoken," Muhidin had once said. She thought she might go to Rabi'a for reassurance. She had not carried the water-stained green book Muhidin had given her so she turned to Google. Rabi'a al-Adawiyya counseled, "The matter falls to the heart."

Koray showed up after four hours, with chocolates and an apology. "Stress," he said. "Not quite the holiday I wanted for us." He had also set aside the rest of the day to show Ayaana more of his city. She was wary. They wandered off the tourist track and traps. Ayaana stopped at every antiques shop she saw. She did not buy anything. They went to the mosques, and, to Ayaana's relief, she found the adornments of her faith, the art and color and beatific expressions. Tears before the sight of the Basmallah calligraphy.

Three cats followed them. There were cats and kittens even inside shops. On the streets, several young voices cried, "*Edeny felos.*" "Whose children are these?" Ayaana asked.

"Beggars. Refugees," Koray spat. "Shall we go to the Hagia Sophia now, or would you prefer the Grand Bazaar?" An irritated sound. Then, "Ayaana, please do not encourage them. Put your purse away. You will start a riot." Koray seized her hand, hurling invectives at the children swarming around them. Whatever he said scared them, because they all ran away. "Look to the margins—you will see their parents." He pointed in three directions. "Disgusting racket."

Circling birds, a spring sun, the bluest of skies, and the songs of muezzins. The world moved in and out of Ayaana's gaze. The assorted music of the land, the scents and food, and Gülbirlik rose oil, which was the most intense she had experienced. She chose several for her mother. When she went to pay for them, she found that Koray had already done so. She whirled around to face him. "You are our guest," Koray told her. "Indulge us." He paused. "Mother . . . She always wanted a daughter to spoil." Koray laughed.

Ayaana stood uneasy. Was she being ungrateful? "Where are your brothers?"

A shadow passed across Koray's face. "They . . . moved. Decided Canada and Chile are better homes. They'll never belong." Koray took their wrapped-up purchases from the counter. "They'll have to come home," he muttered. They crossed to Istiklal Street. Koray led Ayaana into a patisserie as he said, "Mother is pleased that you are here. She has always . . ."

". . . wanted a daughter to spoil," Ayaana finished the sentence for him.

She regretted it when Koray added, "Miss Ayaana, we are in sync." Ayaana paused to watch the elegant street scenes, so different from her island world. Koray observed her. "Istiklal Street."

He said, "I bestow it on you."

A rush of color and privileged noise; a bazaar for the finest everythings through which the varieties of humans from the world passed. Koray kissed her on the forehead. "Your eyes are so wide right now . . . We have a few more hours, but we must return home soon. My father is . . . to our surprise . . . coming back today." Koray glanced down at her with a grim smile. "He *will* approve of you," Koray said.

"Must he?" asked Ayaana, envying a woman in tight jeans and a white peasant blouse, the careless freedom of her gesturing hands, which she moved as she spoke.

Koray's voice was tight when he answered, "Yes."

Ayaana looked at him. She turned back to the crowds. Unease. A sense that she was being herded into something unseen, as if the crowds were in on the plan. Human traffic around them. She peered down the street. At its extreme end, where the cobblestones ended, fluttering on a pole was a red flag with the white crescent and star—the Turkish flag. Her mouth moved faster than her thoughts. "Koray, I do not know who my biological father is. I *chose* Muhidin." An almost smirk. "Mlingoti Baadawi."

Koray was silent for a long time as they walked. Then he said, "Chose? Muhidin?"

She offered, "My real father might even be the wind."

Hooded gaze, tightened lips—Ayaana was sure Koray would erupt. "It is . . . *vital* to know what you are dealing with." Ayaana was mocking Nehir.

Koray ignored her sarcasm. Ayaana looked about her, watching a street vendor cross the road. Koray then grunted, a decision reached. "We can stand forever like this, or cross the road and buy one of every *halwa* on offer, which we can then eat on the Tünel."

"*Halwa?*" she sighed

"*Halwa!*" he answered, laconic.

Ayaana was straining for the unserious freedom of their immediate past. She skipped away and tried to shrug off the firm tap of foreboding on her shoulders.

Emirhan was a fat, formidable, and forbidding presence with searching eyes that communicated a voracious appetite for things and people. When he stood, he supported himself with a specially crafted black cane that introduced a *tap-tap-tap* into the rhythms of the house. He walked with a limp constrained by a rigorous discipline that limited his expression of pain. He smelled expensive: of cigar smoke and bespoke cologne, of murky and dangerous wealth. His very dark hair was sprinkled with strands of white that looked as if they had been carefully placed. The effusive greeting with which he met Ayaana did not quite jibe with the aura of ugly remoteness he exuded. He held on to her shoulders, his grip too strong, too intense, too adhering. They stood around in a smaller, brown-and-black-leather library where classical music played out of speakers discreetly embedded within the cozy room. The effect was of being sealed off from the world in a leather-perfumed song capsule.

"What is your feeling for our land?" Emirhan breathed over Ayaana.

She scrambled for words, confused by the sheer presence of this man. "It is . . . everything."

Koray added, "Ayaana is most charmed by our resident vagrants."

Emirhan beamed at Ayaana. "Life and its vagaries . . ." He fluttered his hands, suggesting evaporation. "I gather you are some sort of Chinese artifact? Good, good. Africa? August 2011," he said, "I was with our prime minister on his visit to Somalia. Turkey is Africa's brother. 'Virtuous power,' dignity and happiness for all. Equal partners, that sort of thing." Emirhan grinned as a hyena faced with a thin goat might—insincerely. "What is our business? Do you know?"

"Shipping?" she answered.

He laughed. "Yes, you may call it that, too. We do sustain the old sea-trade routes. Yes, Korayğim? Ah!" He pointed at a map on the wall. "Isn't that smudge in green your little island? In the womb of the seas. Good. Good." An arm over Ayaana's shoulder, he directed her to a seat. He sat down heavily and huffed as he chose one of four glossy black rectangular devices. A tap, and suddenly the music changed. "Zbigniew Preisner," Emirhan breathed. "Ahhhh! Do listen."

The "Lacrimosa" from *Requiem for My Friend*. Emirhan sank into a black leather chaise longue, his menacing cane next to him, squeezing Ayaana's neck: "Come, *kuzucuğum*. Close to me." And Koray stood as still as a statue.

His father turned to contemplate him.

"I reflect on last things . . . as you should." Koray watched a vein pulse on the side of his head. "Our nation is now the Styx. It will get worse."

Koray made a scoffing sound, turned it into a sneeze.

"Indeed, Korayğim,"—he glowered meaningfully at his son—"*I* have every reason to contemplate death. As you shall. Now listen to Preisner." A command.

Ayaana almost leapt out of her seat. Koray plunked down on another, glowering at his father. They listened to Preisner's "Lacrimosa" in silence, again and again.

Later, buffeted by sizzling emotions that were oozing out of the invisible fissures of that day, Ayaana sought the lyrics of the song to study as a clue. Dinner and drinks had been a forcibly cheerful affair, dotted with place-names and an inquiry into the well-being of many people. Yet, though every turn of phrase was a riptide, the Terzioğlus seemed to be experts at avoiding the catastrophic tug. Ayaana watched them. She looked from Koray to his father as they engaged in a terse exchange in French. They returned to English, suddenly genial. Ayaana saw Nehir drift from flirtatiousness to sarcasm, seemingly baiting Emirhan.

Nehir: "How are the *commodities* doing, darling?"

Emirhan: "Paying your bills, darling."

Nehir: "Anything nasty out there that will hurt *us*?"

Emirhan: "Nothing that you will not benefit from; do make the usual arrangements. And we must speak about the restaurant in Askaray. We need it . . . *darling*."

Nehir sighed dramatically, her dancer eyes exaggerating her exasperation. "Again? Just redecorated it. It *will* cost you, darling."

"Doesn't it always?" Emirhan turned to Koray. "How are your brothers?"

"Well."

"What does 'well' mean? Will they return or not?"

Koray started, "If they choose to . . ."

"Choose!" Emirhan erupted.

Nehir intervened with a laugh. "We have a guest, gentlemen."

"A most delightful addition to our home." Emirhan's smile was radiant. "I shall enjoy getting to know you very, very well, little one." He reached over to stroke Ayaana's hand. "Such a fresh look."

Ayaana would have removed her hand and self, as every hair on her body sprang on edge. True fear.

Nehir snapped, "When do you return to the boats?"

"I shall complete all new undertakings from the sublime comfort of my home . . . *darling*."

Koray and Nehir both winced. Nehir gulped down the remains of her Grappa di Vinaccia and performed a yawn behind an embroidered white handkerchief. Then, half rising, she leaned over to kiss her husband's cheek and murmured, "Good night, Emir." She put out her right hand in the direction of Ayaana. "Come, girl, let's give the boys room to do what boys must do."

Koray cast Ayaana a quick panicked look, which he then disguised by reaching for the wine bottle.

"Ayaana," said Nehir, her tone unyielding.

Ayaana got up at once, dropping a toothpick. Nehir continued, "Isn't this a *bee-yootiful* evening? How lovely is our moon—so white, so fecund, so pure this night—and, see, our dear Emirhan returned to us most unexpectedly. So much to be grateful for."

No sooner had the door closed behind the two women than the quarreling started. Nehir hurried Ayaana down the corridor, and her lips were thin. "In a house like ours, Ayaana," she said, clamping on her arm, "you select one stream with which to move your life, then stay the course. After all, there is only one destination, isn't there? Now, child, do not worry about the noise. Quite normal." A half-smile.

They paused in silence.

Nehir spoke. "My husband has offered me a new hotel to design. We girls shall select colors for its décor." Ayaana deflated. She had intended to lure Koray with a ferry trip along the strait. Nehir continued: "It shall be our *adventure*. I want to invoke the spirit of Marrakech in this new work, in your honor, my dear. Lots of pinks and salt-white." She turned to Ayaana. "We must take what we are given and make it work for us. Do you understand?"

Ayaana looked at Nehir and said, "No."

Surprised by the challenge in the girl's direct answer, Nehir glanced away before taking a breath. "Oh, you will." She let go of

Ayaana's arm. "The things a woman despises she learns to bury in her heart . . . Now go to our little library. Find the music of Latif Bolat. He is good for the churning soul. Good night. Tomorrow we shall discuss what his music means to us."

Nehir turned left, leaving Ayaana standing there.

The sense of disquiet in the house was now a slow-breathing presence. Inside the small library, Ayaana not only picked out the music of Latif Bolat, from duty, but also sought the Preisner Emirhan had played earlier. Later, in her room, she logged in on her phone to find translations for the lyrics. "Lacrimosa"—Weeping. It was Christian and old, from a ritual reserved for the dead. Ayaana imbibed the English words:

Ah! That day of tears and mourning
From the dust of earth returning
Man for judgment must prepare him
Spare, O God, in mercy spare him . . .

Ayaana pored over the phrases, her heart pounding. Entanglement. To what had she come? A few more days, she thought, and then she would make up an excuse to leave.

Knock on her door. Ayaana jerked awake. Expecting Nehir, she was surprised when she saw Koray there. "I . . ." he started. "I . . . Look, sorry . . ."

Instinctively, she said, "It's okay."

He stumbled in. She closed the door. He tumbled into her arms, sobbing. He clung. She wrapped her arms around him, thinking of the lyrics she had read and their music in her head. She was silent as Koray wept. His tears stained her dress. He shuddered and exhaled, then wiped his face. He cupped Ayaana's face and kissed her full on the lips. "Thank you." He kissed her again and left the room.

Ayaana touched her mouth and stared at nothing. She returned to the edge of her bed and sat, unmoving. The undertows. Muhidin's warning words during ocean lessons: "There is a reptilian tinge to particular rip currents, a sense of deliberate intent. There is a mean streak in the subtle nudge that eases luckless people beyond safe water zones long before they realize that they are at the mercy of all the unrestrained forces of life." Ayaana turned to her phone, keyed in "Latif Bolat," and picked a random song. It played while her mind roamed inside the spare lyrics of the "Lacrimosa." Ayaana did not sleep. She spent the night studying Nehir's pure, fecund white moon.

[71]

"When I say Marrakech, what do you see?"

Nothing, thought Ayaana. "Sand?" she offered. She sighed at all the fabric samples laid out, covering every space available in the living room.

Nehir exclaimed, "Sand and purples! The Koubba el-Badiyin. Camels—filthy creatures, but we must think of desert constancy. Stark simplicity, yet elegant. *Bee-yootiful.* Sand is beautiful. Clever girl . . . Microscopic sand is simply *bee-yooo-tiful.* Each room consecrated to a grain of sand." She bared even teeth at Ayaana. "I am happy with you." She shrugged gracefully, and her Kathak-dancer eyes curved upward.

As the morning wore on, Ayaana understood that her primary role was to applaud Nehir's choices. Nehir, pleased with her seeming acquiescence, said, "Will you and my son announce your engagement?"

"Engagement?" she squeaked.

Nehir ignored her.

Ayaana groaned inside her soul.

Nehir paused. "Africa had never occurred to me before. I confess I was gravely concerned. One hears such terrible things. I insisted that he bring you here." Nehir beamed at Ayaana's red dress. "I can see why you make sense. I, like my son, am besotted." Nehir squeezed Ayaana's hand. "The shimmering purple fabric, with the silver thread—do you see it as a curtain?" Ayaana opened her mouth. Nehir supplied the answer. *"Bee-yootiful."*

. . .

Koray was nowhere in sight. Ayaana could not take up the meaning of "engagement" with him. She was looking up bed-and-breakfasts to which she might move. Yet she was also seduced by what she was experiencing. She looked glamorous in her new getup. She felt that she was close to the sort of put-together-ness that she had yearned for, like all the sophisticated females she had idolized in the films she and Muhidin used to watch. She suspended the search and decided to immerse herself in Han Song's novel *The High Speed Railway*, which she had carried with her.

Ayaana took to waking up at 4:30 a.m. to wander into the garden amid the flowers of dawn. It was time that was hers alone. At that time, whenever she walked out, a thin man—a pale, English-speaking man with red-rimmed eyes who accompanied Koray's father—would walk in as if he had been waiting for the door to open, as if he had been waiting awhile and had been afraid to make his arrival known. At first Ayaana's morning appearance had startled him, and he had flinched as if expecting some kind of retribution. But after the fourth morning, he had ventured a tiny smile in return to her Arabic greeting. The man carried two briefcases. He kept his gaze low, his demeanor humble. He kept glancing sideways, as if expecting something to accost him from there. He had a red-and-beige weal on his forehead in the shape of a triangle. He may have been over forty. He was one of the nine or ten new constants that would hurry down the Terzioğlu corridors, and who entered through previously barred doors.

A semblance of an old order returned in the evenings, when a civilized dinner followed by drinks proceeded. Ayaana sat brooding next to Koray when he was there. He asked her the same question: "Did you have a good day?"

"Almost," she always answered, loading the phrase with sarcasm.

"Good," Koray answered.

One evening, as everyone got up to retreat to the drawing room,

Ayaana tugged at Koray's sleeve. "Koray, with less than two weeks left, I want to visit İzmit . . . or Konya."

"Konya! A damn Rumi adherent?" he mocked.

Ayaana added, "I also wish to see the mouth of the Bosporus in Beykoz."

Koray rubbed his hair. "None of us expected Emirhan to return so soon and . . . and . . . with such news."

"What news?"

Koray made a dismissive gesture.

"Then I will visit these places alone." Her voice was firm.

Koray took her arm and spoke with low intensity. "No, you will not. Things are . . . The situation is . . . dicey." He closed his eyes. "Our family . . . has enemies. Dangerous beings who will hurt anyone connected with us . . . That, unfortunately, now includes you. You will have been seen with us. Makes you a target."

Ayaana exhaled. "I want my passport, Koray. I'll return to China. I'm safe there."

Koray cupped her chin. "I think not." Amusement in his eyes.

Footsteps. Then, "*Ooooooh*," cooed Nehir, "to be young and *bee-yoo-tiful*. Hurry, children, get married. Bring me my grandchildren from two . . . no . . . three worlds."

Ayaana stiffened. She scowled at Koray. "Did you tell her we are engaged?"

"Not quite that way," Koray whispered. "Listen, *güzelim*, tomorrow . . . I visit one of our ships . . ."

"May I visit with you?"

"I'll return in the afternoon. İzmit together?"

"Your father . . ."

". . . will survive a few days without me."

Yet Koray frowned.

Father and son were arguing again. It had started in the living room, where Nehir was tinkling with the piano keys. She ignored everything. Father and son walked out to continue their battle out of view.

"Good night," dared Ayaana, fed up with the tensions.

There were unspoken rules about who left the room first—the elder before the younger. "Ayaana," said Nehir, still playing random scales, "hear them . . ." Raised voices. "What you have provoked?"

"I . . ."

"*Shhhhh . . .*" said Nehir. "It is necessary. Such fierce passions. They need this airing. They deal with difficult things." She looked at Ayaana. "They are alike, you know. This is our sea, our passageway. These are the winds that blow. Those are the creatures it forms. The ones who are afraid drown, or get served as meals." An arpeggio. "Do you like my son?"

Ayaana lowered her head. "Right now I don't."

Nehir smiled. "Enough to become his wife?"

Ayaana gaped at Nehir.

"Wife!" A squawk.

Nehir stopped playing. She got up and ambled over. "What a wild look. I am not entirely sure you like me much, either. It doesn't matter. *I* like *you.*" She laughed. "Stay with us; we shall confuse you, and you will amuse us . . . and your children—three would be just right—will help us forget the things we must." She stroked Ayaana's face with a finger. "Stay with us." Nehir stroked Ayaana's head. Nehir then headed for the door. She looked over her shoulder. "Koray . . . will ask you to marry him. Please say yes. We *shall* have fun." She laughed. "I will teach you what questions to ask. Moreover, if you still want a ship to navigate—so your Chinese education does not go to waste"—Nehir laughed—"Koray can offer you one." She winked. "Tell him it would delight me."

By the time Nehir closed the door, Ayaana was kneeling on the carpet, hugging herself. She could feel the tickle that heralded an asthma attack. She did not have her inhaler—she had not needed one for so long. Her chest began to tighten; her heartbeat quickened. She was breathing too fast. *Breathe*, she commanded herself. *Breathe one, breathe two, breathe . . .*

[72]

His gaze was always lowered. Today she followed its trajectory and noticed his brown, shining shoes. Creased, laced, overused. Uneven soles. Spontaneously, she exclaimed, "How far have those shoes walked?" He looked at her then, and his eyes widened. He stuttered something she did not understand. She gazed at his face, at the fear that had left its marks there, at its scarred beauty. She stepped closer to see and at once thought of the Christian God, the naked, scarred, bleeding, broken one struggling on a cross.

And the man smiled into her heart.

"Hello, who are you?" she whispered.

He turned away.

She fled into the garden.

The next day, he answered her first question to him: "Infinite distances; they have walked past eternity."

She listened to the musicality of his voice. Ayaana asked, "What is your name?"

He murmured, "I haven't decided." He looked at her with dark eyes—today they were almost violet. He breathed, "Be careful." He waited until he believed she understood him. "Be careful here," he breathed out.

Because he had whispered the warning, by the end of the day Ayaana thought she had only imagined the words.

The next day, he spoke first: "Where are you from?"

She answered, "Kenya."

"Can't be too far," he joked, "sounds like Konya."

She laughed because she needed to.

"I am from Damascus," he told her.

Damascus. Roses and blood. A visual litany of world fiascos; she read the harrowed face. The silence. His aloneness. Within her, a need to annihilate such desolation, in order to repair existence. *Topography:* the contours of life are edged with horror. She would try to banish these lest they follow her home, as his face and voice had done. She touched his forearm.

He focused on her hand on his arm. He knew there should be burn marks where an unexpected dawn creature had touched his arm in caring. "Be careful," he breathed. "Please, excuse me. I must go in." He stumbled near the door.

. . .

At dawn the next day, Ayaana opened the door and bumped into that man. He stopped her rush with both hands, dropping the briefcases. Electric sensation.

"Sorry," she murmured.

"No," he said. His hands were on either side of her waist. Deep-reaching eyes. "When do you leave?" he asked.

She swallowed.

He let go and touched the side of her face. Flushing, he stooped to pick up his briefcases. He had forgotten himself. They stood together.

"Keep safe."

Ayaana hugged her coat close to her body and stepped sideways, heading to the garden. The man glanced back at her.

The next day, when Istanbul's muezzins had started their morning summons, Ayaana gave the man the box of chocolates Koray had given her. Inside the box she had inserted a piece of paper on which she had drawn the Basmallah. The following morning—she did not know she would never see him again—he was carrying a cardboard box upon which he had positioned two briefcases. Ayaana teased, "What are you trading in today?" He hesitated, fumbled. Two tear globules broke and slipped down his face. The morning light made them extra-large and blood-streaked. "We trade in doomed souls."

Ayaana did not understand.

"Leave while you can," she thought he said again.

But when she did look at him, his eyes, though red-rimmed, were tender. He said, "The chocolates are nectar, their essence a song. They have bandaged, for a season, the holes in my soul. I cherish them as I do you."

Ayaana brushed fingers with him, and his hand ever so briefly curled around hers.

"Tomorrow?" he murmured.

She nodded.

At around 2:00 a.m. that night, in between the sounds of thunder, a hideous, drawn-out human grunt eviscerated the night, followed by three definitive popping sounds. A gurgling existential scream followed, and then there was stillness. In her bed, dreading the unknown, Ayaana made a map of sounds, trying to create meaning. Muted voices. Footsteps. Thumps and whispers. Shuffling. Scrambling. Twenty minutes later, a car started up. It was driven out. Ayaana went to her window to look out. Thunder. Lightning. Odd. She had not imagined rain in Istanbul. Electric gates in shadow swung open. A black car passed through. She returned to bed, drenched in fear. *I must leave.* She covered her body. A fleeting thought: the Syrian. She slept fitfully and woke up to irate thunder.

It was past 4:00 a.m. when a loud knock on her door forced her into wakefulness. "Koray," said the voice on the other side.

"Yes?" she said.

"Open the door."

She stumbled out of bed to turn the key. Koray entered the room. A rancid tang followed him in. Ayaana returned to her warm bed, propping herself up on the pillows as Koray paced the breadth of the room. She waited. He stopped by her bed. "You shall refrain from an overfamiliarity with the servants. Distance maintains balance. It is why the things you enjoy here run smoothly. Distortions have consequences."

Ayaana, heavy-headed from a restless night, sputtered, "What?"

"You will postpone your morning wandering."

Ayaana rubbed her eyes. Had Koray discerned her morning intentions? "Why?" she demanded.

Koray paused as if considering something. "Don't leave the house today."

She flopped in her bed and covered her head. She uncovered her face, counted his receding footsteps, before saying, "Someone screamed in the night. Who was it?"

Koray did an about-turn. His eyes glacial, he asked, in a monotone, "What . . . exactly are you referring to?" The pungent scent that had entered the room with him spread. It infused Ayaana's bedclothes. She turned her head away from the smell as something awful throbbed between them.

The warning.

Be careful.

Koray waited for her answer.

"Thunder," she said carefully.

A chasm closed.

Stillness. "Koray?" Ayaana whispered, suddenly afraid.

"Yes."

"I'll return to Xiamen."

"Not without me."

Another tack: "Your mother has married us off."

Taut look.

Ayaana added, "She said you ought to give me a ship."

Koray asked, "Do you want one?" He leaned over. "I'll give it to you."

The season's undercurrents, like the thunder outside, bore down on them.

"I . . . don't know you well enough," she stuttered.

"I'll teach you me." Koray bent over, lifting her out of the bed and into his arms. "We can be anything." He was lying. "I am not such a terrible marriage prospect, you know." She shook her head. "I want to settle down, Ayaana. I want a deep connection with one person. Wouldn't you like children? Three, maybe?"

His mother was a prescient woman. This was how it would always be. Ayaana's heart gnawed in her. Outside, a drizzle started. There was another layer to the pungent scent. She sniffed. "Do you smell that?"

"What?" Koray frowned.

It might have been the rain, the peculiar moods it wrought. It might have been guilt. The ship leader was still a phantom lurking in the peripheries of her gaze. She stroked Koray's face. What did she want? Within the house, in a room nearby, voices were raised in clamor. Koray raised his head, alert. He then kissed her hard. A hand on her left breast.

She studied him as if he were a Zao Wou-Ki visual—a riddle.

She asked, "May I visit the ship with you?"

He gave her a sideways look. "Ayaana . . . do not ask that question again . . . for your protection . . . and mine."

Silence. A door somewhere slammed shut. Voices. A shout. Koray was alert and still. Watching him, Ayaana imagined that, to be happy, all she needed to do was conform. Koray said, "I have targeted your heart for myself; I never miss."

In Ayaana, a smarting of eyes. A sting spread to her bones. It became goose bumps. A vision: a looming net designed to trap migrating ortolan buntings.

She was flying blind.

The house was in disarray that day. A single official-looking car. The usually invisible servants raced to and fro. Still, in the afternoon, Ayaana decided to dress up and wait for Koray in the small library. After an hour, she ventured into Emirhan's office. The door should have been shut, as it usually was when Emirhan was not in the house. Ayaana poked her head in. The floor was bare. There were carpet outlines. Several pieces of paper were strewn on the floor, including a large map of the kind a large navy might use. On the opposite wall, there had been an attempt to wipe some dark spatters off the wall. The sense of menace in that room was tangible. Ayaana backed out. She needed air. She walked out of the house in defiance of Koray's warning. She needed air.

Outside, the clouds were heavy and black with rain. The threat of another all-engulfing storm brooded over the estate. She followed the Byzantine track up to a hill behind the house. From the top, she would view the city and its waters. As she swung left toward the hill, she saw the shoe. It was stuck in a nameless bush of brown-green leaves. As she reached for it, it fell into fallen leaves on the ground. She knelt to look. It was a man's shoe. It belonged to his right foot. A single brown-laced overused object. Its sole had been worn into a thin layer. There was a hole near the uneven heel. The oxford shoes of a once-successful man. The insole was stained with a dark leak. The toe cap and tongue were as stained as the laces. She looked at it until she was again seven years old, keening over the still corpse of a cherished kitten. *How has the world been changed by the fact that you no longer exist?* Sinking into darkness. But she would get up slowly. She would keep walking as if she had not encountered anything out of the ordinary. Blind, deaf, silent. What had Muhidin told her? "The most important things are concealed in the unseen; the most essential truths inhabit the unspoken." She would keep walking. She needed her passport. Which was Koray's room? She had to go home.

When Ayaana returned from her walk, the shoe had disappeared. As she had suspected it would.

. . .

Ayaana stared at the white walls of her room, seated on the edge of her bed. This day. Istanbul, the world's heaving crossroads, gateway to feckless human hopes and all the opportunities war afforded. She prayed that those who could not pay did not have to die. She prayed that the man of the morning whose shoe had evaporated was alive. She prayed he would find his way home. She prayed that when he had said "doomed" it did not mean himself. There was no Internet signal. All her attempts to speak to her mother had failed. She kept trying. She needed her passport.

She could not see a way out. *What is real?* At the family dinner that evening, Ayaana practiced wearing a mask of gracious blankness that was similar to that on Nehir's face. The look suited her Audrey Hepburn black dress with a cinched waist. Her dinner conversation was adequate. She stayed close to Koray. He was like a lodestone as she tried to figure out which way was up and out. He had her passport. How had she let that happen? She listened to Emirhan's expostulations on the economic destiny of Greece and the wars surrounding their boundaries, and glanced left. He said that ISIL were a purging force, a mirror of human choices. Ayaana nodded in the right places. When her gaze grazed Nehir's, the woman raised her wineglass at her, her look amused and vulturine. Ayaana blinked her acknowledgment of Nehir's recognition. Nehir mouthed, "Good luck." Ayaana was struggling to breathe. Now she knew what it felt like to drown, to inhale water and hope that it was air while her body and soul howled in desperation.

[73]

"I would like my passport back."

"It's safe with me."

"I would rather have it on me."

"No, Ayaana."

"You will return it."

"Nope, Ayaana." Toying with her.

"Why?"

Koray smiled. "Because."

Ayaana stepped back, rebuffed by the horror of unreasonableness, disgusted by her helplessness.

She ambushed Koray and raised the matter at the dinner table. "Koray, I need my passport. Having it will ease my mind as I walk the city tomorrow." She smiled.

Nehir exclaimed, "Walk the city? My dear. With all this uncertainty . . . Koray, why are you not protecting our Ayaana better? Have you explained things?"

Emirhan was watching Ayaana. "In a realm of flux, passports are bounty. My beauty, surely you don't feel . . . unsafe . . . here with us?"

"No . . . I just . . ."

"It is settled, then."

Emirhan, Nehir, and Koray exchanged glances. Ayaana stopped speaking, knowing that her every word would be turned, twisted, changed, rolled as a ball of wool for three human cats to play with. A chill. A tigthtening of lips. This was a game she needed to learn very quickly. She looked daggers at Koray.

He said, "A little wine, *canim*?"

"No, Koray." Cold-voiced.

"I've been most remiss in my duties as host, sweet Ayaana. I promise to set aside the weekend to show you my intimate *cosmoi*."

His parents offered a murmuring laugh, and Ayaana wondered why there was no sense of joy in this, either. Six more days, she told herself. Just another six days before their flight back to China.

[74]

Esmeray. The restaurant was named after a dark moon. It was located within the labyrinthine Tarlabaşı Quarter, which evoked the East African city-states for Ayaana, so much so that she had lowered her guard. They had walked southwest of Taksim Square, allowing the crowds of many nations to move them. The hard throb of life, music, lingering glances. A statuesque European woman who turned out to be a man. The smells of wicked things amid the citrus and spice. Ayaana clutched Koray's hand, nervous about the many looks directed at her.

"They are mesmerized by you." He drew her closer to his side, then indicated eastward. "Tarlabaşı Boulevard. Renowned for its brothels. Think about it. These were once family homes. Greek. Before the exodus. If you had landed here illicitly, it is to this part of Istanbul that you would drift." He suppressed a smile.

Dark and light brown African faces, too, filled with frustrated hope, as if everything they had viscerally believed in when they had started their fantastical quest to an earthly idyll had, upon their arrival, simply evaporated. There was food on sale everywhere. But Koray was looking for a specific no-man's zone. Only Tarlabaşı could have an Esmeray, a space thriving on paradoxes and trompe l'oeil façades. Anatoli rock music played as a crone in a colorful headscarf met Koray and Ayaana at the restaurant door. A round table was set for them toward the back of the room. Ayaana sat down heavily, her perception of her world enhanced. She narrowed her eyes. Koray was reciting a litany of unexpected foods: *cacik*, *lahmacun*, *pogaca*, *bazlama*, *manti*, *biberiye tursusu*, *pirincli tavuk cigeri*, *baklava*, *gyro*, and *labaneh bil zayit*. Koray added, waving expansively, "*Tahini halwa*, *sembosa halwa . . . pişmaniye . . .*"

Ayaana asked, "All this?"

"And more." Koray's eyes danced. "No senses left unstirred."

Ayaana stared in silence.

The woman whose features had been buried in the millions of lines crisscrossing her face showed up offering *mercimek çorbasi* with a lemon wedge planted on the tureen's plate.

Koray looked at Ayaana. "We all needed a break from the house."

Stillness. "I made arrangements. We will not be returning there for a few days."

Koray rubbed his face. He sighed. Ayaana's eyes darkened. Her pulse throbbing, light-headed and almost blubbering, she exclaimed, "K-Koray, I d-do not have a change of clothes."

"Pick up what you need from the shops." He rubbed his eyes.

"Been a tough few days, *canim*. I owed you a holiday." He collapsed into his seat, looking at her. "Uh . . ." Koray's eyes shifted sideways. "News. Emirhan . . . to be expected . . . reason for his shittiness . . . pancreatic cancer. Confirmed. Trust the damn buzzard to find the most grueling way out." A shimmer in Koray's eyes.

Ayaana half melted. Was it true? She lowered her head, partly in surprise at how much the miasma of the home on the hill had penetrated her.

He looked at her. "Desperate handover season. That is what you saw. I am sorry; I had intended an entirely different holiday for us."

"I am so sorry about your father," Ayaana said. Still she shifted, bending her neck forward. Uneasy. "Desperate handover season" did not explain everything in any way, not the mosaic of terror made of the faces of those who walked the passageways of the house, not the single bloodstained shoe in the garden. Not Koray assessing her as he did now, as if testing the impact of his words. She schooled her face, trying for bland sympathy.

He lowered his voice: "Miss Ayaana, you can trust me," Koray said. His touch lingered on her arm.

Ayaana started. Was she so transparent? Just then, a young man with a faint haze of a mustache set out their food order. Koray said something to him. A minute later, the music changed. Koray listened for a second. "Omar Faruk Tekbilek," he said. "Can just about tolerate that." He smiled at Ayaana. "*Gül serbeti* to drink? I recommend it to you, Miss Sweet." Though still wary, Ayaana eased back into her chair, and her stomach muscles unclenched. Breathing a little easier. Koray immediately started to speak of the news of the day: the implications of the stock-market crash in China, the depressive effects on ordinary people. "*Chao-gu* mentality," he observed.

Ayaana took a deep breath before retorting, "The so-called small people also have a right to their dreams."

Koray watched her. He dipped a finger into his Campari. "Unregulated fantasies that lead to collapse. This is a necessary purging. Fortunately, your China is too big to fail." The young waiter delivered to Ayaana the rose sherbet Koray had ordered for her as they spoke of the sea, life, the end of the nation-state, career options, and shipping. Koray cracked jokes about the austerity in Greece: "What's the biggest charity organization in the EU? Greece." He spoke of al-Dawlah—ISIL—his fascination. "Strategic asset turned Frankenstein! The grotesque and death as aspirational brand!" He chortled. "Poor fucked-up world."

Ayaana tucked her hands in her armpits, mesmerized by this Koray: the charming chameleon, Koray the raving prophet, Koray the protective tour guide, Koray the man in control of fate and destiny, Koray the charm-oozing male with presence. He had revealed to her his Istanbul, the hole-in-the-wall outlets filled with treasures, secrets, and whispering people who offered to and could sell her anything, even a purple elixir for eternal life. He had led her into a cartographer's shop that looked like an alchemist's laboratory, and she had been lost in the universe of maps and their permutations. Her face mirrored her confusion and beguilement—awe, disgust, nausea. She was seduced. She could look at his face and find, again, its potency, its beauty. He had discarded his earring. This Koray was a palatable blend of campus Koray and Istanbul Koray. Koray the shape-shifter, able and willing to redesign her life so she need not think about the contours of the unknown. She imagined Koray meeting Muhidin and Munira. Muhidin, she knew, as she sipped her sherbet, would lure him into a fishing trip, and drop him in the deep waters to observe how he might cope . . . or not. She smiled. A carafe of wine appeared next to her. Koray reached for it and poured her a glass.

"Big-girl drink. Was that a smile, Miss Ayaana?"

"Emirhan," she asked, "can anything be done for him?"

A momentary bleakness in Koray's gaze. He veiled it. "Life can be shit." Koray tilted his head at her then reached over to hold her chin. "Little Ayaana, you *do* understand that life is not a human right, it is a roll of dice." She gave him the look of a child whose one dream had been grabbed and smashed. "We are served our number," he added.

Ayaana sagged in her seat and scratched her skin. Koray tossed down his wine. "What can *you* do?"

Ayaana waited for an answer. Outside, a wind started up on a thin whistle. Stillness pierced the room. Ayaana looked over her shoulder at the entrance as if some fanged fiend might saunter in. Dread, and its special questions: what was true or real? Ayaana's fingers traced the Basmallah on the tabletop as her mind whirled before the meaning of so many wicked truths. Soiled fabric of being—what was she to do with it? Yet, in every mad muttering, she could still hear the resonances from her island's muezzin call: the simple, imperfect, spare human truthfulness; despite everything, the many small gestures of joy. And then again the sense of the world in flames, visions of exodus, the agony of women, broken children of this, her broken age. And now the blurred montage of home: Nahodha Ali's fishing fleet, his yearlong preoccupations with the run of the billfish, the blast of his belly laughter when the fishing was good, the *insha'Allah* to Life's will when his boats returned empty; a mother's garden pulled out of the dry, salt earth, and within it the mother humming her favorite songs, unaware that her voice was like incense. One of Pate's storms. Thunder-rumbling, lightning-crackling, swell-and-wave-churning darknesses. Worlds, she concluded, were never meant to be the same.

Outside, sounds of life. Bleating livestock, hooting cars, human voices, music, music, music, and the sudden screams from unseen woundings. Ayaana started then and remembered where she was.

Koray contemplated the tenor of the moods of Ayaana's face. He murmured, "If I could, I would never allow another to glimpse your face directly. But I would paint you and share my experience with only a few. I would paint you in the colors of my choosing."

Ayaana turned to him. Koray added, his voice low and soft, "I would protect you, *yavrum*. Just ask." Ayaana blinked. Exhaled. She took the pot to pour spiced tea into a clay cup, focusing on the heat of the tea and the smoothness of her cup. "Ask," Koray insisted.

Ayaana spat out the tea she was trying to drink.

"Your father . . ."

Koray, grim: ". . . is dying. The pragmatist is unable to barter with death; he is unhappy with death's insolence."

"Nehir . . ."

". . . who has made my father's choices her life mission, is a worthy inheritor of his habits." A glimmer in Koray's gaze. It went out.

Ayaana asked, "You have brothers . . ."

Koray scoffed. ". . . who do not have the balls to grab hold of their fate. I am the sole heir."

Ayaana then asked, "What exactly is the family business?"

Koray glared at her. He stared. He said, "Such questions are not healthy." Koray then ordered a glass of cranberry juice. "No . . . change that . . . Bring me a bottle. Shiraz. Choose right." He gestured to Ayaana. "Your glass?" She shook her head.

"You will drink wine someday."

"Not again." She was certain of that. The wine she had sampled with her friend Shalom had tasted like a version of her mother's wicked concoctions.

Koray held her look. "I will tell you my secrets, but I want to be able to blame the wine. Join me."

She smiled, "If I drink, I will hear your secrets?"

Koray still held her look. "My secrets: are you sure, Miss Ayaana? You cannot 'unknow' afterward. If I open that door, there is no return. Think."

Door creaking open and out of a Stygian cave. She could crawl away. She could run back to find the sun. Ayaana glanced at Koray. Circles under his eyes; she had missed that. Hands: long-fingered, large, with hair on the back, two gold rings. Her heart: hammering. She was sweating. She was drifting.

Koray cocked his head. "Shall I tell you?" He watched her.

Ayaana then recalled how her dirty-white kitten had waited a full day for a single mole to emerge from its safe subterranean home. It seized the mole. Even as a child, she had been struck by the mole's resignation. It did not whimper. Here the clock ticked away. The playing music was a simulation of a Sufi's *dhikr*. Sea nocturnes and underwater darknesses. There is a point when the desire to breathe ends. She relaxed, knowing time would recede. Touching her throat, Ayaana then looked directly at Koray, mouth half open, aware that she was sinking. "Yes," she finally breathed.

Koray offered her a slow, slow smile. He drawled. "We are pragmatists, Miss Ayaana. Have always been. Boats. Trade. We control passageways. Sea routes. We make our rules. If we say something is legal, then it is. We make money. That is our mission, our purpose, our compulsion. If the earth is a war zone, we make money out of that, too."

Koray continued. "Father is brilliant at sniffing out opportunities in the dark cracks of existence where most souls are too frightened to look. Goods, licit or not, must cross worlds, and when they need to, we are there." Koray sniffed his wine. "This rotten portion of the city is probably mostly ours, too."

Music dribbled from the speakers. The singer carved a soundpath in lacerating notes. Ayaana listened to both the singer and Koray.

Koray spoke. "Father knew souls in peril needed . . . extraordinary services and were willing to pay large sums for the privilege of access to . . . safety. We offer, for prime rates, a middleman's infrastructure." He paused. "Yes, there are those who, in turn, need access to souls in peril." He shrugged. "For the right price, we deliver.

"The food is good," added Koray, his jaw crunching the bread. He continued, "We supply life jackets, lifeboats . . ." He reached over and took one of her kebab sticks.

Silence.

Koray scrutinized Ayaana's face, its confusion and hint of fear. He said, "Remember, *canim*, nobody quibbles over the color of money, or its source. The point of war is money—industry, jobs at home—power. People are and have always been"—he smiled—"tradeable." He reached for his soup.

She ought to have cried out. She ought to have protested. Yet now she understood the surrender of the mole in her kitten's mouth. Ayaana picked at her salad, shredding its leaves; her thoughts were crackling, and she was no longer hungry. Koray's words were more grays in the malignant shades of a world that was a riddle. She asked him, "So why do you bother praying?"

Koray shifted in his seat. "Strange question."

"Answer it?"

At a Siming mosque, months ago, glancing down the hall at men prostrating themselves, she had been drawn to one body that had conveyed a sense of prayer as a dance of abandonment. She had watched the man for a while. When the man stood up, she realized it was Koray. Struck as if by light, she had been embarrassed by her sudden need to get close to him, to see and taste what he knew.

Koray asked, "Do I pray?"

"You do."

Koray leaned over to wipe a sauce stain off her chin. "Maybe I have this need to hear from Someone Other than Me." He laughed. "And . . . the mosque is a great place for strategic contacts. It is important to be read a certain way . . . and"—eyes hooded—"fine, I admit it . . . I *am* curious. Always felt that death was such a bore. Especially now . . . with Father . . ." He stopped abruptly.

Track change: an inscrutable smile. "My father says I am wasting you." Ayaana tilted her head, waiting. "Emirhan," Koray continued, relishing his words, "considers himself a connoisseur of women—a hobby. There are others who share his . . . predilection. Men who would pay prime rates for the pleasure of your company, and even higher premiums for the ownership of your body."

Ayaana's skin turned cold.

Koray reached across the table. She shook off his hand. Her voice was ice. "I've met such demons." Her eyes were dark.

"Where?" Koray growled.

"At home."

Koray said, "Aha! The mystical island is not so benign after all."

"Strangers."

"They hurt you?"

"They tried," she said.

"You hurt them?"

"Mother did."

Koray's look was predatory. "Good."

Ayaana's eyes were huge with the emotions wrestling within her. Her awe and revulsion, her fear and enchantment, her sense of all she did know and would never understand, her avid curiosity. Koray guffawed. "Ah, *canim*, your face!" She looked away quickly. "Hey," he now said, "hey . . . a theology must withstand the test of reality." He cupped her chin. "I am in the market for one . . . if you have a suggestion."

Ayaana opened her mouth, and then shut it firmly.

Koray grinned. "Don't worry so much. Ask me to protect you. I can. Even from the world and its . . . strangers."

Ayaana folded her arms over her body. Koray told her a Turkish joke. Ayaana then asked, "Koray, what happened to the Syrian employee?"

A swift frown that faded. "Who?" he asked. "Oh! You mean your enthralled migrant?"

She started to object. Koray lifted a hand. "I know that nothing untoward occurred between you." Koray waited, calculating risks, his pupils dilated. "Our work attracts all sorts. Qualified refugees—they are affordable—we hire them. He was good. Meek, obedient until he fixated on you. We had to let him go." Koray paused. "He did throw his shoe at us. Did you see it?"

"The *bloodstained* shoe?" she asked.

Koray's eyes were again predatory, yellow with hunger and potent with knowledge of superior strength. He said, "We are successful because we do not take hostages, Ayaana." His look was hard. "And this, my darling, is where your tour of my hidden cave ends."

The evening juddered on, interspersed with the clash of jostling contradictions. When Koray spoke, Ayaana's fears subsided. He mocked their campus lecturers, making up a conversation between them in their different accents and voices. Koray performed and proclaimed and then got up to dance to Turkish pop. Ayaana was now weeping with laughter. When the plaintive music ended, on a warbled screech, Koray said, "Tell me more about your mythical island."

So Ayaana talked about Munira. And Muhidin. Koray listened. Ayaana told him that, one day, Ziriyab disappeared from Pate. Koray listened. Then Koray said, "Life is crafted from absence to absence."

She asked Koray, "Your brothers?"

He hesitated before admitting, "Yes." Now he spoke of the music he loved, and confessed to Ayaana his secret expeditions to a Mawlana Rumi center. "When I was a child, I wanted to be a dervish. I would wrap myself in sheets and whirl." He reached across the table to touch her face, her hair. "Dance obsessed me. If it wasn't for so many things—this—maybe I would dance."

Ayaana's fingers twirled her hair and remembered her vision of Koray at prayer. She lifted her head to say something when she glimpsed the glow in his gaze. She propped up her chin as he recited, his hands gesturing: "'*Gel, gel, ne olursan ol yine gel / Ister kafir, ister mecusi, ister puta tapan ol yine gel . . .*' You've heard it? 'Come, come, whoever you are / Wanderer, worshipper, lover of leaving—it doesn't matter . . .' I took Farsi lessons. Oh, I had intended to inhabit the Mawlana."

And silence dropped upon them. Koray frowned, and his mind roamed.

Chameleon man. *What is he?* Ayaana had followed Koray here. Might she . . . escape? That word. As if she were imprisoned. Could she pick up her handbag and race into the night and release herself from the magnet that was this man? She saw the lies woven into partial truths. The Damascene. She *had* heard a human scream that night.

She had heard the popping sound of a gun being fired. *Bloodstained* shoe. She had seen a car being driven out that night. She had . . . Koray—the seduction of this night, his frontierlessness. He was not a "good" man. He did not pretend to be. He was Koray, a man who brandished his flaws, her guide into the sunless geographies that were the world. He offered few apologies. He did not stop for chasms, either; he created them, he expanded them, he was paid to build bridges over them. He turned uncertainty into profit. He treated lie and truth as one thing—anything for power. He was interested in light, only if it served his purposes. All this flashed through Ayaana's senses in the second it took for Koray to switch from wine to a pale green juice in that slowing-down night. His words were dragging Ayaana downward, into a whirlpool. The spell had sunk tendrils into her soul, and in this replaced her instinct to flee Koray with desire.

Ayaana waited for "next."

Koray's voice was low and warm and sure, and when he laughed it was a rumbling. Ayaana rested her head on the table. Becalmed heart.

His voice said, "You know I could love you."

She waited.

Koray reached over and wrapped her hands with his. He said, "I want you to have this." He placed a small black box between them. He opened it for her. Inside was a sapphire ring. "Madagascar sapphire," he added.

Ayaana's voice was so quiet he had to strain to hear her. "What does this mean?"

"A gamble," he said.

Ayaana shook her head: "What is this for?"

"Take it."

The music of Erdoğan's Turkey. Melodies that wanted to soar but consistently crashed into the Bosporus. It sounded like an ode to loss. Ayaana was descending, with no idea of how to be or where to go. Koray got up and murmured, "Come, *güzelim,* now let us dance."

"But . . ."

"I'll dance us," he whispered. "Stand on my feet."

Within the brew of homelessness, exhilaration, ferment, and weariness, Ayaana crumbled. Tomorrow. She would take up wondering again. Tomorrow. Now she needed to be led, guided, moved, raised to someone's feet, held, and pressed into a man's body—the opposite of hers and its curved fragilities. She clung to Koray as if she were tumbleweed. But then there emerged a sudden, secret counterpoint, a tune once heard in the company of the phantoms of the doomed: "*Lacrimosa dies illa / Qua resurget ex favilla . . .*" Ayaana ignored the warning; she closed her eyes. She stopped listening. Tomorrow, she thought. Now she allowed a man with broad shoulders to dance her, and Koray asked, "Why would I let you go?"

Ayaana heard him. She would give him an answer tomorrow. Koray lowered his head. She could taste blood and wine and sweetness and sour in her mouth, and still she did not speak. *It is raining.* Pattering sounds from the street; the flustered shrills of those surprised by the downpour. And she was here, dancing in silence, her body molded to fit into another's. Turbulent twisting. Downdraft. She was spinning freely into a maelstrom.

For a timeless moment, she was inside a ship cabin, enclosed in the arms of another, so that when she opened her eyes, if Koray had been paying attention, he would have noted her shock that it was his face before her. Still swaying, they left the restaurant. It was long after midnight on a moonless neon-lit night. The wind flung debris at them. Ayaana gripped Koray's hand, grasping for certainty, imagining his could transfer itself to her. She was immersed in the darkness, but as long as Koray was whispering to her, she was not afraid. A night mist offered by the waters settled and numbed footsteps. Koray pressed Ayaana to his side. She imagined passageways through his heartbeat and reveled in the fact that he was at ease in this dark. He laughed. He referred to foghorns that she could not hear. A sliver of fear . . . *tomorrow*, she told it.

The whisper of passing ghosts: A father unknown, Fazul the Egyptian, Wa Mashriq, Suleiman. The empty, hungry thing that consumed the beloved things: a kitten, Muhidin. A mother's vaulted silence. Koray spoke, and his voice was a thin flute. She forgot to remember the Damascene. Koray's arm was tight around her. A buzzing around her, dizzy, as if she were intoxicated. And she was. As on that night on the ship, again, a streak of lightning. Ayaana was clutching a chameleon man who was offering words to night deities, and leading her up to a doorway, through a doorway where an impassive doorman stood guard.

Koray said, "Tell them, should anyone ask, that this is our Nikāḥ al-Mutʿah."

A traveler's marriage.

He laughed.

She laughed.

[75]

He told her she would be his bride. She did not care. But for this one night—one night when she ached to know, to feel, to fall—for one night, she suspended waiting.

That was all.

Later.

Metamorphosis.

Him. Intimate touch. Ensconced, surrounded by him, his wounding, the dark, the freedom it proposed, and she had drunk of pleasure and pain and gnawed on these, but then she had also plummeted into the roaring abyss, its sinister emptiness.

Later.

. . .

He murmured to her:

"You, mine."

Longing, containment, and disappointment. This—the secret, whispered, sanctioned, intimate thing—was not infinity, either. She looked at him. She had scarred his face. Bloodlines. Eyes narrowing, he asked her, "Do you see as I see? Do you, *gülüm*?"

Cartography of possession. What had she expected? Now she was the hostage. They stank of each other. Sticky, clingy bodies. Her mouth was swollen. His face was scarred. Her body scourged; his appeased. From within the web Koray had spun, his red-rimmed eyes.

"Mine." He wrote his name across her bare breasts.

A bloodstained covenant.

Her blood.

Not his.

Both her wrists locked by his hands. He squeezed them and told her matter-of-factly, "I would kill for you."

Bloodstained brown shoes.

She hid her gaze.

He whispered: "And now, I want your soul."

Never.

Inside her body, within the spaces of dreaming, she peered over the rim of this seductive chaos, its moans just like the sea but without the sea's truthfulness. She ought to have leaned closer to Delaksha's heart to learn how to fall.

~

She watched Koray in the filtered morning light. A piece of sun had fallen across his large body. It made a circle rainbow. Hooded eyes, angular face, lips she used her lips to brush against. He was watching her, his face taut with thought. More streaks of red: she had deliberately tried to draw blood. "We are hunters," he had said, meaning himself. But hers were the gleaming eyes. Reaching for her: "I want your thoughts." Half-closed eyes. He added, "I could love you, *birta-*

nem." He stroked her face. "The day I heard about you, I knew you would suit me."

Ayaana walked her fingers on his body. A wisp of thought, a reaction, like an itch. It blinked. It escaped. And Koray was breathing hard, sweating, and grunting. His hands and fingers and mouth everywhere, and he cajoled, "Your soul," and she screamed out her ecstatic "never," her absolute "no."

Real, concrete, solid.

She could stay hidden inside Koray, in spite of the acerbic aftertaste of blood-iron on her tongue, its sweet bitterness when he touched her. His body had swallowed her, and for a minute she was secured, and she craved this weight, this pounding, tearing, breaking, shattering sense of having and losing again and again.

Stillness.

She read a future on Koray's face. There she was reflected in his gaze. Here, in this crucible of yearning, she saw herself in pieces.

He said, "I have something for you." She waited. He reached into the pocket of discarded jeans to reveal a small black velvet box. He opened it. It contained a sapphire ring that was a precise copy of the one he had given her at the restaurant.

"Here," he said.

A riddle. "The other?"

"*This* is real, *gülüm*." He held it up to the light. The blue of the stone was bluer than the other one. "See? Inclusions? Let me put the truth on your finger."

Ayaana's large eyes studied Koray. "Inclusion?" She did not care. "It's too large."

Koray tapped her nose. "The foreign thing enclosed within a forming crystal. Like water trapped inside a rock." He whispered, "High value." Then laughed at a private joke. "It will fit."

Ayaana's lips were numb.

Ebbing. Hearing her heartbeat anew. Understanding in another way the language of bodies straining toward a concealed nothingness that spilled into fragments, like shards of blue light. What was true?

Koray stroked the gem. "This one is alive; its color changes. It breathes."

She looked. Saw violet.

Koray had lifted the gemstone to the light as if it were a sacrifice.

And a sliver of blue light sprinkled Ayaana's body. A lightning strike that evaporated the threat of tears.

Hatred of an incandescent six-rayed star glimmering inside the stone and Koray's gravitational pull, its consumptive impulses; the power of his seductive hunger had been undermined by a gem and its fake. And Koray, thrilled with something, was talking about the Descendant, asked if she realized that she was of strategic import for the future of the Terzioğlus in China, the dazzling future.

Ayaana half listened. Adrift again, clutching to her soul.

Unmoored. Remembering. It had niggled, the talk of Chinese heirlooms and artifacts. Perhaps in all intimate relationships each person had to bring something tangible to the table. Koray his networks, she her perceived influence.

Koray was now advising her about risk management, its necessity in, particularly, the important aspects of life, like the choice of one's woman.

He added, "I shall keep you."

Never.

But she moved, unresisting, into his desolate otherness. The paradox. Now she was almost reoriented.

Later.

Ayaana said, "We should return home."

His look was unreadable, shadows tinting his gaze.

She watched. He was studying her, too, with penetrating eyes. His left hand was on her neck, a finger beneath her ear, feeling its pulse. "We shall design our own." A finger stroking her cheek.

Never.

Ayaana breathed, hefting Pate, her home, as another talisman. The outside wind dropped its high-pitched lamentation. Eavesdropping wind. Ayaana's thought: *Today, my ghosts, you have witnessed my tumble.* Transmutation. What she knew: currents were bearers of destinations. A putrid fish smell seeped into the room through an open window. Ayaana lifted the edge of the sheet to cover her nose. Koray seemed immune. The more she watched him, the less she saw him. Thick silence. Limbs entwined. Koray's hand was flat on her stomach. "I will adjust the ring for you." Her fingers combed through his soft curls of their own volition. His eyes flickered. His eyes closed. "My mother wants you to have it."

Of course she does. "Is this Nehir's house?" Ayaana asked.

"And mine," Koray murmured.

Stone-heavy weight on Ayaana's chest, as if the old asthma were stirring awake. She held her breath, a shield. Reflections from the day striped the room and their bodies. Pungent scents of living. There was also that special loneliness that can come only from being with another.

Before dawn the next day, Ayaana scrubbed her body with the assorted oils that adorned the shower walls, testing them all. Nehir's distillates. She dressed up in sweat-stained clothes and left the den and the sleeping Koray surrounded by his true and false sapphires. Outside, transfixed by light, even though it was a drab day, she carried the riddle of herself, touching her mouth, noticing her flushed skin, seared at the core. She made her way through dimming worlds, the stink of smoke, and the centuries saturating narrow pathways. She ignored the leering eyes and derogatory catcalls of hungry-thirsty strangers who imagined that a woman alone at this time in this district was peddling her soul. Refuge in the memory of the rhythm of tides as they flowed into her in the company of Delaksha's question: "Is it true that there are bats that can suck your blood as you sleep, and all you might feel of the draining is a sweet-sweetness, and only when you wake up do you realize how grievously mutilated you are?"

[76]

When Ayaana reached Taksim Square, she snapped to greater wakefulness. Crowds, faces, people of the world at the crossroads, bumping their heads against low-hanging ancient stones. Beggars. Time. A booming voice, American? Despair. Inarticulate heart-wail: "Where am I?" She looked and looked. Standing before the desired shores of the Bosporus, but instead of awe and wonder, for no fathomable reason she saw, through borrowed memory, the souls scattered and still scattering beneath waters: all those pilgrims who, like her, had fantasized about elsewhere-bliss. Nameless, invisible, and already abandoned. *Speak to us of earth*, she heard them whisper in many voices; Ayaana fled. "Where is the Embassy of the Republic of Kenya?" she gasped.

Hunting for home. "Ankara," an information bureau informed her.

"I need a new passport." She was tearful.

"Ankara."

Disassociated. She wandered through the city, another child of Daedalus, that euphoric fool who flew with wax wings toward the sun. A gnawing sense in her heart, her belly. Screeching birds, discordant notes. Ayaana peered through Istanbul's open doors, passageways, and windows. She noticed the cats and their humanlike eyes. They noticed her. Wandering through the cacophony of the Grand Bazaar into exhaustion. Lurking in bookshops drowning in music, picking names off book titles. There was Gurnah. There was Agualusa. There was Iduma. There was Tadjo. Names from her continent. And here Selasi. She touched these. Late in the evening, when she returned to the villa, she was a delirious sepulcher stumbling past Nehir, whose mouth was moving. Ayaana heard nothing. Without a word, she sought and entered her designated room and locked the door. In her bed, Ayaana folded her body into the shape of a mollusk shell, knees drawn up, her head resting on a tear-stained pillow. Both hands were wrapped around Han Song's novel *The High Speed Railway*. Forgetting by entering into another's hurtling imagination. It painted over her ineffable sense of loss. A dull throb. When her phone rang and rang again, Ayaana ignored it.

[77]

Koray was beating at her door. Ayaana heard other doors creak open as he doubled his pounding. Ayaana got out of bed to move the chair she had used to lever it. Koray stood, unshaven, on the other side. "What the fuck's wrong with you?" She was wearing a T-shirt and shorts. He strode in. "This is no game, *canim*." He tried to stare her down, then slammed a black velvet box into Ayaana's hands. "You left this behind." He pursed his lips. "You look a mess." He paced the room. "Why did you leave?" He pressed his fingers into her arms and scrutinized her face.

Ayaana looked back, voiceless. Koray shook her. A scowl. "Women disappear off the streets of the boulevard, never to be seen again. You took a grave risk."

"You taught me well."

Koray moved back as if slapped, and then he laughed and wrapped his hands in her hair, pulling at it. She refused to react. "*We* are expected for dinner, together, *canim*."

Pinpricks on Ayaana's skin. Gelid wordlessness. Koray's words were clipped. He stroked her skin. "Clean up." He paused to squeeze her chin.

Ayaana pulled away. Koray's eyes gleamed. "Curious creature. Dinner in thirty, my *lover*?" An edge to the word. His lips brushed her right ear. Ayaana shuddered.

Now familiar Terzioğlu routines: breakfast, lunch, dinner, and drinks; the small talk—the weather, the markets, the literature of Pamuk. A deeper level of scrutiny was attached to Ayaana's person. Koray sat close to her, implying by his actions that she was his. Nehir's pleasure was palpable. It was at the dinner table that Ayaana learned that plans for her public outing as Koray's mate were already under way. "Just family and close friends." Nehir overrode Ayaana before she could object. Among the benefits she would gain after the event would be to have her belongings moved into Koray's in-house apartment. Nehir was already working on a list of likely invitees. She wanted African lilies for the table. Nehir turned to Ayaana. "I am *dee*-lighted, my darling." Nehir was eager for a shopping expedition for the two of them. There was so much to do.

Ayaana listened. Hemmed in, encircled by the Terzioğlu-making process. She was being ingested into the family. Ayaana stood to watch dawn's muted colors from her window, watched her breath on the pane. *I must breathe*. Later, she matched one of the large handbags with a red Audrey Hepburn dress. She wore the black patent-leather pumps. Terzioğlu shopping uniform. *I must breathe.*

Shop managers and myriad assistants fussed over Nehir, having already clucked over Ayaana, who was to present herself at the weekend event in a frothy rust-colored frock that reached just below her knees. Nehir, caught up in the drama of preparation, did not see Ayaana wandering away from the shop's private salon. Somewhere between the ice-cream parlor and the men's shoes shop, Ayaana was distracted by a plaintive repetitive phrase from a song. She looked about her. Nobody seemed to notice it. So she decided to seek after the grieving chords.

Ayaana wove in and out of streets and stalls amid a curtain of daily noise, and citrus scents in the streets. Just within sight of the Eski Istanbul, the live music became louder. She turned left and saw a bandaged arm: the wound it covered oozed something yellow. It belonged to an elderly busker who was playing an oud. Wrapped in a dirty white shroud, on top of which sat a heavy green jumper, his body was withered and dry, his skull visible, as if it had been borrowed from a recent grave. The music from his oud mourned something, beautiful and desolate. Inside Ayaana, a despair she had not known gushed to the surface, where it transformed into unexpected light with which to see. The old man stared into a space, his eyes fixed as his music cried for him.

Ayaana hugged the wall, not seeing the public passing by. From above the music, the musician, assuming she was Middle Eastern spoke to her in old Arabic:

"What do you see, child?"

"Dusk's boats coming home laden with fish," she murmured, her Kipate seeping through in her language cadence.

The musician paused. He was fascinated. "Where?"

"On Pate, within the Swahili seas. Our fishermen sing."

"What do they sing?"

Silence.

"Sing it."

"My voice . . ." Her singing voice had not improved with age.

"Sing."

Ayaana sang: "*Ua langu silioni nani alolichukuwa?* . . ." She stopped, because the vision of that other world was a moan in her soul.

The man asked, "Why do they sing?" Then he answered his own question. "They sing because life is a dragonfly: flutter, shine, fly, die." He strummed the oud. He looked at Ayaana. "So—there are still places in the world where the human can hear homecoming songs?" His sunken eyes acquired a faraway gaze. "Blessed be their dreams. May the enemy remain blind to their existence." He paused. "Where is this place?"

"Kenya," she answered.

"And this Kenya?"

"In the east of Africa."

The man cradled the oud close to his chest. He made it weep and weep. Ayaana felt all feelings for which no words existed, the unheeded cries of uncountable beings. She burst out, "Why play that?"

"Does it hurt?" the old man asked Ayaana. "So then cry for me. For once there was a hearth in exquisite Ma'loula. Turned to ash overnight while its keepers slept. A single rocket came through our roof." He strummed the oud. "Seven children. Gharam, my wife, my waterbird, slim as the twig of the *Sanawbar el hhalab*, even seven births later." He played. "The human body burns like roast meat." He paused. "The end." He cried. " 'Death,' girl"—he tugged his oud—"is an abominable word."

The musical elegy conjured the sinister absence of an English-speaking Damascene with no name, a hapless dirty-white kitten, suffering ortolan buntings, and a soul she had wounded and the body she had used to betray it with. Ayaana wept for things she had not cried over before. A few passing humans dropped coins into the man's open case before they continued on their way.

The elder stopped playing to ask, "Where to now?"

Broken. "I . . . I must . . . go . . . home."

"*Home*. Yes. You want to find it while it still exists."

Ayaana dug into her handbag and found a clutch of liras to press into the busker's case. Impulsively, she stooped to cup his pinched face.

The man grasped her fingers and said, "This present darkness is a death shroud." The sun drizzled in their corner of the world. He rasped, "Run, child." His voice was bile. "Tell your people that the world is turning blood-red as they sing." He plucked the strings of his oud. "Go!" he howled.

Ayaana tore down the big road, urged on by primal dread. She threw her phone into the nearest bin. A twinge of regret: this was the first phone she had bought for herself. She ran past a haggard woman trying to nurse a baby who would not stop crying. She skidded when their eyes connected. The woman was so close to tears herself. "*Ana asfa*," Ayaana told her—I'm sorry. Ayaana ran. Taxis idled at a rank on a corner. She asked to be taken to the Chinese consul general's office.

[78]

Ayaana, the Descendant, guest of the Chinese state, reported a bag containing her passport and most of her money stolen. Pickpocketed by a vicious vagabond. She relished saying that—a grubby creature who had bruised her and given chase. She had fled to the consul general's for safety. She rubbed her eyes. She looked around the office. Lassitude, the miasma of dense bureaucracy. Beijing was five hours ahead in time, and no easy references could be exchanged to verify her story. But she could not stay in Istanbul another day.

An official, not the consul general, stared her down. Ayaana sobbed. "Please," she asked. And she started to tremble, then wiped her face. "If you search the Internet, you will see my story. Please call the Xiamen Maritime University; they will confirm who I am, please."

Ayaana was directed to wait. She sat on a chair with one weak leg and perched, unmoving.

In defiance of the usually low bureaucratic expectations, Ayaana's role as the Descendant was verified in a record six hours. She had made a police report, and the junior official took it upon himself to lecture her intermittently on the perils of leaving her study base without informing her hosts, even if it were for a holiday. Gallivanting! He tut-tutted. Her only job was to study, he told her every time he opened his mouth. Ayaana, her head lowered, did not answer. She just needed to leave Turkey. Time had slowed down. Her heart raced and ached. Uncertainty. She needed a place to stay, and did not have enough money. The official sighed in irritation, would have tossed her out to fend for herself if she were not something of a state guest. Well, she would have to make do with the office storeroom and a foldable bed. Another six hours passed. Ayaana, who, though cold, had slept quite well, was summoned into the dingy den of a main office to be issued a temporary emergency travel pass. Her return ticket had been retrieved from the system and changed. Unwashed, hungry, exhausted but elated, Ayaana was on a flight back to Xiamen that evening.

[79]

The luggage carousels at Xiamen Gaoqi International Airport belched into life. Ayaana watched other people's bags turn up in assorted shapes and colors. The airport's space-age design gave it a sense of anonymity that could place it anywhere in the world. She crossed the arrivals hall. To the left of a café, a television flashed news of the release of the journalist Gao Yu before returning to its regular programming, which revealed the image of sinewy arms around a pottery wheel, crafting a vessel. Ayaana idly watched an elongated earthen pot emerge. A transition of seasons on the screen: the tides, birds, wheat, skies, flowering trees, clouds, and dust, then back to the potter and his vessel. And then his hands ritually broke the pot he had created, and Ayaana recoiled. A river of arrivals pushing luggage carts drove her into the Xiamen evening. Outside, East African botanical exiles—the flame trees of Xiamen had exploded into red flower, and in the late light these looked like giant lanterns. The distant glimmering line of the South Sea, and inside Ayaana an odd sense of arrival. And Ayaana remembered that she needed to buy a new phone.

Later, inside her hostel room, Ayaana called Munira. Hearing that suddenly most beloved voice, she whispered, "*Ma-e*"—tasting the words—"how I love you." And her voice cracked.

Munira cooed, "What's wrong, *mwanangu*?"

Ayaana wiped tears. She could not continue. "*Ma-e* . . . it's been too long."

Munira crooned, "My jasmine, my rose baby."

Ayaana shut her eyes and could feel the ache of her body, its new knowing. She had broken through a side window to steal some of the secrets in the cult of life. "*Lulu*," Munira said, "I have a surprise. I must speak of it to you soon." She paused. "Please, pray very much for me. Pray for us."

"Muhidin?" Ayaana was suddenly terrified.

"What, that one? He grows fatter every day." Munira giggled. "You should hear him. He has a theory for everything, now that he captains his own ship."

"How is . . . M-mozambique?" The word stuck to her tongue.

"It is good to us." Munira laughed. Ayaana made a face. "You are well, child? You were doing exams? That is why you were quiet? I told your father. But you know him. His crazy mind creates trouble where none exists." Munira laughed. "He was certain you had been eaten by Chinese sea monsters!"

Ayaana touched the phone to her head, gave a wry smile. *Close*. Muhidin. "Where is he?"

"Gone to Pate. Call him there. You have his number? How were the exams?"

Within Ayaana, silence: *If I could find again the God, who contains the allness of existence, including the story of this China, maybe I would learn to pray again. I wish you were in Pate, Mother; I would come home to you tomorrow. Learning about the sea is not the same as being with the sea. I should have apprenticed myself to Mehdi. I gave my body to a man I fear; he is trying to swallow my soul whole. I am not Chinese,* Ma-e, *and I never shall be. My heart is drifting in waters that have no name. I am also afraid of shadows.* "I am well," Ayaana replied.

"God is kind," Munira said.

Then: "*Ma-e*," Ayaana said, "do you sing in Mozambique?"

"Not yet." Munira cleared her throat.

"Can you sing now?"

A high laugh. "'*Ua langu silioni nani alolichukuwa*'?"

"Yes, that one." Ayaana hunkered down, the better to hear her mother's voice.

Ayaana needed a new passport. She extracted money from her account and bought a second-class ticket from Xiamen to Beijing, looking forward to sleeping overnight on board. From Beijing South Railway Station, she headed for the Kenyan Embassy. When she saw the red, green, black, and white of the Kenyan flag, she had to wait for a paroxysm of a most unexpected emotional yearning to pass. Inside the embassy, while her new application was being processed, she indulged in a frenzy of speaking Kiswahili and guzzled Ketepa tea with rice-flour mandazi, paged through the Kenyan newspapers—she read about the usual swindles by Kenyan politicians with indulgent affection. Wanting to stay close to the bulwark of the embassy, Ayaana decided to go shopping for clothes. On impulse, she stopped at a cinema. The film was one of those that featured a grand emperor in bright robes who falls in love with the nightingale voice of a blind peasant girl, who sang as she tended to her meager fields. Ayaana wept in all the right places. In the afternoon she learned that the embassy would have her new passport ready after twenty-one days. She spent one more night in Beijing—the Beihai Old Town Holiday Seaview Inn in the Dongfeng area had a sixteen-dollar room available. The next day Ayaana was on the return train to Xiamen.

The university hostel was still mostly empty. The start of the fall semester was nine days away. Ayaana missed the annoying cacophony of pop music of many nations spilling out of different rooms. To while away the time, she arranged and rearranged her books. That night, she picked a book from her shelf to read: *The Book of Chameleons*. She fell asleep with the book next to her.

Freshly made morning. Crisp air. While bicycling around, Ayaana had stopped to admire the fresh rust color on the university training ship, where she would be doing her new semester practicals, when it dawned on her that she could accelerate her lessons, take more classes, and complete her finals a year early and leave China as soon as possible. Contented, she spent the next day twisting her hair into braids, seated on her bed, legs crossed, mind blanked. She added coral beads to her locks. Still restless, she spent the next day tracing and retracing the Basmallah, using Thuluth calligraphy, finding voice in an old refugee's oud melody. Then Ayaana wept.

Two days later, not really looking for anything, as she ate her lunch while reading a newspaper, Ayaana saw an insert with the thumbprint image of the Zao Wou-Ki print she now had. Her chopsticks clattered on the table. She pored over the text, which announced a Zao Wou-Ki retrospective in a Shanghai gallery.

Studying schedules, she found a train would be leaving Xiamen North Station at 09:34 the next day. If she got a ticket on it, she would reach Shanghai Hongqiao at 17:42. Shanghai, like most of the big cities in the country, did not sleep.

Ayaana wandered up and down from the Bund to the gallery, her face turning often toward the water. Smog obscured a clear view of the city on the other side, giving the edifices the sheen of a dream. Ayaana had made note of a boardinghouse that was one stop after Shanghai Central; she would spend the night there. She entered Zhongshan East Street and located the Shanghai Art Gallery. And there were the works of Zao Wou-Ki. She had to pause to keep herself from foundering. A rush of emotion. She settled on a bench, staring, remembering. Life had seemed to stretch out infinitely on the ship; it had felt charmed. She raised herself to immerse herself in the Zao Wou-Ki painting: "*4.4.85*, 1985. Oil on canvas." Wistful. "What do you see?" he had asked. *An echo*, she might have answered him now.

"*Histoire sur la mer*, 2004. Oil on canvas, Zao Wou-Ki." Ayaana sat before each print or painting until she ran out of day and dreams; she was the last member of the public to leave the gallery. Later that evening, in a city filled with movement, Ayaana joined a river of souls. She flowed with them one way and then another, hemmed in by a surging populace. She wandered onward, belonging to nonthinking nothingness, and trying to remember the sea, only the sea. She returned to the gallery the next day and lingered there until it was time to catch the train back to Xiamen.

A bright dawn marked the start of the new semester. A torrent of students and their sounds filled the space. Chen Sheng—Shalom—saw Ayaana in braids and exclaimed, "You look *exactly* from Tibet." She took several selfies with Ayaana. Ayaana's mouth turned down. She had intended to underline her African-ness.

[80]

Ayaana ran from her maritime-ecology classroom, heading for the hostel and her room. She jumped over a bucket before skidding to a stop in front of two brand-new pink suitcases on wheels parked outside her door. Her head drooped. She had hoped to catch a nap before heading for her night classes. The bags, she knew, carried all the things she had abandoned in Istanbul. Koray was back. She looked around before rolling the bags into the room as if they might also hold grenades. She stared at them before stepping around them, and out of the room. She fled to the library where a "strict silence" rule was rigidly enforced.

. . .

"Ayaana." Koray found her on the breakfast line early one morning. Intense whisper. "Well done. You pissed Mother off." He was grinning, but his eyes were searing. "How did you leave?" There was unalloyed rage in that question.

Ayaana laughed to annoy Koray, to mock herself.

"Searched everywhere for you. Can you imagine the shame?"

"No," she answered. And she scooped extra shrimp *shu mai* onto her plate.

His voice in her ear. A shiver. Lust. "We are betrothed, my love."

She was serene. "No, we are not . . . my love."

His eyes: lonely, greedy, restless. Koray leaned over to whisper, "Life is war. We pay for our victories in advance. That is why we own the future. We do not fail." Ayaana turned to fill a cup with jasmine tea. He continued, "I choose you. Learn to like it, for you will live with it, whether you want to or not."

In the awful warmth of the room, Ayaana wanted to howl. Behind her, Koray said, "You may want to take a step forward, baby; you are holding up the line."

Ayaana laid aside her tray and walked out of the dining hall.

Ayaana left her hostel room, where she had closeted herself, to go to her pond-view bench and listen to the night. The place felt uninhabited but safe. Stillness. A soft and salty breeze. "Koray is back," she murmured. She was neither happy nor sad. That darkness. That night. Eddying thoughts: the seduction of surrendering, of forgetting, of numbness. But then a familiar sound reached her from the far waters. *Zar.* The murmuring cry of djinns at night; other saltwater whispers, urgent and garbled.

Three days later, storm sirens sounded. A typhoon that had been pummeling nearby Taiwan had switched direction and was heading straight for Fujian. At once, emptied streets, barred buildings, sheets of rain, and all the moans and groans and howls of wind. Ayaana sneaked into a storeroom at the top of their building to see what a typhoon looked like. She listened to the screeching hundred-kilometer-an-hour winds. She saw one of the largest flame trees roll across the main street as if it were cardboard, and strained toward the sight of giant waves breaching the sea walls. The water reached for the avenue. The djinns were roaring *Ni shi shei?* today. Strangely exhilarated, she listened to the boom of life at its fiercest. Some of the building's windows facing the sea broke in tinkling symphony. The typhoon, though, was a summons. If she were Fundi Mehdi, she would have known how to read it.

Udongo utakuita.

The clay will call you.

[81]

He was turning his life into a clay-borne liturgy. He traveled with ghosts—his fire-eaten wife, his fire-eaten ship, and the sea creature, Ayaana, who floated in the turbulence of all his dreams now, and in whom sea, ship, and wife had converged. He turned his story into water and soil and the pinching, pulling, turning of his body and hand around a wheel. His hands as wings, as small birds in flight, listening, throwing clay. Passages, transforming, and he had become a scarred vase, a scarred plate, a scarred bowl.

[82]

This was a land unfazed by the sea's dramatics. After the typhoon, a return to routine. School was no exception. Clanging of machinery. The *tang-tang-tang* of the tools of students learning, rebuilding, and testing metal parts. Oil and fuel, the aroma of latent fire. The training ship was out at sea. Koray joined Ayaana in the simulation engine room, where she practiced, ear plugs in her ears, protective glasses over her eyes. She was on her back in blue overalls, examining pipes as part of an exercise. Cables and all manner of gleaming tools were arranged beside her. As she held a screw between her teeth and cleaned a gap, Koray's face loomed over hers. It was somber, with wariness in his hooded eyes. He signaled to her; his mouth opened and closed.

"What?" She was brusque.

He gestured outward. "News," he mouthed above the din.

"What?" she said, tapping at a knob with a wrench.

He pointed at his watch. "You need to come now." He then wrote it out and placed it over her face.

Ayaana checked a nut.

"Admin office says it is urgent," he added in blue ink.

"Koray . . ." she started.

He added, "They sent me to get you."

She dragged herself out from under the machine. She smelled of diesel and oil. She removed the protective gear and wiped her blackened hands on a greasy brown cloth.

Their footsteps hurried along the corridor. A distance from the noise, she asked, "What's wrong?" Her voice was shrill.

Koray said, "Just come with me, *canim*. Do you have your phone?"

Ayaana looked at him and started to quaver. She adjusted her overalls. She was suddenly dumb. Koray offered her an arm. She did not react. They walked into Xiamen's world, its air redolent with rain, a blend of blossoms and invisible spices. Wind created ripples on water, stirring leaves. Ayaana's heart cudgeled her ribs.

It was Muhidin.

[83]

Enchanted by his new life, entranced by his increasing wealth in family and matter, in love with existence again, Muhidin had felt invincible. He had taken leave from his work in Pemba to make a jubilant return to Pate Island. There were things to do. He intended to convince Mehdi to return with him to Pemba and set up a boat-building-and-repair yard there. He wanted to commission a *dau* for his wife. He also wanted to surprise her by repairing and repainting both their houses. With this in mind, he had arrived on Pate with three workers from Pemba and Mombasa.

. . .

These were details Ayaana would collect much later, when she went from soul to soul on Pate asking what the islanders had seen and heard and sensed about Muhidin before he disappeared.

Muhidin had declared, "This realm shall be known again." He had distributed some of his old books to the school. He had teased the boatmen and said they needed to diversify their businesses: There were immigrants from Europe looking for uncomplicated ways to enter Mozambique and Angola by sea from Oman, where they waited. They were paying in euros up front. The young men listened to him and sought contacts. He had supervised the house repairs by day, and offered additional work to the long unemployed. He had harangued, bullied, taught, laughed, and slaughtered a goat, both for gratitude and to share his bounty. He had administered some more of his herbs and tonics, including a few he had acquired in Mozambique. He refound his corner in the evening *baraza* and regaled the men with stories of life in Mozambique, of working as a sea captain on oil-prospecting vessels. He had praised the wonder that was his wife, Munira.

Hudhaifa would tell Ayaana, "Muhidin radiated the joy of paradise. He had no one to hate anymore."

The tailor would tell Ayaana, "Your father descended upon us like the sun."

Dura, Ayaana's former classmate, now married with three children, would remember Muhidin's attempts to comfort the desolate Mama Suleiman. "Amina," he had said, "your son is on *hutubu*." He had meant YouTube. "He has a long beard. It is thick. He wears a black headscarf. Very advanced. Many men wear headscarves these days. He was carrying a grenade launcher all by himself. He has become a strong man. His voice caused the black flag he clutched to flutter. Your son is ambitious, Bi Amina. He is working for the caliphate. It includes us here. He now calls us infidels. Which is truthful. For who here is without sin? The good thing is that he says he is coming back to us as a raging fire. I suspect he has been infected by some foreign fervor. But Pate is an old place. When he comes back, we will calm him down." Mama Suleiman had moaned and groaned and wailed, Dura would tell Ayaana, her eyes sparkling. Muhidin had looked confused. He had gestured and asked, "Have I said anything wrong? I told her he *is* coming back home. Here, doesn't she want to see?" He had pushed buttons on his phone to access the Internet. The link had failed to open.

Muhidin had also taken to spending most of his time on Pate with Fundi Almazi Mehdi, who had been joined in his enterprise by Mzee Kitwana Kipifit, who mainly focused on etching symbols on the boats, and stitching sails in silence in full view of the sea. The ship-repairing enterprise had grown steadily over the last three years. Mehdi and Mzee Kitwana became entwined, as companion boat makers, and in their shared silence had found something of a comrade in each other. They listened to the tide news together. They walked, worked, and ate together. Mzee Kitwana then built a shed close to Mehdi's. Muhidin had at once understood that now Mehdi would not go anywhere without Mzee Kitwana, but Mzee Kitwana did not care to ever leave Pate. At first Muhidin sat with them to try to change their minds. But then he started to enjoy being with them, in a season surrounded by October's dragonflies. He would speak of his pride in Ayaana's progress in China. He asked Mzee Kitwana for words in Mandarin he could use to surprise her with. He also told Mehdi that he was experimenting with forgiveness.

"How?" Mehdi had asked, interested in it for himself.

Muhidin had tapped his nose, and his eyes had twinkled. He had said a miracle would make itself apparent on his next return to Pate.

"We spoke of Ziriyab. His absence," Mehdi would one day mutter to Ayaana. "Then we spoke of the sea." His eyes became distant with remembering—not the conversation, but the sea.

Two mornings later, Muhidin had come to the two men with his eyes red, his hair uncombed, and, for the first time in his new days on Pate, unsmiling. He plunked himself down in silence. After about an hour, he said, eyes darting hither and thither, "My son Ziriyab came to me in a dream. Wherever he is, he is not doing well."

. . .

In the dream, Mehdi would remember Muhidin saying, Ziriyab had been on a metal bed in a small room drenched in fierce light, so Muhidin could see that his entire body had become a wound. Muhidin had smelled the foul green pus of death within Ziriyab's slowing crashing heart. Tearing up, Ziriyab had said to him, "My father, it is good you came. I am dying." Muhidin said he had shaken his son, slapped him awake. "No!" he had commanded. Ziriyab had then pointed. "See my heart. It is rotting." Muhidin had shouted, "Is it a heart you need? Then take mine. It is large. It is enough for you." And in the dream he had torn out his heart and shoved it into Ziriyab, and did not let go until that heart started to beat inside Ziriyab's body. "And you, Father, and you?" Ziriyab had apparently clung to him. Muhidin told Mehdi that he had informed Ziriyab that since he carried his heart now, he would have to live for him, too.

Muhidin had asked Mehdi and Mzee Kitwana, "What can this dream mean?"

And the mood had turned somber.

"That dream infected us, too," Mehdi would tell Ayaana.

To reassure themselves, the men then spoke of the sea. They spoke of boats, of fish, of currents and tides. Muhidin spoke of watermen he had known. And because he needed to talk, he also spoke of the time he was "Abd" and how the sea saved him. The muezzins called the noonday prayers. The three men paused to pray in their own ways. After the silence, Muhidin said, "The sea is an old story."

"A song," Mehdi offered.

"True," Muhidin replied, "and I have heard many. There is one that bears the fragrance of citrus and honey. I have tasted it."

Mehdi replied, "As I have."

Mzee Kitwana, who had been listening, exclaimed, "How does one savor this thing?"

"It finds you at sea," Mehdi said.

Muhidin then asked Mehdi if he could build a *dau* to be named for Munira. Muhidin said he would pay for the boat up front.

Mehdi would one day point Ayaana to the vessel, which he was still working on.

And Mehdi remembered how they had spoken of Kenya, and why, whenever it took two steps forward, it also took eight steps back. Muhidin spoke of Pemba, of Mozambique, of the people. "Look at me," he said, "how stylish I have become: *Gome la udi si la mnukauvundo.*" To live among the civilized rubs off on a person.

And they had laughed.

Mzee Kitwana insisted, "How does one taste that sea-song?"

Silence.

The Pleiades had been an especially luminous blue that evening. The men stared at them. Mzee Kitwana had pleaded again, "Will I ever know the sea and its citrus-scented song?" And Muhidin had then said, "I will take you to the place in the water where the song first ambushed me. But I cannot guarantee that it will appear."

Two early mornings later, Mzee Kitwana and Muhidin set sail on a rehabilitated *mtepe*. No one thought to worry about them until four days had passed and their phone signals had ceased. Passing fishermen did say that, two days before, blue phosphorescence had covered the night waters and blinked out unfathomable messages, but of Muhidin and Mzee Kitwana, nothing. A flotilla went out to search. On the sixth day, Fundi Almazi Mehdi gave himself the heart-shattering task of calling Munira to tell her Muhidin had not returned from the sea.

After hearing the news, Munira had waited a day before phoning Ayaana's university. She had begged the authorities to guarantee that someone would be with Ayaana when they gave her the message. The university, for whom little was secret, had enlisted Koray's help for the task.

~

In a hard-angled rectangular room, full of green files on shelves and smelling of just-eaten pork *shu mai*, the light fell golden and soft on the corduroy-wearing message-giver's face, making his lips glow pink. Ayaana experienced the delicacy of this culture, how a people reshaped their bodies to convey bad news. Husky-toned formality that contained the proper essence of emotion, the gentle bow, the almost tender voice that delivered a terse report without euphemisms, the pause so that the news could fill the space, that gentle bow again. So that, even though she would have preferred to hurl herself out of the window to escape the soul-searing, -tearing, -bursting monstrous awfulness that invaded her body, even though she might have torn out her hair to ease the pressure on her head, she could not. That gentle nod. And here was Koray, a rock, with both arms around her in case she did not wish to think, move, or plan. The shadows floated like frisky crimson phantoms around her vision. But after the messenger finished with his soft words, and expressed tender sorrow for her pain, Ayaana dragged herself away from Koray. She murmured, "Thank you. But my father is the ocean. Therefore, he does not drown. He is a wave. He is also the tide. He will return."

~

Every day, Munira and Ayaana spoke. First they listened to each other's silences.

Ayaana asked, "Has he returned?"

"Not yet, *lulu*."

Silence.

Munira said, "We have petitioned the sea and its deities for mercy."

. . .

One Friday evening, Ayaana told Koray, who was standing next to her, "I will speak with the water." Koray was talking to her. She did not hear him, beyond random words: "emotional paralysis . . . delusional . . . irrational . . ." She observed his mouth move: "accept . . . fate . . . submit to life . . ." Ayaana felt herself float away, as light as fluff, leave the room, take the elevator and stairs, walk out the main door, dull pain in her stomach, hollow in the heart, sting in the abdomen, fog in the head. But the more she walked, the more she felt the sea come close to her, and if the sea was close to her, so was Muhidin.

Zar: A murmuring cry made by djinns at night.

She could not unhear it. Under the water of her half-world, she looked for Muhidin's face. "Where are you?" he breathed. 哀愁: *ai chou*. Sorrow. Palettes of life's shadows. Topologies: painful, heartbroken, bitter; sorrow, wounded, separated; anguish. When Munira called the next night, and Ayaana heard her, Ayaana moaned until those near to her had to wrench the phone from her hand. Roaming realms without a map. Here she could not wail in her mother's language. The waiting had metastasized in her marrow, her fiber, and her pores, and then there were those other whispers from the sea that she heard, and she concealed these from her watchers in the blandness of a smile, the diligence of her work.

She was being crowded in by the well-meaning, overseen by Koray who wore his role as "curator" of her life as a dark, heavy, rich coat. Ayaana loathed words. They did not produce Muhidin. They pretended that they could explain the feeling of the not-being-there of her father.

Muhidin.

Sometimes Ayaana just said his name.

Yesterday the djinns sang to her. They told her that she ought to be used to disappearances by now. She told them that absences are capricious. They attach themselves to different people in different ways.

Ayaana had stopped eating.

Ayaana was dehydrated.

So they sent a doctor, a roly-poly, bespectacled man who spoke to Ayaana in soft Mandarin and broken English and laughed at his own obscure jokes. He thought she wanted to drown herself.

"No, no," Ayaana protested. "I just need to *speak* with the water."

The doctor left. Later, a nurse came to Ayaana's room with a hydrating IV line. To show that she was in her right senses, Ayaana let the woman insert it into her wrist. They had mixed it up with a drug that would put her to sleep. Ayaana woke up thirty-two hours later, light-headed. And the world had tilted some more, and she was no longer attached to the IV, and the grief had gone deeper, so it was a low hum, as if it were crying in secret.

~

The Embassy of Kenya sent Ayaana her new passport by registered mail. She took it as a sign that Muhidin would come home soon.

[84]

A medium-sized package came for Ayaana. She studied it. The return address in Mandarin, a place she had not heard of: 破釜, 嵊泗列島, 杭州灣, 舟山群島新區; Po Fu, Shengsi Island, Hangzhou Bay, Zhoushan Archipelago. She opened the package with care. A black-lacquer-painted vase in the shape of a large teardrop—with broken red, green, and amber sea glass embedded in it. The images, whirls, and whorls had created a three-dimensional landscape, feathery gestures burned in so that a fire-drawn, almost blue mythical creature raced through a dark lacquer night, which seemed to move depending on how the light fell on it. It emitted a vague scent of night-blooming jasmine, as if this essence had been interlaced with its clay. The vase filled Ayaana's hands with its smooth roundedness.

Koray visited Ayaana's room at noon and found her contemplating the vase in her hands. "This is different," he said.

Ayaana lifted the vase up to her face.

He asked, "What is it?"

She shrugged.

"Something to do with that 'Descendant' thing?" asked Koray. "Let me see? Who sent it to you?"

He grabbed the vase from Ayaana and lifted it to the light. Those who knew what to look for would have recognized the work of a reclusive contemporary ceramicist whose work had appeared as if from nowhere, who was known as 破釜, Po Fu, a play on the words "broken vessel," which, in interviews the potter had given with his face in shadow, he had said referred to himself and the world.

Ayaana rose to take it back from Koray.

She tilted it upward.

"It is beautiful," she said.

Koray pursed his lips. "You did not tell me you liked pottery. We have a large collection in storage back at home."

Ayaana turned to Koray. She wanted to tell him that the vague aroma of night jasmine embedded in an etched vase received at dusk in a season of sorrow meant something.

He watched her as she cradled the vase. His gaze returned to the vase, then back to her. Ayaana's fingers stroked the vase, a caress, before she took it to her shelf.

Koray left her room in silence.

Footfalls in a thick, lightless night, as if sea djinns had left the water to seek her out and, if they could not reach her by song, they did so by means of dreams in which they chanted, until grief drenched her face with tears that she wiped when she woke.

News from Pate Island:

Muhidin had not yet returned.

Rain: thunder at midnight. Ayaana slipped out of class at 10:00 a.m. and went down an emergency staircase to find the gate to Baicheng Beach and access to a sea from which she had been temporarily barred—for her own safety, the counselor had said. She squeezed through a fence and dashed down a side road and along a rotting jetty that stopped at a rocky shore. She slid on seaweed, and picked herself up to jump from rock to rock until the sea spray could soak her body and hair and fill her. And then she looked past the gray, gray water, the breaking surf, and saw a large dead feathered bird ebbing with the currents of that time of day. Above her head, circling gulls. She tilted her head to follow their dance, their whirl and return and swoop. She lifted up her arms, stretched them over the water. She waited for a tingle at the tip of her fingers, something to indicate that Muhidin had heard her heart screaming out to him.

Nothing.

Nothing.

Ayaana returned to the campus dripping water, trailing beach soil, shivering, and silent.

In her room, Ayaana phoned her mother. Munira answered, "No," to her unasked question.

Ayaana said, "I heard the djinns last night."

Munira's abrupt "*Don't* answer them."

A second package came to Ayaana by mail. It contained a white lacquer vase with sky-blue flecks that seemed to extend not only its contours but also its dimensions. It had a rough finish that scintillated the nerves on the skin, so that Ayaana returned to it often, to rub her palms and the backs of her hands on it. She lifted it to press her face into it. This one smelled of the deep, dark earth.

[85]

The door to Ayaana's room swung on its hinges, moved by a breeze that traveled down the corridor, having swooped in through large open windows. There were no thieves. The consequences of crime on campus stopped a mere half-millimeter from the penalty of death by firing squad. Expulsion was the kindest sentence. So Ayaana was unworried when she walked into her open room that evening. The wind blew in through her open window. Had she forgotten to lock her door?

Pieces.

Both her gift vases.

The shards were in a blended heap on the floor.

She knew the wind had not gathered the broken portions into one pile. It was this, seeing the pieces, that made her rage. The tears trapped between her heart and soul seemed to bleed through her ragged breathing. Delirium. Madness. *Never!* She screamed from her core as she emptied her olive canvas rucksack, upended its contents, and gathered the shattered pieces and poured them in. She bruised her hands as she rummaged in the wastebasket in her closet for the address on their original packaging. She wrote it out, and she was burning. She retrieved that packaging and transferred the broken pieces into it. Securing it. In her eyes a dangerous smoldering, and, single-minded, she set out before dawn.

Ayaana secured her rucksack as she strode. Inside the bag were her purse, a notepad containing an address, some water, the broken pieces of vases, underwear, and an extra T-shirt. She traveled, fueled by rage. *Never!* And as she stood at a platform of the Xiamen North railway station waiting for a bullet train, she had no plan other than to find a potter.

Kusi huleta mvua.

The south monsoon brings the rain.

[86]

In a northeastern trajectory, Ayaana's train hurled itself across immense landscapes, whizzing past city after city, which mirrored those she had seen before. View from a window. In the foreground, concrete uniformity oppressing even the sky, box after box after box, fence after fence, and in between, smog and fog. In the background, a blur of stillnesses, as if, in reality, nothing moved, nothing changed. Ayaana sat in a large red chair inside a fast-moving rectangle, sealed from the terrain. Except that now she had time to reach for Muhidin, hands flat against a sealed train window, the fleeing, shrieking train, and she in it, clutching a bag that contained pieces of broken clay. Glimpse of ocean in portions; as if it too had been taken and smashed into manageable pieces.

Brown cliffs, gray mountain peaks. Beneath these, another city, another bridge, another district, written out in flat-screen lights that touted all the commodities of human existence. Her fellow passengers slurped their food while reading books on their phones, or had closed themselves off from everything with earphones. The voice that addressed them was the one that announced stops and starts and warned them not to step off a moving train. Through the window she found the flight of wild geese. She pursued them with her gaze. They prevented her from noticing the eruption of new stone cities.

Destination Zhejiang. Subway, then bus. Traversing seas and rivers on vast bridges, icons of human madness and genius; the willful shrinking of the world, the evidence of a culture's spiderlike focus to weave itself deep into spaces, places, and already frayed worlds. Eight hours after leaving Xiamen she entered Hangzhou, Zhejiang, which was, though she had not thought of it when she set out, within sight of the ineffable and mercurial Qiantang River, lair of the Silver Dragon, the best of those solitary waves that carried tides upstream. *Tidal bore*, she remembered from her lessons, as she walked across roads, oblivious to stares, heading for the bridge, trying to think beyond her churning anger. As she looked at the octagonal Six Harmonies Pagoda emerging from the greenery of the Yuelun Mountain across the bridge, she finally gave way to a few quiet tears. Holding on to the day's light warmed her and melted the wintriness of her losses. Crying over broken vases? She almost laughed at herself. She breathed in deep. *Muhidin*. She allowed the sensation, but the bite from his absence was far less searing than it had been in Xiamen. As she shifted her rucksack from one shoulder to the other, the broken pieces of the vases jingling within, her stride was long. She hurried to find and take a bus to Xinchang County, and meet the ferry to Shengsi Island, and from there figure out which of the nearly four hundred islands hosted a potter who had sent her the gift vases.

Ayaana trod a sand slope dotted with browning seashells, delicate things that crumbled under her footsteps. She trod softly. Her rucksack on her back, she followed an ox track that abutted fields of green wheat. Shimmering in the distance to her left, a fog-shrouded bay. A chill wind circled her as she stopped so that the scents of the sea might suffuse her being, soak into her.

She paused to catch her breath. She surveyed the greenery; holding her face up, she felt for the direction of the wind. She ran down a small hill. Breathing. Breathing. Down, down, down, until she reached the thick pearl-gray sands, into which footsteps and seaweed pieces were implanted. The sands stopped in front of a makeshift jetty that stretched out, a grim, cobbled road to a confluence of rocks upon which a lighthouse stood stranded, like a forgotten, fading legend. Even the wild sea it had once guarded seemed to have receded far from it, after an earthquake. This was Ayaana's destination. Rehearsing a speech she must make to a stranger: *These are broken. Please fix them. I can wait.*

Evening. Far-breaking waves split on the black pebble beach. Small boats in the distant sparkle of water. Inside the roughly repaired lighthouse, a wooden floor, shells of abalone on smooth shelves. High, fractured windows opened out to the horizon and cast shadows on the cliff edge.

Ayaana's first steps across the threshold.

A potter's wheel and a long table; he was sitting on a curved bench in the middle. He smelled her rose fragrance before he saw her standing at his doorway, hair over her forehead, intensity in dark eyes deepened by experience, made beautiful and fevered. He kept to his seat, struggling not to react. Slow steps toward him. She looked again, squinting. She was startled, and then not startled that it was he. The potter. Perhaps she had known.

He was in partial silhouette, his gaze level. The dusk light framed her features, her mouth parted. The last time he had seen her was when he had traveled to be in her presence in the night gardens of Xiamen. He had told himself that he had come to bring her news of Delaksha. But, as then, now he said nothing. She dropped her bag. Footsteps across the floor. Shivering now. "I . . ." she began.

She sought and found the burn scars on his face. The familiar eyes now deeper set, as if he had recently suffered. He was thinner. He wore his hair longer. Hollowed features. His hands were colored by gray clay. She stepped close.

He returned to his work in slow motion.

"*Ni shenti haihaoba*"—You are well? His words were soft on his tongue.

"*Haihao*"—Fine—she stammered.

He squashed clay. She watched him in his earth-stained apron that might or might not have once been brown. White-painted walls. She tilted her head at the two Zao Wou-Ki prints and heard the faraway water. *From sea to soil,* she thought as he wove the clay and, outside, waves slithered on rocks. She turned on her toes, picking up scents: abalone, sea slugs, and cucumbers; dung of seagulls, the sweat of the sea. She huddled in her jacket, stomach churning. What words: "These. They broke." She added, "I didn't break them."

When she found herself on her knees, grieving, she scrambled in panic. *What now?* Noiseless tears puddled the ground. The fractures, the fences, these fragments.

Lai Jin listened. He threw clay, wove worlds and comfort with molding-making hands. She was here. She shouldn't be, but she was. The rose whiff was now in his nostrils, the promise of new life, like citrus. His old lighthouse was suffused with the scent of light and wild roses as a sea wind howled. Outside, the stumps of a forest of petrified wood, calcified by sea salt and time's crouch. Tuning in to the rhythm of the turning wheel. *Ni shi shei?* whispered the waters, *Who are you?* they demanded.

She rose from her knees. She said, "I lost the sea." She retrieved the box from within her rucksack. The broken vessels clanged. "Will you fix these? They are smashed. I brought them back for fixing." She carried the box to his table.

He drew the clay out. She watched as he slowed down the wheel, his hands still pushing, pulling, kneading. Entranced, she slipped into stillness, the better to see his hands create. He worked, and some of the congestion in her heart dissolved. "Will you fix it?" Meaning the vessels, meaning her core, meaning Muhidin, meaning the world. He reread the sorrowing worn by her body, the bent head, the sadness and hunched shoulders.

He stopped his work to take her hands.

The half-made vessel dissolved.

Touch.

She curved her hand around his.

Time died.

She cleared her throat. "You are here now?"

"Yes."

"The ship?"

"She was killed."

Ayaana closed her eyes. The MV *Qingrui:* another phantom in the landscape of losses. She had stopped asking, "Why?"

His new Zao Wou-Ki, it was mostly sky-blue. Violent blue, red, and black brushstroke signals, like colored scars on a page of light. There was a word she would have used if she had known it: "palimpsest." Dusk, and the shine of an ever-new, unfolding glimmer, revealing new skin on a now old soul.

Rain pattered. A stirring on the roof. Sparrows roosting on eaves. Ayaana turned from Lai Jin and flowed out the door to witness their presence.

She said, "Forgiveness birds." Then she wiped her face with the backs of her hands. Tears. Rain. It soaked her clothes and skin. The purging water trickling into a place of the heart. Lai Jin knew when to meet her at the door with a thin red towel. A hot shower was already running. He led her to it. His beige robe lay folded on a wooden bench for her to use.

Later, supported by soup, they would talk until the dawn. Mostly, they would remember Zao Wou-Ki and smile about plastic ducks and frogs still floating on ceaseless seas. Ayaana would tell him about being the Descendant, and how she had needed to escape it: "I sought the sea." Stillness. "Then the sea left me." They would reach for the silence that sat between words. They moved into it. They shifted to sit close to each other. Bodies touched. The fluttering of roosting sparrows. They both looked in that direction.

Forgiveness birds.

He imagined she alluded to the Great Sparrow Campaign disaster that still haunted the psyche of the nation, which she would have heard about by now. He imagined she was observing that the sparrows, despite the horror visited upon them, had returned. *Forgiveness birds.* That was what Lai Jin would call them from now on.

"My father," Ayaana said, "Muhidin, he went to the ocean. He has not returned." Eyes met, entangled. She whispered, "We are waiting for him." Her gaze searched his for his knowing. Gaze to gaze. Within his eyes, the image and likeness of her tears. It was what, today, she needed to see. That was why she flung her arms around his neck, and he lifted her to himself, and she grieved into his body, and he knew enough of life to know when listening was the only word.

. . .

Nightfall. For the first time in Ayaana's Chinese sojourn, she saw Teacher Ruolan's Tou Mou, the empress star that never set. How much she had longed for the darkness of real night, away from the confusion of commerce's neon and sky-clouding smog. In the depth of that night, as Lai Jin slept, Ayaana heard, as if from within, an oud played by a chimerical soul on the fringes of a street that was a crossroads between worlds, between wars. She soared out of bed to reach for a large window out of which to look. A woman wearing a man's shirt while scanning strange skies for a song. She was still crying.

She wanted to tell him that she had lost the strength to try to keep negotiating existence in Mandarin. She wanted to explain to him that her dreams were inundated by a torrent of languages. She was drowning. Silence. There were no words for what she wanted to say.

The next afternoon, they sat together on a bench, which Lai Jin had crafted beneath an overhang next to an ancient willow tree. It was positioned so that, when they squinted a certain way, they might imagine the sun over Hangzhou Bay, beyond a curtain of smog that ventured to obscure vision. Sometimes, cirrus clouds. Tendrils like calligraphy etched into the sky. The water flickered with copper highlights. Four plump ducks waddled close by. They belonged to nobody. They had turned up one morning, murmured Lai Jin. They must have got lost along the way. They had arrived exhausted and had not thought to leave.

"Why are you here?" she asked.

He spoke to her of events. The accusations, a damning voyage-report. A prison sentence. He imagined she might balk at that; she did not. He told her his ship had been put on trial and murdered by fire.

As Ayaana turned to stare at the browning sky, he said, "I did drown the containers with the slaughtered animals."

She said, "Good." And then she smiled. "Good." And her hands were on either side of his face and her eyes were aglow and he was elated, for she had kissed him and said again, "Good."

Late dusk; birds were going home. Rustle of leaves, lolloping wind. As she watched the earth, something reminded Ayaana that life was passage, nothing lingered. She shut her eyes and clutched Lai Jin's hands. The silence between them absorbed extraneous words. Somewhere in the lighthouse, a clock chimed. Ayaana remembered: "You found the watch."

"Yes."

"You came to Xiamen?"

He dipped his head.

The temperatures outside plummeted, and they shivered.

Lai Jin had gone to Xiamen to tell her something about Delaksha and Nioreg. No, he had needed to content himself with a glimpse of . . . not her, but the idea of alternative spaces. No, he was a man. He had gone to Xiamen to see a woman. No. Return to silence.

Ayaana said, "Now you work with earth."

Lai Jin stooped to stroke the loam. He smiled as he remembered. "First, after prison, I tried to cook—I burned the food. Tried trade. Bought things in Hong Kong, sold them in Myanmar. Credit, credit, credit. Nobody returned with my money." His look was desolate. "I returned to my beginnings." Ayaana stirred next to him. "To fire."

Ayaana absorbed his words as a prayer.

She asked, "This is your home?"

Lai Jin looked around him. "It was broken." A distant murmur. They listened to the receding sea, pieces of breeze. *Ni shi shei?* the ocean was still crying. As before, neither of them replied.

Ayaana rested her head against Lai Jin's right shoulder. Her words were caught in her throat. "That watch. The *ping* . . . has gone from it." Fresh tears settled beneath her jaw. *Muhidin*, she remembered. She was wearing Lai Jin's waterproof jacket, the one that had once sheltered her. She leaned in to him, with ease. He watched her. Her fingers were on his arms. The seduction of the deep—its bewildering layers reflected the colors of longing, the memory of a shimmering blue wick that set the sea on fire, and with it two bodies. His eyes were on hers; fingers traced her mouth, fluttering. Her fingers reached up to search his face. Flowing. And then he gathered her to himself. Her face was pressed into his chest, but she had borrowed enough air from the surface not to mind. There, in the middle point between top and bottom, she connected to a heart. And the demons of her present life vanished. She descended; she descended in the bubble of their silence. Cocooned stillness. The temptation to linger. She stroked him.

His hands bruised her arms. "This time . . ." he warned, "this time . . ."

"What?" she whispered. She faced him.

"What?" he asked.

Unveiled—everything was there to be read.

Lai Jin's gaze darkened.

She said, "I went to Shanghai to see Zao Wou-Ki."

Lai Jin nodded.

She rested her head against his neck.

His arms enfolded her.

In the afternoon, throwing herself into activity, Ayaana used up all Lai Jin's spices to make a rudimentary chicken biriyani. She also watched Lai Jin fire the clay. His hands, focus, stillness. She knew his body: its feel and taste and touch. She knew the feel of outward scars. And then—a tug in her soul. Stirring outside wind. A chime. The truth: transience. He caught her watching him. Embarrassed, she equivocated. She told Lai Jin of something she saw on a Shanghai street corner. "Someone had carved a Buddha out of a blood-streaked elephant's tusk." She then looked over her shoulder, as if expecting something awful to appear.

What are you running from? Lai Jin wondered. But he would not test fate; whatever this was had brought her to him. He listened as she told him that she was waiting for Muhidin to return. She clutched her stomach. *Home*. Of late, it had become an ephemeral place she inhabited, which refused to guarantee its endurance. She did not speak of Pate's expectations for her, or the one thing she was beginning to sense she could no longer do: stay in China. She was not Chinese. "What if there is no home?" she asked, her breath caught in her throat. She looked at him as if he had been privy to the sequence of her thoughts.

. . .

Later, Ayaana ate her portion of the biriyani in a small wooden bowl with chopsticks. She lifted the chopsticks. Lai Jin laughed at her ease with them. She cast him a wry look. He looked down at the rice on his plate, frowning as if he might speak. Her friend Delaksha, he remembered. He needed to say something.

Ayaana said, "I'm like your ducks."

He laughed instead.

A view of the night: no curtains, no veils, and sometimes the wind found a way in through the holes in the window. She was wearing one of Lai Jin's large white workman's shirts. His futon was small. She was to his left. He settled on his side. She turned to him after five minutes of dense silence. She touched his mouth, the burned side of his face. He blinked. He touched her face as if it were made of clay fragments.

Ayaana told him, "I saw a man in Turkey. I think he was a lost prophet."

Lai Jin stroked her eyelids, wiping away tears, drawing them on her face as if his finger were a paintbrush. Her warm body, warm breasts, warm thighs. Warm voice.

"I met another who evaporated. All he left behind was an old brown shoe. There was blood on the shoe." She painted the air. "The shoe itself disappeared." Tears reached her jaw. He wiped them away.

"Does anyone in the world find exactly what they need, ship leader?" Her voice petered out.

Lai Jin recoiled. "We hope to every day."

Silence.

She accused Lai Jin: "Even you abandoned the sea."

He heard the break in her voice. He shook his head. Fingers on her skin. He had so many questions for her. He wanted to know about the fissures in her gaze.

Her hand was on his belly, his on her breast.

She asked, "Po Fu?"

He mulled that over before choosing words. "A name for exile." A light smile. He turned to her. Ayaana saw his soul shimmer, as if it still lived in the sea.

. . .

Ayaana inched closer and closer to Lai Jin until she was melded to his arms, which tightened around her. *Touch.* She was drifting to sleep, breath by breath. He stroked her body, reviving memory. The storm, their storm. Its colors. She was here. Ayaana slept long and deep, right into the middle of the following day. When she opened her eyes, a thick smokelike fog shrouded the area, its lighthouse, and its few inhabitants. Desolate weather. Ayaana was cocooned.

She lay beneath him, guiding his erect penis into her softness. Enclosing him. Another beginning. In. Timelessness. They were its sole occupants. Thrusting, thrumming, and starting again. And, again, both dissolving into fire. And currents of dreams and salty dampness and need.

The next day, Ayaana scrambled to the top of a rock to try to get the phone signal that she would use to inform a university administrator that she had gone away to a quiet place. She had gone to a shrine close to the sea.

"*Houyi!*" the woman screamed. "This is most dishonorable. You come back immediately . . ."

Ayaana switched off her phone. And tossed it in the air—catching it before it fell.

"There are no secrets in China," he told her.

She was bartering with existence, trading ghosts: Pate for Muhidin.

Ayaana and Lai Jin walked all the way to a sea that had fled its old shore. A three-kilometer walk before the water glistened like a silver table in front of them. They looked out of place. They endured the gaze of the few others, the unstated questions. They oozed silence as they walked the bleak shoreline, listening to water. He stooped to pick up sea glass: white, green, blue. She copied him. Lifted up to the light a red one smoothed by the whole weight of the sea. Only later, after the sun dipped into the water, did Ayaana find the portal at the water's edge from which she could call out to Muhidin in a high cry that split winds and forced them into listening-waiting, as Lai Jin watched over her, and the sea asked, *Ni shi shei?*

They were a strange pair, sitting as they did, blurred by a darkness that had sewn them into a shoreline as they looked over a night sea. Lai Jin watched the waters for a message. And, with dark light, Lai Jin saw how he would repair Ayaana's broken vessels. He knew he would use gold paint for the darker vessel, and copper for the light.

Throwing clay at night. In a soft, soft voice made of single words and long pauses, she asked him why the world was the way it was. He told her that he could not say, but that he had settled for the basics: soil, clay, water, fire, and silence. Touch, too. He told her that touch was necessary. The next day, he untied the carton in which she had placed the broken clay vessels. He picked out the pieces one by one. She watched his face. He tested the broken edges with his finger. He blew on others. He transferred all the pieces to a separate rectangular tray, then retreated to a cupboard and returned with the tools and equipment he might need to make sense of the fragments and bring them back to wholeness. She watched his face, his body. At last, he lifted his head to look back at her. He smiled. She breathed.

The next day, she woke up before dawn to run to the sea and walked into the cold, cold waves until they reached her waist—the extent of her tolerance of the icy water. There she prayed to the God that had ebbed from her life as she crossed from Pate to Xiamen. She informed both God and sea that Muhidin was her heart, her spirit, her breath. She told God and the sea that they owed her his life. She gave them a deadline. The tide was coming in. Driftwood buffeted her body. She brought it back to shore and into the lighthouse.

~

She took to sitting between his legs. Leaning in to him, turning her face so his warm breath could touch her skin: the building up of body tension and desire, of strained longing, skin to skin, and craving wholeness. He was creating a vessel over her shoulder, dipping his mouth into skin. She tilted her head so he could taste the part of her neck beneath her ear. Silent days. Few words.

Lai Jin waited for her footfalls; he anticipated the sense of urgency with which she threw herself into the day, and, more recently, into his arms. Fate. He had been contemplating his relationship with fate. "*Haiyan.*" He tested the name, feeling its power, as if it were destiny. She was here.

She saw her life's otherness as if she were a detached spectator. What would have happened, she wondered, if she had not received that dry pink petal from the Chinese visitor's hands on Pate?

Clear lacquer. Gold leaf. He started with the tear-shaped vessel.

Her voice cracked. "You can make it whole?"

Lai Jin answered, "I will try."

"It will be scarred."

"Yes."

"It's not the same as before."

"It is other and more."

"But not as before."

"No."

He applied a thin brush with lacquer to a piece of ceramic. The round palette containing the clear lacquer balanced on his left thumb. His delicate touch, delicate gestures. She sat cross-legged, watching. She imagined that the sea was flowing in now.

. . .

Muhidin.

Her father.

This absence was the worst of all.

Ni shi shei? the oceans cried.

An answer stirred just out of her hearing.

~

In the evening, the two of them sat together on the stone bench beneath the ancient willow tree. There were clouds. The distant bay was shrouded by mist. Ayaana laid her head against Lai Jin's. Surrendering to the unknown. Not asking for more than the present. Dinner was oyster porridge with rice and dried seaweed, served with instant noodles. They spoke of worlds they knew, books read; they spoke of the sea and some of the puzzles of navigation. They spoke into the early dawn, before they remembered they ought to sleep.

Later, she wandered into the shower, where the water was pouring over his body. She said he had become thin. She asked him if he remembered their storm. "Every day," he answered. She said she wanted to taste the water on his mouth, and his eyes, and the scar on his body. So he asked her if she would stay in China. But she did not have an answer yet. She watched him turn off the shower water. He was aroused, erect. She watched him dry his hair. She watched him tie a towel around his waist. She watched him and waited, and he asked her again if she would stay. She said, "I don't know."

"Come here," he said.

Slow, small steps to the waiting man.

Exorcism. Scraping her heart and skin bare of the stain and shame of an other with an other. Disarticulated. So she could choose what spaces to include as part of her other selves. He woke her up to ask if she would stay, not for him, but for the sea, and he used her wakefulness to bring her into his body. Sharing ghosts. And then he told her the pale brown of her eyes was a map to a galaxy. And she remembered that her mother had already seized for her Orion. But he was calling her "Haiyan," his name for her. It would always be so, and she knew now that Haiyan had something of the sea in it. She was listening to him, absorbing him, storing him so that when she must she would pull the memory of now from the shelves of time. And when his fingers traced her body inch by inch, soft as down, she dissolved and floated away. When she dreamed he was still there, watching over her. When he roused her because the glow of dawn was on her naked form, he had been at once mesmerized by the riddle of a curved human shape, this female being, and how and where the light stroked it, and stayed on it by way of his still ravenous body.

Her lidded eyes only half open, a sad whispering. "I cannot see who I am."

"With me?" He was distressed.

She at once turned to cup his face; she pressed him to her. "This nation. I am not its Descendant." And she rested her head against his.

Crumpling of space.

Of unformed imaginings.

Syntony.

He whispered, "You will be leaving." Statement of fact.

Disentanglement, she thought. *It is a word that looks like what it proposes.* Yet the ache of leaving was already a stabbing sob within her, and then she hoped he might protest and ask her to stay so she could imagine trying that. But he was silent, and therefore, so was she.

"Tears?" he asked, turning his face so the tip of his tongue could dip into the salt on her face.

Speechlessness and morning shadows.

Streaks on two entwined bodies.

A dog-eared, folded timetable indicated that the last train to Xiamen on Monday would be at 8:37 p.m. Lai Jin had escorted Ayaana to the station in Hangzhou. Their progression had been awkward. Still shadowboxing. The previous day, they had argued, not about the shape of the desire that engulfed them, hurling them into and out of each other's arms, but about the meaning of words. He had not expected to dread her leaving. The fear disguised itself as exasperation. "What do you need?" he had erupted, his fingers in her hair, tugging. She had rebelled: "How can I know?" Her tone was lacerating. As was their way, they skulked into their coves of silences until the flaming undercurrents threw them together again. Quickly, mouth to mouth. Wordlessness again. Breathing, and opened. And that silence spread within them, swirling, flowing, ebbing, and dragging them down to the ground as their sparrows roosted in the eaves. Crooning. Listening. Feeling herself drowning in clearer waters, her core being transmuted, and she succumbing, Ayaana twisted her body away, thrashing for a surface, fleeing the man; she went out through the door and into the evening. She breathed the cool air and looked back at the lighthouse. There was a man looking down at her through a window. She stared right back at him with everything she felt written out in her eyes: *How can I know?*

He kissed her again and again, and this time did not ask, "Will you return?"

The last southward-heading train of the day. It was already 8:15 p.m. The two people sat on a stained steel bench, their bodies pressing against each other, watching people mill about.

Lai Jin cleared his throat. "*Haiyan* . . ." Ayaana turned to him. "Your friend on the ship, Delaksha . . ."

Ayaana smiled. "Yes?"

The rush of the approaching train interrupted his next words. "What time is it?" he shouted as if shocked. A scramble. He carefully placed Ayaana's rucksack over her shoulders as she watched the train stretch out its halt. Lai Jin's arms on her shoulder, he spoke into her ear, said, "I will mail the repairs."

Ayaana stared fixedly at the milling passengers. Lai Jin then took her face to make her look at him. She squeezed her eyes shut. Ignoring the watchers, he locked his arms around her. "Look," he said, "there. Autumn's sparrows." She opened her eyes. A swift pressing of lips that left the impression of everything and nothing.

They waited for more passengers to board the train. Some announcements. Ayaana kissed the burned side of his face, the fingers of her right hand stroking it. She turned abruptly to board her train, stumbling a little on the bottom step that led into her carriage.

Lai Jin saw Ayaana disappear into the train. He heard the train's baleful honk. His shoulders slumped. After half a minute, he straightened his back. He inhaled the night: its scent of salt and sea and, today, a hint of wild rose. With slow steps, he started the long journey back to his shelter.

He did not know when she had done it, but the next day, as he stripped off his clothes to sleep, he found the Basmallah she had sketched for him, black ink on white paper; crafted as a sparrow in flight.

[87]

Insomnia. The gold-tinged hours before dawn, and it was almost quiet in the city. Ayaana was watching the sky as she swirled in a force of life currents that had converged within her: absence, desire, choice, certainty. An hour later, she was scrabbling in the suitcase where she had concealed nostalgia's trinkets: Muhidin's now silent watch, the yellowing map she had taken from Muhidin's chest, her mother's essences, which suffused the room with their life, and Lai Jin's Zao Wou-Ki print. She sat down with her knees drawn up and stared at these artifacts as if they might reveal a way.

Ayaana dressed up in a demure pink suit and open-toed shoes, and tied up her hair to look severe. Camouflage. She took herself to the university administrator's office to wait. After an hour, a woman with viciously sheared black locks that made her look like an animated cartoon superheroine dealt with Ayaana, who was made to understand that her desperate excursion had displeased the authorities. The woman studied Ayaana surreptitiously as she indicated a seat. Ayaana sat in decorous silence, her head humbly lowered. It would be another two hours before the acting main supervisor called her in.

Ayaana entered the room, stooping. She embodied regret. She commenced her performance in as perfect a Mandarin as she could muster. She had learned her lines. "I apologize for causing you such distress. I thought only of myself. But I could not contain my sorrow. I needed help to keep my head from exploding." She hesitated. Was "exploding" too dramatic a word? "In pursuit of my father's ghost, I have brought shame to you, who are my honorable hosts. I beg your forgiveness." "Father's ghost"? Perhaps she should have left that out; she did not want to invite a psychiatric evaluation. "I needed another sea." This was true. Here her voice cracked. She stopped and kept her eyes low. Ayaana counted the faux-marble tiles of a sickly beige and white. In that posture, she listened to a detailed lecture on the values of protocol and procedure, of manners and good conduct, of the shame that a disordered person brings upon her country. Ayaana's mind drifted, returning to the lighthouse, and to Lai Jin looking down at her from a high window.

The lecture eventually ended. The room was still. Ayaana said, "With your permission?" Her supervisor nodded. "I am dedicated to working three times harder. I will complete my studies within a year."

Her acting supervisor was impassive. She started, "The Descendant . . ." Her voice faded. The whole "return of the Descendant" experiment was wearisome. The machinery that had brought Ayaana to China had moved on to other emblematic ways of excavating, proving, and entrenching Chinese rootedness in Africa—archaeological expeditions, cultural collaborations, infrastructure projects, mass migrations, and the seduction of credit. The woman sighed. "Pass your exams with success." Ayaana nodded. She was very good at passing exams. "*Xuexi jinbu,*" the woman added—Study well. Ayaana nodded again. She walked to the door, then dashed away as it closed behind her.

As she rushed back to her room, her heart felt stuck. Later, huddled under blankets, her hands damp, her look stern, Ayaana phoned her mother.

"Daughter!" Munira exclaimed.

"Ma," Ayaana replied. She paused, "Any news?"

"None."

Ayaana said, "Ma?"

"Yes."

"Who is my father? The one of my blood?"

All silences in that moment. Mother and daughter trembled. "I need to know," Ayaana added. Her voice was frantic. Munira was quiet. Ayaana cried, "The question is like a hole inside me. I look at every man and wonder . . ."

Munira said, "I don't know."

Ayaana waited, her hands sweating, hearing resonances from her own "don't know"s.

Munira then asked, "Wasn't I father enough for you, Ayaana? What about Muhidin, whom you chose? Is he not 'father' enough?"

Munira heard Ayaana's faintly whispered "No." She was now on her knees in her house in Pemba. "*Lulu*, those questions are consuming ghouls."

Ayaana cried, "I live with them. I live inside them."

Silence. Munira, alarmed, asked, "What has happened to you?"

"Why?"

"Why now?"

"I have asked before."

In Pemba, by the sea, Munira knelt. Somewhere in the house, a child started to cry. She lifted her head to listen. She paused. More than anything else, it was this, the crying child, that inspired her next words. "*Zamani za kale*"—Once upon a time—Munira's voice sputtered. She started up again. "There was a creature. She thought that it was her right to be best loved by all. She knew herself as queen of history and could therefore write any dream for herself." Munira began to cry.

"She imagined she would leave Pate and go to England, to Paraguay, to Italy, to Iran . . . anywhere her heart desired."

Ayaana listened.

Munira continued tearfully. "She was the most beautiful of her generation on an island of the most beautiful women of the seas. She was desired. She was envied. In secret she imagined for herself an enchanted being as consort who would be worthy of her, to whom she would bestow the honor of leading her away from her small island." A withering sound.

For a second, Ayaana heard again the rustle of the leaves on an island evening; the shadows that hovered, the rhymes of her seas. Soft-voiced, Munira continued. "One day, in Mombasa, where this girl was sent to study, she caught sight of a shining being adorned with gold. He glittered with promise. And when he spoke, men listened to him. She looked and loved him on sight."

Ayaana made a sound. "My father," she announced, as if meeting him for the first time.

"Yes," Munira said.

"What does he look like?" Ayaana asked.

Munira wrestled with her heart, dug around to try to remember the face of that one she had imagined she adored more than life, more than death. Residue of feelings—that was all that remained. Her dart of triumph: one completed exorcism. She told Ayaana, "I can't remember. I do not see his face. He was tall. Like you." Uncertain.

Munira did not speak to Ayaana of abandonment, of existential terror, of the death of self. She offered the minimum: "We were not married. I believed in him more than I did God. Him I could touch. Do you understand?" Ayaana's "Yes" was stagnant on her tongue. "When I conceived you, he left. I looked for him. I discovered that not even the name he had given me was real."

Another sound from Ayaana, a splintering. Munira added, "I was alone with you when you were born. You were destined to live. I worked. I went back to Pate." Quietness. Munira ended: "My family left when I returned."

Each waited for the other to speak.

Ayaana finally asked, "Because of me?"

"No, me," Munira countered. Breathing softly.

"Why didn't you marry?"

"What I could salvage of life, *mwanangu*, belonged only to you." Silence. Munira conceded, "I also needed to grow up."

Ayaana rubbed her heart. Some absences, she was beginning to see, were part of existence: faceless and nameless forever. She wiped away her tears. She *did* have a father. Ayaana's voice was strained. "Will our Muhidin return?" Munira choked. "*Ma-e*," Ayaana suddenly said, "how I miss you."

Munira paused before whispering, "And I you, my *lulu*."

After that phone conversation, for almost two hours, Ayaana sat by her study desk, lost in silence.

[88]

Sitting outside, Ayaana shuddered as the waters changed color to look as disgruntled and wrinkled as an unwanted prophet. She was wrapped in a coat, eating a chicken spring roll on a bench close to a fountain in front of the lake, and feeding curious birds with pieces, her bicycle on the ground at her feet. She sensed Koray before she saw him. He sat down next to her, his hands leaning on his knees. "Tell me, Ayaana," he said. She continued tossing pieces at the birds. "It is rumored you took yourself into some seaside shrine; was the expedition useful?"

She did not answer.

"Must have been. You are also likely to finish your course requirements ahead of the class? You did not care to let me know?"

"No," Ayaana answered.

"*Halwa?*" he offered.

She said, "No, thank you."

"*Halwa?*" Koray insisted, his voice soft. His hands were on her elbows. "My lover?"

Ayaana shivered. She feigned her indifference and chewed her food.

"Adultery and apostasy are offenses punishable by death," Koray suggested. "For all sorts of verifiable reasons," he chortled, "I have a right to exact retribution." He smiled, and then drummed his hands against the back of the park bench.

Ayaana briefly contemplated the threat, and then resumed her chewing.

"What say you, *sweetheart*?"

"Go die, Koray."

He leaned in to her ear to whisper, "Were you alone in your 'temple'?"

A malicious impulse. "Of course not."

"A man?" Koray asked.

"Oh, look at those naughty green birds." She indicated the water with her chin.

He insisted, "Did he touch you?"

Ayaana glowered. "How are your studies going, Koray?"

Koray was fencing her in with his body. A glint in his eyes. "Where did you sleep?"

"Did you destroy my vases?" she asked; she was scowling at him.

With his pupils dilating, Koray pressed his nose to her neck. She struggled to free herself. Now Koray applied pressure on the nerves of her arm and thigh, and when she tried to move, searing pain shot up her spine and caused her to crumple over. Koray was breathing against her face. "Who was he?"

Ayaana whimpered, "Ahhh!"

Koray pressed hard. Her eyes watered.

"Koray, stop it," she cried.

He pulled her hair. "Who?"

She gritted her teeth. "Get off me."

"Wrong answer, *canim*. I can do this"—his hand wrapped around her neck—"and this." He squeezed. "In a public place, with a view of a lotus-filled lake . . . nobody knows you are dying except me . . . and you, naturally. *That* is power."

Ayaana scratched at the air. Koray laughed. Ayaana shut her eyes. Her occasional asthma was something like this sensation. The darkness of underwater also had something of this. There was always a point when the human urge to breathe ceased. She relaxed, waiting for it. Time receded. Voices dissolved into Koray's whispers into her ear—vile words to describe her, her race, her nation, her island, her body, and what he would do to her. "Fight me!" he demanded.

Never!

It was the last thing she thought.

This was power—her detachment.

Ayaana came to. She did not know when Koray had gone. She was alone on the bench, with five birds at her feet, and the day had turned orange. Her bicycle was propped against the bench. There was no Koray. She touched her neck. Later, when she returned to her room to shower, she would see the bruising. She would lock her door and reinforce the handle with a chair and lie in her bed, watching the ceiling and listening for footsteps in the corridor, remembering Delaksha. No tears. She had glimpsed how a woman might become haunted. Basmallah, she remembered. She would draw it out, as Muhidin had suggested, a reliable means of exorcism.

The next day, Ayaana walked into the evening class with her laptop bag, wearing a tank top that revealed her neck and exposed the bruises. She had tied up her hair so that there would be no disguising the discoloration. Koray was the first to exclaim, "Oh, *canim*, did you fall?" He walked up to her as if to embrace her. He whispered, "Cover up. What are you doing?"

She wrapped one arm around him.

He gasped.

She murmured, "A long, sharp steel point is piercing your chest. It is pointed at your heart. If you move, I will push it in."

Koray's voice was thin, but he was still. "You *bitch*. You dare to threaten me?"

She said, "No, *canim*, I am telling you." Stillness. "Smile, Koray, you have turned green."

He asked, "What do you want me to do now?" She moved the tip of the steel, and Koray, with fury in his tone, suggested, "You want me to apologize and vow never to choke you again or something similarly banal, yes?"

Ayaana stepped away from him, palming her calligraphy pen. "No, I wanted to see if the threat of death affects you. It does." She nodded. She slid the pen into her bag.

Koray's eyes were cold and yellowish. "You would be so easy to kill."

Ayaana's voice was cool. "True. But I swear, you will bleed to death with me."

Ayaana then pivoted. She waved at Ari. She mouthed something to Shalom, making a phone gesture. She moved to a chair next to the wall before her knees gave way. She leaned back, just as she had seen Bollywood gangsters do on film. She then stuck her phone earpiece into her ears, nodding to the silence of a turned-off phone while her heart pounded and she tried not to vomit on her books. She wanted the maritime-cartography session to begin at once.

Koray seemed to have disappeared soon after. This made Ayaana nervous. Looking over her shoulders. Ayaana spent days and nights in the library. She signed up for on-water assignments. She waited for news from home in increasing despondence. Where was Muhidin? She considered traveling back to a certain lighthouse. The passing days brought filtered news of a restless world and all too soon, it was her birthday. She thought she would mark it in silence. Early in the morning, when she opened her door to step out, there was a hamper filled with peaches, teas, dates, lotus seeds, a bunch of lilies, and some rose *halwa*. A red envelope. A note. The note contained five words: "Still charmed. *Always* your Koray."

Lenye mwanzo lina mwisho.

What has a beginning has an end.

[89]

She sat by the lake to feed the swans for what would be the last time. She remembered the friends she had made, the fleeting acquaintances who would end up in so many other parts of the world. Dispersions. Her hands swirling in the water, she conjured a vision of a potter in a lighthouse.

A phone call in the night had secured her decision to leave.

No preamble. Koray was matter-of-fact. "I am in Istanbul." Ayaana blinked. "Last evening, my father, Emirhan Terzioğlu, died. We were with him."

A groggy Ayaana said, "I am so sorry."

Koray said, "He did not die well." Ayaana's thoughts scampered. "You will now come."

Ayaana had reacted as if an ice block had fallen on her. A clear memory of a promontory: a desire to jump. Ayaana turned to stare at the full-blooded orange moon of the night through her window. Silence.

Koray said, "Ayaana?"

There was a theory among fisherfolk that in the season of the full moon extra caution was needed by blooded beings, for blood, like the tide, was drawn to the moon: the fuller the moon, the greater the impulse to fling one's being in its direction, especially by way of the turbulent sea. In cultures where exorcisms happened, the first act was to demand the name of the ghost: *Koray*. Renouncing, detaching, and annulling its power—*the suggestion of a planned, secured future*—was a brutal and absolute act. A force burst from a nook of Ayaana's soul and drove her fingers to switch off her phone with all her strength.

Ayaana sat through that night with hands half covering her face. On her way down into the depth of her heart, enclosed in the hum of refreshed mysteries, she saw Emirhan and smelled the grief of all the world's unmourned. She swam past Koray, his face, this stranger, this lover, and the universes he offered her, for the price of her soul and its ghosts. And the moon's light was on her body and offered itself to her as another witness. Wetness ran down Ayaana's arms. And then she was done. Another lesson: endings were a rehearsal for death; death was in the constitution of life.

Two nights later, Ayaana opened the door to her room to discover a large brown package waiting for her. She opened the parcel at dawn, after a sleepless night. Inside were two bubble-wrapped ceramic vessels. Her potter had used clear lacquer, gold, and copper to repair them. They were even more perfect with their burnished flaws.

[90]

Two weeks later, Ayaana returned to the site of her hair disaster. The hairdresser recoiled at her approach and smothered the panic on his face. "Cut it all off," she told him, and plunked herself into a chair that was too small for her hips. The hairdresser's initial paralysis gave way to zeal once he was wielding his special scissors and a fine-toothed comb. With renewed confidence, he summoned minions to oversee different roles in the experiment that was Ayaana's head. When she emerged from the snipping and shaping, the hairdresser and his assembled hair team were certain they had turned Ayaana into Rihanna. "Liana," he announced. Shorn, Ayaana endured new photographs, the final record of her China sojourn. She looked at the woman in the photograph; the world and its experiences had reshaped her face.

Ayaana left Xiamen and China.

The feeling of departure: the stomach hardening into a ball. Her life was in her mouth as the Kenya Airways plane pointed its nose skyward, rising and rising as if never intending to return to earth. At the midway point, Ayaana looked down at the land from her window. An impenetrable haze covered it. She attended to her seatmates. The plane was packed with Chinese citizens. Ayaana had smiled at the hostess—name tag "Achieng." Hours later, touchdown, in Nairobi. Everything stopped mattering when the Kenyan sun, never brutal, reached her face. The scent of homecoming. The sweat of dawn smelled of mango mixed with clove, earth, and fire.

A stout immigration officer in a black suit and tie asked Ayaana, "*Umerudi?*"—You have returned?

"*Nimerudi,*" Ayaana answered—I have.

Mtumbwi wa kafi moja huanza safari mapema.

The boat that has one paddle leaves early.

[91]

Seven months after Ayaana left China, a most curious event took place in an art gallery in Guangzhou. The gallery was exhibiting the most recent works of the reclusive ceramicist Po Fu, titled, "About This Earth, Woman." These were assorted pieces that suggested the curves and shape and roundedness of a female body. The press heralded them as "sensuous, dramatic, and evolutionary." Black and brown lacquered vessels. There was a triptych that, if placed together, produced a reclining form, the back of which bore henna-colored whorls and lines, and was infused with a scent—in this case, night jasmine, a trademark of the ceramicist's work. An art critic who hyperventilated with hyperbole had featured pictures of these in the *China Daily*. The effusive praise drew the attention of a man who was returning to Xiamen from Istanbul on a plane, who was browsing idly through the newspaper's pages. He read and reread the phrase "inspired by his experience of the Western Ocean learned through the gaze and touch of a Descendant."

Three days later, a gallery curator's words bashed into themselves as he babbled on the phone to the gallery owner. A foreigner had walked in to purchase the most expensive trio of pieces. Four days later, the owner, an unnaturally thin woman who had returned after living in Australia, clopped into her gallery space in a tight black designer dress and red platform shoes embedded with diamonds, to meet the buyer who had paid up front for the triptych. The check had just cleared. The purchaser strode into the gallery—closed to the public—an hour earlier than expected. They had arranged a private viewing for him.

. . .

The dark-haired man with hooded eyes, in a Hugo Boss suit—she noticed such things—was curt. He wore dark glasses that tinted his upper cheekbones. His customized timepiece was made of platinum. The gallery owner studied the man, a beautiful, *rich* foreign man. The gallery owner simpered. Her assistants and curator hovered.

The man drawled, "Check okay?"

"Yes, sir."

"The pieces are mine?"

"Yes, sir."

"Excellent." The man approached the triptych. His long fingers stroked the three pieces. "Exquisite," he said.

"Sir, how would you like us to prepare them for you?"

The buyer lifted the first of the pieces and deliberately dropped it. It shattered. The curator shrieked and rushed over. Koray stopped him by lifting up his left hand. He stared the weeping curator down. Soon the second and third pieces were fragmented heaps beneath their intricate stands. Koray studied his handiwork. The woman owner stumbled on her heels to stand close to him. The woman looked up at him. "Dinner?" she suggested. She proffered a card.

Koray looked at her, raised an eyebrow, and smiled. He took the card. She walked with Koray toward her employees. Koray paused and placed a hand on the curator's shoulder. "Curator?" The man bowed. Koray's Putonghua was passable. "Tell the potter that this"—he indicated the broken pieces—"is private territory. Those seas and what they contain . . . Trespassers will be smashed."

The curator nodded with vigor.

"Now, repeat the message . . ."

The curator stumbled over the words a few times, to the nods of his gallery owner. Koray then patted his shoulder. Koray turned and kissed the gallery owner on her cheek before sauntering out, whistling a phrase from an irritating but catchy Korean pop song.

The gallery owner sent Lai Jin his portion of the money from the sale. She did not inform him of the fate of his work. She swore her staff and curator to secrecy on the pain of death.

Months later, Lai Jin was being subjected to self-righteous officiousness by eight state officials who had been lurking in the vicinity, circling like nervous serpents. They waved massive blueprints, these bureaucrats who now laid claim to the lighthouse, the island, the area. These plans were for a brand-new resort. Lai Jin halted his wheel and wiped his hands before turning to stare at the public servants. Estrangement from space and country was a slow-drip process. He had expected this. Outside, the ducks quacked in contentment. Lai Jin picked clay flecks from his fingers and shirt and thought of the sparrows, who would return in the spring and find no roosting ground. He glanced out a window toward a misted horizon to tune out the men. "In the beginning there was . . ." Looking back: "Events cast shadows before themselves," it has been said. "Water?" he asked the men, trying to be courteous.

Later, he watched one of the men brand the lighthouse with a massive black "X" on behalf of the nation.

Lai Jin spent the night after the visit studying the old compass Ayaana had given him. Seeking north.

Within a month, Lai Jin had packed his home in eight boxes. He had forged a hollowed silver bracelet. In this he rolled and stored the Basmallah Ayaana had left him with. Days later, he would attempt to drive the surprised ducks away. They were outraged by his behavior. They waddled away for a while before returning as a flock.

"Abandon ship," he commanded the ducks, sparrows, earth, lighthouse, and sea.

Lai Jin left for Hong Kong.

It would take more than three months to dissolve most of his assets and then imagine another destination.

Kilichomo baharini, kakingojee ufukoni.

That which is in the sea will wash up on the shore.

[92]

Ayaana's return coincided with that of a different kind of sea visitor, a harbinger. Pate's Captain Mohamed Lali Kombo and two crew members had retrieved it from their fishing nets and brought it to shore. "Sea dog," they called it. They laid it on the jetty, where it peered in genial curiosity at its watchers. The news spread. It was delivered to a radio announcer, who broadcast it. The message brought to Pate those who would then identify it as a Cape sea lion. It was so far from home. It belonged to the farthest of seas. A harbinger, it was understood. But its destination was elsewhere. After a discussion among many, the islanders decided to bless the sojourner and its mysterious journey. They returned it to Captain Kombo's boat, and he and his crew restored it to the sea. Harbingers—birds borne on the *matlai*, moon-drunk dragonflies, and dolphin schools, a sea lion, the changing seasons of earth. Stars disappeared. Time and the debris of souls moved by the monsoon showed up on Pate's dark sand shores. Ayaana reappeared on the archipelago that held her island. Her head buzzed with the sense of this return. Words. Language. Home. It was the light over the jetty. It was looking at other skins and seeing shades of her own. Words, an iridescent river. Her senses remembered the colors of thought, the savor of words, the scent of images, the way to inhabit the here and now.

Ayaana eavesdropped on the wind, picking up song fragments. The tide report, the Kenyan nation in its unending election cycle, the preoccupation of the passing citizens with the character of their politicians: "scavengers." Synonyms: *wabeberu*, *washenzi*, *kingugwa*, *adui*, *wahuni*. Ayaana laughed—the familiarity of national discontent. She shifted from foot to foot on the jetty, her two pieces of luggage near her.

Listening. Discerning, again, those in-between spaces that transmuted ordinary things: hyenas could gossip with hares; Fumo Liyongo, legend and leader, could still walk in fire-emitting footsteps; braying donkeys were harbingers; and not every person who stared at you was a person. The plane that had deposited her on Lamu Island took off with a new set of passengers. Ayaana watched it before turning to read her seas again, as if they were a childhood story whose every word she had rubbed and tasted and stored inside her best dreams.

Ayaana faced the ancient city on a waterfront. The children: laughter. They dived into the sea. And she realized she might bawl. Ceaseless greetings of passersby. Colors, colors, and she was dizzy and drunk. Home: incoming souls. Some tourists. Listening. Mostly Germans, ignoring travel advisories. The *watu wa bara*, upcountry visitors, humorless civil servants. *Home-comers*. Today, she was a home-comer. Circling boats, and the light on prows, the light on the water. Blue light, purple light, orange light. Light that lit up light. She had forgotten that light could also be this. On a nearby field, chickens, goats, sheep, and a single cow. Ayaana's heart finally slowed down. A wind traversed the channel, twirling gold and brown leaves in its wake.

And then the Asr Adhan resounded:

"*Allahu Akbar* . . ."

Herald. Promise.

"*Allahu Akbar* . . ."

The song ripened.

"*Hayya alas Salah* . . ."

A relay of offbeat summonses from mosques across the water. Ayaana exhaled and lifted her face skyward. From there, a whisper from another time reached her: "Greet Yourself / In your thousand other forms / As you mount the hidden tide and travel / Back home . . ."

The public ferry to Pate was at the Lamu jetty, overladen with goods plus a few goats and souls, waiting with the captain for high tide. Babble of voices in the lyrics of home. Etchings of life woven into the land in Kiamu, Kimvita, Kipate, and Kiunguja words, and the voices of others who had found a home here. It would be a three-to-four-hour ferry ride to the jetty on Pate, and another hour or so to walk into Pate Town. A sudden inspiration: Ayaana decided to hire a speedboat instead. She chose the newest one and persuaded its young owner, Captain Ali, to let her pilot it after they had reached the Mkanda Channel. Ayaana sped home.

[93]

Those who had known the child were jolted by the sight of the elegant, foreign-seeming woman in short hair, large sunglasses, and high black boots who had returned to them, who rode into the harbor on one of Lamu's new speedboats. She stepped ashore with confidence and a coolness that created temporary awe.

Ayaana looked around her, just breathing, as the island welcome-and-hospitality machinery took over. Men offloaded her luggage at the jetty, exclaiming their greetings: "Could this be you, Ayaana?" Word passed down the island trails: Ayaana had returned. Ayaana had returned as Chinese. Those who came to see, and sought it, did find a hint of the old creature, like the light rose fragrance that still suffused her.

"Ayaaana!"

Mwalimu Juma reached Ayaana. He took both her hands in his. Merits from her school exam results had eventually caught up with him and brought him ample reward. When the time came, he had been made county education officer. He exclaimed, with a wide grin that showed his gums, "You have returned to us." He noticed the new lines on her face, the cloak of weariness she wore. The world had worked her hard. "*Alhamdulillah*," he added.

Ayaana lowered her sunglasses to gaze into her old teacher's eyes to say, "I'm *here*."

One of the passing fishermen sang, "*Angepaa kipungu, marejeo ni mtini . . .*"—An eagle may soar, but must return to its tree.

Ayaana laughed. And there were prayers and songs, exhalations and exclamations. *Pole kwa safari*—Sympathies for the traveler. Dips in the conversation to accommodate the griefs, all the losses. A young imam announced that he was praying for Muhidin's return. "The ocean is a cipher." Assent. "We can only wait."

True.

They walked an hour and a half southwestward to Pate Town, this welcome delegation and their returnee. Stepping over ruins, and rubble. The familiarity of decay: the Nabahani ruins, the graves and tombs of the many. The inscriptions of Pate's poets, its scholars, its saints, its wanderers.

Ayaana crossed into the market hub where a hollow-cheeked, voguish woman in gold and brown who was about to bite into a stick of *oudi* pivoted to glare at Ayaana. "You! You are back?" she huffed.

Mama Suleiman.

Within Ayaana, a mosaic of emotions, vestiges of childhood fears. The woman looked Ayaana up and down. "You look like a boy, China," she noted. "So thin. What? Dog and snake do not a meal make?" Mama Suleiman tittered. "They deported you?"

Ayaana sniffed. From a tree, some of the island's omnipresent crows serenaded them. The scent of sea mingled with that of wild jasmine; the rhythm of the tides was a familiar tune. Well-being. Ayaana exhaled with care. "Good to see you again, Bi Amina. You look well." She resumed her unhurried passage along the path leading to her mother's boarded-up house. Hudhaifa bolted the doors to his shop to hurry toward her, waving the tinkling house keys that Muhidin's workmen had left behind. In the manner of unsupervised workmen everywhere, they had abandoned their repair of the houses to take up other commissions.

Ayaana exclaimed *Mashallah!* when she glimpsed her childhood home. It still looked as if it had sprouted from the coral of the land. How small it was. How . . . old. A short distance away, the now wild plants of her mother's garden drenched her with their unbridled scents. The pawpaw tree was heavy with overripe fruit. Ayaana took the key from Hudhaifa and inserted it. The lock turned. She pulled open the door and entered the house, the accumulated dust anointing her head. Within the dark and musty space of the house, Ayaana set down her bags. She dropped to the ground. Struggling with words. Ayaana wrapped her arms about her chest. Pain: home.

In a land like this, of arrivals and departures, there were many ways of reconnection. An embrace. Laughter. Prayers. Food and drink: tea, coconut water, *mkate wa mofa*. Others showed up, welcoming, commiserating. "Your father," they said, and left it at that. An elder prayed for Muhidin's return. He added that they were grateful for Ayaana's safe return. The day slipped to darkness, and someone lit three hurricane lamps. The scent of smoke from hidden fires. *Home*.

A woman's question: "So, child, how is China?"

Ayaana paused. "Good," she answered three seconds later.

"Did they like you?"

Ayaan smiled, implying nothing.

"Are they really like us?"

Ayaana resisted the urge of the traveler to embellish tales. "They are themselves."

"Will you be going back?"

"I don't know."

"*Duu!*" The questioner was disappointed.

Ayaana added, "There was nothing for me to do there." Within her breathing, the truth: *If I had stayed, I would have evaporated. My heart is tired. Now my dreams speak to me in Mandarin. Even my demons have become red dragons.*

"Tell us about the plane—the one that still cannot be found."

Ayaana frowned. Then she remembered Flight MH370. She had seen how its disappearance had crushed hearts in China. As a class, they had studied the process of seafloor sonar surveys being undertaken to locate it.

"A riddle," she answered.

A man said, "They should consult our prophets." "Or fishermen," a woman piped up. Laughter.

"You have heard that a sea dog has visited us?"

"Yes," Ayaana answered, eyes bright.

"What did this China want of you?"

From Ayaana, wordlessness.

"What is your degree?"

"Bachelor of science, nautical studies."

"What does it mean?"

"I can bring a ship home."

"You?"

"Yes, me."

"Duu!"

Stillness.

They watched her.

So Ayaana asked after old acquaintances. Some had died. Some had left for Mombasa or Nairobi or Oman or Zanzibar or Dubai or elsewhere. She was told of the persistence of the ignorant, heavy, deaf, blind, stupid hand of the state, the open-ended "War on Terror" they had adopted as their own. Executions, murders, Friday roundups in Mombasa. The slaughter of the sheep by the shepherds to feed the lust of strangers. Yes, some of the young had gone over to al-Qaeda, al-Shabaab, al-Dawlah, imagining paradise. Stillness: the formlessness of futile rage. Now subdued voices. Ayaana heard of betrayal, death, and anguish. Life, and other people's wars. Cold crept over her body when she was informed that the eternal Mkanda Channel might be closed, that a new harbor was to be built by the Chinese. An oil pipeline to traverse Lamu was to be built by the Chinese. A coal factory would rise in pristine Lamu and turn the island black and bleak. The Chinese would build that, too, and Ayaana remembered her vision of a spider weaving a net over worlds.

"Will you speak to them for us?"

Ayaana bent her head and shifted to sit on her heels.

Giant shadows on the wall: the shape of the hungry, hungry world she had thought to leave behind. A specter, and she recognized the open, stench-filled mouth salivating at the promise of her island. Gas. Oil. Coal. Her seas. "Will you speak to them for us?" Upward glance, glimpsing her people. What could she say? What language could she use? Here was the smell of kerosene, the familiar gurgle of sweet water in the *djierbas*. Small crimson lights of charcoal fires. The honey smell of fried *mahamri*. Here the timbre of the sea. She stared at her people, these remnants with their sea-borne dreams, their hospitable, uncomplicated eyes. If they were to be scattered, what distant crossroads would ever understand their luster? Ayaana looked away, fresh tears causing her eyes to smart. She wiped them. She would say nothing about the disarraying forces marching toward them. She blinked away her thoughts, then straightened her spine. On Pate, there was always another way, wasn't there?

"Will you speak to them for us?"

"I will try," she answered.

Next topic. The more confident, always renewable anti-Lamu grumblings, soap-opera episodes from an ancient bickering that was pleasurable to recall. In the retelling, the Pate of memory was a distinguished place, renowned for enterprise, civilization, and scholarship—the Swahili seas' trendsetter. Pity about time's ruthlessness, pity about Lamu's perfidy. Then that silence that ghosts use to assert their presence descended upon the gathering. Outside, a wind bubbled like a brook. Birdcall, and then, at last, Ayaana heard the sound of the sea of home. She wiped away silent tears. This time, though, she did not weep alone. Her island snuggled around Ayaana. It nestled within her heart. It returned her to belonging. A child laughed. There was more bread to break. *What is to become of them all?* A low-whistling wind. She listened and remembered that other sinister forces had entered Pate many times before. But Pate had survived the lusts of the bloodthirsty.

It was close to a new morning when the last of Ayaana's welcomers left. She then settled into Pate's particular lonelinesses, among its drifting primordial ghosts. To these she could show the contours of a densely populated inner topography, the portions of China she had brought back to her island. Reaching through clouds, grasping at . . . nothing. It was only then that she realized that all her musings had been in Mandarin.

Ayaana stood at once to go into her old bedroom.

Small, bare, deficient by the standards of the places from which she had come. She stopped by the old desk with its objects: Rabi'a's poetry, the last Basmallah she had traced on Pate, Suleiman's pearl; a beachcomber's plastic duck; fading photos of Munira and Muhidin. She touched these. The note from long, long ago left to her by Muhidin. His scrawl still dark, and replete with promise: "Abeerah, I've gone to find our Ziriyab. I shall return. Be brave. Protect your mother. Study hard. It is I who am your father, Muhidin." A sensation struck her like a cold knife under her ribs, and she gasped. The words "It is I who am your father, Muhidin."

. . .

And then Ayaana wept.

Afterward.

Ayaana slept naked. She would not have done so before. She listened to her sea, tempted by its moaning to go to it. She waited. Listened as the house creaked in new places. After Ayaana shut her swollen eyes, she did not wake up till the evening of the next day.

[94]

Tuning in to the cool landscape—it had been drizzling, and sea smells pervaded the atmosphere. Jumping puddles. Ayaana was wrapped in her mother's peach shawl when she reached the water's edge. She carried a squashed scrap of paper. Otherworlds. She waded in, leapt, and landed on rocks jutting from the water. Listening in. Sea nocturnes, boom of distant deep-water waves. She had been here before. When she raised her arms to throw out feelers across the sea for the sense of Muhidin Baadawi, her father, her only father, she did so with the familiarity of ritual. She sensed other night watchers, night listeners, night gazers, the susurrus of night ghosts who knew the hiding places of the absent. Climbing to the promontory. Her neck craned toward the stars, summoning a wind. She wanted a whirlwind to carry to Muhidin his portion of a guiding yellowing fragment that had been living in the insides of a dark brown book. A slow breeze eased the fragment from her open hand. The fragment spiraled. It spun. It soared and scaled altitudes in order to circle the land. It plummeted to the sea.

In the daytime, she would return to comb the beach, searching for spoors—was that a man's footprint?—crossing dunes, poking into crevices for something that might have fallen from Muhidin's pockets. *I am here; you come back*—that was the tune to which her heart was beating.

She called Munira to let her know she had returned to Pate Island.

Munira listened to her daughter. And then, emphatic: "But you will return to China?"

Ayaana replied, "Don't know."

Silence. "You are there to look for him, aren't you?" Munira murmured.

"Yes."

Munira said, "Think of your future."

Ayaana did not answer.

Munira asked, "What will you do?"

"Maybe find work at the port. For a while. Till I can decide."

"Ayaana!" Munira was exasperated. A sigh. "At least go to Mombasa. Don't molder on Pate, you hear me?"

Ayaana chewed on her lower lip, saying nothing.

The next day, Ayaana hired three *ngarawa*s so she could imagine Muhidin's trail and follow it. And there—on calm blue sea, with a view of forested islands and white beach, under a stark sky in which a single bird soared, amid the rhythm in the voices of the men, her people, who rowed with her on seasoned wooden boats, souls reading the water for clues of life—in all this, something of beauty, that blazing event, flooded Ayaana's deep self, and, without her expecting it, she started to wail and she seized the thing to herself, pressing it to her heart, and her assent emerged as a wordless prayer.

Seeking Muhidin.

Her focus absolute.

They would search the seas for a full day. They returned to the water the next day and the next, when they returned to shore in the early afternoon because the seas were restless.

On the fifth day after her return to Pate Island, Ayaana walked from house to house, asking people what they had seen and what they knew. Mwalimu Juma told her that Muhidin had vowed, "This realm shall be known again," as he handed over his old books to the school.

Muhidin had told Hudhaifa that he now knew the answer to the riddle of happiness. "He hated no one," Hudhaifa told Ayaana.

The tailor said, "Your father returned to us a sun. Pemba is good for him."

Dura told Ayaana of how Muhidin had attempted to reassure Bi Amina about Suleiman her son.

On the seventh day, Ayaana walked to the cove to speak to Mehdi.

He would have the most to offer.

Almazi Mehdi had set aside two pieces of driftwood: one for Muhidin, the other for Mzee Kitwana. "Place markers," he told Ayaana. "Muhidin had wanted a *dau* to be built for his wife. Am working on it."

Ayaana touched the hull, and the prow. Mehdi continued, "Wanted me to go to Pemba. Couldn't leave Mzee Kitwana. Has no one of his own, you see." Pause. Fleeting sorrow. "Couldn't go." Mehdi turned to Ayaana, a speculative look on his face.

They watched the return of the boats at dusk, and with these, the calm that filled such evenings. Mehdi then added, "He spoke of Ziriyab." He coughed. "Dreamed of his boy. In the dream, he said he had handed over his heart."

Ayaana stroked the boat. Mehdi said, "A prophecy of sacrifice." Quietly: "How could we know? Would have told Kitwana to wait." Suddenly Mehdi buckled into himself. A single sob eased out of him. But, just as suddenly, he stopped. They then watched the raven family that had moved into Mehdi's territory. The three adults and four juveniles strutted nearby, confident of their place. One of them had taken to bringing pale pebbles to Mehdi. "Couldn't keep driving them away, could I?" he told Ayaana.

She watched the birds.

"Your father. Spoke of water. Spoke of his uncle. Terrible man. Remember him playing the *zumari*. Had a sacred quotation for everything. Yet what human can claim to know the innermost truth of a man, tell me?"

Cawing.

Mehdi waved the birds away. They barely lifted their wings. "Your father went to sea," Mehdi told Ayaana. "Craving mystery. Mzee Kitwana went with him. They sat there when they decided to go." Mehdi pointed at two places near to him. He then squinted at the sea. "'*Bahari usichungue, utajitia wahaka,*'" he recited, recalling an old sea minstrel's poem about the mysterious seas. "They have not returned."

Silence.

The pair watched the silver-streaked water. "Went to look for them myself." Mehdi paused. "Asked the winds; they are not talking. Had to call your mother. Tell her. Terrible day." Mehdi stared at the ground as the tide news resumed. Ayaana and Mehdi heard that high tide was expected at 1947 hours.

Ayaana sat close to Muhidin's driftwood and picked up a torn sail Mzee Kitwana had been repairing before he disappeared. She looked for the thick needle with which to complete the work. Mehdi watched her for a while. He studied the bent head, the life-marked face, short hair stirring in the wind, the slender woman of unusual beauty. His glance shifted to the pockmarked sail and the large needle in her hands. He said nothing. He said nothing when she returned after dawn and stayed by his side until the evening. The owners of the sail were from Unguja. He reasoned to himself that they would never know it was a woman who had worked on their sail. A sense of mischief lit up his mouth. He had always delighted in Ayaana's company.

Mehdi told Ayaana, "We shall look. Until we know. We shall look. Even after we die."

She continued with her work. *It is I who am your father, Muhidin.* Her tears stained the sail.

[95]

Migrant fishing boats from other ports, beached on Pate Island to wait out a quick approaching storm. Like the other islanders, Ayaana wandered over to hear tales of their seas. Echoes of the same cries: declining fish stock, the gluttony of ocean-emptying trawlers from the ravenous lands, the silence of authorities, a nostalgia for the season of the Somali pirates, the heroes, who had scared away the ocean plunderers and restored the run of the billfish. Ayaana then asked the visitors if they had any news of a seaman named Mlingoti. They said not recently. They had heard rumors, though, that one with such a name had, about two years ago, commissioned seafaring acquaintances with piracy as sidelines to look out for and detain a vessel named *Bathsheba*, should it ever be seen to approach the East African coastline. His seafaring friends were to put the vessel's souls to compulsory work somewhere unseen, for minimum wages, for as long as they wanted. Beyond this, these fishermen had not heard anything more about the man Mlingoti. Ayaana hugged this news to her soul: a lost father's protective canopy reaching in to erase a daughter's fears. Wa Mashriq were not ever likely to show up on these shores again.

Two weeks later, Ayaana traveled to Nairobi by road. She glimpsed the progression of a Chinese-built standard-gauge railroad snaking across the landscape with moral messages emblazoned on massive signs: "Today low skills, tomorrow chief engineer." Ayaana's name was in the book for her early-morning appointment at the Embassy of the People's Republic of China in the Republic of Kenya. Banners at the gate announced a "Seminar on Deepening China-Africa Cooperation." The red-paper-wrapped package she was carrying in her big violet handbag was also scanned. A man ushered her into the office of the adviser on culture and education. Two minutes later, Shu Ruolan clickety-clacked in, in pointy patent leather shoes. Ayaana shot up.

She held out her package with both hands. In it was a green-and-white *leso* set woven with the aphorism *"Elimu ni kama bahari, haina kuta wala dari." "Xie xie nin,"* added Ayaana—Thank you.

Shu Ruolan studied Ayaana. *"Bu ke qi."* She hesitated before accepting the offering.

Ayaana stretched out her right hand. Shu Ruolan took it. They held hands for a moment.

"Xie xie nin," Ayaana repeated.

She bent her head before leaving the room.

Teacher Ruolan watched Ayaana make her way through the embassy's gates. Her hands idly unwrapped the gift. She studied the colors on the cloth and patterns. She read and translated the aphorism to herself, "Knowledge is an ocean, it has neither walls nor a roof." A student should honor her teacher.

Usiku mwaka.

The night is a year.

[96]

Fates. The children, the next generation of islanders, had run down the hill to Mehdi's workshop to seek out Ayaana, who was welding in greasy overalls. "Bi Ayaana!" they shouted in unison. She turned off the metal cutter and lifted up her rusted helmet, to listen to what the children had to say.

Ayaana tore out of the shed full-tilt, the children at her heels. She saw him, the giant. Attenuated by time, still and sedate, a huge green canvas-wrapped object positioned next to him. He carried a simple black leather bag.

"Nioreg!" Ayaana screamed, forgetting herself. As if she had not already caused sufficient scandal on the island, she leapt into his arms. Nioreg lifted her up, his face wreathed in so many lines, his hair now white. "What're you doing here?" Ayaana cried. "Where's Delaksha?" Ayaana looked around for her friend.

"She is here," said Nioreg.

The porter carrying his bag handed it over to him. Nioreg slipped him a few euros.

"Where?" asked Ayaana, scanning the road behind.

Nioreg pulled out an engraved wooden box. Inside the dark blue felt, a painted urn. He did not need to speak. It is in stillness that stark truths emerge. It is in moments when pasts, and what is unspoken between them and the present whisper, but not in words. There is a way of knowing that bypasses mundane words. Then Ayaana knew, but she denied truth entry.

She looked into Nioreg's eyes, her voice breaking. "What's that?"

Nioreg lifted his eyes to survey the island. He looked up at the sky, its endlessness, and how it met the sea. The in-betweens. He smelled the age sweating off the skin of the coral land, scattered by winds with strange and lyrical names. He looked at the slight young woman looking at him with all her life inside her gaze. He wanted to say, *This is what the passage of life is, here its culmination. Unlike your tides, we do not always hear it coming. Sorrow is our fate, but we sometimes live enough to recognize it as the finger of a friend. Everything gives way, at some point of its being. Even hauntedness gives way. One truth remains: I was loved. And I loved. How I loved.* A soft smile suffused Nioreg's face. "Ayaana-*petite*," he says, "I've brought Delaksha home. I trust that a discreet person exists who will help us commend her to your earth?"

Two tear streams lined Ayaana's face. She bowed her head. At last she said, "Yes. Follow me." They walked in the direction of Sheikh Shamum's house. The sheikh's application of the faith was broad, creative, and greatly accommodating of human vicissitudes. "What happened?" Ayaana hiccupped.

Nioreg glanced at her. "This beautiful girl . . . she fell."

"Fell?" repeated Ayaana.

"Hard."

Quiet.

They walked. Their feet crunched the sand.

Something had split, and metals had groaned, as the MV *Qingrui*'s gangway jerked left and launched Delaksha forward. She had tumbled to the ground. Her head had connected with a jutting metal object. The crack that broke her neck was audible. Bags tumbling around him, Nioreg had reached her side in a single leap and heard her mutter "Fuck!" before she had gurgled, "So sorry, my dear big love." There was nothing he could do for her. Because he did not know yet how to cry out loud, he had shuddered from the inside out.

"Don't leave me," Delaksha had lisped. "Pray."

"How . . ."

"'Now I lay me down . . .'"

"Delaksha . . ."

"Love me . . ."

"Delaksha . . ."

In that atmosphere of quiet catastrophe, baffled watchers saw wrinkles and shadows wreath the face of a black colossus, a muscular foreigner who clamped down his lips, and who, bit by bit, turned sallow as a bleeding woman twitched in his arms. A medical team raced in with a stretcher between them and went into action. Watching over Delaksha in the speeding ambulance, the passing lights on their faces, Nioreg understood that there was no theory or philosophy for what hospital emergency doctors would confirm to him: *Delaksha is dead.*

~

Two weeks after she died, a lead coffin was loaded into a China Eastern plane heading to Rome. An unspeaking man accompanying the corpse had sat in Business Class, studying a document written out in Mandarin and attached to a brutal English translation, and an even more horrible French one. His eyes had focused on the section of the document that noted, "Delaksha Tarangini Sudhamsu Ngobila, wife of Nioreg Marie Ngobila." Death did not disturb the plans they had made. He implemented their travel itinerary in full. A few adjustments: A hearse was now on standby in Rome. He drove it. He had also included a destination he had earlier disputed—the Church of the Sacred Heart of the Suffrage, where there was a Piccolo Museo del Purgatorio. He spoke to Delaksha there. Months later, his constant conversations with her had transformed the timbre of his voice into a soft hauntedness that those who heard leaned toward to hear intimately. His security-service life ended. Those whose job it was to find out what happened when one of their own went AWOL reported that some of the demons they were familiar with had caught up with their brother Nioreg.

Nioreg told Ayaana, "They prayed for her at the *museo.*" A pause. "A liturgy for her soul." Remembering with a soft smile. "Couldn't leave her. Couldn't leave her in Kerala, either. Her mother's mind is not . . . whole. She would not know what to do with her. We've traveled a long way, Delaksha and I. We have cried. We've waited in many places. Couldn't leave her. Bought her a place in a cemetery in Spain with a view of the sea. Cremated her there. When they gave me the urn, I couldn't leave her. She needs to be with those who love her, you understand? One day I had a dream. We were all here." He looked about him. "I was not certain you would be here. But it is destined." Ayaana wiped her eyes. Nioreg added, "She'll be content here."

Ayaana nodded. She lifted her hand to knock on the sheikh's door, but it was already opening for them.

They buried Delaksha before sunset. They burned incense for her and consoled themselves with the mystery of its scent. Her resting place was shaded by a tall pawpaw tree, beneath which lay the small bones of a long-dead kitten. Delaksha was interred with an additional name: Ra'abia. The name secured Delaksha's belonging to Pate and its people. After a simple ceremony, Nioreg decided to walk the length of the beach. He had lost his voice. He stumbled into a fisherman's shed that had last been used by a seeker in exile who had now joined the long list of Pate's "disappeared." It was a good place to sit and not know what to do for a while.

Ayaana phoned Munira that night.

"We buried a friend today."

"Who?"

"Delaksha. We met on the ship." Ayaana's thoughts skittered.

"She was good to you?"

She was a lighthouse.

"Yes."

Munira's voice sounded thin. "This thing, death."

Stillness.

Later, Munira added, "Soon, Ayaana, soon, I too must return to Pate."

. . .

Almost a month later, Nioreg re-emerged. He came to Ayaana to say his goodbyes. Ayaana was silent as she walked him to the jetty. Nioreg left Pate, promising to return. He left on a fast boat to Lamu, where he caught a short flight to Mombasa. Weeks later, Ayaana would read a small news item in the *Coastweek* newspaper. A long-established coastal magnate, a man of European origin whose vivacious wife had disappeared a few years ago and was now presumed drowned, was driving home from his private club at night when a jalopy appeared from a side road and crashed into his Mercedes. He leapt out to berate the offender—the magnate's temper was renowned. The offender was described as a large African male, who delivered such a beating to the businessman that he was left on the roadside with a fractured spine, broken ribs, teeth, jaw, and nose. The magnate would recover, but, unfortunately, would never walk straight again, nor would he be able to eat without dribbling. The male offender had disappeared into the night. It turned out that the jalopy was unregistered. There were no fingerprints on the steering wheel—a strange thing indeed. But such was the character of life in these uncertain times. Ayaana read the article several times over. When she lowered it, she knew East Africa would not see Nioreg again.

[97]

Harbingers. A cloud appeared over Pate. At its core was a rainbow. The temperatures on the land plummeted briefly. Some islanders glanced upward and waited for the winds to show up and deliver the message.

Thirty-one days later.

The disembarking three-year-old had her father's popping-out eyes. Her name was Abeerah. A strong-willed soul, she preceded her mother off the boat, acting as if she knew what to do. She tumbled into the water. Emerging from her immersion, stoic, she attempted to wipe her soaking-wet dress. Her presence on the island was as surprising as that of her mother.

. . .

Munira, noticeable in the fuchsia sweater she had thrown on against the cold breeze, was greeted as a grieving and honored sea widow. She was treated as if her past had not happened. She was welcomed as a mother of the island.

When she had stepped off the boat, she turned around to stare at the sea.

"My rival, my wicked co-wife, this sea; must it always seize my men?" Tears in rivulets ran down her face. "How did I ever offend this witch?" She clung to the hands of the little girl.

A fisherman asked, "Who is our guest?"

"She is not a guest; she is his daughter."

"Muhidin has a daughter?"

"He named her Abeerah."

And those clustered around the child cooed and oohed and praised Abeerah, who peered at the crowd from behind her mother's back.

News reached Ayaana that Munira, whom she had been expecting, had at last arrived. Three days late, but she was now here. Ayaana ran all the way to the jetty. She started screaming from a distance the moment she glimpsed her mother. She reached her and grabbed her. They clung to each other. Crying, laughing. Talking. Crying. Laughing.

Ayaana turned to help with the luggage, and then she saw the child. At first she thought the girl belonged to some other passenger, but when she caught sight of something of Muhidin's being in the creature, Ayaana dropped the bags, and time scattered. A metallic bad taste in her mouth, her palms wet, and her eyes narrowing, she pivoted to face Munira. "Who is this?"

Munira leaned over, half smiling, and touched Ayaana's face. "Your sister, Abeerah."

"Abeerah?"

A complex silence followed before Ayaana's drawn voice asked, "Your . . . daughter?"

"Yes." Munira's stretched out her hands to Ayaana. "We wanted to . . ."

Ayaana's tone was chilly. "I see. We had better get to the house; you must be tired."

She lifted the bags on her shoulders and set off ahead of her mother and sister, marching toward their house. Her face was flushed, and her stomach roiled: *I. Will. Not. Cry.* Unreal reality. Falling apart within. *A sister?* No one had told her anything. *Their* daughter. *Abeerah*. Jealousy in procession: her father, her name, her mother. Melancholy. It tasted like loneliness and the horror that she was not necessary to anything. *Abeerah.* She had even been robbed of her name. When Ayaana reached the house, she dumped the luggage, went into her small room, and shut the door. She crashed. She did not know how to stop the breaking of a patched-up heart.

~

The family again endured curious and commiserating crowds. Food appeared. It was served. Ayaana emerged from her room. She listened to many voices in silence. She avoided her new sister's watchful gaze. She did not need to know how she was supposed to be.

Long past midnight, when the house was quiet again, Ayaana stood at her mother's door as she watched her soothe Abeerah, who was fussy. Munira saw her there. "How tall you are. How well you look. How were your studies, child?" she asked.

"Good."

"What did they give you?"

"A bachelor of science, nautical studies."

Munira's eyes shone.

Then—uneasy silence.

"We were waiting to tell you together . . . before . . . before . . ." Munira gestured as she cradled Abeerah. Shadows on her face, she sighed, "What's so wrong with this, *lulu*?"

Ayaana snapped, "Others know"—she pointed at the child—"before me? A whole baby?"

Munira laid the child on the bed. She walked to Ayaana. She opened her arms. "*Lulu* . . ."

Ayaana turned away from her.

Munira's hands fluttered. "She surprised us." Ayaana rolled her eyes. "So unexpected. Didn't know I could carry her to term. Everything . . . Allah's hand . . . this child, a gift. A woman my age . . . and

Muhidin . . . This . . . He was so happy. He said we must tell you together. He named her for you, the first one who had truly loved him—that is what he called you."

Munira's voice faded.

Muhidin was missing.

Munira's mouth trembled.

Both women then touched the wounds of far too many absences, the losses and silences, all the things they could no longer talk about.

Numbness.

Pushing herself away from the whirlpool of strange emotions, Ayaana glanced in the direction of the child. Cold-voiced, she said, "Mother, we are related by blood, the child and I, but that is all. She is nothing to me." Ayaana spun on her heel and went back to her room. She closed the door.

Whenever Abeerah tried to enter Ayaana's room, Ayaana screamed, "*Toka!*"—Get out! Ayaana would not carry Abeerah, or help feed her, or dress her, or soothe her when she cried. Ayaana would rush to work at Mehdi's workshop when it was still dark in the morning, and return late in the evening. She took her food in her room, with her door shut. Soon, when Abeerah saw Ayaana approach, she would freeze and wait for her to pass.

The island gossiped: "*Du!* Ayaana is possessed. Chinese djinns!"

"Ayaana!" Munira once shrieked.

"*La kuvunja halina ubani*"—Incense cannot disguise something rotten—Ayaana retorted. And she walked out of the house, despising herself for escalating things, unwilling to do anything about it.

Confused and trying to shrug off some shame, some guilt, Munira threw herself into the repair of their houses, chasing after repairmen and moving supplies from Nairobi and Mombasa to the island. She and Muhidin also had a boat in the high seas, heading out to Aden, carrying passengers and goods. She monitored its progress by phone.

She was immersed in work, paralyzed by sorrow and denying the broken link with her elder child. She had difficulty reading Ayaana and the impassive face she wore. Her daughter's eyes were all too often turned inward, as if debating some unknown fate. Munira fretted. What was this cloud over their lives? Munira felt the island had returned to whispering "*kidonda*" behind her back. She started tending her garden to calm herself. She muttered her fears to the plants and the earth. When she went to the mosque to pray, she caught sight of Mama Suleiman there. They nodded at each other. Ache in the soul as she thought of Ayaana, grief when she remembered Muhidin, and then deep gratitude for her child Abeerah.

One early evening, Munira decided to seek out Mehdi. He got up to greet her. Without her saying anything, he said, "Time corrects. She misses her father. I miss her father and my brother." He rubbed his eyes before adding, "*Bi Badaawi, liwapokuwa, lakuwa*"—What will be will be.

Abeerah now dared to shadow Ayaana, whose aloofness had only made her think her big sister even more magical. Ayaana would sometimes turn and find a little face with big eyes staring at her from behind a cupboard or bucket or chair, with something akin to worship. When she wandered outside, she often turned in time to glimpse a small being darting from bush to bush behind her. She crushed her laughter. She pursed her lips. She needed to ignore the child.

Six weeks later, an increasingly emboldened Abeerah trailed Ayaana to the mangroves, where Ayaana had taken a detour to watch approaching boats before returning to Mehdi's workshop. Back at work, Ayaana was drawing rough blueprints for a cell-phone app that fishing boats might use to send out intermittent coordinates to others on the shore.

She was wondering what it might take to activate the system so that the data would update themselves when she heard a bloodcurdling "*Ayaaaaaana!*"

Ayaana rose to meet her mother, who came flying down the pathway. "Abeerah!" Munira seized Ayaana's shoulders, looking around. "Abeerah! Where is she? Isn't she with you?"

"*Nooo,*" Ayaana huffed. That interloper was so annoying.

"I've looked and looked everywhere." Munira was sobbing, "Where is she? She was following you. Didn't you see her?"

Ayaana's heart tumbled; her body juddered. "Let's look."

They ran up and down the island, shouting Abeerah's name. Some of the Pate Town dwellers joined the search. Every call, every "Abeerah!" was a blow on Ayaana's body. She had not seen Abeerah. She had taught herself to be blind to the child. Ayaana screamed, "*Abeeerah!*" Fighting self-loathing. *What have I done?* "*Abeeraaaaah!*" she cried, offering new and forever promises: *Come back. I will love you. Forgive me. I will love you.*

Abeerah had slipped and fallen down a slope into a mangrove grove not too far from where Ayaana had been sitting in the morning. A sluggish current had sent her drifting about twenty meters away from where she could be seen. She was stuck in sea mud by thick mangrove roots. Ayaana, who had been circling the island and had returned to the mangroves, heard, between the anxious cawing of crows, the faintest of sounds. Her name: "*Ayayana!*" She hurtled in the direction of the call, urged on by a feeling, and saw the tracks in the mire. She jumped into the brackish water. With the tide coming in, it was up to her thighs. She saw mangrove branches upon which dangled the gossamer wings of a thousand dragonflies. Clinging to a stump was her mud-stained sister.

It was twilight.

Mud-marked, Ayaana carried her sister all the way to their house. Her sister clung to her, not moving. Those who saw them assumed the worst, because Ayaana was mute. Those who saw them turned away, lamenting the losses that afflicted the family—too much, they cried.

Munira, visible in her fuchsia sweater, was told that her daughter had been found. She was asked to prepare her heart. Munira heard the silence. Then she heard Ayaana's howl, a horrible sound as if something infinite and good and beloved were gone forever. Munira fell to her knees. She refused the hands reaching down to help her. She crawled all the way to her house, her knees scraped, her sorrow dumb.

Ayaana rocked Abeerah in her arms. When Ayaana had seized Abeerah, she had had to let go of Muhidin, and to do so she had touched the bottom of fathomless grief. It was for her father that she cried out—the one who had never shown up, and the one she had chosen. She cried for Muhidin.

Then.

A heart whisper, feather-light in the soul: *Promised you I wouldn't leave you. See, you* have *found me again.* Stillness. *I shall love you.* Even Abeerah heard those words.

"*Baba?*" she whispered.

"Yes, my love," Ayaana whispered back.

Munira dragged herself in. Then it dawned on her that both her children were whole. Pate Town heard a woman's terrible laugh, the laugh of wild, fierce, ceaseless life.

The next day, Ayaana, veiled and red-eyed, tore out of the house before dawn. She accosted the stooped Abasi, eternal muezzin. She had to talk to someone. "I have hated a child," she told him, her voice cracked. Abasi, toothless and cataract-eyed, would listen to her. She would speak from dawn to noon. She would weep. She would tell him about Koray. Everything. Abasi would cry with her. Then he would wipe Ayaana's eyes with dry, scaly hands. He had become a human being. "So," Abasi would comfort Ayaana, "you have been offered the gift of falling and failing; you encountered the mystery of human wretchedness and powerlessness." And then his eyes would shine. "Use it wisely." And Ayaana would stare at him, speechless. Afterward, Ayaana would retrieve her secret trove of words—"yearning," "searching," "longing," "desire"—a topography of living.

At evenfall, Ayaana was eating damask roses, stuffing small pink petals into her mouth. She chewed rose hip, knowing that the thorniness that scraped her tongue was the rub of life. Sucking rose water from her fingers. On the stove, green neem-leaf water bubbled. It would treat forty ailments. Ayaana dipped her fingers into the liquid. She tasted its bitterness, a basic taste in existence. It filled up her tongue. It blended with the rose flavors that were already there. She offered a petal to her sister, and watched Abeerah's face as its essence suffused her.

A day later, at low tide, within the mangroves, the two sisters watched home-comers arrive on boats. They made up stories about them. And then Abeerah asked Ayaana, "Our father—he is on that boat?"

Ayaana froze, and time fell away. For a moment she was that child again. She answered, "His ship is the biggest. The sea he crosses covers the sky. But first he must harness two stars for you and me. Only then will he return."

Abeerah digested this.

Another question: "You are my Ayaana?"

Tears and a smile. Ayaana's arms clung to the child's shoulders. Her voice caught as she answered, "For always, forever."

Sometime later, when the tide was higher and the sea warm, the sisters swam together without caring who saw them. One day Ayaana would introduce Abeerah to Bollywood. Tonight, though, they were content to examine the stars to try to identify the sky-sea where their beloved father sailed.

Simba kiwa maindoni, hafunuwi zakawe ndole.

A lion sheathes its claws when hunting.

[99]

Eons ago—for what does time matter now?—three strangers had leapt from beneath the waves and seized Ziriyab Raamis. Three beings in black had torn him away from his home and his Buthayna, his Ghazalah, his soaring Huma. They had twisted his limbs, tied him up, covered his head with a black cloth, and thrown him on a boat to Diego Garcia. He had embarked on a long and hideous voyage. When they finally uncovered his face, weeks later, he found himself huddled, cramped, and naked in a cold-shower cell in a nameless, faceless bay, in a concentration camp in alienated territory.

He was dragged out of the shower by more snarling men. An orange jumpsuit waited for him, his costume for the timeless years. Men mocked his diarrhea, his hacking cough. Men bled him, and replaced his name with a number. They forced tubes down his throat to feed him until he gagged and still hoped to die. But when he would have faded away completely, he invoked his Buthayna, his Ghazalah, his soaring Huma. He would close his eyes. The whisper would emerge from inside shadows. It was a lone blue note, a settling sound, like his wife's perfect heartbeat. So that, when he could open his eyes again, he might return to life. One night, when he was about to die, he had bled from his soul. But then his father, Muhidin, appeared. They held each other. They spoke. When he woke up, his heart was quiet, and he could hear the sound of seabirds and imagine the brush of wings against his face. It was the first time he had smiled in that place.

Two words into which he had retreated in his season of darkness: *kabsh alfida*, كبش الفداء—sacrificial lamb. The scapegoat. For, in the same senseless manner as his incarceration, he was released. He was escorted to a waiting cargo plane that dropped him off in Al-'Ain, Abu Dhabi. No explanations.

"You are going to kill me." He spoke with a rasp, declaring the obvious, and his voice was colored with hollowed-out age and defeated rage. A still point amid the flow. He had not yet recognized the flow as people.

"You are free to go."

He swerved as if turning from a blow, and waited for the lie to come to birth—the death they had prepared for him, so he grieved his life.

A tear dropped between the men.

"Our investigations are complete. You are now free to go."

". . ."

"You are free to go."

He gasped and ogled his handler's bulk, the thick, unkempt ginger beard, mirrored dark glasses. Ziriyab dared a glance so he might start to believe. He saw twin images looking back at him. He did not know the man in those reflections.

"Free to go."

The man gave him a label-free black rucksack. "Everything you need is in there." A bland voice.

Inside the bag, Ziriyab would later find a brand-new Yemeni passport, a wad of cash in two currencies, which he did not count, jeans, cheap sneakers and a shirt, and a shiny new suit. A pat on his head, a tap on his right shoulder, the wickedly accented "*Salaam aleikum.*"

Ziriyab Raamis stood frozen. Concentrating on the prickling sensation that filled even his heart with pins and needles. When he opened his eyes, what he saw made him stumble, and if he had not still been voiceless, he might have shrieked. What he saw was people moving, crossing streets, planes taking off from the airport bustle of another life, and he was standing unchained. He turned and saw an elderly woman in a bright-blue hijab, and her face was lined with bright-eyed worry.

"*Jaddah-ti?*" he murmured.

My grandmother.

She had heard him. *"Nem, aliabn?"* Sweet voiced, warm, a mother's gaze.

Son.

In him, a choking sob; he bit it down. *"Shukraan,"* he grunted.

She was real, and he saw toothless joy in the wreathed face of an exquisite old woman whose voice was honeyed and curious. *"Min ayn anta?"*—Where are you from?

Haawiyah, he might have said. But then he would have also had to burden another soul with the details of the topography of hell. So, instead, he leaned forward to ask her, *"Ayn 'ana?"*—Where am I?

Grandmother giggled, wagging a finger at him. "Naughty boy, teasing your own mother." She trotted off, still chuckling, and her laughter bounced around in Ziriyab's head and landed at the top of his heart, where it waited for him to respond.

Ziriyab started to move. One limp into another, and his body tilted left. Left was the side he had favored when he slept in his steel bed. Ziriyab walked into the realm of free-to-go-ness, waiting for the bullet. He clutched the rucksack to his front to shield his heart. Only after he had walked for an hour did he dare to look at the signs. They informed him that he really was in the garden city of Al-'Ain.

Ziriyab walked. He carried what he knew: the nature of lies, ugliness, and hatred; how to invert good and evil; the vulnerability of humans before the roar of power, how only a few could resist the temptation to roll the dice of life or death over another; living under the daily threat of a terrible dying. He walked with fresh memories of sleep deprivation, sensory deprivation, food deprivation, water deprivation. He understood that uncertainty was a weapon of mass fear. He carried trace marks of blindfolds worn for days. The invisible disfigurement caused by human bullying. As he walked, he tumbled back into an abyss of harsh lights, loud random noises, and the ghastly musical brayings of alleged artists.

To survive, he had discarded time. To survive, he had shed his need to know the time of day or night. He had hidden inside memory. There he had, one day while in solitary confinement, heard his class teacher's voice remind him and his literature classmates that "an actor's role is to reflect humanity." There and then, he sought a role for himself. He took on *kabsh alfida* as his sobriquet.

The Scapegoat, performed by Ziriyab Raamis.

Then he had laughed at himself. Yet, through the role, he had learned to pity his tormentors and to read the gradual emptying of souls from eyes. His gaze washed over the faces of men who strapped him down to feed or beat or half drown him. One night, they threatened to pluck out his eyes, so he shut them. They had forgotten that even the senses have eyes of their own. He could watch them through the eyes of his nose, ears, skin, and heart, these other prisoners of war.

Yet there had been seasons when the ocean of horror inside had engulfed him, and he was ready to die. But he would have died wrong, because accompanying the anguish was the undercurrent of a malicious thrill that these men, when they returned home, would deliver into the womb of their own families the malignant gift that now possessed them.

As Ziriyab walked, he remembered that he had managed to hide his heart. He had distributed its portions evenly. One portion he kept in silence; another he had left beneath the breasts of his Buthayna, his Ghazalah, his own soaring Huma; a third he hid among ghosts of the family he had lost to drones; and the fourth part he had tossed to the God who had forsaken him.

Ziriyab traveled across Abu Dhabi.

A voice in his head murmured in poetic meter to orient him. He heard:

> *At the end of the river,*
> *The wolf star plows into the sheep flock of Algenib*
> *The phoenix dances*
> *Into the navel of the mare*
> *The shining one bristles*
> *At the follower of al-Dabarān . . .*

It was night in the desert, as scorching there as it had been during the day. Ziriyab relished the heat and the thick air, which he needed to gulp down in order to breathe. The sweat that poured out of his soul purged him as he traversed the fissured land. He was in Musandam, in Oman, on his way to Khasab and its port. He crossed Bukha, stopping for sweetmeats and spiced rice. He was unable to endure meat. It brought back to him the memory of the slow putrefaction of bodies at that prison camp. The stars at night: how he had ached for them, how he had longed for them. So he stopped. He fell to the ground to gaze at the heavens. And then he could not see for the tears in his eyes and the howling of the ghosts in his soul.

He had given himself no choice but to return to his wife by way of the sea. He was wary of confined spaces. He wanted neither to see nor to meet a Caucasian any day soon. He would never board a plane again. He found a ship, a *jahazi*. It was under the captainship of one Nahodha Aboud Khamis, born in Mombasa in 1964. They took to the blue sea on the tail end of the *kaskazi*. Ziriyab tuned in to the winds of his ocean. Inside their song, he listened to his wife whispering him back home.

Hakuna bahari, isiyo na mawimbi.

There is no sea without waves.

[100]

Nine months earlier, in the January time of departing dragonflies, a corpselike man had appeared like an apparition on the island on which he had been born, from which he had been exiled, to which he had returned for refuge, and from which he had been stolen. Now, on the decayed cusp of a late Thursday in October 2016, this man wearing Munira's fuchsia cardigan splashes through a freshwater pool teeming with minuscule C-shaped dragonfly nymphs. The waves swirled warm around his legs. He inhaled and shut his eyes. He closed his eyes, the better to hear the bass-infused chord of longing that had brought him home. At Pate, he had cried to his unseen father, his betrayer: *Why?*

He had been at this for months now.

Home.

But his heart had not found shelter yet, had not yet understood that it needed a new language to contain his life. Everything had changed. Nothing had changed. Flash of blue. *Kerem-kerem.* A bee-eater. His eyes locked on the rhythm of its wings. Its beauty pulled his memory back from echoing the gross blaring of a nation's anthem. His gaze sought the bird again. Nothing had changed. Everything had changed, and he shuddered because in the sound of the wind he also heard the horror he had hoped to outrun slithering in their direction.

Everything had changed. He now had a daughter.

A *sister,* he corrected himself.

Abeerah had already informed him that Ayaana was *her* sister, not his.

Newer wounds from an unremitting darker struggle with volatile emotions, with disillusionment: his father's child, his wife's daughter.

Ziriyab unclenched his fists.

He *had* died.

Death had filled up the emptied spaces of life with other beings.

Life, it seemed, had not missed him.

He could read the story of his death in the glances of those who had experienced his absence, in the habits of his Buthayna, his Ghazalah, his soaring Huma, who still averted the guilt-shame-defiance look of one who had betrayed faith.

She had not waited for him. She had not proved to death that love was infallible.

"Forgive me," she had told him. Those were her first words to him when she saw him, and he her.

Munira had said, "When you disappeared, we died."

Munira then added, "Now you have returned, you can see we are no longer the same."

She had repeated, "Forgive me."

After the silence, which lasted two days, Ziriyab had spoken. He told Munira that it was the memory of her existence that had kept him from being devoured.

Then he had a question for her: "Why him?"

She was silent. Then she said, "He loves what he knows."

He grabbed her forearm. "And I don't?"

She shook her head. "You love what you do not know."

He had cried, "Is that so wrong?"

"No," she whispered. "But I am both."

Hudhaifa waved at Ziriyab from the seashore while hurrying on, making it clear he did not want to speak. Ziriyab watched. The islanders were suspicious of his materiality. Most did not wish to be alone with him, half expecting to see him transform into a djinn. A tiny smile—he was not entirely sure he would not.

Ayaana observed Ziriyab when she could. She hesitated with her questions because of the otherness of his face, as if it was Ziriyab, but not entirely. He had taken to observing the behavior of land birds. The ravens, the doves. The pigeons he thought he might keep. One day, she walked out to the veranda, where he was squatting and looking out at the world. "It was a bad place?" she asked.

He nodded once. Could not speak yet of many things. *It is a wound that never heals. It infuses you with the enduring stench of human evil.*

Unchecked tears.

They both watched the world in silence.

Minutes later, Ziriyab would tell Ayaana, "A young man from Yemen—he has not eaten for eight years. They have to force food into him every day." Ziriyab's voice receded. "He was only a child when they stole him from his mother." And when he looked at Ayaana, his eyes were crushed inside a sunken face. His voice was inflected with rust. "They bleed souls—that is their hunger. They are possessed, you understand. When they kill us, they do not think we are real."

A warm wind stirred the land. Distant waves bumped into the shoreline. *Bahari haishi zingo*—The sea does not stop moving.

Ayaana hugged herself. She said, "We looked a long, long time for you." From the outside, wind sounds in the mangroves, and the songs of the island's new children at play.

Stillness.

Ziriyab listened. Then he said, "Now I'll go to the sea."

Munira was on her way into the house, carrying a bucket full of dried clothes. As she crossed the threshold, she glanced away.

Ziriyab put out his hand. "Come with me?" he asked.

"Soon," Munira murmured, her eyes focused elsewhere.

The hot wind swarmed Ziriyab's body as he stepped out into the pale yellow evening. Without a word, Munira and Ayaana watched him glide toward the sea.

[101]

The howl of djinns before dawn, a harrowing din. When Ayaana heard the wildness, the anguish of it, she wrapped her body and raced to the ocean to see what creature this might be. She ran to the end of the pathway. She crossed the threshold between the red land and black sand, and she saw—buffeted by waves, arms flailing at sky and water, beating his heart with an open palm—Ziriyab Raamis.

[102]

Ziriyab returned to his first room in Muhidin's house in the night. *When my father, my betrayer, returns, he will find me here.* But when the doors closed, he paused to imagine Munira's knocking on the door. Against this door, he often cried unseen. Not sleeping. Counting minutes until the dawn, when he had permission to walk through half-labyrinths into Munira's house for the day and glimpse his Buthayna, his Ghazalah, and still, his own soaring Huma.

They often poked at each other's tender scars, probing new boundaries.

Munira asked him one day, during breakfast, "Will he return as you have?"

Watching her, Ziriyab replied, "The thought haunts me every day." Clash of cutlery on utensils. Spoon to plate, spoon stirring sugar into a ceramic mug. "How will you choose?" he asked.

Munira turned to watch her late-life daughter attempt to eat. Her silence splintered Ziriyab's heart again. Munira pointed: "Abeerah."

Ziriyab's spoon slipped from his hand and clattered to the floor. He bent over to reach for it. "A daughter." His voice was faint.

"His daughter." She looked him in the eye. "Your sister."

They ate in silence after that.

. . .

One early morning, after breakfast, Ziriyab decided to visit Mehdi's workplace. On the way, he was distracted by the sight of a little being dressed in yellow slinking toward the mangroves. Out of concern, he followed it.

There, just behind the dunes, beneath a grand old mango tree, a parliament of crows greeted her, fluttering like doves as she approached. Ziriyab watched as Abeerah scattered the food she had taken from her mother's table that morning. He heard her admonish a brown bird with an orange beak that had dived in to steal portions from her hands. Ziriyab knew that the current county administrator had, on Jamhuri Day, launched yet another futile war against crows. Abeerah was obviously with the rebellion. As Ziriyab watched her, a tender, warm, molten honey eased through his heart, and, from within, a chortle. At first, the unfamiliarity of his own laugh unnerved him, and he slapped a hand over his mouth.

Abeerah froze when she turned toward the sound and saw Ziriyab. She tensed, eyes large in fear. She considered tears; this always deferred punishments. She waited for Ziriyab to scold, but then he planted a finger on his mouth, as he exaggerated sneaking away. How she laughed.

The next morning, when Abeerah's and Ziriyab's eyes met across Munira's breakfast table, Ziriyab slid a *mahamri* portion into his pocket. They would feed the birds together from now on. The birds deigned to approach him for food. Their simple trust. Heads twisted at him in curiosity: he was of special interest to the ravens. He discovered he was smiling, and the child was beaming at him. Stillness, the tides, the child, and the birds. A raven with a deformed foot hopped toward him and pecked at the edges of his *kikoi* for bread fragments. Only then did Ziriyab allow his heart to contemplate the matter of Abeerah, his most unexpected sister. She was staring at him, her head tilted far back, and within her eyes, the totality of mischief, an invitation to play again.

Still, at dusk every day, Ziriyab went to the sea, as if to purge his life of its human-inflicted bruises. He was shrouded in those threads from

Munira's life that he wore as a talisman—today it was her fuchsia cardigan. He did not yet know how best to re-enter life outside the shelter of home and family. He had ceased wondering about the rest of the world and its silences about demons that roamed the earth unimpeded and unquestioned. So he went to the sea to ask why he lived when better, braver, bolder, more beautiful men had been murdered. What would it be like to see the world whole again, and not through the seared-in vision of barbed wire and prison bars? He scratched his skin. *Where are you?* he asked the phantoms as he scanned the waters for the shapes of the men who had died. Then there were the day memories of nightmares. Terrors that hid from light would cause him to rise like a bird on fire at least three times in the night, crying out like a cat being sacrificed alive. At least three times a week, before the night terrors, his spirit tried to escape his body through the top of his head. Ziriyab would yank it back into his body, clinging to its fiery heels and refusing to let go. It was such an effort that when he got up in the morning he would be panting and stinking of sweat.

On an October Thursday of 2016, on a timeworn island that had sprouted off the Western Indian Ocean, a corpselike man, dark eyes flitting, wearing a too-small fuchsia woman's cardigan, would splash through a freshwater pool teeming with minuscule C-shaped dragonfly nymphs. Twelve meters away, dusk's incoming spring tide—his destination. There the sea would swirl and froth warm around his thin, scarred ankles as he inhaled the salt-seaweed-earth smell of the season. He would close his eyes, waiting for a whisper from inside shadows. He would hear, as always, a lone blue note, that settling sound like the perfect heartbeat: a bass-infused chord of longing, the song of home. After forty minutes of pure listening, he would turn to wade back to land. But, close to the shore, something would wink and glint at him from the shallows. He would wander over to look and find it was red sea glass that had been worn by the weight of the sea into a smooth, shiny pebble. A portent.

[103]

Stranger signs have been summoned from out of the sea by those who crave an answer. A fisherman, not one of the best, had hauled in an exceptionally bountiful catch. Among his miscellaneous sea bounty, shivering, shuddering octopuses, *mkunga*, *tengesi*, *kilualua*, *pono*, and *suli suli* was a blood-rusted frayed rope. In that frayed rope was a red glint. And the red glint was a ruby ring that had last been seen on Muhidin's right ring finger. And the fisherman understood that the sea might have been speaking. He only wished it had not selected him to deliver the message. As with such situations, as soon as the man docked his vessel, he did not bother with unloading his sea harvest, but bore the ring straight to the sheikh, who he felt was better placed to interpret the meaning of this happening for the family concerned.

[104]

Munira was in her garden, clearing the weeds as she listened to the crickets and their plaintive mating songs. The evening threatened to turn everything into a silhouette.

"We must talk," Ziriyab whispered to her.

She turned to study, again, the shape of hauntedness in his gaze. Her heart twisted.

He asked, "Where are the children?"

Munira stuttered.

Tears on Ziriyab's face. "*He* will not return." She was wiping the mud off her hands. "You may want to speak to Ayaana." Munira's body shook. She rubbed her eyes, but still they smarted with sour tears. "Here," Ziriyab said, and he placed a ruby ring on her open palm.

It was Munira's dreadful keening that suggested to the rest of the island that there was no further need to wait for Muhidin. After the sound, the vision of Ayaana tearing away, a silent and furious, unstoppable tempest. Islanders hurried toward Munira's house.

Mwalimu Juma intoned three times, "Whoever dies by drowning is a martyr."

Pate heard from the elderly Abasi how meaningful the return of the ring was, but his words were garbled and bound by an undercurrent of uncertainty: The return of Ziriyab and now Muhidin's ring did not necessarily mean death. These signs could also mean "lost," "misplaced."

The island reshaped its body to accommodate the hint of calamity. It sorrowed with the family, but not too intensely, lest they all curse the hazy possibility of Muhidin's return.

Munira offered these visitors her rose-essence-scented tea with coconut *mahamri* and did not know what to think or feel.

Ayaana had huddled close to Fundi Mehdi. She was avoiding the crowds. "There is no body," she informed Mehdi. "He will return."

A Salat al-Janazah for Muhidin took place the next day in the courtyard of the crumbling mosque. Ziriyab stood with the island's men in front as Pate tried to free itself from the shadow of waiting for Muhidin and Kitwana Kipifit. Pate half mourned Muhidin and the former seeker now entrenched as Kitwana Kipifit. Prayers of repose for the presumed dead, prayers for the bereaved, prayers for protection, ceaseless prayers that were the evidence of the reluctance of the many to let go of Muhidin, seafarer, keeper of secrets, healer of intimate wounds, owner of Books and Other Things, Ayaana's chosen father, Munira's husband, Abeerah's and Ziriyab's father, man of Pate,

Ziriyab's ghost. Abasi intoned the Basmallah. Stirring winds, temperature drop; the quality of light deepened to a purer orange. Change of season. In Abasi's intoning, Ayaana also heard echoes of music from another time inside a large house that was a tomb: "Ah! That day of tears and mourning / From the dust of earth returning . . ."

Later that evening, quietly, Munira retrieved the ring from her brassiere, to give it to Ziriyab. "It was always yours."

"Keep it," Ziriyab pleaded with her.

She studied his face, and then nodded.

Muhidin.

Inna Llilahi wa inna Ilayhi Raajicuun.

We belong to Allah and to Him we shall return.

Or, perhaps, not yet.

[105]

Two and a half months later, Munira pounded on Ziriyab's door. It was after his third scream that Tuesday night. First she had called him on his cell phone to say, "You are crying again."

A confession: "When I close my eyes, *they* come, with red eyes . . . eyes with fangs. I smell their breath." He gasped. "They are here."

Stillness.

Munira said, "Unlock your door." She switched off her phone.

Ziriyab was sure he had heard her wrong. His craving often bewildered his thoughts. He went to the door anyway. He unlocked it.

Munira was there.

Eye contact.

Both looked away.

Munira walked in.

Ziriyab shut the door.

They walked slowly up the stairs, bodies almost touching. Munira preceded him into his bedroom. She stepped out of her slippers. She dropped the *leso* covering. She unzipped her dress. She lifted up her hair and made a bun.

Ziriyab and Munira, veterans of those battles that unfold in between spaces, both graying and sadder, would peaceably thrive. Munira flew once to Pemba and then returned. The next time, Munira sent Ziriyab ahead of her. When he returned to Pate, he had fattened up and his face now glowed.

"*Bom dia família*," he would announce every morning, while trying to forget that the first Portuguese phrase his mind had retained was *dor da alma*—pain of the soul. Later, in the refined laughter Ziriyab shared with Munira, as they lobbed phrases in Portuguese, Shangaan, and Makonde at each other, Ayaana sensed, perhaps before they did, that they would leave Pate Island again.

[106]

One night, close to 4:00 a.m., soft footsteps led up to the dunes where Ayaana sat, waiting for the morning, as she struggled to imagine what she could make of her life. Ayaana turned at the sound and saw a woman shrouded in gray and white, her veils aflutter, her eyes hollowed, her mouth frozen in a rictus of horror. Ayaana had leapt up and was preparing to flee, to scream, when the woman, Mama Suleiman, groaned in the voice of a void, "Help me, please."

And Ayaana's body came to a complete halt mid-flight. The woman said, "My eyes . . . I can no longer see." But Ayaana could see that her eyes were fine and were looking at her with death. A gleaming object in the woman's hand: a tablet computer. "Look for me," Mama Suleiman said. She pointed to the screen. "Is it him?"

A scene from the wars of the day: pockmarked palaces, rubble on the streets, bloodstained craters that used to be roads, ceaseless screams frozen on human faces as if the earth itself had become a single groan; trucks burned black, cabbage and tomatoes and eggplants. This had been a market before the detonation. A still-veiled man—wearing a niqab? Ayaana wondered—bullet belt, bloodied camouflage gear, a body caught in the act of retrieving an AK-47 from mounds of flesh, former boy-men and their casualties. Ayaana scrutinized the trade objects, as Koray would have: the price-tagged grenade, bullets, cartridges, guns, rockets, missiles, tanks, and uniforms, the portions of a single blood-and-brain-spattered mosaic showing on a tablet screen. But what Mama Suleiman wanted to know was if the man alive in the foreground could be Suleiman, if Ayaana agreed that the other—a cracked head with the skull exposed and bleeding, popped-out eyes in the background—was *not* her son.

Ayaana said, "No, it is not."

"I look every day," Mama Suleiman grunts, her voice relieved and human again. "I look, but today . . . I don't know . . . today I could not see."

Ayaana took the tablet from her hand.

YouTube, Facebook, Twitter, memory: the ephemeral maps a mother and a girl she loathed were using to search for a soul caught up in a war of worlds that should never have touched their lives. On a lit-up screen, the pair focused on the eyes of boys and men, dead or alive. They imagined they would recognize the long-lashed gaze of a mother's only son. His name was Suleiman. He used to play marbles and football. Eminem was his icon. Tableau of human anguish revealed by a tablet. Now two women who had been formed by a mostly invisible island studied the geography of Syria's Ar-Raqqah and Idlib and Homs. They drew finger lines to measure distances between Iraq's Dahuk, Fallujah, and Samarra. They smiled because in that map they saw a city called Sulaymaniyah. It sounded like "Suleiman."

"Does it mean the same?" Mama Suleiman wondered.

Ayaana replied, "Probably."

Other images from the same kind of hell—the still-smoldering ruins of cities older than time, returned, literally, to the Stone Age.

Rubble. “There are no other places to go,” Mama Suleiman said later, “only here.” She caressed the tablet’s screen. Later, she added, “He is here.” They were still studying faces on the screen, the dead as well as the living.

Ayaana turned away from the screen and the mother to watch the sea. Its sweat washed away the memory of what they had seen. The blue-silver light of the fading moon tinted the waves’ edges. Ayaana observed that, on the night of a mother’s sobs, the djinns did not cry. A new day started, luminous. Mama Suleiman’s face and body were calm. To Ayaana she said, “This does not mean that I like you any better.” Ayaana shrugged. Mama Suleiman said, “We are not friends.” Ayaana agreed, “No.” Stillness. Mama Suleiman asked, “Do you still throw yourself into the sea?” Ayaana’s head swiveled to gawk at the woman. The woman’s gaze was on her. Ayaana looked away. She watched the sky, now tinged with orange and violet. She considered again an island that hemorrhaged secrets. She did not even bother to laugh. Mama Suleiman said, “Soon I must plunge into *my* ocean. I shall bring my son home.” The woman lifted herself up from the ground. She carried her tablet. She left Ayaana without another word and faded into the new day. It was as if she had not been there at all.

Mvua haina hodi.

The rain needs no permission to fall.

[107]

A ponytailed man from China wearing frameless glasses disembarked from an airplane in Nairobi. He was about to learn a country in as many of its textures as he could contain, acquire some of its cadences and senses, before he took another plane and then a boat to an island that was his real destination. Elsewhere, harbingers—birds borne on *matlai* winds that coincided with the departure of yellowfin tuna from the seas, moon-colored dragonflies, the signs of earth's changing seasons. Sometimes the jetsam of the seas collected on monsoon-fed shorelines. Sometimes these included strangers: passers-through, and those destined to stay, stepping across thresholds into the lives of those who, though almost incinerated by so many recent darknesses of the human heart, still set up a ritual of hospitality for the guest.

Almost four months later, a slow ferry that had broken down twice and turned a five-hour crossing into a seventeen-hour odyssey limped into Mtangwanda. One of the men on board did not mind the delay. He disembarked, carrying a rucksack and two dark blue metal cases. He looked around. Two boys who had been diving into the water from the jetty surfaced. They stared at the arrivals, but this one was the most obvious outsider of all who had landed on Pate that day. They laughed as they saw the man sniff the air as a dog might. The man turned to take slow steps to the place where the land met the sand.

. . .

Thresholds—treading softly into the mysteries of others' lives. He hesitated. A breeze drew his attention to a beckoning plant with delicate flowers. He crossed to look, and there it was, a wild-rose bush. He cupped a floret as children sneaked up behind him to look, discussing what he might be up to. The man turned to them. They darted backward, laughing. He smiled. Then, in hesitant Nairobi-acquired Kiswahili, badly spaced, abrupt words, he enunciated with care: "*Hamjambo. Ninaitwa Lai Jin. Natafuta mtu wangu. Anaitwa, Haiyan. Tafadhali.*"

The children laughed.

Then, to his left, a crackling voice intoned, "*Masalkheri*"—Good evening. The visitor looked over his shoulder at a white *kanzu*-clad wizened presence, a dark golden man of the sea, bent with his age, who looked back at him with the most open gaze he had ever seen.

"*Ni hao*," he blurted, and then remembered where he was. He lowered his head, as if he had erred. "*Umekaribishwa*," the elder pronounced, and offered him a hand, and then called for others to help Lai Jin with his luggage.

Tender-voiced, "*Pole sana.*"

We are sorry. *For what?*

Karibu na pole, from so many mouths. *Pole.* Only later would he understand that it was assumed he had come to bear witness to the life, loss, and meaning of Mzee Kitwana Kipifit. And he would do so.

~

Two boys pranced around Ayaana while she soldered a joint on an anchor she was working on for Fundi Mehdi, as the radio delivered news of the state of the tides. The children shouted over her work, to tell her in disjointed words that a guest had arrived on the island and was asking for her. They told her that the man was right now being escorted to her mother's house but would be hosted by Mwalimu

Juma. Ayaana paused. "I have heard," she informed the children, and then proceeded with her work. Fundi Mehdi glanced at her and shrugged. They heard from the news deliverer that a storm was expected at sea, and that all boats should return to shore. They glanced seaward at the same time. Silver-tinged dark shadows on cumulus clouds.

~

At sundown, after prayers, Ayaana walked up to her mother's house. She listened for the clattering of pots, heard her little sister's voice, her numerous whys. When she approached, Abeerah sang out her name and dashed out on fat legs for a hug. Ayaana carried her back into the house. Her mother met her at the door and took Abeerah. "Wash up," Munira said, looking flustered.

"Who?" Ayaana whispered.

Munira fluttered her hands. "China."

Ayaana's back stiffened. She inhaled. She then slid into the kitchen to wash her hands and face and postpone her entry into the living room. She scrubbed her hands and reached for a tattered dishcloth, hearing the pounding of her heart. Somewhere, her sister prattled. She peeped and saw Lai Jin standing in front of the Zao Wou-Ki print she had framed and hung next to a tiny alcove in the wall, next to the two repaired lacquered vessels.

Ayaana stepped out, her heart in her mouth. Without turning, Lai Jin said in Mandarin, "The rose of your skin—I have now seen its flowers."

Silence. He turned around and smiled at her. "I met the descendants."

"They are of Pate," Ayaana said.

Lai Jin simply watched her as she circled him, relishing her discomfort. Ayaana flexed her fingers. "Nioreg from the ship . . . He was here." Lai Jin lifted his head. "He came to bury Delaksha." Ayaana watched him. "You knew?" She stepped closer to him. "That she died?"

Lai Jin said, "I should have told you." His face tilted away as he recalled how he had been sprawled next to Nioreg, who covered Delaksha's body with his own. Together they had watched Delaksha's eyes dilate as blood trickled out of her nose and ears. It had soaked their clothes. Nioreg's cries: *The diction of fire*, Lai Jin had thought then. Stupendous stillness. He had propped up his head as if it were the heaviest of boulders. He would be accused. He would be implicated in this tragedy. He would suffer for it.

He turned back to Ayaana, gesturing, palm open. Ayaana turned her gaze to the outside view. The sea was churning in anticipation of the storm. Her mind was jumping in all directions. What could she say? "Sit. Coffee?" she asked.

He shook his head. He did not sit.

She said, "On my plane home . . . there were more of you than there were of us on board. China is our typhoon." Her mind grasped for clarity. At last she really looked at him. "Why are *you* here?"

Lai Jin's hands opened and closed; opened and closed. "*Haiyan*," he said through gritted teeth, "I'm not 'China.' I am Lai Jin. A man. I am here. My purpose is to find you. A man. He has come to find *Haiyan*. A man, not 'China.'" Pain spots in his eyes. He approached Ayaana, his look troubled.

She looked down at her hands.

"A man," he repeated.

"I owe you nothing," she stuttered. Surprised by how easy it was to slip into Mandarin, how different she felt in another language.

Lai Jin moved to face her. "I saved your life."

"The ship was yours," she countered.

He was smiling. "Your debt." Lai Jin stroked her face. Remembrance. "I have traversed your country. It is a deep country. In some places . . . where the roads are built by our China"—a shine in his eyes—"in the bus I have lied; I said I am from Japan. We design good roads." A snort. He had enjoyed saying this, his poke in the eye of a hateful stepmother. He was embarrassed by the convoluted mess of tarmac, those unfinished edges, the slapdash signs that did not honor his people. Confronted by the hideous quality of his nation's projects, in an act of private protest, Lai Jin had presented himself, when the question of identity and infrastructure merged, as not-Chinese.

Ayaana raised a brow. "What are you here?"

"A man," he repeated.

Desire: its confusing reach. She stuttered. "For how long have you been in Kenya?"

"One hundred and eighteen days."

Ayaana gasped. "What?"

"I try to know to what I come."

Ayaana turned again to face the sea, turbulence on her features. One hundred and eighteen days? Her voice trembled as she rushed to fill it: "The vases are beautiful." She gestured to the alcove. "Thank you for fixing them." Her voice faded. She was still bemused by Lai Jin's presence in her mother's house. She was not entirely certain she was not asleep. This could be a dream layered upon a tempest of memories of lacerating, unexpected, and unsettling intimacies. Ayaana tried to demur. "What if it is only a brother that I now require?"

Lai Jin breathed slowly, choosing a thought, a slight flush on his face. First, disarm. "The treasure you left me," she looked up at him. He added, "The prayer . . ." She nodded. "I carry it on me." He tapped his bracelet. "Here." When he was captain, he was most at ease in deep waters, far from known horizons, immersed in the imagination of uncertainty. These here were uncharted waters. "About your question"—a gambit—"*name wo shi ni di gege*"—then I am your elder brother.

~

On a promontory, two beings stared down at a sea stirring itself in a sudden high-tide frenzy, as if it had been caught snoozing by an authority figure. The melody of the tide, a resolute and confident flowing now that the anticipated storm had evaporated. Moonlight on water. A curious creature—a goat, perhaps—foraged nearby. Ayaana inched closer and closer to Lai Jin until their bodies touched—just. With the corner of his gaze, Lai Jin attempted to reread Ayaana within the geography of her home and its waters. Lai Jin groped for a word to complete the picture.

An odd sensation of falling out of time had shaken Lai Jin's balance at the Lamu jetty before the iridescence of a storm-threatened violet-silver sea. It was as if he had stumbled into a warp that ignored expected spatial and temporal relationships with the world. He recognized in silhouettes another past and future imaged in the crumbling infrastructure and seductive desolation of an older history upon which the present hovered. Ghost presences would brush against skin and cause the hairs of his head to stand on end. Fifteen minutes into his arrival, as he crossed the ancient trails toward his rooms, he had seen a crow standing one-legged on a moon-shaped Chinese tomb with the sun in its eyes. That was the moment when he understood that memory was also matter.

Afterward, he had seen Ayaana.

A sense of inevitability had staggered him: the knowledge that, whatever else he had done, his journeying would have ended right here. He exhaled, and below them the waters splintered themselves on the rocks. Beneath her lashes, Ayaana studied the former ship captain. She tested him: "There is a man. His name is Koray. He and his mother have designed a future for me in Turkey. Their imaginings are so vast that they swallow even my fate. Just like China dreaming Kenya . . . without our elephants and lions, without our land, without us." She watched Lai Jin for his reaction.

Lai Jin's hand moved to her arm. She leaned against his shoulders, then dropped her head against his chest. "How long will you stay?" she whispered.

He did not reply.

She murmured, "How is the lighthouse?"

"Now dust."

Silence.

"Come." Ayaana pirouetted. She grabbed his arm. "I'll introduce you to Mother . . . my dear *brother*."

Lai Jin hesitated, saw the challenge in her eyes.

He would play along.

Ayaana called as she approached the door, "*Ma-ee*, our brother. He has come from China." She smirked at Lai Jin. "See the little girl? Doesn't she look like me? The right age for a daughter." Munira appeared, laughter in her eyes, seeing more than Ayaana gave her credit for. "*Maaaa*, this is Lai Jin." Ayaana said. "He is a ship captain. He is also a potter."

~

Lai Jin took two rooms in the back of Hudhaifa's shop. After two weeks, he moved out. Mwalimu Juma had made a deal with an absentee landlord who was based in Oman, who had a house Lai Jin could rent for a token fifty dollars a month, and he could do so indefinitely, as long as he repaired and maintained it.

[108]

Pate Island insinuated itself into Lai Jin's core. Returning to Pate Town in the *matatu*, he had sat next to Mwalimu Juma, who proceeded to tutor him, answering his questions about Pate, its life, its meaning, its shadows. Mwalimu Juma asked him if he knew what he wanted from life. Lai Jin said he was a pilgrim. Their conversation stretched long after their arrival at their destination, and then crossed into the doorway of the things of faith. Lai Jin said he did not know what faith meant. A drizzle started over the land. They listened to the drip-drip of water as they sheltered in a makeshift café.

When Lai Jin visited the village of Shela, near Lamu, he imagined he could apprentice himself to one of the re-creators of the architecture of the space. But when he returned to Pate with some of the fishermen who had recognized him, he helped them haul in and sort their catch and wondered if he might consider the art of fishing. Mimicking their words, he acquired more of Pate's words and worlds. On some days, he would be at the jetty, talking engines and sea routes with assorted vessel captains, watching the time; the rhythms of Pate were converting him into another kind of man. It was among these men that he was first renamed "Nahodha Jamal."

. . .

A moment in dusk. Migrant dragonflies flitted above Lai Jin's head as he stopped to stare at Pate's old crescent-spaced tombs. Tang, he suspected—not Ming, as was presumed. Downturn of mouth, the wind on his skin. Goose bumps. A realization: there was nothing unique about his presence here. He stroked the curves on a tombstone. Ebb. Flow. Repetition. Rhythm of the ages. Nothing new or unusual about the arrival or departure of souls from here or elsewhere. It was the warp and weave of existence.

Lai Jin stumbled into ancient whispers: the presence of persistent ghosts. And, breath by breath, he allowed the island into himself, this ruined trading state, this moldering realm. Ebb. Flow. Some days, he waited for Ayaana to find him at the dunes or promontory; other times, he wandered some more along the seashore. What he understood: the more he knew of life, the less it made sense.

He grimaced.

Waiting.

She was already at the promontory waiting for him.

"*Wo de airen,*" he called out to her—My lover.

She answered, "Yes?," as if it were normal. Ayaana had tied a green *leso* around her waist, he noted. "Where did you go?" she called to him.

He had ventured to the north of the island. "Siyu."

"Alone?" She raised a brow.

"Yes." He smiled.

She crouched. "Why?"

"Kuchi."

The fighting chicken.

She frowned. "To gamble?"

"No."

"Then why?"

"Breeding."

"Breeding?"

"They are good birds. Very strong, very heavy."

"You'll eat them?"

"Chinese eat everything."

She looked up at him, ready to attack the statement. He was teasing her. "Very funny," she said.

"Yes."

Eyes met. The same pull, the same storm. She touched her mouth. He watched. Ayaana lowered her head. Warm hands, soft touch. The ocean still asked, *Ni shi shei?* Insects fluttered. Lai Jin's gaze followed the flight of a bee. "Soon the dragonflies?"

Ayaana nodded. "Their destiny is kept by the wind; they must return." The lilt of her Kipate voice reshaped her Mandarin. "But they don't stay," she added.

[109]

Only the tip of the sun still showed, red and low on the horizon—a clear evening. Lai Jin knocked tentatively at Munira's open door. His hair was wild and stood on end. He found Ayaana blowing air into a charcoal stove, a saucepan of water by her side. He had a favor to ask. She agreed to it with a grin.

Half an hour later, she slipped into his house with a blue bucket full of water into which she had mixed a portion of coconut oil and a cup of aloe vera. Lai Jin was waiting, shirtless. He crouched in front of another basin full of water, a long plastic bottle containing a tiny bit of beige-colored shampoo in hand. Ayaana recognized it as one of a set that had first brought grief to her hair in Xiamen. She sniffed at it, then placed it on the ground beside her bucket. Next, her hands warm on his shoulders, his chest. Remembering. Too many eyes would be watching, she knew. Lai Jin's presence was a riddle. Her behavior and habits were under scrutiny; she had become an enigma. This did not bother her. She stroked the back of his neck. He tilted it, eyes shut. Ayaana ran fingers through Lai Jin's extra-dry, long gray-flecked hair.

Before he went to Ayaana's house, Lai Jin had found himself ensnared by profound doubt. Feeling his otherness keenly, he had groaned, asking himself what he was doing on this shifting island of an Africa where history was a shroud, the news of the world was a lusterless rumor, the water he used was from a brackish communal well, and sometimes when he looked sideways, he glimpsed odd-shaped shadows peering at him. The scented vision he had pursued treated him like a mirage, while his life yearned for all that was her and hers. It was as if another man had possessed him.

He had got up to seek Ayaana.

"I need you," he had whispered.

She had come. Her hand was on his forehead. *Touch*. She had asked, "Will you cut it?" *Not yet*, he thought. *Touch*. And then his fear left him.

"What is China to you?" he asked. *China?* He had meant, *What am I to you?*

The used water ran into the outside drain. Ayaana lathered his hair and remembered crossing the sea with him, the world she had found, the profession she had gained. She had been marked by China. But "marked" could also mean "bruised." Or blemished, or scarred, or written into. She lathered Lai Jin's hair. She wanted to trust in his presence, its life. Life was wild, beguiling, and dangerous. It peddled desires, and could abandon the beloved at will.

The sun still rose and shone after a disappearance, a death, an exile. She stroked Lai Jin's head. His raspy breathing, eyes closed.

Every day she watched him—of course she watched him. She wanted her island to tether him. She coveted his time. She raced to Mehdi's because she knew he would be there. She listened for his thoughts. Yet she needed space to surface from the depths of the unknown into which she had plunged. She asked, "What is China to you?" as she rinsed his hair. "Have you seen the American salt well? The pit latrines they built?"

He smirked. "The goat shelters?"

"Yes," she answered. She continued: "I was young when they came. They landed with noise." She scoffed. "Their dream for us? An unusable well." She flicked the suds off Lai Jin's head and poured more rinsing water over him. "China says she has come back. An 'old friend.' But when she was here before, we also had to pay for that friendship. Now she speaks, not with us on Pate, but to Nairobi, where our destiny is written as if we don't exist."

Stillness.

"We hear China will build a harbor, and ships will come; we hear that an oil pipeline shall cross our land. We hear a city shall emerge from our sea, but first they will close our channel. These are the things we only hear. China does not talk to us."

Lai Jin listened to Ayaana, heartsick for her, for the island, unwilling to lie about assurances. Outside, other night voices: Mama Suleiman yelling over some offense, Munira calling for Abeerah, Ziriyab hammering some wood into shape, fish on fires, and the smell of steamed coconut rice, night jasmine, cloves, lemongrass, and rose; moths, and the fluttering of several other shadowed night fliers—bats, maybe. Lai Jin exhaled. Ayaana sprinkled more conditioning water on his head. She said, "We hear the Admiral Zheng He has emerged from out of time to resume his voyages." A twist of her lips. "Me, though, I desire Pate's dreams." She paused and shook her head, softened her voice: "If they can be retrieved. You see, we have lost even the memory of the name for our seas." She patted his head dry with a frayed green towel. Evening cicadas added to the night chorus. Lai Jin shifted to get more comfortable. Ayaana added, "China is here. With all the others—al-Shabaab, everyone else . . . China is here for China." She shrugged. "What do we do?"

Lai Jin felt, for a moment, the paralyzing weight of insane historical forces and their cacophonic slogans pressing both of them down.

Ayaana dropped the towel and leaned over his neck. "Done." Her head tilted over him. She crossed her arms over his chest. He held her arms. Her face was pressed against his. She added in a whisper, "But maybe, as it approaches us, this earthquake that is 'Zhongguo,' it will do us the honor of recognizing that Pate Island is also the keeper of its graves?"

Lai Jin shivered. Still, he lifted Ayaana's hand to his mouth. "*Xiexie xiao . . . meimei.*"

She turned to kiss his face. "Not '*Wo de airen*'?"

They laughed.

[110]

Lai Jin had become a grounding rod of sorts for the family. He had joined their meal. Little Abeerah was already in bed, faking sleep. Lai Jin had become a crucible for their memories of Muhidin. Though speaking of Muhidin opened their hearts and changed their voices, he also noticed that the repetitive mention of Muhidin's name gradually turned Ziriyab mute.

As Ayaana had escorted Lai Jin partway to his house, she had suddenly burst out, arms flung forward, "I need a storm." The next afternoon, Lai Jin, having already learned from one of the fishermen of Fundi Mehdi's past as one of the coast's legendary wind-whistlers, had approached Mehdi mid-work to ask what, hypothetically speaking, a person might require in order to purchase from him a storm-raising wind. "Why?" Mehdi had asked. Lai Jin had hemmed and could give no answer.

Ramadan came and went, and a few more of earth's new exiles, the Yemenis now, showed up on the island armed with shared genealogies that guaranteed that they had a place to settle into. Lai Jin went with Ayaana, Munira, Mehdi, and Abeerah to Lamu for Maulidi and, for the first time in his adult life, dared to dance in public. Mama Suleiman was present, making deals and catching up with old friends. Lai Jin had, naturally, attracted Mama Suleiman's disdain: "Made in China Bandia," she called him. She took pleasure in pointing him out even to strangers as "Mtu Bandia Made in China." He ignored her, his thoughts briefly preoccupied with the e-mail messages he had received: demands for his ceramics, his agent's desperate appeals, and more requests for interviews. Maulidi. Music and prayer and dance, and the loud arrival of boats and souls from other Indian Ocean islands. Timeless rhythms. The dusk's orange light reflected on sand dunes, and all around him the warm, warm sea. "I am betrothed to the Western Ocean," he wrote back to his frantic agent, "and to its ineffable bounty, including its light." The music from this land bounced off his browning skin. "I am unable to respond to you now. I am dancing."

Lai Jin sometimes accompanied Ayaana as she prepared rose-and-jasmine attar for Munira. Slowly, he was co-opted into the gathering of materials amid the ruins of cultures past. He was learning the terrain and what it carried. One dawn, Mama Suleiman found Lai Jin collecting wild-rose florets for Munira. "Mtu Bandia! Stealing knowledge!" she hurled at him.

The morning had been pleasant and tender until that moment. Lai Jin felt the fresh breeze falter, as pained as he was by the unexpected sourness. In defense of the morning order, he placidly told her in Kiswahili, "*Umerogwa. Nenda zako!*" Testing a new repertoire of insults: You are possessed. Get lost.

Mama Suleiman froze. She peered at him, and her face flushed. He waved her on. She huffed. He touched the plants to his lips, ignoring her. Yes, he could learn the secrets of rose attar and the meaning of its sprinklings on a woman's skin, this uncommon map that had steered a seafarer to this most unexpected place. Receding footsteps. He did not dare turn to see if the woman had really gone.

Lai Jin found he was most contented when he was in Fundi Mehdi's ship-repair yard. Among boats. Close to Ayaana. In view of the sea. Without intending to, he found himself under Mehdi's tutelage, learning how to craft boats with mangrove poles, and repair them with cotton rope soaked in coconut oil, and hearing about Mzee Kitwana Kipifit, another ghost with whom his fate was entwined. Like others who had found a way to Fundi Mehdi, Lai Jin worked best in silence save for the reassuring cadences of the teller of the tide news.

[111]

You are facing your older child. She is so much taller than you, her breasts and mouth are fuller, her body is more contoured. She is a woman. She has her grandmother's face and gait. You, too, are a reader of signs, and you know, in a way that she does not yet, how everything in life has turned upside down, how certain arrivals change the course of currents. But this is not why you want to talk to her. "It is time," you tell her. "Come with me." She follows you, and on her face are traces of the distance that China had first imposed on it. It is a chasm that wounds you, too, because you would have preferred that none of your children should know pain. But you have faith now, for you trust the one who has been willing to journey so far to be close to your child. He is older than you would have wanted, but you also know that the spirit of your girl is old. You stroke her face, this daughter born of your first encounter with fiery desire. She is a woman now, older than you were when you gave birth to her. She has a degree. She speaks Mandarin, English, and Kipate. She is tethered to an island that is a death sentence to its many. You do not know why; you do not understand many things. You do not know what will resurrect the fullness of your Ziriyab's soul. Your daughter—ah, but she is lovely. You are in the garden you created to perfume faith, hope, and a beauty you imagined would restore life. You knead the earth of the garden you wrestled from the salted earth and made fecund and rich. The wind lets you eavesdrop into the whispers of your transplanted roses. They are dropping their petals today. The rose hips have burst into orange-red. Your daughter says, "The seed harvest is good." You shift on your feet. "What do you know?" You pretend to frown. Your daughter reaches up and plucks and skins a yellow-green loquat. She sucks the flesh and spits out the brown seeds. You follow her and pluck one of your own. She laughs. "I spy on you." The mischievous child shimmers through. "Babu . . ." A pause. A smile. "He asked me to tell him the secret of your *halwaridi.*" You pinch your daughter's cheek, half in jest. "Tricky hawk!" Fake outrage, the presence of beloved ghosts. Your daughter giggles, "I didn't tell him about the seeds. I spied for me." Now she cups your face. "To find you." Heart in her eyes. You want to weep. Somber: "And?" Your child reaches for the rose hips. She brings her nose to these. Nutty, earthy, gentle—you know. "Harvest seeds before dawn." She adds, "You sing to them, and tell them how necessary and beautiful they are; that is why they grow for you."

She asks you, "You will be leaving soon?"

"Leaving?" You step away from her. You look at the garden. You carried livestock manure from Mombasa to feed this soil. You massaged the dung in, centimeter by centimeter. You smuggled in dirt from fertile places in paper bags. You have borrowed, begged, and stolen herb, flower, shrub, tree seedlings for this garden. You learned about the character of plants, how human they were. Some take, some give, some share; others must have everything for themselves. You found the ones that purged the salt that would have burned roots. And the earth yielded to you. It helped you raise your daughter. You stoop to scoop some of it with both your hands. You squeeze it, and the light of day tints you and the earth yellow-gold. You ask your daughter, "Could you keep her for me—this co-mother of mine?" Perhaps you are mad. Your daughter reassures you by asking the right question. "What is her name?" Your daughter crouches next to you. You want to ask her to go with you to Pemba. But, then again, you understand that fate makes its own plans. You press the name of your earth into her ear: "Bibi Alilat Dhat-Hamin." She is still, absorbing this. Now you sit holding hands, as sisters might, your legs stretched out in front, surrounded by birdsong, the buzzing of bees, the undertone of the tide, and the memories of worlds shared. The laughter of new children, and the unease of a wind you suspect Mehdi has summoned for company. It is a young one. It is warm and loping. Its habit, you notice, is to reap scents from your garden. A sweet-nosed wind: it lurks most among the jasmine, lavender, and rosemary. Your daughter's head is against your heart. Tomorrow you will show her which one of the chests contains your seed bank, now hers. You will later tell the story of these to your grandchildren, whose closeness you sense, for you have started to dream of them. You want to give your daughter the pale amber of the first rose-hip-seed oil you ever made. You have stored it in your brassiere, close to your heart. First you will rub three drops into her forehead. The bottle is almost full. She will know what to do with it. You will add to her knowledge of herbs. You will tell her why and for whom to mix what and when. But, for now, linger in this moment of existence, for all is well, and you and your daughter are perfect.

[112]

Preparations. A few weeks later, the Adhan crescendoed as early-arriving water-seeking dragonflies rode in on a mid-September wind. The *kusi* stormed seaward and unveiled storm-darkened skies. But since life's small creatures were calm, and the season's fish showed up as expected, the fishermen were not worried. It was on this day that a visitor now living within these—the farthest edges of life inside an invisible, old, and ruined land—pronounced Shahada, reciting, "*Ash hadu anlla ilaha ilallah . . .*" He cut his hair short. He took a purifying bath. He adorned himself in a clean white garment. He re-emerged transformed, and belonging to God and Pate. The imam had told him that he really did not have to change his name. He could still be Lai Jin. He replied that he could also be Jamal. And so he was both. Because of the seas in his blood, his name was preceded by "Nahodha."

[113]

Four months later, Munira left with her once-and-again husband, Ziriyab, and her daughter Abeerah for Mozambique. Ayaana haunted Pate Island, roaming its contours with a doleful look. Gaps in the heart; family was completion. Yet, given the chance, she had not left with them. In the house, she studied a tattered green-and-gold photo album filled with images of antecedents that Munira had bequeathed to her, saying, "We are *still* that constellation, my love, my child."

Seven nights later, Ayaana waded into her sea. At low tide, she drifted out with the current.

~

She dived in. Now she offloaded the cacophony of the world. She propelled herself down. Slow release of breath. She hovered at that point where, if she turned, it would be easier to sink than to surface. Daring. Dropping into the soul of the sea, where she could feel the whole of the ocean cocooning her again and offering its dimensions for her to expand into.

Drifting.

Breathing.

Her generation was supposed to develop a taste for a world that was being manufactured elsewhere. She had not found anything in it that mattered enough for her to own. There were things she was supposed to want, ways she was supposed to speak, and images she was supposed to adopt for her dreams. Yet, the more she had experienced of the world, the less she was certain of it. She had returned to Kenya supposedly armed with options. Ayaana kicked her heels to start her ascent. She could move to Mozambique. Ayaana somersaulted beneath a slow-moving dolphin pod, old friends introducing moonlight to sea depths. Breathing out, a bubble at a time, Ayaana floated and wondered if the traveling sea dog was already on its way home.

Ayaana surfaced.

Glimpsed a human silhouette on the beach. She lowered her shoulders into the water, squinting to make out who it was.

~

Nahodha Jamal had stumbled upon Ayaana's nighttime sea sojourns. The sultry humidity had driven him outdoors, and the moonlight on the water beckoned. On impulse, he had headed down to the coves to rummage through Mzee Kitwana's things. He wanted to be alone to think. What was he still doing here? And, just like that, there was Ayaana, wrapping up her body in a torn *kikoi*, having emerged from the waters. Moonlight on her skin. Somehow, when she saw him, it was natural that she would head straight into his arms. It was natural that he would enclose her in them. "What? A sea spirit?" he had asked.

She giggled. They shifted, still attached to each other, to watch the moon on the water and see how it lit the ocean as if from within.

Mahtabi. Akmar. Ayaana remembered.

Resting her head on his chest: "Did you want to be alone?"

He hugged her close. "Not at all."

She stuttered, "The water is warm."

He was somber. "Do you still want a brother?"

She studied the silver light reflecting off his bracelet. "No." An upward glance. "Not at all."

So they moved even closer. He pressed her against him. Breath to breath, heart to heart, and the tide swirled around their feet, casting the sea's detritus around them. Seaweed wrapped around their ankles, and they stood in shifting sand beneath a soft bluish bucket-shaped moon. *In dreams,* she remembered, *I travel inside stars, on stars.* Her arms wrapped around Lai Jin's neck. *In dreams I am a tunnel made from darkness and I know the way. I'm not alone, even when there is nobody with me.* His scars, the burn marks, on face and back. She rubbed her hands against his mouth. There was the scar beneath his lower lip. She would drag him down to her, because she needed to feel again the sense of his body on hers. In this place where they could be found and seen, every suppressed tension turned into yearning and its appetites. Slipping into yet another unknown, submitting to yet another call of the promise of moreness. Enveloped again, but this time she knew the currents, she knew where they would lead. Submerged again, seeing through the darkness, the motionless vastness, and now she knew she would not drown, she could not drown. Breathing. Life as passage always: *Here are thresholds.* And all that Lai Jin sought was in the softness, the wetness, the moaning, the pulsing, pounding, slippery rhythm of this, of everything sought and wanted and ached for so terribly, so terribly. Cartography not of possession, but of, how odd, belonging. Lai Jin groaned out, unheeding, and she, cradling him, tightened her body, arms, thighs, and heart around him. And there was soundless stillness, and the sound of waves lapping close by.

~

Early-morning mists filtered the new light.

"*Allahu Akbar . . .*"

The beckon of another day, this soft-voiced summons. Experience had mellowed the old muezzin's voice, vesting it with heart.

Elsewhere, and between them, a good silence.

Homecoming.

They retreated to their different shelters before the day's fishermen could discover them.

Breakfast. Wash. Rest. Work.

Later, with Fundi Mehdi, they listened to the tide news, working near each other, brushing skin. They were building a ship for an Omani merchant. Mehdi would teasingly dare Jamal to recite a sea journey from memory. Mehdi said, "Let us go from Cape Town to Malacca in March." And Ayaana and Mehdi heard lyrics imagined for such a water passage. Mehdi intervened to remind Jamal of a rocky headland and a seasonal swell he had neglected to mention.

A convergence of echoes in Kipate.

Mwendo dahari hauishi.

The infinite road never ends.

[114]

It would take a little more time. First Ayaana had to forgive the sea for swallowing the father she loved. She would also need to find the courage to surrender to the truth that life made of its own meaning. She then returned to blending flowers and herbs and spices in the ways she had learned from her mother, so that she could propose ways of fragrant wholeness to those who now whispered their suffering to her, as they once had to her father, Muhidin. It would take a few more months, and a red moon that melted time, before Pate Island was able to bear witness to the nuptials of the seawoman Ayaana to the seaman Jamal.

The event was hastened by a most unexpected happening:

One midday in March, Ayaana had secured a fishing boat she had borrowed from Mehdi in order to traverse the morning waters. The fish she had caught floundered in a reed basket as she hurried along a trail. At a bend, beneath the old neem tree, Mama Suleiman, in a broad lemon-green sun hat, sat on an idling purple Vespa that she had had shipped in from Dubai and launched in Pate Town the previous November.

"*Shikamoo*," Ayaana said at once, still inclined to curtsy.

Mama Suleiman said, "Come close, girl."

Ayaana did, wary, perspiring, sunburnt and stinking of salt and fish. Mama Suleiman considered her and pursed her lips. "Swimming, young lady, is *one* thing. *Fishing*"—she paused—"from a scooped-out *log* is quite another. However, you are not to blame. You have not benefited from access to a *somo*. That is over now." She gestured expansively. "I shall be she. Now, tell your mother I will accept eight *leso*s and three bottles of her *halwaridi* as payment. A token, really . . .

given how much"—she considered Ayaana again, and a pained twitch passed as a ripple across her face—"we must undo." She peered at Ayaana, pinched her cheeks, assessing the quality of her pores. "You may call me Shangazi"—Auntie. "You will move into my home. We have so little time. I have informed Bi Mwadime and only the worthiest of women to work with me to prepare you." Ayaana was goggle-eyed; her mind was blank. "You shall be a model bride, a template for women everywhere. Now you may kiss my hand." She extended her limb. Ayaana kissed it. Amina Mahmoud revved the engine of her scooter. As she puttered away, she announced, "At my house. Tomorrow. Nine a.m. I do not tolerate lateness."

It took time. But Ayaana was at last inducted into the arcane society of women who also lived in, with, and through their senses. She was invited into the art of purification, of cleansing, of perfuming, of being and inhabiting and sharing her body; of color and allure; of using the potent forces in coconut oil, rose, jasmine, *langilangi*, patchouli, sandalwood, and cloves to the gut-twisting tempo of seductive cadences and intimate invocations, of turning life into an enchantment. Ayaana was layered and rubbed down as invocations were made, and memory shared: how to beguile the beloved, how to receive what is desired, how to hope when life's winds changed, how to love with the soul anyway. Mama Suleiman insisted that she smear the *singo* on the bride. Ayaana could not move as fine essences seeped into her bones and transmuted the past. Munira would arrive from Pemba just in time to adorn her daughter's body with henna, her finest work. Weeks later, a delicately made-up and bejeweled Ayaana emerged in a flowing gown of ivory silk and lace. She floated across infinite thresholds, this rose-scented Ayaana, Jamal's betrothed.

"Our girl is a true dolly," Mama Suleiman sighed to Munira. They had stared at each other before bursting into a profound cackle that vaporized the stench of a long and almost-fatal quarrel.

On the fifth day, the wedding festivities acquired new life when a *jahazi* showed up from Tumbatu, carrying a merry troupe of fishermen that included a seagoing bard. Three men pounded on a giant drum. Its reverberations stirred the bowels of the island. It was *matlai* season. An itinerant photographer who specialized in weddings was losing his voice, cajoling another generation of sea-formed souls to hold their poses as he tried to compose a family portrait. Months later, the bride would choose one of his photographs and carefully insert it into a fraying green-gold album. After the photo session, an inquisitive little girl wandered away from the revelries to chase after the season's first golden skimmers. When she reached a wild-rose bush perched at the thresholds between sea and time, she was distracted by a mewling sound. She crawled to look, and discovered a shivering ginger kitten with big green eyes hiding beneath a beached *mtepe*. The stowaway had traveled from Vanga to Pate by mistake. As the girl reached for it, it purr-meowed. The echo of her mother's voice drifted to the shoreline.

In rhythm, the sea ebbed.

"*Ua langu silioni nani alolichukuwa?*"—My flower, I do not see you; who has plucked you?

As she lifted the kitten to her shoulders, a sudden stab of yearning for her father's presence caused her to crane her neck and scan the seas for him.

"*Ua langu lileteni moyo upate kupowa*"—My flower, bring your heart to me and find wholeness.

Munira sang.

"*Ua langu la zamani ua lililo muruwa*"—My flower, from of old, a gracious flower.

In rhythm, the sea flowed.

No mar estava escrita uma cidade.

In the sea there was a city written out.

—Carlos Drummond de Andrade

Acknowledgments

For the development of this story, I am especially indebted to the University of Queensland, Australia, and its UQ Centennial Scholarship, the UQIPS, and the School of English, Media Studies, and Art History. In particular, I thank Dr. Venero Armanno, who first offered this story and me a season and space to learn and grow in the rich humus that Australia was for me. Your wisdom, sense of story, advice, and encouragement pushed me into making daring choices. To dear Professor Gillian Whitlock, thank you for the inspiration, questions, questions, questions, and motivation.

Although inspired by actual events and historical texts, in constructing this tale I took inspiration from many other sources: *Shukraan* to the exquisite old man of the sea, seafarer, minstrel, poet, living library, and world treasure, Mzee Haji Gora Haji, who is the sonorous voice for the Swahili Seas, and from whom the character of Muhidin materialized; to the filmmaker Sippy Chanda, who long ago celebrated her vision of a bold little girl ocean swimmer of Lamu (lyrically illustrated in her film *Subira*); to Ed Pavlić (*But Here Are Small Clear Refractions*, Kwani, 2013), who "sees" Pate Island; to Dr. George Abungu, a marine archaeologist involved in excavating the China–Eastern Africa buried histories; to the staff at the Zanzibar International Film Festival (2003–2005) and other Zanzibari, who made of me a Swahili sea citizen; to friends from the 2010 Pilgrimages project, who watched the premise of the story spring up at the banks of the great River Congo. Kiswahili aphorisms applied in the tale are drawn from common use and acquired from a great resource, a compilation by Albert Scheven (of the University of Illinois) that is accessible through the Internet; others have been suggested by individuals listed below, and borrowed from assorted *leso*s (*kanga*).

Mea culpa! I took all sorts of creative liberties with geographies, languages, and topographies. I even borrowed little bits of this and that from the other "Ziwa Kuu" islands and transported these into the Pate Island of the story. The muse made me do it!

Thank you to the Wylie Agency and Sarah Chalfant, wonderfully supportive in all ways, and especially to Jacqueline Ko, who has so lovingly and fiercely journeyed with this story from its inception; you are a treasure. To Alba Ziegler-Bailey, Charles Buchan, and Sarah Watling, enthusiastic cheerleaders, who show up with floodlights when dark clouds obscure confidence. To the Knopf team, including Vanessa Haughton, Kathleen Fridella, Zachary Lutz, Soonyoung Kwon, and Linda Huang, and especially my luminous, so-patient editor, Diana Miller; you are a writer's gift, a blessing; every story adventure shared with you is a lesson in becoming better. From my soul, thank you. Thank you, dear Angela Tsakiris and the Dumont family, for calling into being new worlds in another tale.

Others who informed/influenced the shape of this story (it takes a village) include Hildegaard Kiel (thank you for the shelter), Abdul

Sheriff, Khadija Musa (you will recognize adaptations of your hilarious China adventures), Angela Köckritz, Ngari Gituku, Abubakar Zein Abubakar, Bettina Ngweno, Samson Opundo, Anya Pala, Aaron Bady, Garnette Oluoch-Olunya, Sheila Ochugboju, Achieng Onyango, Salvina Kelly, Barbara Flynn, Kay and Paul Bertini, Michael Onyango, Clarissa Vierke, Nancy Karanja, Andrea Moraa, Paul Ostwald, Phoebe Boswell, Ken Oloo, Pierre-Emmanuel Maubert, Doreen Strauhs, Margaretta wa Gacheru, Stephanie Wanga, Maryanne Wachira, Ann Gakere, James Ogude, Uni Dyer, Ezekiel ole Katato, Michael Karinga, Lucy Mulli, Taiye Selasi, Oyunga Pala, Pete Tidemann, John Githongo, Rebecca Yeong Ae Corey, Agiso and David Odhuno, Wangechi Gitobu, Raphael Omondi, Pinkie Mekgwe, Subraj Singh, Sharlene Teo, Deirdre Prins-Solani, Wambui Mwangi, Eunice Githae, Hamza Aussiy, Captain Ali (Lamu), Gabeba Baderoon, Marie Kruger, Klaus and Iris Schneider, Farouk Topan, Joe Kobuthi, Emmanuel Iduma, George Wen, Bernd Harbug for the unconditional support and photographs, Abdulatif Abdalla, Françoise Pertat, Munira Humoud, Muhidin Kutenga, dear Binyavanga Wainaina, my truth-teller, and the late irrepressible raconteur, Emerson "Babu" Skeens, who first told me about the Admiral.

Family! Thank you for the strength, encouragement, and love offered when these are most needed. Mary Sero Owuor, your faith fires my heart, and keeps life sweet. This book is especially for you, woman of heart. Remembering you, Daddy; there is so much of you in Muhidin the father, you know. Beloved siblings—Vivian Awiti, Caroline Alango, Rob de Vries, Genevieve Audi, Joseph Alaro, Chris Ganda Owuor (gifted brother, mapmaker for this story, protector, transcendent artist and renaissance man. You rock! You are a rock), Joanne Achieng, Frank Laroque, Alison Ojany, John Primrose, Patrick Laja—and the beacons that are the new generation, inspiration, informants on the nature of a child striving for magic and light—Karla, Angie, Gabriella, Taya, Thomas, Nyla, and Tahera—you are my sunshine.

I am most grateful to the Rockefeller Center in Bellagio, Italy, for the residency that was a space of encounter with a tribe of exquisite souls who provided fresh impetus for the evolution of the story; Pilar Palacia and your wonderful team, thank you. Andreas Delsett and the House of Literature (Oslo), thank you for the gift of space and silence to complete the writing of this book. Thank you also to the IWP 2017 cohort, and in a very special way the wand-(correcting pen-)wielding, no-nonsense, fiercely gifted Audrey Chin; also to the Grinnell College autumn writing class, who taught me again—not in words—why story.

I enlisted the help of the front line: "story darling assassins." They are a formidable, brilliant, focused, story-loving band of friends who give no quarter. They were exposed to various drafts of the book and took time and energy to critique, question, refine, remove, and channel a semblance of flow leading to the version of the story in your hands. Any enduring errors are entirely mine. To these the truly brave and beautiful, I am in your debt. Not enough words to thank you: Keguro Macharia, Leila Sheikh Rutteman (and Naël), Annette Majanja, Mshai Mwangola, Anja Bengelstorff, Ashminder Kaur (and Sahiba), Tina Steiner, and Gregor Muischeek.

To the inspiring community of friends and fans, Kenya's reading groups, and those random readers who stop me on streets, in restaurants, in public transport, atop mountains, under the sea (no escape for the procrastinating) with *that* look in their eye, to ask, "Is it done yet?" You scared me into delivering this one on time (relatively speaking)! Thank you. To "the fellowship"—Alfajri: the Content Creators Collective and the Chimurenga Chronic, who affirm and egg on my Swahili Sea follies, thank you; and to all readers and friends I am unable to thank individually, my gratitude and affection.

Pate Island, the Lamu Archipelago, its souls and ghouls, and the many lives of its seas: thank you for the inspiration, my love, my love.

A NOTE ABOUT THE AUTHOR

Yvonne Adhiambo Owuor was born in Kenya. She is the author of the novel *Dust,* which was shortlisted for the Folio Prize. Winner of the 2003 Caine Prize for African Writing, she has twice received an Iowa International Writer's Program Fellowship. Her work has appeared in *McSweeney's* and other publications, and she has most recently been a fellow at both the Stellenbosch Institute of Advanced Study in South Africa and the Wissenschaftskolleg zu Berlin.

A NOTE ON THE TYPE

This book was set in Janson, a typeface long thought to have been made by the Dutchman Anton Janson, who was a practicing typefounder in Leipzig during the years 1668–1687. However, it has been conclusively demonstrated that these types are actually the work of Nicholas Kis (1650–1702), a Hungarian, who most probably learned his trade from the master Dutch typefounder Dirk Voskens. The type is an excellent example of the influential and sturdy Dutch types that prevailed in England up to the time William Caslon (1692–1766) developed his own incomparable designs from them.

Composed by North Market Street Graphics,
Lancaster, Pennsylvania

Printed and bound by Berryville Graphics,
Berryville, Virginia

Designed by Soonyoung Kwon

Lamu
Manda